Stellar Navigation

Elena's Story

Susan Michalski

GEODESY SERIES

BOOK 2

This is a work of fiction. Names, characters, places, and incidents either are the product of the author's imagination or are used fictitiously. Any resemblance to actual persons, living or dead, events, or locales is entirely coincidental.

ISBN 9780692441473
AISN B01E3BRZZE

Cover photos by Paul Woodruff

Cover design by Skye Hospod and Susan Michalski

For my father,

who taught me to see the possible, but to live in real.

TABLE OF CONTENTS

ဆ 1 ര

BACK HOME

Worn leather and laces
Dust left to those places
Cathedrals and castles
Trails and skyways
Winding backward
Upside down and sideways
Lost and alone
To find a way back home
Back home to you again
"Secret Passages"
        - Luna Rayne, 1992

The heavy ocean air breathes me. I'm a grain of salt dissolved in wind, both less and more than when I first stepped onto this strand. Until a month ago, I'd never been to a beach or much of anywhere, really. I'd never been drunk on my own power or aware of my ultimate insignificance. I moved through a life that was only half mine. Now I've traveled through the stars and landed on a planet light-years away. The air has substance; I can wrap my arms around it, or spread them wide and let it lift me off the ground as it sings my name, Elena. Even the ground has a will and desire of its own, shifting and sucking my feet until I tire of fighting it and collapse into its warm embrace. The star-studded horizon stretches into a silk thread and falls away just beyond my imagination. I'm inconsequential under the moonlit sky, and at the same time the secret me inside rises up with the tide, authentic, suddenly whole and real and more than what I was before.

Every afternoon for three weeks, poor tortured Finn was there beside me, but not really with me as he stared expressionlessly out at the water, waiting for it to quell the flames licking at his head and heart. I should hate him for the things he's done. I should thank him for the things he's done. But our past feels like nothing more than a weathered shell that has no purpose anymore. If he'd just let me, I'd help him. I'd reach inside, find the source of his agony and extract every shard and ember. All it would take is a touch. I reach for his hand again and again, but he pulls away every time. Maybe his torment is too much a part of him to be without it; maybe I get that more than I'd like to admit.

Downstairs the door opens and bangs shut, pulling me back to the present. I get out of the tub and wrap the towel around myself as Ethan climbs heavily up the stairs. I got back from Florida this morning and begged off the museum excursion that my housemates, my twin brother, Ethan, and bestie, Sage, had planned. Of course, I missed them over the three weeks I was away, but I wasn't ready to struggle with where I fit in this world that dances to Sage and Ethan's beat. I wanted to have a few more hours to be Elena, alone and simple, just me.

I'm about to open the bathroom door, but Ethan beats me to it. I know by the inward curve of his shoulders, the tremor in his chin and the lines creasing his brow what happened, so I don't ask. I touch his hand, but he won't lift his gaze. I close the door behind him. Not so long ago he would've reached to me for comfort, asked me to help him get sorted out. Now he'll suffer the humiliation, angry and alone, as he changes out of his wet clothes. It's a bitter pill that I can heal anyone I touch, except the one person I'm most connected to, the one person who needs my healing gift the most.

Voices drift up from the living room. Sage isn't alone. I dress quickly and sprint down the stairs. Jo is standing at the bottom of the stairway, like she's thinking about coming up. I leap into her open arms from a few steps up and wrap myself around her, almost toppling her onto the sofa. Luckily, I'm tiny and she's strong. She laughs low before kissing me and putting me carefully down. I run my fingers through her short, dark hair while she twirls one of my shoulder-length curls, and I close my eyes to imagine holding her kiss much longer, savoring it like the last bite of a dark chocolate mousse.

"You're blonder," Jo says, smiling her approval. Sage drifts in uncomfortably through the archway from the kitchen. Jo drops my hand and I follow her lead.

Jo and Sage have known each other beyond forever, but I came into the picture as Jo took a brief hiatus from Sage. When she came back, I'd taken her place in Sage's life. It would make sense for her to resent me, but our mutual attraction to Sage and then each other dissolved that potential energy, and a much more complicated dynamic has emerged.

"What a fab surprise." I can't stop smiling.

"Wild horses couldn't keep her away," Sage says. Jo shifts away from me a little.

"Guess we aren't celebrating tonight," I say to distract from the awkwardness. I look up at the stairs where Ethan went.

"It was my fault. I forgot how long it would take to get home during rush hour, even in a car. At least we weren't on the bus or in the museum," Sage says.

"He had a great day, though. And even when he . . . you know . . . lost it, he didn't lose it completely like he used to. You know what I mean?" Jo says.

I have to smile, despite the sadness of the subject, but I don't prolong the conversation because Ethan's descending the stairs, head down with a handful of ink pens in different colors clutched in his hand. He doesn't look at any of us as he makes his way through the room. We follow him into the kitchen, where he takes the chart off the refrigerator.

He was so excited to show it to me this morning when I got home. "Thirty days," he'd said. "If I make today, I'll have a whole month with no daytime accidents." At nineteen, this is a huge accomplishment for my precious and problematic twin, who spent fifteen years of his life as a four-year-old, living and reliving the trauma of the fire that took our mother and sent our father on the run. Now he looks at the chart like it has betrayed him. For half a second, I think he's going to rip it up or crumple it. Instead, he sits at the table and begins to draw.

"Hey, Mouse, tell Elena what we saw today," Sage urges, trying to bring him back to us.

"Later." He doesn't look up.

I take a step forward to see what he's drawing, but he shields it with his arm like a kid taking a test in school. Jo comes up behind me and slips her hand into mine. Her touch is magical in the corniest of ways. I just want to take her upstairs and close the bedroom door.

"Who's cooking tonight?" I ask absently.

Ethan looks up at Sage ,and I wonder if he's communicating with her telepathically, the way he and I used to, but rarely do anymore.

"No one," Sage says. "We're going out to dinner tonight to celebrate your homecoming."

I raise my eyebrows. "You sure you're up for that, little brother?" I ask, putting my hand on his shoulder.

He shrugs it away. "Why not?" His voice has an edge I've never heard before. It stings like a sharp flick to the temple.

I let it go. "Is Jo coming?" I ask.

"Sorry, sweetie," she says. "I'm just the taxi service today. I have music stuff, rehearsal, you know, big performance coming up. Next time, for sure." She motions with her head toward the door.

I walk Jo out to the car, stopping to look in the back window to see how much damage Ethan did to her upholstery.

"You gotta love leather seats," she says, reading my concern. "Sage cleaned it up, no worries."

"Thanks for being such a good sport." I shuffle a bit closer to her.

"What am I gonna do? Be mad? It's Ethan. How could I be mad at an angel?" Her eyes go soft as she talks about him.

"Sage should've made him wear a diaper." I shake my head.

"Controlling Ethan is not Sage's gig."

"I see," I say, half-insulted. "That's my gig."

"Hey, if the fiddle fits..." She flashes her adorable, tough girl smile.

I stand on my toes and kiss her. "When do I get to see you?" I try not to sound as desperate as I feel.

"As soon as I can get my shit together. Promise." She looks into my eyes until I have to look away.

"Tomorrow?" I ask.

"I'll do my best," she says. Then she's in the car, backing down the driveway. I could've done with one more kiss, but Jo's not there yet.

Back in the kitchen, Sage is putting dishes from the sink into the dishwasher. Ethan and his pens are gone.

"Check it out." Sage motions toward the chart on the fridge.

I take it down to examine it. There in the box labeled with today's date is a tiny picture of a boy with curly hair, a sad face, a dark spot on the crotch and a puddle on the ground. I bust out laughing. "At least he's developing a sense of humor about it," I say. "That's good, right?"

"Maybe. It's a way to deal with his embarrassment and disappointment, at least," Sage says.

Ethan comes into the kitchen. He takes the paper out of my hand, holds my eyes for a beat and puts the chart back on the fridge. "Let's go eat. I'm starving," he announces. Then he whispers in Sage's ear. Sage grins like a chimp.

"Whisper. Whisper," I mock.

"Don't get your panties in a twist, Sister. We have some surprises for you," Sage laughs.

Ethan hands Sage the keys and her purse, then bolts out the door ahead of us. Sage locks the house and makes a great show of sauntering to the driver's side of the old Volvo we share. She's swinging the keys in a spiral on her finger. Just before she opens the car door, she lets the keys fly in a high arch over the roof of the car. Ethan plucks them from the air with one hand. I hold my breath as the two of them circle around the car, like a Chinese fire drill, and take each other's places. Ethan slides into the driver's seat. Sage looks at me over the top of the car and I mouth, "Have you lost your fucking mind?" She shrugs and drops into the seat next to Ethan. I get in the back hesitantly and fasten the safety belt with exaggerated care.

Ethan turns the engine over, checks the rearview mirror and backs out of the driveway. My mouth is catching flies, no doubt, but I've temporarily lost control of the muscles that might close it.

Sage patiently coaches Ethan through the intersections and on and off the highway ramps. It's clear this isn't his first time on the road. He's calm and adept in a way I would've never imagined. Even his parking is smooth and accurate. "Wow," I say when he turns off the engine. He smiles brightly, confidently, maybe the happiest I've ever seen him. He puts up his hand for a high five that Sage returns, along with a little, hipster, fist bump. I can only shake my head.

On the way into the restaurant, I grab Sage by the upper arm to let Ethan go in ahead of us. "What in the name of hell and all its manifestations made you think it would be a good idea to teach Ethan to drive?" I demand when he's out of earshot.

Sage stares me down. "He's a teenage boy. What do normal teenage boys love almost as much as girls in tiny bikinis?"

"Cars," I say quietly.

"Ethan needs to feel normal to be normal."

"Sage, he's not normal," I remind her.

Sage looks away, then back at me. "You need to let go of that, Elena. Let him grow up already."

A part of me knows she's right, but she's wrong too. She can't make him into something she wants him to be. Her expectations are too high.

Ethan comes back out of the restaurant. "What's taking you guys so long? I'm hungry."

"You're always hungry, Mouse!" Sage says as she slips her arm around his waist, and they put their foreheads together.

Inside the restaurant, I pull back and watch them. Sage gives the hostess her name and asks for a booth. Ethan hides behind her like a little boy. What's new is that when the hostess says hi, he responds in kind, making eye contact, albeit briefly, and he shows no sign of the terror that would have consumed him in a situation like this a year ago. I'm sure he appears shy to her, but maybe not abnormally so.

After we're seated, there's no avoiding Ethan's elation. "What do you think, Lanie? I can drive a real car!" He laughs like a little kid. "By next month I'll be ready to take the test if I want."

"Really?" I say, shaking my head at Sage.

"Sage says I'm good enough." A small flash of anger colors his cheeks and tone.

"You drove amazingly well, E. I'm really impressed…"

Sage signals me with her eyes to not continue the 'but' phrase that was set to follow. I bite my tongue and leave it at that. We'll have to talk about it later, but I can let him have this moment.

I scan the restaurant. We come here to this little, roadside, Italian dive a lot. It's usually pretty empty, and the tables are oceans apart, so Ethan doesn't feel crowded. Repetition and routine are the keys to success when it comes to my brother. I'm not sure if Sage has internalized the rules.

A group of girls a couple of years younger than we are comes in. They look sweaty and happy, like they've just won a soccer game. Every one of them slows as they pass our booth to gaze at my brother. They stare in hungry admiration as he holds hands with Sage, and she whispers in his ear. They don't see him, though. They see the pretty wrapper: the golden, surfer-boy curls carelessly framing his gentle face, the bright red lips shaped into an angelic pout, the intense gray eyes with impossibly long, blond lashes and the turned-up nose that makes him look much younger than he is. What they don't see is that he's gripping Sage's hand for dear life because their attention is making him panic, and she's whispering words not of love, but of comfort to assuage his anxiety, so he doesn't freak out, start crying, or worse. If those girls knew the truth about this boy, their stares would be quite different. Not normal, not close.

Ethan and Sage have one more surprise for me. When the waitress finally graces us with her presence, Sage nudges him gently. Ethan swallows and looks down at the menu. He points to the chicken Marsala and mumbles his order without looking up. The waitress writes it down on her pad, completely unaware that she's witnessing a milestone, a miracle. I let it sink in. Ethan ordered a meal in a restaurant. It's a small thing for most people, but for a boy who never left the house for six years and hid in his room anytime someone new came through the door, this small act is earth-shattering. I'm so thrown I almost forget about the news I've carried from Florida. Almost.

I've had a week to mull it all over, and I'm still a bit flummoxed by the development I've yet to impart. I have no idea how Ethan and Sage will take it. I plan to break it to them slowly, give them enough information to figure it out for themselves, so there's no killing of the messenger if that's the upshot. It could really go either way, though. I know I'm taking a big chance throwing this at Ethan in a public place, but what the hell. If he can drive a car and order a meal, this should be easy. I hope. When the food arrives and silence settles over us, I edge off the cliff.

"How long have your mom and our dad been living together?" I ask Sage.

"Rachel and Jesse?" Sage answers. "Six months I guess, about as long as we've been in the apartment."

I pause for a few seconds. "How old is Rachel?"

"Ask weird questions much, Elena?" Sage is looking at me kind of funny, and I think she might guess my news.

"Just answer the question," I say.

"Forty-five," Ethan says, happily joining the game.

I wink at him.

"Sage, do you think of us as family, like siblings?"

"Really, Elena, enough with the disconnected questions." Sage puts her fork down in annoyance.

"Yes or no, please," I insist calmly.

"Of course, I do," she says, looking nervously from Ethan to me. "Where are you going with this?"

"Well. . . in about six months we're going to be related for real."

"What the hell are you talking about? Rachel would never, ever, ever get married again, even to Jesse. Besides, he can't marry legally; that would put him back on the grid." Sage is shaking her head like I've lost my marbles, but Ethan's eyes are growing huge with the realization that he stole from my mind. "Cheater," I think, but he doesn't care.

"A baby?" he thinks. "I'm going to have a brother?"

"Or another sister, if you're very, very lucky," I respond in my head.

The smile spreads across his face slowly as his imagination goes to work on the idea of a baby in the family.

I watch him and think, "One more reason for you to grow up fast, little boy. Let's see if you can get out of diapers before the baby does." It's a cruel thought, but it's there before I can stop it, and Ethan hears it. In an instant his smile vanishes, replaced by the creases in his brow and tilt of his chin that signal the peculiar pain of shame. I might as well have punched him. Ethan starts to bring his thumb up to his mouth, but I reach out and catch his hand in time. He pulls away and sits on his hand, scowling at me. "I didn't mean it, Mouse. I'm sorry," I think as loudly as I can. I don't know if he hears me.

All this drama goes on without Sage. She's still trying to add up the sums.

I finally spell it out for her. "Rachel's pregnant, you big idiot!"

Sage's mouth falls open, and her eyes go blank for a second. Then in typical Sage fashion, she explodes. "No fucking way! Rachel's too old! I can NOT believe this! Great timing, Madre mio! All those years I begged for a sister and now that you decide to give me one, I have to share her! Really, Mother!"

"Ah yes, I forgot. It's all about Sage." I lean over and give her a playful punch in the arm. She looks at Ethan for support, but he's lost in his own thoughts. His eyes are sparkling with the tears he's fighting, thanks to my unfortunate mean streak. That's new too, Ethan fighting back tears and not just melting into them. He succeeds in regaining control of himself and picks up his fork. I watch him push the food around his plate. He glances at me because I'm staring and manages a fairly vicious return glare. I look away, completely chastised by the thought he directs at me. "At least I'm trying; I don't see any charts on the refrigerator dedicated to your little problem."

"Who are you?" I say out loud. He turns away from me, frowning.

The rest of dinner is a combination of Sage's restless, self-centered energy, Ethan's barely concealed disappointment with me or himself or both, and me desperately jumping through hoops to make everything seem fine. On the way out of the restaurant, Ethan turns the keys over to Sage and gets in the backseat, where he curls into himself and immediately begins sucking his thumb. I give up trying, and Sage drives us home in silence, each of us lost in the reality of what it could mean to be a sibling, or for some of us what it already means.

On the way through the kitchen, Sage grabs Ethan's chart off the fridge while he heads upstairs to get ready for bed.

"What do you need that for?" I ask.

"Ammunition," she explains. "He's going to expect me to sleep in his bed with him."

"Right. Because of your magical, motivational intervention in my absence," I say.

"Hey, it worked. Didn't it? Twenty-nine days without an accident is a record, I think," she says.

"But he didn't make it today, so no reward tonight, right?" I ask. I want Sage with me.

She nods. "That doesn't mean he won't try to negotiate anyway."

"I think I'll just stay down here while you guys work that out." I collapse onto the sofa.

"Suit yourself, but you'll need to go up and spend some time with him before bed. He missed you like crazy." Sage stands over me.

"Sure," I say, but I'm not sure. "You go first, and I'll be like the clean-up crew."

"Very funny. You can go up first if you want to," Sage offers.

"I'll take it." I jump up with an enthusiasm I don't really feel.

"Sold to the highest bidder." Sage drops into my place and takes Finn's letter out of her pocket.

"You haven't read it yet?" I delivered Finn's letter to her this morning as soon as I got home.

"I haven't memorized it yet." She smiles sadly. A year and half is a long time to not talk to someone you're in love with. I'm sure that letter is small comfort.

"Better get to it then," I say and begin the long climb to Ethan's room, completely unprepared for who or what might be lurking around the next psychic bend in the labyrinth of my twin's mind and heart.

He meets me in the hall, ready for bed.

"Where you going?" I ask half-smiling, hoping he's forgotten my nasty comment.

"Downstairs to hang with Sage," he says, without returning any of my goodwill.

"E," I put my hand on his arm to force the connection. "I'm sorry for being mean at the restaurant. I don't want you to be mad at me. I missed you. Didn't you miss me too?"

He looks down at his feet and nods. I take his hand and lead him back into the bedroom. His room in our little rental house near the university is tiny, with barely enough space for the bed, dresser, and a small desk. Sage and I share a slightly bigger room, so that the third bedroom, the largest, can be used for Ethan's art studio. A gallery in town sells his haunting paintings. While it's hard for people to imagine, Ethan brings more money into this house than Sage and I combined. Ethan sits on the edge of the bed while I fiddle with the stuff on his desk, sketches, notes, and elaborate math problems with symbols I don't understand, worked out in perfect miniature print, filling three or four pages, front and back. "What's this?" I ask, holding up a page.

"Don't mess those up!" He jumps off the bed and grabs the paper from me. He organizes it back into the pile while I look over his shoulder.

"Sorry," I mumble.

He turns around to face me, and I feel oddly intimidated. Ethan's nearly a full head taller than I am, though no one would describe him as tall. At 5' 8", he and Sage are actually about the same height, but in the last year or so he's put on a little weight and filled out some through the shoulders and chest, so he doesn't seem as small to me. I step back to let him through and notice the sprinkling of blond whiskers over his top lip and on his cheeks and chin, one more thing to add to the growing list of changes in him. "So, what's the stuff on those papers?"

"Dr. Roschan from the university started working with me online a couple of weeks ago, remember?"

"Oh, yeah. I forgot Sage set that up. How's it going?"

For a second, Ethan forgets his annoyance, and his eyes light up. "He's giving me extra problems and stuff he does with the graduate students. It's way cool." His voice drops at the end.

"Sounds awesome. What's the prob?" Ethan sits in the middle of the bed, cross-legged with his head down. After a couple of seconds, he looks up halfway.

"He wants me to come to his class at the university, but. . . I can't."

"Too scary?" I ask, and he nods. "Nobody's going to make you go, E."

"I know, but—" He doesn't finish. He pulls at the fuzz on the blanket, and his eyes cloud over.

"What is it, E?"

He takes a deep breath and looks at me with something akin to desperation. "I don't want to be afraid of everything anymore. I want to be like you and Sage, not like me." Now the tears spill over, and I feel him reaching out for me emotionally. I sit next to him on the bed, and he puts his head in my lap, curls in knees to chest, and puts his thumb in his mouth. I run my fingers through his tangled hair, trace the lines in his forehead.

"Give it some more time, E. Look how far you've come in the last six months. Riding the bus, going to museums and restaurants, and driving a car." I give him a playful poke, and he manages a fleeting smile. "Who knows, maybe next year you'll be ready. Maybe by next year, it won't seem so scary."

"Maybe," he says wistfully, wiping his eyes with the back of his hand. Gradually, Ethan relaxes, and a comfortable silence settles between us. I wonder if he's falling asleep.

"Hey, Lanie. What did they do to you in that place in Florida?" Ethan asks quietly.

I shift a little, and he sits up to face me. His brow is knit in concern. Since when does Ethan worry about me? When he was stuck in time as a four-year-old, his selfish anxieties took all his energy. How old are people when they begin to worry about others? Eight? Ten?

Now that Ethan's unstuck, this age thing is becoming a kind of obsession for me. I ask Rachel, Ethan's and my therapist, over and over, "So, how old do think Ethan is now?"

"Nineteen, same as you," she laughs. "The mental age measurement is not that literal," she explains. "He'll make amazing progress in some areas, like the agoraphobia, and no progress at all in others, like the enuresis."

It's a reasonable explanation, but I still wish I could have an age thermometer, so I know what to expect from him.

"Lanie? You're staring at me in that weird way again. Why do you do that all the time?"

I look away. "I don't know, E. I guess I just don't recognize you sometimes."

"You're kind of freaking me out. Can you stop?" He gives me a little grin.

"Freaking you out? You sound like Sage." I reach out and caress his face.

"What did they do?" he asks again, leaning into my hand.

"Actually, it was kind of amazing, like something from the future or a movie." Ethan isn't looking at me anymore, so I pause and follow his gaze. Sage is standing in the doorway.

"Mind if I join?" she asks.

I motion her in. "Saves me from having to repeat myself," I say.

She walks around the bed to sit behind Ethan. He immediately relaxes against her, and she wraps her arms around his waist. I envy the easy, comfortable way they fit. Before Ethan can put his thumb in his mouth, she gently catches his hand in hers. The way she caresses his thumb has to feel much better than sucking it. She rests her cheek against his head, and they breathe in sync. Sometimes, I think that maybe this is how it's meant to be, that Finn was some sort of temporary disturbance in the force that is Ethan and Sage, and all of that's over now. Then I remember the fire in Finn's eyes on the beach and the catch in Sage's voice when she says his name. And I know without a doubt it's not over, not by a long shot. My heart aches for my brother.

"You're doing it again, Lanie," Ethan whines.

"Sorry, little brother," I tease. Sage rolls her eyes knowingly, waiting for Ethan's indignant response to the moniker, but Ethan's not stuck at four anymore.

"Just tell your story, littler sister," he responds, giving me a mock glare.

I have to smile. "Well played, E," I say. "I'll tell you the story." But not the whole story, I think. Not the part about Jamie. Not the part about you, Brother.

Ethan's gray eyes lock on mine, and in the back of my head I just make out his thoughts, like a voice whispering from across a noisy, crowded room. "I already know the whole story. I knew it before you did. I knew it before it happened."

℘ 2 ∝

ALL THOSE SHADOWS

All those nights I held you tight
Demons tearing you apart
All those shadows
Terrors tattered hearts
Beat back come morning's light
I kept you safe and sound
Promises and flight
You held me down
Trying and desperate not to drown
    "Light and Shadow" -"- Luna Rayne, 2002

When Ethan's screams rip through the 2 am silence, I'm still awake, trying to figure out if I imagined his voice in my head. I'm not startled; in fact, I think I'd subconsciously been waiting for it. Sage warned me that my absence had been the catalyst for another round of nightmares that had come consistently since the first night I'd been gone. I didn't bother to ask her what he'd dreamed because Ethan won't tell even Sage about the things that torture him in his sleep.

Sage and I sit up at the same time. "I'll go," I tell her, grabbing my robe. "I wasn't sleeping anyway." She drops back onto the pillow with a sigh of relief.

Ethan's awake by the time I get the light on. He's gasping for air and trying desperately to untangle himself from the sheet and blanket. I help free him.

"You okay, E? Are you awake?" I ask.

He nods his head, but he backs himself up against the headboard and wraps his arms around his knees. I sit next to him and smooth his sweaty curls. He's trembling and crying with his head down, like he doesn't want me to see. It's ridiculous. All our lives I've been with him through the bad dreams and wet sheets. There's no embarrassment or indignity that I haven't witnessed and, more importantly, wouldn't suffer myself to free him. He knows this, yet here we are. It was easier before, when he would wake up, cry it out in my arms, let me sort him out and sing him back to sleep. Now there are lines that cannot be crossed, lines that are changing all the time. Lines that are cutting us apart.

"What do you need, E?" I ask, wondering if he'll tell me. I put my hand lightly on his arm, inviting him to let me hold him.

His bicep hardens. "Leave me alone," he mumbles into his knees between sniffles.

"It was a dream, E, just a bad dream," I try again.

"What do you know?" He sobs harder. "You don't know."

"Then tell me. I want to help," I say.

"I don't want your help, Lanie. I can take care of myself. Go away." There's that flash of anger again in his tone, like this is all my fault somehow.

"You sure?"

He nods into his arms without looking up. I kiss the top of his head and leave without closing the door. From the hallway around the corner, I watch him gradually come out of the cocoon he'd created with his body. His hands and shoulders continue shaking while he changes. Then he crawls back in bed without turning off the light.

I finger the earring in the pocket of my robe. It was my mother's. I pulled it from her ear the night she died. The paramedics found the tiny fairy holding a moonstone clutched in my unconscious hand after they pulled me from the fire. I only know this because of Ethan. I have no memory of that night. I press the post into my palm until it pierces my flesh. I wait for the bead of blood to rise and contemplate how good it would feel to drag the dull metal up the inside of my wrist. I can taste the iron and salt as I imagine it.

Ethan's still crying. I wish I knew what to do. I'm a useless lifeguard in an outlandishly tall tower. My brother's drowning, but there's no way I can get down in time to save him.

He sees me lingering in the hall and rolls over to face the wall. The spasms rippling through his shoulders betray his torment. His resentment of my presence radiates off him like heat, but I go to him anyway, sit on the edge of the bed and start to sing softly. It's the only tool left in my bag of tricks, but I have to use it with the greatest of care. There are songs that are off limits now, the ones that remind him of when we were small, when we were living with Grandmother. I choose a favorite of Sage's and sing in a whisper, hoping he won't turn around and scream at me to leave.

As I start the second verse, he rolls over. I turn my palm face up, and he takes my hand, finally accepting the little bit of comfort I can offer him. I sing a little louder and caress his fingers with my thumb. By the end of the song, his eyes are closed, and his breathing is deep and even, though I can tell he's not asleep. There's no pulling my hand free without disturbing him, so I lie down. I'll go back to bed in a few minutes, after he's asleep.

Light streaming in the dirty window in a single, arrogant beam rouses me from a sinister and futuristic underground lair where I'd been armed and engaged in a heated, tactical debate with Sage about some kind of conflict with someone or something I suddenly can no longer remember. The clock on the desk blinks 6:12. Ethan stirs beside me.

"What time is it?" His voice is so low I have to look twice to see if it's really my brother.

"Way too early for me to be up," I say, rising groggily to a seated position.

"Don't you have to go to work?" He sits up too, turning his back to me, like my presence is making him uncomfortable.

"Not today. Tomorrow." In the old days I'd tease him, bean him with a pillow or push him off the bed, but I can't fathom how not to annoy or upset him now. "I think I'll go back to sleep in my bed," I say.

"'K." He glances at me over his shoulder.

"You going for a swim?" I ask on my way to standing. It's a dumb question; Ethan swims every morning in the heated pool in the yard, just like at Grandmother's house. For at least an hour, he immerses himself in a world where he can be powerful and free from the gravitational forces of the past that pull so heavily on his psyche.

"Uh-huh," he grunts. I pause in the doorway, waiting for him to say something more, but he doesn't, so I stumble back to my own bed, hoping to return to the narrative of my dream and find out what I'm fighting against.

Sage is still snoring in the bed next to mine, so close I can touch her. Ethan will come in here in a second to wake her up before he goes down. Until then, I marvel at the total abandon of her expression. I've never known anyone who sleeps with so much pleasure as Sage. Insomnia - never; nightmares - not a chance. She says I provide the mystical magic behind her easy sleep, that somehow, I induce this peacefulness in her with my gift, that this is one of the reasons she loves me. Whatever that means is anyone's guess. I love Sage, have loved her, will love her, but in a very different way than she loves, loved, will love me. Ethan, Finn, Jo, and I all vie for her, and she balances our love on the head of a pin, fitting all of it into her heart like a magical suitcase that can hold the contents of an entire kingdom, blissfully unaware of the chaos ensuing under the clasp.

Her straight, chestnut hair spills off the pillow in a tangled, mocha waterfall. As I drift back down, I conjure the sweet memory of our first kiss in Sugar Creek Park. Even though it was part of Finn's fucked up dare, it was real, too, or maybe it was too real, I reason groggily with a smile before slipping under.

I wake up at 8:30 to the sound of silence in the house. No splashing from outside, no conversation or giggling from below, complete and utter silence. Ethan must've gone running with Sage. She won't venture too far from home with him along. For some reason, the anxiety of leaving the house is worse for him on foot. Hoping they made coffee before they left, I stumble down the hallway toward the stairs in my pajamas. Halfway down, I see them in the living room and pause.

They've moved all of the furniture against the wall and are seated in the center of the room, cross-legged, back to back, close but not touching. Their eyes are closed. I sit on the stairs and watch. I can almost feel the electricity in the room raising the hairs on my arm. Sage must be trying to work with Ethan on controlling his gift— or curse, if you ask him. I close my eyes, too, ground myself and bring my chakras into balance the way Jamie Fleming, my mentor at the Parapsychology Science Initiative, taught me. I open my mind to their energy and slowly, like turning a tuning knob on a radio, Sage's and Ethan's thoughts come into focus.

I'm immediately caught in the stream of Sage's memory. She's maybe five, hurrying through an airport behind Rachel. A stuffed dog in a shop catches her eye, and she swerves away from her mom for just a moment. When she moves back into the rushing stream of humanity, she flashes into an instant of panic. Rachel isn't there in front of her. She isn't anywhere. Sage rushes forward, her heart beating wildly. Then, suddenly, Rachel's beside her, smiling down, completely unaware of Sage's momentary absence and her terror.

Unexpectedly, I realize that while the memory is Sage's, it's not coming from Sage. I'm reading it from Ethan. I search Sage's thoughts to see which one of Ethan's memories she's been thrust into.

That's how it works for him. He accesses someone's random memory, usually without meaning to and without focus. In the process, he drives his own memories violently into them in a kind of consciousness swap. He has little control over what he sees or what he passes on, and the other person experiences the exchange like an aneurism. Physical contact is the catalyst for the exchanges and the root of Ethan's agoraphobia, in my opinion.

I focus my concentration on Sage to see what Ethan's passing on to her. I search deeply and come up empty. Her thoughts are vaguely on her own memory as well. This is amazing progress for Ethan, but it's all so controlled. Could Ethan keep it together in the heat of the moment with someone other than Sage, I wonder. Sage and Ethan have pushed specific memories to each other before, but with fairly serious consequences and with no control over where they themselves ended up in the other's psyches. Being able to push or receive a memory and stay in control would be a game changer for Ethan.

"I know you're here, Elena." Ethan's in my head now. He can't see my memories, just as I can't heal his pain, but we've always shared this telepathy that he somehow amplifies now to include Sage. Unfortunately, the twin thing short-circuits our deeper abilities. "Those tricks you learned in Florida are cool, but I've been practicing too," he thinks. I don't have to open my eyes to know he's smiling. He sounds almost arrogant; it's disconcerting.

"What do you know about the tricks I learned?" I think apprehensively.

Jamie's sitting across from me in the lab at the Initiative. Ethan's pushing my own memory back to me. I'm looking into Jamie's dancing, light brown eyes, smiling back at his goofy, crooked grin, with our hands resting palm to palm on the table between us. Jamie's playful voice flows clearly from Ethan's mind. "'Close your eyes, Elena." He gets up from the table and moves behind me. "Place your hand at your second chakra, here." He guides my hand to the place just below my belly button and rests his hand over mine. I giggle. "Concentrate on opening the petals. Radiate pure, orange light into and out of that space - "

"Stop it, Ethan!" I yell out loud, jumping up and cutting the connection. I pound down the stairs and into the kitchen, breathing hard. This isn't like the anger I feel when he wets his pants or refuses to eat something I've cooked. This is battle-ready, spitting-fire angry.

He picked a memory he knew was private. He invaded my mind, my memories, and what's worse is that he isn't supposed to be able to do that. How the hell was he doing that?! I pace around the kitchen, slamming things from the counters into the sink. I grab a glass and hurl it at the wall. It explodes with a satisfying crash. I pick up one of the shards off the counter and trace a line across my fingertip. The blood immediately rises in bright, scarlet beads. I put my finger to my lips and instantly feel calmer.

When I turn around, Sage is standing there. "You want to tell me what's going on with you two?" she asks.

"What the hell are you doing to him, Sage?" My tears are going to spill over any second.

"What am *I* doing to him? You've got to be kidding me."

"What was that in there? You're screwing around with shit you know nothing about, Sage!"

"*That* in there isn't the problem. This started before you left for Florida, and since you got back, it's worse." Her voice is rising.

I carve another slit into my fingertip, below the first, and watch the blood surface as I search for a point of reference. She's wrong. "No way. This started the day you walked through our door!"

"Nice, Elena! Real nice. I'm not gonna let you do that misdirection thing." She knocks the shard of glass from my hand. "You've been home less than twenty-four hours, and Ethan's totally falling apart. We didn't even make it to the end of the block this morning before he had an accident, and yesterday in the car, he was fine until the conversation turned to you."

"I see. So, I'm the cause of all of Ethan's problems. If I just went away, he'd be fine. You could play house here and lead him on until one fine day when Finn walks through the door, and then what, Sage? What are you going to do with Ethan when Finn shows up again?"

She looks away as I draw blood, and I wait for her to walk out, but she takes a deep breath and turns back to me, her jaw set and determined. "Look, I'm not saying you're the cause of Ethan's issues, but did you ever stop to notice that his accidents are triggered by anxiety? He had twenty-nine dry days and suddenly he fails twice in less than two days. What changed?"

I'm shaking my head because the tears are blocking my ability to speak, but I know she's right. She touches my hand and goes on. "I'm trying to tell you that something is happening between you and Ethan that's messing with you both." She turns my hand over and watches the blood dribble into my palm. "When's the last time you cut?"

I pull my hand away and don't answer.

"I'll bet you a month of dishes it was before you left for Florida."

I glare at her. This is not a topic of conversation she's allowed to broach. She knows the rules. "Go ahead and play at fixing my brother, Sage, but I don't need you to fix me." I push past her to go upstairs.

"That's the problem," she yells at my back. "To you, Ethan's a problem to fix!"

On the bottom step, I turn to look at my brother. He's still in the middle of the room where I left him, with his knees up against his chest and his thumb in his mouth. He's rocking back and forth. He doesn't make eye contact, but I can feel him reaching out to me in my head; he's sorry for what he did. I don't care. In this moment I hate him with every fiber of my being. I hate his pitiful weakness and his power over me. I hate that his ability works on me, but mine doesn't work on him. I have to get out of here before I suffocate.

I throw on my clothes without showering and pull my hair into a ponytail. On my way through the kitchen, I grab the keys off the counter. Neither Ethan nor Sage is around, and I don't particularly care if Sage needs the car today.

I'm just about to back down the driveway when Jo pulls in behind me. Just my luck. She gets out and comes over to the driver's side door. I roll down the window.

"Jo, what're you doing here?"

"Nice to see you, too." She looks me up and down. "You okay, sweetie?"

The concern in her voice melts me, and tears burn behind my eyes again. I shake my head.

She opens the door to the car and pulls me out and into her arms. I really don't want to be crying on her, but at this point I can't rein it in.

"Come on," she whispers in my ear. "I'll buy you a cup of coffee."

I nod and get into her car. Sage comes outside before Jo can get the engine started, so she gets out and meets Sage by the back door. They engage in a brief exchange. Then Jo's taking me away. I have the ride to the cafe to pull it together, and Jo's smart enough to give me that time. I'm grateful she chooses Starbucks, not the Bean Scene, where I work.

"What's up?" she asks, once we have caffeine in hand.

"Sage and I had a fight," I say.

"So, she said, but that's not really what's wrong, is it?"

"Not really." I pause. "It's more about Ethan," I say quietly.

Jo nods, looking at her coffee. "That's a huge burden you've been carrying all alone for a long time, baby."

"I just want to go back and stay in Florida."

"Running, hmm." She licks the foam off her cappuccino. "The final refuge of the cowardly and the desperate. Away or toward?"

I laugh without mirth. "Both, I think. Ethan is… different now. He's changing. It's scaring the shit out of me. Sage says I'm holding him back, making him worse."

"Damn. That's pretty heavy coming from her. Not really fair either."

"I don't know. Everything's so weird with us lately."

"I know I'm no expert on Ethan, but I'm thinking his problem with you might have more to do with your absence than your presence."

"Maybe," I say.

"Since I've known you, Lane, I've watched you go from being Ethan's mother to his sister. You're gradually leaving him behind, inch by inch, and that has to terrify him. Think about it; would you want to depend on Sage to be your safety net? Particularly if you were as dependent as Ethan?"

"Scary thought. But he keeps pushing me away. What's that about?"

"You'll have to ask him. Knowing Ethan, it's something totally out there that you wouldn't guess in a lifetime, Rumpelstiltskin. Now for the more interesting part. What're you running toward?"

Jamie's face flashes through my mind. I close that thought down. "An ocean of possibility, no pun intended," I say, smiling. "I'm like someone special at the Initiative, a VIP, a celebrity even."

"A valuable resource." Jo has a ruthless way of bringing truth to bear.

"I guess. But I can see a future there that belongs to me, where I'm doing exciting, important things, not washing sheets and serving bad coffee."

"What kind of exciting, important things?" Her interest is genuine, but I hesitate. Saying some things out loud in the 'normal' world will make you sound decidedly freakish. I take my version of reality down several notches.

"I could be a doctor or nurse or counselor. Who knows?" I look down and take a breath. "Enough about me, Jo."

"Not nearly enough, if you ask me." She winks and reaches for my hand.

"What're you doing at my house at like 9:30 on a Thursday morning?" I ask, lacing my fingers through hers. "You missed me that much?"

She smiles. "That too. But, actually, I was there to help Sage and Ethan with some sort of experiment. Sage was a little short on details in her text last night, but I have a feeling it's not going to be America's Test Kitchen. I should get back. I did promise, and I have a piano student at noon."

I know immediately what Sage is planning. "She wants you to touch Ethan," I mumble, letting go of her hand.

"What?" Her eyes get wide with the memory of when she accidentally touched his arm over a year ago. "Last time, my head nearly exploded. I still have nightmares about it."

"They're working on Ethan's control over his thing, you know, but they can't fully test his progress because Sage is kind of immune or whatever. You don't have to do it."

Jo is lost in her own thoughts for a minute, shaking her head. "Sage never changes, does she?"

"She's only trying to help Ethan. Her heart's in the right place." I'm not sure why I'm defending her.

"Sage's heart is always in the right place," Jo says a little bitterly. "It's her head that's fucked up." She downs the last of her tea and gets up.

"You're gonna go anyway?"

"If it were for her, I'd blow it off, but—"

"It's for Ethan," I finish for her.

"Can I drop you someplace?" she asks.

She leaves me at the Bean Scene. Even though I don't have to work, it's where I want to be.

Despite the clever name, the Bean Scene isn't the hippest cafe in town. It's actually more like a road-kill diner, trying too hard to be a European coffee-house. The coffee's pretty bad most of the time, and the clientele tends toward the aging, university townees and the wannabe whatevers of the world. Sadly, I kind of fit in perfectly. Marco, the manager of the place and grandson of the owner, greets me with a hug. He drags me to a table and yells for two cups of brew and a grilled blueberry muffin, the house specialty. Since most of the tables are empty, half the staff joins us to dish about the goings-on while I was away.

Marco and I bonded in my interview when we discovered our mutual love for TV and movies that deal with the occult, and our intense dislike of the writers and directors who play fast and loose with the real "facts" about demonology, witchcraft, mythology and the like. "*Charmed, Buffy*, and Anne Rice — love them! *Bewitched, Vampire Diaries* and Stephanie Meyer — hate them!" Marco's mantra. 'Sparkling vampires — for real?!' Most of us work here because of Marco. It certainly isn't the tips that keep us coming back every day. Not only is Marco smart, hilarious, and totally unique; he's nearly always smiling. Someday, he'll be a famous movie director. At least, in a perfect world he would be.

After he tells me about the near breakup between Heather and

Hunter, the resident love-bird baristas, caused by totally unfounded jealousy over a new dishwasher who only lasted a week, he confesses he hasn't done a lick of work on his opus, an avant-garde animation film, since I left.

"Didn't know I was such a muse," I joke.

"Angel-face, you have no idea," he says. I don't take him seriously. We all know his heart belongs to the short, curt, hyper-organized hostess, Myra. She keeps Marco and the restaurant humming.

"Enough procrastination, Elly. Tell us all about your Florida vacation already," Myra insists, planting herself in Marco's lap.

They think I took a vacation to see my long-lost, recently re-found dad. I didn't tell them about the Initiative; that would've entailed explaining my gift. "I never imagined the ocean would look so ginormous!" I tell them. "Oh yeah, and I met a guy."

Oohs and ahs from the crowd. "I didn't think you liked that flavor," Marco comments, one eyebrow raised in surprise. Myra smacks his arm hard.

"No rules against sampling all the flavors," I say. They laugh.

"Details, details," he demands. "And give me something juicy to work with."

"His name's Jamie, and he taught me how to open my sacral chakra."

More oohs and ahs. Everyone's hysterical now.

"That's plenty of detail, girl. My imagination will take it from there." Marco grins salaciously.

"I'm sure it will," Myra says, kissing him soundly before getting back to her duties.

Customers start filtering in, the early lunch bunch. Everyone gets back to work, so Marco and I are finally alone at the table. "What about Jo?" he asks, suddenly serious.

"That's the million dollar question, isn't it?" Then he gets up, too, leaving me to my rumination and muffin dissection. I can only hide out here for so long. Eventually, Sage is going to need to go to class and because of the time Ethan burned down the garage apartment that

Sage and Rachel lived in when we first met, we tend not to leave him alone for too long. I'm just about to ask Marco for a lift home when my phone rings. I'm sure it must be Sage, but it's the Initiative.

"Elena?"

A single word and I'm immediately returned to the fantastical world I left behind only two days ago. Or was it twenty years ago? Jamie Fleming, graduate researcher in Parapsychology from Flagler Beach, Florida, stands before me like the first time I met him, tall and lanky, hands shoved deep in the pockets of his faded jeans, unkempt hair swept distractedly to the side, goofy-grinned and hawk-eyed behind the requisite horn-rimmed glasses. After the screening phone interview with a minion of the Initiative, Jamie showed up here to do an in-depth assessment in person. We spent four days together, forehead to forehead, testing my "potential," measuring my psychic energy levels. He seemed increasingly amazed by my responses to his "games." That's what he called them, games. At first, I took this personally, thinking I must be pretty damn special, but by the third day, I realized this was just his way of getting a subject, me, through the tediousness of the tasks.

At the end of the fourth day, Jamie bid me a fondish farewell. Two days later, he called to "invite" me to come out to their lab for three weeks. Sage and Ethan were less than thrilled. Sage went all *X-files-Fringe* on me, filling my head with dire and horrific scenarios ripped from the Sci-Fi channel. And Ethan cried and cried, terrified I'd never return. I must admit in retrospect that I had a few qualms about going there, too. When I saw the ad on the bulletin board at school, I totally made fun of it. I mean, really, how many people are walking around with psychic gifts like mine and Ethan's? And why in this age of social media would someone put a lousy poster on a bulletin board at a small local college, instead of tweeting or using Facebook? Impractical at least; questionable at best. Still, after seeing the ad every day for a month or more on my way into psych class, I took a tab with the number, deliberated with Jo, and made the call, setting the rest of my life in motion. The serendipity of the lab being in Florida, only twenty miles from the ranch where Jesse, Rachel, and Finn live off the grid, sealed the deal.

The last time Jamie called, he sheepishly offered me $3,000 to take a leave of absence from school and come down to their facility for three weeks, as if this were an embarrassingly small sum of money. I make $8/hour plus tips at the coffee shop. Sage makes $15 an hour tutoring at the writing center, so $3000 is a lot of ramen noodles to us.

I know why he's calling now.

"Jamie. Can't live without your favorite subject?" I try to sound light and breezy.

"My personal feelings notwithstanding, I'm afraid this is a business call." Why does he always sound so apologetic?

"That's too bad," I say.

"You've had a couple of days to think over what we talked about," he begins.

"I have."

"The details of the offer stand. I need a decision, Elena. Lots of people here are counting on you to make the right one."

There are people here counting on the same thing, I think. Unfortunately, the happiness of the one group completely, irrevocably precludes the happiness of the other. I shake my head to clear the confusion. I know what I'm going to do. Courage, Elena, I tell myself. I clear my throat and give Jamie my answer.

ℰℴ 3 ℭℛ

RELEASE

The clock in the hall is ringing
You know the time has come
Your back against the front door
Arms across your chest
Tears in your eyes betray you
So, I'll slip out the back door
Sweet release in time
Note left on the kitchen table
The story of our tears
I know what I told you
I know what I said
But the train whistle's blowing
Calling in my head
        "Tracks" - Luna Rayne, 2012

The unexpected sound of raucous, silly giggling greets me when I get back home. Sage and Ethan are upstairs in the bathroom. What they could be doing in there that could be so outrageously humorous is beyond me. In fact, I'm not sure I even want to know. They exhaust me sometimes. I mean to curl up on the sofa and listen to some music when another wave of laughter piques my curiosity. I creep up the stairs halfway and peer over the remaining steps, through the open door. Ethan's standing in front of the mirror, stripped to the waist. In one hand he cradles a red balloon about the size of a head; in the other he holds a safety razor. Sage smears shaving cream over part of the balloon. She dabs the end of his nose with what's left on her hand, and he lets out a playful shriek. In the process of wiping off his nose, half the shaving cream on the balloon ends up on his chest, and Sage nearly falls over at the mirth of it all. She rinses her hands and dries them off on the towel that's draped over her shoulder as she steps behind him. She takes his hand in hers and guides the razor over the balloon. Together their hands rinse the razor in the sink and come back for another pass.

Judging from the number of balloon carcasses on the bathroom floor and the amount of shaving cream on them and the walls, they've been at this for a while. I'm so enthralled with the details of their actions that the importance of what's happening here nearly escapes me. When all the shaving cream has been removed from the red balloon, Ethan bats the balloon into the air to high-five Sage, and I finally catch on as a lump begins to grow in my throat.

"Let me try by myself now," Ethan insists gleefully. Sage sprays the shaving cream into his palm, and he immediately splats it onto her cheek. They both howl uproariously. Then, gently, he takes the cream from her face and rubs it over the surface of the balloon he's caught on its way back down. Sage turns on the faucet, and Ethan rinses his hand. To dry it, Sage wraps his hand in the towel with both of hers. It's an act of supreme affection and intimacy. Ethan leans in like he might kiss her, and my stomach wrenches. To my knowledge, they've not kissed since the summer of the fire. That kiss happened after Sage and Ethan swapped memories, and Ethan got her memory of kissing Finn. I guess you could say he channeled Finn, but I know it awakened something in Ethan, too.

Thankfully, Sage hands Ethan the razor, and he concentrates on carefully scraping the balloon clean. When he accomplishes the task without a pop, Sage bats the balloon into the bathtub, like a touchdown spike, and Ethan giggles with delight.

"You're ready now, Mouse. Time to do it for real," Sage says semi-solemnly. Ethan nods, like a soldier going into battle. Sage smears the shaving cream expertly over his chin, cheeks and upper lip. I want to run up the stairs and end this whole thing right now. Half of me is sure Ethan will slit his own throat; half of me feels ridiculously guilty and left out. I should be teaching Ethan to shave, not Sage. The boy belongs to me, not her, but I creep back downstairs, swallowing the tears threatening to expose me. I slip outside and crumple onto the back step. All of this should make my decision easier to live with, not harder.

I have only two weeks to get everything organized. I start by boxing up all the summer clothes and books under the guise of spring cleaning. I scan all the papers and load our music up to the cloud late at night. Gradually, so it's not noticeable, I pack the few knick-knacks and mementos I'll keep. I pay the rent through the end of the semester, so Sage won't have to scramble to handle the financial burden of an entire house. A couple boxes at a time, I ship my life to a storage location in Florida. It's wrong not to tell Ethan and Sage what's happening, but I need to do this peacefully, without drama or recriminations.

Giving notice at the Bean Scene is rough. Myra actually cries and Marco promises that if it doesn't work out, I'll always have a place to come back to. He holds me in a gentle bear hug for a full minute before letting me go. Tomorrow begins the one-week countdown. In the morning, I'll tell Jo. I didn't want to put her in the position of keeping a secret from Sage for too long, but she deserves a little time.

When I get home from the Bean Scene, Sage is sitting at the kitchen table, bouncing an envelope up and down between her forefinger and thumb, tapping it until she gets to the bottom, then flipping it to begin again. She doesn't look up or say a word.

"Where's E?" I ask.

She turns the envelope over and holds it like a game show host showing me the prize. "You got something you want to tell me?"

I can tell the seal has been torn open. "You opened my mail? Spy much, Sage?"

"I had to open it, Elena. When my roommate gets huge contract-looking envelopes from the Parapsychology Science Initiative, I go a little crazy. I start thinking maybe she's leaving again and not telling me. Damn it! I thought we were done with PSI! Why didn't you tell me?"

"This is none of your business." I grab the envelope out of her hand and turn away. She stops me dead in my tracks.

"It's very much my business. I love you and Ethan, but I didn't sign on to do this gig solo. We're a team." She pauses. "I can't take care of Ethan alone."

I pull up a chair, so our knees are touching. "Please try to understand. This is my chance to have a real future. I have to see where this is going to take me—" I take a deep breath. "—take us."

Sage's eyes get wide. "You're taking Ethan with you." Her voice is flat.

"I'd never ask you to do this alone. Ethan's my brother, my blood, my responsibility. I think the people at the Initiative can help him." I speak slowly, softly, hoping she'll understand.

"Does he know?" she asks.

"I haven't told him, if that's what you're asking. That being said, I'm sure he knows."

"Explains a lot," Sage mutters.

"I'm sorry, Sage." I take her hand. "I don't want to hurt you."

She pulls away. "Sure," she says, her voice heavy with sarcasm. "When?"

"I'll be flying down a week from tomorrow to find a place to live and get settled. The Initiative is giving us a car. I'll drive back and get Ethan in a couple of weeks."

Sage nods, chewing on her bottom lip, either trying to hold in her anger or her tears. I lay my hands on her knees and absorb her pain into my palms. A slow ache runs up through the muscles in my arms and travels into my spine. I can taste Sage's emotions, like the complex palette of a gourmet meal. When the blood and pain cycle into my brain, a kind of explosion occurs that pours through me, like a burning hot shower emanating from the center out. Bit by bit the burn cools, leaving me exhausted physically and mentally. Almost instantly, Sage brightens, though, and she gets up from the table. "I hate this. I just want you to know I really, really, really hate this!"

I hang my head. More words won't make this okay for either of us.

"You need to talk to your brother," she says.

"I know," I say, but I don't move from the table.

"Maybe, like now." Sage says, a storm brewing behind the forced patience in her voice.

I nod and try to will myself up from the chair. "Are you ready for the fallout? He's not going to forgive me for a while," I say, hoping to postpone the inevitable nightmare this conversation is likely to unleash.

"Elena, I've been dealing with the fallout for weeks." She sounds exhausted.

"This is not how I planned it, Sage. I was hoping to just…"

"Throw him in the car like a piece of luggage." Sage shakes her head like I'm a huge disappointment to her.

"You must really hate me right now," I say.

"And you must really hate Ethan to think so little of him." She goes to the sink on the pretext of loading dishes into the dishwasher. I watch her back for a few seconds, then pick up the contract and go.

At the top of the stairs, I turn right. Ethan's art studio is at the end of the hallway; the door's open. He paints with his back to the door by one of the windows, where the light's best. I stand in the doorway and watch the mathematical precision of his work. He's not the kind of artist who paints from life, though his works are eerily lifelike. His brush strokes aren't loose and energetic; they're small and subtle. He goes into every piece as though it's fully conceived and sitting in front of him, no hesitation, wiping, layering or backtracking, like the painting's already on the canvas and he's just pulling it out of hiding.

The piece he's working on is a boy and girl, startlingly similar, yet each unique. The conflict between them comes only from their eyes locked on each other's as their hands are joined in a white-knuckled grasp. They appear to be moving forward as though the frame is a doorway, and behind them in the room they're leaving is a mirror, where they're reflected in reverse, moving in the opposite direction. My heart skips a beat. It's us. Ethan's painting us. Why did he reverse the images in the mirror, I wonder? It's definitely not a mistake. Ethan doesn't make mistakes in this realm. I tear my eyes from the creation to study the creator. His head's tipped to the side in concentration. He holds one brush in his left hand and one in his teeth. His right hand pushes the curls out of his face every few seconds. I need to trim his hair, maybe tonight, I think. His face is absolutely peaceful, like he's gone from this place to another, easier one. I wish everything weren't so hard for him.

Suddenly, an alarm goes off beside him and it takes him a couple seconds to return from his other world to this one. He shuts it off and puts down his brushes. When he turns around, he's surprised to see me. "Lanie?"

"Hey, E. How you doing?" I try to smile nonchalantly.

He's wondering why I'm here. "Okay." He gestures toward the door. "Be right back."

I ruffle his hair as he passes, and he grants me a tired smile. He glances over his shoulder at me as he makes his way down the hall to the bathroom. I turn away and step into the studio to get a better look at his paintings. Sketches of the current painting are taped all over the wall behind the easel. Several other paintings that have been started are stacked on the other side of the room. He has no idea how utterly talented he is, but I guarantee he'd trade it all for ten minutes of normal.

"Whatcha looking at?" Ethan's voice startles me out of my thoughts.

"I love the new painting! It's us, isn't it?" I ask.

He thinks about it for a couple of seconds. "I guess so."

This is the part where I wrack my sluggish mind for the best way to break the news to him and still end up doing it all wrong. I look away, searching the walls for cue cards that refuse to appear.

"Why are you here?"

"I've got something I have to tell you, E, and I don't want to." I hang my head, rotating the envelope around and around in my hands.

"Oh." He looks at me intently, waiting.

"I'm going back to Florida, but you probably knew that," I begin.

He looks down at his feet and nods. "When?"

"A week from tomorrow."

"How long are you staying this time?" He won't look at me.

"That's a complicated question." I put the envelope on the table by his pallet and take his hand. "The Initiative has some interesting work for me, but I can't be away from you as long as they want me to stay." I wait for it to sink in.

Ethan shifts his feet uncomfortably. Then he pulls his hand away and pushes past me to get back to the canvas. "Please, E, we need to talk about this." I touch his shoulder.

He shrugs my hand off and dips his brush into the crimson paint. It drips onto the envelope. He doesn't notice. I tear my eyes from the droplets that look like blood and watch as he takes a couple of measured strokes.

"What is there to talk about?" he mumbles to the painting.

"Ethan, please try to understand. I need to do this, and I think it will be best for you, too. I think they can help you get control of your abilities."

He won't turn around, but I can see his chin and shoulders beginning to shake.

"E, I know this isn't going to be easy for you, but you're doing so much better now, and you survived the move here. Plus, we'll be near Rachel and Jesse when the baby comes. You'll like that, right?"

He looks out the window to his left. "What about Sage?" he asks in his head.

I answer him out loud. "She'll come visit us."

He turns around and despite the tears spilling over, he levels me with his stare. "What if I don't want to go with you? What if I just stay here with her?" Even telepathically his tone is belligerent, frustrated.

My turn to look away. "That's not on the table," I say silently.

"I don't belong to you, Elena. I can do what I want," he thinks, but he drops the brush, sinks to the ground, leans his head against the windowsill and puts his thumb in his mouth.

I sit next to him and wrap an arm around his shoulder. "Not yet," I think. "You're not ready to make it on your own yet, little boy." He leans into me for a moment, then pushes me away.

"Get out of here, Lanie," he says, warming to the anger that's rising.

I get up and stand over him for a couple of seconds. "It's going to be all right," I say. "Better than all right. You'll see, E." I pick up the contract and hold it away from myself, being careful not to get paint on my clothes.

"It's not going to be all right. You have no idea what you're doing, Elena," he thinks. He's given in to the tears, and his head is buried in his knees.

I hate doing this to him. Hate it more than anything, but I know this is the right thing to do, despite what Ethan thinks. I'll send Sage to pick up the pieces.

Alone in my room, I take the contract out of the envelope. It's about a thousand pages longer than the last one. My plan is to read it all, every single line of small print, but my mind keeps wandering to Jamie, Ethan, Sage, Finn, and Jo. The words on the pages aren't nearly as important as the pot I have only begun to stir.

I imagine a new life in Florida where Ethan and I are alone again, and he has control over his powers, over his life. I see Sage and Finn happily together at last and me with. . . Jamie. . . or Jo.

I try to remember the first time I felt attracted to another person. Was it a guy or a girl? There'd been Finn, of course, all the way back in the sixth grade, but I'm not sure that really counted as attraction, at least not at first. Even later, I wouldn't swear to wanting him in that way so much as wanting to be with him, with anyone, really. I just wanted to belong. Then the incident happened. I don't dare call it what it was even in the privacy and silence of my own mind. That word is just so violent, so unredeemable. I wonder, though, if the incident is the root of my sexual preference in some way, like my mind twisted itself into an utter distrust and distaste for men, so I became attracted to women by default.

It's not as though I've ever had a girlfriend, though. I made out a few times with Mindy McConnell under the bleachers during lunch my junior year. Then there was Sage, but even though she kissed me like she meant it, she's always been all about the penis. And now there's Jo, but she's almost as confused as I am. In my deepest fantasies, it's always a girl I'm with, and I really do love Jo, and I really do want Sage, so if I'm gay then what's the deal with Jamie? Why do I feel so confused around him? I can't remember a guy, besides Finn, ever affecting me that way.

The seventy page contract is opened to page five in front of me on the bed, and I can't remember a single word I've read. I have to fax this back to PSI by close of day, and I can't even read it. I flip through all the pages a dozen times, glancing at phrases here and there. There's a bit about the car and stuff about housing, the salary numbers, and tax information that I manage to fill out. In the end, I just sign the pages and hurry to Kinko's at 4:45, hoping I make the deadline. Jamie told me everything anyway, and the last contract was reasonable and fairly standard, I think, handing it over to the clerk, willing my hands not to shake. I know what I'm doing.

At dinner time, Ethan refuses to come down, even for Sage, so she and I sit and eat his favorite pizza without him. Though we barely speak, her anger isn't tempered by the absence of words. The daggers from her eyes cut through my flesh, all the way to my soul. I finally give up on eating and go outside. The night's chilly, and I didn't think to grab a jacket, but I don't bother going back in to get one. I walk to the far end of the pool, where I can't be seen from the kitchen. Without really thinking about it, I take my mother's earring out of my pocket and turn it around and around between my fingers.

The moon's nearly full, still a sliver or two away from howling round, but it's glowing like it's in love. The silver sheen over the lawn and trees with the slight steam coming off the pool make the moment almost magical. I settle on the hard, concrete deck and brush my fingers across the surface of the warm water, like I'm in a rowboat on a river.

For some reason, Jamie's suddenly there, standing too close like he always does, with that crooked, apologetic grin. He smells vaguely of Indian food and cardamom. He takes a step closer, so all I can see is his mouth, and I want to kiss him. The two times he kissed me were like that, spontaneous and totally inappropriate. We both acted shocked that it had happened. There was way too much giggling, and I protested, defending my sexual preference, but I liked it. A lot.

Kissing Jo is different; it's both easier and harder, means more and less at the same time. I want Jo in the way that means forever, good and bad, no matter what, until time ends, with the deep knowledge that it won't be easy. I trust that if she ever takes that final step toward me and forgives me for loving Sage, we will both be all in at last. Or will we? Will I forgive her for loving and hating Sage as much as I do? Can I muster the courage to step up to meet her, or will I prolong this endless dance? Maybe my decision to leave has pressed that issue to its logical conclusion. Tomorrow when I tell her, she'll either beg me to stay or blow me off completely. Either way, it won't change what's going to happen. The wheel's already in motion.

I run the earring through the water, then bring it to my bare foot. The water droplets, immediately cool, send a shiver down my back and raise the skin on my arms. I trace a triangle with the drops falling from the tip of the post, then dig in hard, waiting for the pain to fill me so completely that Jo and Jamie and Sage and Ethan will cease to exist. Then it will be only me and the physical pain that burns so deep it becomes pleasure, like water so hot it feels cold, or ice so cold it burns. I inhale sharply as endorphins flood my brain.

I fail to hear the back door or see Sage pound across the deck. I only notice her when she grabs the earring out of my hand.

"No way, Elena. You do not get to come out here and play the victim, cutting yourself up to make yourself feel better about what YOU are doing to all of US! You can just suffer like me and Ethan, without your stupid crutch."

I jump up and try to take the earring back, but she has the advantage of height, weight, and strength. I have only my ferocity and desperation.

Sage vents as she fends me off. "You go on and on about Ethan sucking his thumb! Tell me how this is any different. No wait, I'll tell you. Ethan sucks his thumb to comfort himself. You actually get off on this." I make a lunge for her arm and land hard on my knees. Sage shakes her head in disgust and drops the earring in the deep end of the pool where the fairy appears to flutter down and lie on her side. The stone glimmers in response to the moon's rays through the water for a moment. Then the shimmer dissipates, lost amid the steam. Sage turns her back and leaves me to contemplate diving in to retrieve my treasure. For the moment, I have the presence of mind to realize how desperate and crazy that would seem, dressed as I am in jeans, in fifty-five degree weather. Instead, I get the net and try to scoop the earring up. Unfortunately, the pole is just short of the ten feet it needs to be to skim the bottom. Every time I nearly catch it, the net makes waves that push the tiny fairy closer to the drain. Finally, I slam the pole onto the deck. It makes a spectacular amount of noise as the metal hits the concrete and bounces off. I don't really care. I kneel down to make sure the earring's still on the pool floor and find myself bawling like a little kid. I cry so hard I think I'm going to throw up. My throat and stomach muscles feel stretched and torn, but now that I've started, I can't stop. I lay down on my side on the cold, wet deck and wait for the torrent to end, but like dry heaves, every time I think it's over, it starts again.

This goes on for what feels like hours until the back door slams. The thought of anyone seeing me like this pulls me out of a cycle of spasms suddenly. I jump up, expecting to go another round with Sage, but it's Ethan who's standing there. He's wearing his swim suit and a towel around his neck. He shivers as he hands the towel to me, and without a word, he dives in. A moment later, he comes up and holds out his hand to me. I open my palm, and he drops the earring into it. Then, in an impossibly graceful movement, he pulls himself out of the water, so he's standing on the deck. I wrap the towel around his shoulders and collapse against his chest. For the first time in our lives, Ethan, my brother, wraps his arms around me in a gesture of protection; I feel strangely safe and cared for. We stand there for a while as he strokes my hair, and I squeeze him around the waist as tightly as I can. Then he lets me go, steps back, and looks at me wide-eyed. I try to read his thoughts, but my emotions are too high to access that part of my brain. He's shaking and his teeth are chattering from being wet in the chilly air. I take his hand and bring him inside and upstairs. I'm about to peel off and go into my room, but he won't release me, so I go with him instead. When he turns around to face me, his eyes are soft and childlike. He won't ask, but I know he wants me to get him ready for bed, like I used to when he was stuck at four. And just like that, the roles are reversed again, into the balance of before. But after he's crawled between the sheets and I've sung him to sleep, I cannot shake the knowledge that something elemental has shifted between us.

The next morning, I get up before the sun to avoid Sage and Ethan. Sage's bed is empty, so she must've stayed with Ethan last night after his nightmare. I leave a note and head over to the Bean Scene. Jo will be there at eight, and I figure I can kill a couple hours with Marco and Myra.

Marco tells me to do it fast, like pulling off a Band-Aid. Just spit it out, without unnecessary pretext, and let the pieces "fall where they lay." Myra rolls her eyes while the two of us giggle like fifth graders. Marco loves to bastardize sayings, another of his endearing traits. Myra is all business; she tells me to break the news to Jo gently, enjoy some small talk before I crush her. I'm not so sure Jo will be all that crushed.

For all I know, Sage called her last night, and none of this will even come as a surprise. I almost wish she'd stand me up so we can skip over this part, but at ten till eight she comes through the door, takes off her sunglasses, scans the room for me, and runs her hand through her shiny hair. I take a deep breath and swallow hard. Marco pats my arm and gestures to Jo to come take his chair. She thanks him, then leans in to kiss me, smooth as butter. At least Sage had the decency to keep her mouth shut. I'll have to thank her when I get home.

I've pretty much decided to take Myra's advice. Coming from a woman, it just holds more weight. I take a deep breath to ask about how practice is going for her solo recital, but my mouth ignores my brain and blurts out, "I miss you already."

Jo smiles at me in the patient and gentle way she uses with Ethan. "I've got an hour and a half before I need to go." She reaches across the table for my hand.

In another dimension, deep in my brain, I'm appreciative of Marco, who knew me well enough to anticipate my inability to approach any kind of confrontation. He told me to do it this way because he knew I would, and he didn't want me to feel bad about it afterward. I hold Jo's hand, but follow Marco behind the counter with my eyes. He winks at me.

I turn my attention back to Jo, who's still waiting for a logical explanation for the glaring non sequitur. "I'm going back to Florida," I mumble.

Jo blinks twice, attempting to process exactly what this means. She inhales deeply and leans in a little. "As expected, maybe not this soon, but I figured that door was left open. How long will you be gone this time?"

I smile fleetingly, avoiding eye contact, and I feel suddenly like I'm channeling my brother. This is exactly how he would act. I hate it. I pull my hand away and sit up taller, looking into her eyes. "When I left, they offered me a position at the lab, $60,000 for a one-year contract."

She sits back and crosses her arms. "I see. Professional lab rat." Her tone isn't mean, just matter of fact, cold.

"I guess so, but it isn't really about the money."

"I know," she says. "I understand the need to explore your gifts, find out who you are. I get it," she says, like she's already waving good-bye.

"Thanks for not freaking out on me," I say, attempting to veil my disappointment in sarcasm.

"What do you want me to say? You've obviously decided already." She doesn't raise her voice.

I shake my head. Why is she so calm? "I don't know." I choke out the words around the growing lump in my throat. She looks out the window, away from the storm clouds darkening the space between us. I beat it back with a thought — we aren't even together. The thought makes me want to cry more than the disappointment of her lack of reaction.

Finally, she turns back to me. "Do you want me to talk you out of it?"

"No." I pout like a child, like my brother.

"You want me to throw a Sage-like fit and raise hell about what you're doing to me?" Her voice gets a tiny bit higher. "I'm not her. I won't do that to you."

"You think that's what I want?" I ask in a quaver.

"I think that your expectations are whacked."

"How do you know what my expectations are?" I whine.

She looks down, and after a pause, she concedes, "You're right. I shouldn't be throwing the Sage-card in your face. I'm listening. What do you need from me, Elena?"

She's so damn grounded. How does she do that? I wonder vaguely. Then I process her question. This may be the last chance I get with her. I go for broke. "I want to know. . . what we. . . are . . . to each other. I need to know. . . before. . . I go."

I expect her to bolt. We've never been direct about our friendship, flirtation, whatever you call it. But she doesn't bolt or laugh or cry or anything for a moment. Then she starts turning the ring on her middle finger. Hypnotized, I wait for my hopes to be dashed.

Finally, she stops, places her palms down on the table and leans in. "Lane, you have to understand. I love this." She waves one hand over the space between us. "I might even love you. . . someday, but I can't. . . DO this, BE this. . . what you want us to be. My mother would bring a storm of hail and brimstone down on our heads, the likes of a Baptist tent preacher and then some. I know she's narrow and judgmental, and she makes me miserable, but I. . . I just can't."

I feel my heart turning to stone or ice or crystal, something heavy and cold that might fall out and shatter all over the scuffed floor of the cafe if I don't hold it inside. "Okay," I say.

Silence stretches like taffy.

"So, what about Ethan?" she asks, biting off the question and turning her ring again.

"The deal is for both of us. The telepathy between twins is a huge field of study for the Initiative. I think it'll be good for Ethan, too," I say, moving my lips without thinking, without feeling a thing.

She looks up and lets out a low, slow whistle. "Wow. Did you ask him before you committed him?'

I shake my head slowly, unable to verbalize my thoughts. You can't expect me to base my life's decisions on the whims of a four-year-old living in a nineteen-year-old's body. I justified it this way to myself when I made the decision, but now saying it out loud suddenly seems harsh.

Jo's left eyebrow goes up. "Are you sure tearing him away from Sage is best for him?"

I push the threatening anger down into my gut. "Now or later, he'll have to learn to live without Sage. The minute Finn comes knocking, she'll be gone so fast, Ethan's head will spin."

"You sound pretty sure of that. Yet, here she is nearly two years later, having chosen Ethan over Finn. I think you underestimate the deep pull between Sage and Ethan."

I don't want to hear this. "I think you underestimate the deep pull between Sage and Finn."

We stare each other down for a beat or two. Jo looks away first.

"Trust me, no one understands your distrust of Sage more than I. Besides, I know you love your brother. You'll do what's right for him." She takes my hand, and my heart instantly transforms again into something aching, wounded, and most definitely alive.

I suddenly want to tell her about Jamie to hurt her back. But what is there to tell, really? He's an experiment, a temptation, a minor blip on the romantic radar. Jo's a hurricane, a glacier, a desire so deep I'm sure I've carried her with me from another lifetime. On the other hand, it's painfully obvious we're running toward each other on parallel tracks that might never meet. Perhaps the time has come for us to pass each other by and accept the unyielding rails that were laid long ago.

Instead of throwing more words into the air, I get up and walk purposefully to her. She turns toward me like she knows what I'm going to do. So, I take her face in my hands, gently. I close my eyes and kiss her one last time, with all the gratitude I can squeeze out. I pass my healing power through my kiss, so she won't have to suffer the loss. When we part, the pain in my head rivals that of my heart. Jo smiles when she says, "I know what you did."

I drag home, exhausted, anticipating a handful of Advil chased by an extended nap. Sage is sitting by the pool, studying. When I get out of the car, she glares at me with an energetic venom I don't think I deserve. I go inside without saying hi. I've just passed through the kitchen when it occurs to me that Ethan isn't with her.

From the living room I can hear him crying. Out of reflex, I rush up the stairs to find him. The door to his room is open, and he's curled up on the floor just inside. It looks like a team of professionals has tossed the room. Every drawer has been emptied and thrown aside. Every item on every horizontal surface has been dashed to the floor. Even the mattress has been ripped off the bed, as though someone was looking for something valuable.

I enter slowly and silently, clearing a place on the floor to sit next to him. It takes him a minute to realize I'm there. He pulls away from me, curling tighter into himself. I give him a minute or more of silence.

Then I can't keep my mouth shut any longer. "Oh, E. It's been a while since we've been here." I watch him for a reaction, but he keeps sobbing, like I'm not there. "You want to tell me about it?"

"No," he thinks.

I contemplate all the times we've done this before. Ethan's a pretty passive guy, but like everyone, he has a breaking point when the anger he represses explodes out, like a pressure cooker that gets too hot. This kind of mess can only be the result of that explosion. When he was little, he couldn't do much damage, but now that he's nearly a man, the damage is pretty intense. The desk chair is more or less splintered, and it will take hours to clean the place up. As I take in the damage, Ethan moves uncomfortably beside me. I look over to examine his damage, too. He's curled into a ball on the hard floor with his head resting on one arm, while he tries to suck the thumb from his other hand between sobs. His face is dirt-streaked, sweaty and swollen. His hair's a wild tangle. He looks so small and fragile, in a disarray that mirrors the room. Finally, he glances up at me.

"Go away," he thinks. But even in my head, his voice isn't convincing. I slide a little closer to him. He doesn't move away, but he does think, "It's your fault. All your fault." He doesn't bother wiping away the tears tracking sideways over the bridge of his nose and onto his arm. I wrack my brain for what could've sent Ethan this far over the edge. My mind flashes on the look Sage gave me when I pulled up.

"Did you have a fight with Sage?" I ask out loud.

He nods slightly and slides closer to rest his head on my knee. I stroke his hair and wipe his tears away before going further down the rabbit hole. "You asked her to let you stay here when I move?" I ask in my head. He nods again and hugs himself, like he's trying to keep from flying apart.

Now my eyes fill up, too. "I'm so sorry, E," I say, and I mean it.

"She hates me. Grandmother's right. I'm horrible and a baby, and no one could ever love me." His thoughts are beginning to race, making them hard to follow.

"It's not true, Ethan." I say with authority. "Sage loves you. And I love you. I don't want you to stay with Sage. I want you to come with me. Sage knows that. She just wants what's right for all of us."

"I want to stay with Sage," Ethan thinks. "Please, please, Lanie. Don't do this."

He really is breaking my heart now, but there's no going back. I can't undo this. I don't want to upset him any more than he already is, so I don't say anything, but he can read my thoughts so I'm not really fooling him.

"Just once I wish someone would listen to me," he mumbles through his tears. "I know how this is going to end, just like all the other times. Why won't you just listen to me one time?"

"Ethan, you'd say anything to stay with Sage. Wouldn't you?" I ask.

He sits up and looks me in the eye through his tears. "That doesn't mean I'm lying."

I look away. "Let's get this place cleaned up," I say.

"Go ahead," Ethan says, putting his thumb in his mouth and lying back down on the cold, hard floor.

"Come on, E. You need to help. You made this mess." I try to keep my voice gentle.

He takes his thumb out of his mouth to talk. "You made this mess, Lanie! Everything's wrong now, and it's all your fault."

I'm not going to engage in this argument, so I launch a different one. "Clean yourself up, at least."

He brings up his knees to hide the stain on his pants. "Leave me alone!"

I start moving around the room, gathering the trash and putting it in the wastebasket, stacking unbroken items, books and papers on the desk, and tossing clothes toward the dresser. When I get over to the bed and try to get the mattress back onto the box-spring, I run into problems. It's just too big and too heavy for me to manage on my own. I try to get under it for leverage, but I slip on the wood floor and end up on my back, almost under the bed, with the mattress on top of me. I detect a suppressed giggle from the other side of the room. I get up and try again. This time I fall, splayed out on top of the tilted mattress.

Then I'm crumpled on the floor after sliding down the plastic cover, like a cartoon bird hitting a window. Ethan giggles louder, but by the time I've turned around, he's all grim-faced and petulant again.

"A little help here?" I say, picking myself up.

He shakes his head, but he can't hide the hint of a smile playing at the corner of his lips.

"Please, Ethan," I beg.

He shakes his head again and thinks, "It's too much fun watching you flipping and falling all over yourself."

"Fine. You'll have to fix it before you can go to sleep." I leave the bed and continue with the rest of the room. I line up the dresser drawers on the floor near the clothes pile. Ethan watches me fold all the shirts into one drawer, shorts and pants into another, and underwear and diapers into the last one. When I'm done, he takes his thumb out of his mouth and says, "You aren't going to be able to lift those now."

I glare at him and get to my feet. I'm able to almost struggle the underwear drawer up into place, but I can't tilt it at the right angle to get the roller into the track. The whole thing tumbles out of my arms and crashes to the ground, spilling the contents again.

"Told you," He says, smirking.

I pick up a diaper, boxers and a pair of pants, and throw them at him.

"Let me do this in peace if you aren't going to help."

He throws the diaper back at me, but he gets up and takes the underwear and pants into the bathroom. I watch him leave. Then I contemplate the room. I shouldn't be doing this, making his temper tantrum my responsibility, no matter how guilty I feel. If he's so bent on growing up, he can clean up his own messes. I kick the drawer out of my way and go to my room, slamming the door loudly enough for him to hear from the bathroom.

The time has come for me to practice the new skills I've acquired. I may need them to get through this.

Susan Michalski

๛ 4 ๙

THE UNDISCOVERED

Caught in a blazing snowstorm
Whiteout blurs the lines
Burns so cold my bones are ice
My skin ignites like fire
I thought I knew this place
Path like the back of my hand
I swear I knew this place
But each turn leads to new revelations
Truth coming clear as day undiscovered
Cold and swirling round
Somehow, I'll find my way
Tell me I'll find a way
　　　"Ice Storm" - Luna Rayne, 2014

I know I should be worried about Ethan and Sage. They have a couple more weeks to get through together before I'll be ready for Ethan in Florida. It's strange to think of them at odds. I don't think they've ever fought before, so I can't really be sure how this will play out, but for the moment I'm done with being second-guessed and bombarded with emotional blackmail. They'll have to figure it out without me.

I lay down on my bed in a meditation position on my back, palms up. I start with deep breathing. I use the techniques I learned with the Initiative to slow my heart rate and control my breath to access a place of complete concentration. Then I release each muscle of my body one at a time, starting at my toes. It's a long process, but I have to create a hyper-state of body-spirit awareness in order to be able to separate the two. When each muscle has been tensed and relaxed, it's time to ground my physical body and leave it behind.

This is the part of astral projection that's the hardest to achieve. In my early attempts, I was only able to lift an arm and sit up, but as Jamie points out, I'm uniquely suited for this particular paranormal skill. Because of the distance I've established between my psyche and my nervous system, I no longer feel pain when I cut myself. There are Buddhist monks who practice for decades and cannot attain the level of pain receptor control that I turn on at a whim.

Splitting the mind from the body is only part of the separation process, though. The other part is far more difficult. I don't have to wait long for the vibrations to begin. Like sound waves surrounding me, they take up resonance that I try to ignore. Acknowledging the reverberation will shut down the separation and bring me out of my meditative state, like an alarm clock. I concentrate instead on my breathing, and let the vibrations take hold of me and build in strength. Practice has taught me the moment to ascend, though frequently this is the point where I fall through and drop back into reality, like a stone kicked from a cliff. There's an instant of nearly insane terror that most people experience here. It's the terror of being lost in the ether, a disembodied spirit for eternity. I look for the silver thread that holds the two parts of me together and focus on its strength to get through the blinding flash of fear.

At the Initiative, astral projection is a staple of the curriculum, but from what I saw only a handful of people actually achieve it, and even fewer actually practice it with any regularity. The last time I tried working this magic in Florida, I was able to move around the space nearby, but I didn't stray far from my physical self. Jamie placed objects around the room to identify when I reentered my body. While I focused on that task, I was fine, but when I turned and saw myself lying on the bed, I panicked. Suddenly, something in me snapped to attention, and my body and mind flew together like oppositely charged magnets. The reconnection was violent and shattering. It left me disoriented and shaken. Though Jamie had explained to me about the silver thread, he in no way prepared me for this silver rubber band. I must put my memory of that experience to the side if I want to move outside myself again. I file the fear in the box marked for my old companion — pain.

The vibrations reach a crescendo, and I feel a sensation of rising above myself, like levitation. In my mind, I open my eyes and settle myself on the floor. Before I can do anything else, I must find a way to look at my body. Controlling reintegration is the priority for this practice today. I prepare my mind to accept what it will see by fully envisioning myself on the bed in the meditation pose.

I'm about to turn when I hear Sage knocking on Ethan's door. I wonder if my thread is long enough to travel that far, and suddenly I'm in Ethan's room. He's cleaned up most of the mess. The dresser's back together and the bed's made with clean sheets and his favorite blue blanket. He's sitting in the middle, drawing in a sketch pad. His head shoots up when Sage knocks again, and for a moment I think he's looking right at me. I remind myself I'm not really there; he's looking at the door. I move across the room and stand where I can see what he's drawing. The picture isn't complete, but it's his white wolf, the one that appears in so many of his paintings, tethered to a chain and being dragged from the foreground back into the drawing. A girl deep in the center holds the other end of the tether, and the wolf's head is pivoted outward and raised in a howl of indignation. Half-completed and only in pencil, it's still breathtaking in detail and emotion. It fills me with guilt.

Sage opens the door and enters. From behind, I can see Ethan's shoulders and biceps tense, but he keeps his head down and pretends to draw. Sage sits on the bed across from him. She puts her right hand over his left to stop him from sketching. He pulls away. I have to jump back to keep from being hit. Inwardly, I laugh. He can't hit me because I'm not here.

"We okay here, Mouse?" Sage says, unflinchingly.

Ethan shrugs, but his eyes are tearing up. I want to yell at Sage to go away and leave him alone.

Sage slides closer and runs her hand up and down Ethan's thigh in a gentle, soothing motion. He doesn't stop her. He leans in a little closer to her and closes his eyes like a cat being stroked. He breathes like he's trying to find the oxygen in the air. Because of my vantage point above and behind Ethan, I can see the visceral effect of her touch on him, and it totally throws me. I'm wondering if Sage has any idea that she's turning him on. She stops and caresses his face with her other hand.

"You know I love you, Mouse. Right?" Her voice is like a purr and her forehead's almost touching his.

He licks his lips, inclines his head slightly and swallows as he reaches up to caress her face in response. For a moment, they're locked in this intimate moment. Deep inside Ethan, I sense a fire that's being fueled. His hand travels down her neck to her shoulder and arm. He's tracing her lines, leaning closer, holding his breath now. Her eyes don't shift or even blink as she stares at his mouth. I wait for her to turn away, make a joke, get up, anything to stop what Ethan has in mind.

I panic then and fly forward to push her out of the way, but I only end up on the other side of her. I spin around in time to see Ethan tilt his head to the left. I can't do anything to stop their lips from connecting. A small moan comes from Ethan that could emanate either from the pleasure of kissing Sage — a pleasure I've known more than once — or from the pain of knowing he's losing her, or both, perhaps. I'm frozen, waiting for Sage to stop this insanity, but after their lips part, eons later, she only hesitates a second before leaning in to kiss him again. The spark in Ethan rises to a full-fledged flame, driving him up onto his knees, casting the sketch pad and pencil off the bed. I guess this is Sage's wake up call, because before he can encircle her in his arms, she places her hands on his shoulders and presses him away. He leans back on his heels, his face lined with confusion and frustration.

"Why'd you do that?" he whines.

Sage looks away, even as she reaches for his hand. "I shouldn't be — we shouldn't do that," she mumbles.

"Why not? I want to." Ethan leans in again, smiling shyly. "I like it."

"I know." She slides away from him. "You aren't ready for this — not yet."

"What do you mean? I am ready! Really, really ready!" He's half-incensed and half-pleading. I feel nauseous.

Sage looks like she might laugh, but the giggle never makes it out of her mouth. "I'm sorry, Mouse. I just came up to tell you, I'm sorry. And I wish more than anything there was a way — I do love you." She stands up as Ethan drops his head in defeat. I pray for her to leave, but she takes a step toward him, tips his face up to hers and leans down to kiss him again. I count to five-Mississippi before their lips part. Then she rests her forehead against his and whispers, "I like it, too." Finally, she leaves. I follow her down the hall and make the mistake of glancing into our room.

SNAP! I see my body on the bed and an electrical surge of panic pulls my consciousness home suddenly and violently. I actually feel like I've been thrown from a moving vehicle or dropped from a tall building. My eyes flutter open, and I try to make sense of my view of the ceiling. An ice pick must be planted in the center of my forehead. I'm not cold, but I'm shivering, even as a sweat breaks out all over my body. I force myself to sit up and take deep breaths, and I rub my forehead and eye sockets.

Gradually, the shock and pain ebb, so I can process what I saw. I go straight for denial. Astral projection! Really? What a load of shit! Obviously, I fell asleep and dreamed my worst fear. Ethan isn't capable of those feelings, and Sage is in love with Finn. Ethan's a child to Sage, to all of us, no matter what Rachel says about him being nineteen. The whole idea of Sage coming on to Ethan is absurd, nearly as absurd as him coming on to her. I get up slowly, steadying myself on the bedpost until my mind stops spinning. I turn at the doorway and head down the hall. Ethan's door is opened. He's curled up on the bed, facing the window with his blue blanket over him. Perfect, I think. He's been napping. Maybe I hooked into his dream somehow. That would make sense.

Just to be sure, I head downstairs to check on Sage. She's in the kitchen with her head in the refrigerator. She's got a notepad in her hand and she's jotting down the groceries we need. Surely, that's a good sign. If she'd been making out with Ethan, she wouldn't run down the stairs to make a grocery list. I heave a sigh of relief and head into the kitchen.

"Cooking something special tonight?" I ask.

She stands up suddenly and cracks her head on the freezer door. "Jeezus, Elena! Sneak up on people much?"

"Sorry. I thought you heard me come down the stairs."

She pulls herself up, rubbing the back of her head. "I was thinking about making the mushroom soup and soda bread Ethan likes."

I stare at her mouth, like I might see some trace of Ethan there. I'm still not entirely convinced. "Okay."

"I wasn't asking your permission," she says, throwing me her bitchiest snarl.

"Fine." I lift one eyebrow, trying for Jo's nonchalance. I might have to pass on that meal. The chef seems a little hostile. On the other hand, if I really did see what I thought I saw, I might not want to leave the two of them alone. "Sounds great," I add. "Count me in." I don't wait for her snarky reply. I go upstairs to work on packing up Ethan's studio.

When we moved here, we shipped most of Ethan's finished work, including the paintings that hung in my room, to a gallery downtown. Sage made it her mission to find a place to sell Ethan's art after Finn left. She took his canvases to every place in town, sent almost a hundred emails and letters, and made twice as many calls, convincing the galleries that he'd produce even more, better work. It was a victory when Phacets and Phazes, one of the hippest of the lot, returned her call. The sketches and paintings E didn't like we put up in Grandmother's attic, and the ones he couldn't part with or felt he hadn't finished he packed in special boxes that we moved here.

Six months later, it feels like there's twice as much to move out. I can't leave all of this for Sage to deal with. Luckily, I saved the art boxes from the last move in the back of the closet. I pull them out one at a time and start wrapping the work that's dry enough to pack. I'm going have to pack up the oil paints today, so he doesn't start anything new that won't be dried by the time he meets me in Florida. I search the back of the closet for a box to put the paints into. I'm moving the last painting box to look behind it when I notice it's not empty. Why would one of E's paintings still be packed away back here?

I haven't even taken the canvas all the way out of the box when I realize what it is. A wave of emotion takes my breath away. Inch by inch I pull it out, not wanting to, but compelled by something stronger than my own will. I stay in the half-darkness of the closet, afraid to examine the flames and that face in the light. I prop it against the wall and lean away from it warily, afraid it might come to life and send me back in time to the horrifying moment that has defined every moment since.

For comfort, I reach into my pocket. I run my fingers over the pointed wings of the same fairy earring that glimmers from one earlobe of the woman in the painting. Her other lobe is torn and a drop of blood hangs in the balance, about to fall. A lump begins to form in the back of my throat as my vision travels over the feverish cheeks of the woman and settles on the cerulean blue of her determined eyes. They are my eyes and her eyes, my mother's. The fire of the painting begins to lick around her, coming to life, but she doesn't try to escape it. She waits for it, like she's waiting for a lover who might reject her after all. My knees buckle, but I don't cry, not yet.

The first thing that comes back is the smell. I know I'm in Ethan's studio, and the only real smells are of solvents and paint, but all I can smell is smoke — I begin to choke — and burning flesh. I gag. "No,"

I hear myself moan, but it doesn't bring me back enough to quell the sensation of heat that hits me full on. I shiver. I want to look away, but I can't. Instead, I drag myself toward the painting on my knees. The cackle and crackle of flames play like a white noise track in my ears, growing louder as I get closer. Still, I reach out to touch her face and my fingers are shocked to feel canvas and hardened paint where they expected flesh. "Mama, oh Mama, what did you do to us?" I whisper in her ear. Now I cry. I cry with every ounce of strength, with every shredded memory that returns to me whole and unadulterated. I cry and cry and cry for her, for me, for Ethan and our dad, for the life we never had together and the death that tore our family apart. For so many years I thought my father set the fire in a drunken rage, but when Jesse finally returned to us, he confessed to me that it hadn't been his doing. That left my mother. Ethan must've known the secret all along. "Why, Mama? Why?" I ask again and again, until I'm screaming at her.

Then Ethan's there, somehow. I hate him for bringing me to this place, for taking away my sweet amnesia with this dreadful, beautiful thing. But more than hating him, I ache for him, because this image resides in him, and there has never been a moment when he could be free from it. I vaguely wonder if it helped him to paint it. Did it purge the pain or make it swell, like an infection in his psyche? Poor Ethan. Poor me. We're wrapped in each other on the floor in the closet like we were in the months and years that followed on the heels of that day. In the back of my mind, under the screech of memory, I hear him begging me to forgive him. I hear his pleas and penitence, but I can't respond.

Time has stopped, so a second or an hour later, when Ethan gets up and puts the painting back in the box, I laugh, and his eyes grow wide. Can I pack the memory of the painting away that easily? If I ripped out my eyes, would the smells and sounds remain? I'd gotten so good at forgetting. I don't know why, but I find it all oddly funny. Hilarious, in fact, but only for a couple of seconds, until the tears start up again with renewed vigor.

I remember reading somewhere that a person can become

dehydrated from crying, and that dehydration will eventually force the person into a deep, recuperative sleep. I wonder how long that will take because I don't think I can bear this much longer. Ethan's trying to coax me to my feet, crying and cajoling in the same voice I use with him. But no matter what he says, I can't get up because my tears take all my strength. Eventually, he gives up and bends over me, scooping me into his strong arms.

Despite his own tremors, Ethan carries me like a child to my bed. I cling to his neck and cry into his hair long after he's put me down. I can't let go because the images, sounds and smells have not abated. If I don't hold on, he might dissolve into ash, disintegrate before my eyes or drown in the water that held us during the conflagration, the water that went from ice cold to boiling in a matter of minutes that night. Poor, sweet Ethan, so terrified and lost. I can't let go for his sake, for mine.

Sage finally pries my arms away from him, and bit by bit the horror ebbs away, until I'm in the room I share with her in the little, white house with the big pool near the university. When my mother's face recedes into two dimensions and the painting's just a canvas and pigment again in my mind, I entertain the thought of rest. With a deep, shuddering sigh, I allow the promised sleep to come.

Memory's a twisted thing. In the light of day, the memories I have of my mother are few, fuzzy, and far-between. She's more of an idea, a waft of almond extract, a bouncing ponytail streaked with gold, the nap of a corduroy shirt, the color maroon, the whistled bit of an aria. In my dreams, she's whole and complete, with hands and a face, a voice, and a scent like no one else I've ever known. In my dreams, I scream at her and cry for her. We walk together and hold each other. In my dreams, we have a life together, a life that never happened because of her. I wake up angry and confused about why I'm dreaming about this woman I barely knew. How dare she invade my sleep! I struggle to open my eyes, which are cemented closed by dried tears and swelling.

The sun's still beating against the window, behind the thin yellow curtains. Have I overslept; I wonder. I roll over to see if Sage is up, but she's not there. Instead, I find Ethan sitting on the floor between the beds, his back against Sage's bed and his chin on his knees, watching me.

"Hey, pal," I say beckoning him closer. "What 'cha doing? You okay?"

Ethan crawls over and throws his arm over me in an awkward hug. I sit up a little. "Hey, E, what's wrong? Where's Sage?"

He tries to talk, but nothing comes out but a croak. I smile patiently as he clears his throat. "I'm sorry, Lanie." His eyes dart around the room guiltily. I'm not sure what he's sorry about. "Are you mad?" he asks, finally settling his gaze on the floor.

I look him up and down, trying to assess damage I've somehow forgotten. "Why would I be mad, E? Did you have an accident?"

"NO!" he says indignantly, like that would never happen. "No." He stands up to show me.

He's so incensed I can't help laughing. After a second or two, he smiles tentatively. "I'm gonna get Sage." He edges nervously toward the door, like he's afraid to leave me alone for even a second. As he slips out the door, his hand grips the doorjamb, and the streaks of crimson paint on his knuckles and under his nails make my breath catch in my throat. I close my eyes to blink and an image fills the space behind my eyes. I inhale sharply as I remember.

Thankfully, the memory's like an aftershock with diminished intensity, but the impact still shakes me. The painting was real, the fire was real, this is real. Out of reflex, I reach into my pocket and after a beat of panic, I find the earring. I'm studying the details of my talisman, mentally comparing the real thing to Ethan's depiction, when Sage, Jo, and Ethan plow in, then stop short to stare at me, like I've just returned from the dead.

"Relax, y'all." I attempt nonchalance, but I come off sounding defensive. I shove the earring back in my pocket. Sage takes a step back, and Jo surges forward, until she's sitting beside me on the bed.

Ethan hovers behind Sage, wringing his hands and bouncing on his toes nervously. "I'm okay, E," I choke out. "Can you get me some water?" He bolts from the room and pounds down the stairs.

I turn to Sage. "Have you seen it? Did you know?" She looks away and nods once slowly. "Damn it! Sage. You could've told me, warned me, kept me out of that damn closet!" Every word increases the ire burning in my chest. "Jeezus, Sage! Sometimes I fucking hate you."

She looks contrite, even though she justifies her silence. "I promised Ethan," she says.

"When did he paint that thing?" I ask.

"It's not finished," Sage offers.

"What?" It makes me sick to think of him standing in front of it for hours, days, weeks on end.

Sage takes a step closer, lowers her voice and glances back at the door. "He started it long before I ever knew you guys. He showed it to me that first summer when Rachel and Lily went to Florida, before the fire."

"Ugh!" I groan with the thought of that image circulating in his head for years.

"Lanie?" Ethan's at the door with the glass of water. I can't even look at him when he hands it to me. Jo's rubbing my arm slowly, rhythmically, like a bow on a violin string. I feel the vibration deep and comforting inside, and I concentrate on that. Sage ushers Ethan from the room, though he protests loudly.

Left alone with Jo on the bed and the door closed, I can't help thinking ironically that I couldn't have planned this better if I'd tried. I move over to make room, inviting her to join me under the covers. She hesitates for just a second, then slides into place beside me, like she belongs there. I maneuver my head onto her shoulder, and she has no choice but to put her arm around me. Yes, I think, this is how it should be now and forever.

"How're you doing?" she asks. "Sage was freaking out when she called me."

"Sage overreacts," I say, moving my head to a place where I can hear the metronome of her heart.

"Be that as it may..." She lets whatever she was about to say float off. After a pause, she speaks again. "Lane, I don't really know all that happened to you and Ethan, but I know from my own experience that pushing the heavy stuff down doesn't make it go away. I don't mind listening if you want to talk."

I sit up and take in her open expression. "I'm not really good at talking about things," I say. "I'm much better at forgetting." I go for a grin, but I'm sure it must look more like a grimace.

"Okay, Dorrie, but you know you never really forget any of it, right? It's all still there, just waiting to resurface when you least expect it."

"Yeah, I get it."

In the silence that follows, I drop back onto her chest, and she strokes my arm.

When Jo starts talking again, her voice is far away and deep, like she's on the verge of sleep. "Did Sage ever tell you what happened between us? The rift?"

"No," I say, though it's not exactly true. I was there the night Sage watched the video her dad had taken of Jo. I know that Sage's dad, Jake Wester, sexually assaulted Jo, and the video showed the preamble to the crime. The details of what happened after the video were never discussed with me. I didn't know Jo then. It was the first time I'd ever seen her. She was only fifteen.

"Mr. Wester is a predator; I was prey." She says it simply, without emotion. She takes a deep breath. I think about telling her to stop, that I don't want to hear this, but when I look up her eyes are focused on a place far above the dingy ceiling of my room. I doubt she'd hear me even if I did tell her to stop.

"He suggested we make a video for Sage's fifteenth birthday. He was a photographer, videographer. I'd spent the night at his house with Sage more than a few times, been out to eat with them hundreds of times. He'd come to my recitals, for Christ's sake. I didn't think in a million years there was anything wrong with him."

An almost imperceptible tinge of anger edges into her narrative, but her heart beats steadily under my ear.

"I knew that something was off almost immediately. He took me to this weird room with a bed, some of Sage's stuffed animals, a mirror, the camera, and microphone, nothing else. For a long time, all I remembered was him and that room and waking up in my own room the next day, bruised and bleeding. At the trial, he said I fought hard. I broke his fucking camera or something." Her voice goes up an octave when she curses. I really want her to stop now, but I'm afraid to interrupt.

"Before the trial, I underwent hypnosis. It worked. It all came back in vivid detail. His grating voice telling me what to do, the sting of his belt when I refused — at first, the smell of his breath and sweat, the look on his face as he —" She looks like she might hurl or scream now, but her voice remains even. She stops and looks down at me. Her eyes are glistening.

"At the trial, he testified that he never touched my 'private parts,' like that made it all okay. He said it just like that, 'private parts,' like some kind of pornographic prude! Unbelievable. And strictly speaking, he didn't touch me. He made me do it all to myself, fucking freak!" She wipes the tears that spill over with the back of her hand, and inhales deeply.

"I never told Sage any of it. I did tell my mother, though. She didn't believe me the morning after when I came home wrecked. She told me Mr. Wester was a stand-up guy, down on his luck, maybe, but he was so good looking. She accused me of being dramatic, wanting attention. She told me I was sick, took me to a shrink, who gave me Prozac and told me not to lie. Little by little, I think they convinced me I imagined the whole thing. I wanted them to be right. I loved Sage; she was my best friend, and I didn't want to lose her. But every morning I'd wake up and a tiny fragment of him in that room would come back to me. I needed Sage to see it, too. I waited for her to ask me what was wrong. I tried a hundred ways to show her, so she'd guess. I clung to a fantasy that she'd be the one to save me."

"But she did, kind of," I say.

"Not really. Not without it becoming about her first. Everything's about Sage for Sage. Everything except Ethan."

"Tell me about it," I say a little bitterly.

"Ultimately, it was that fact that gave me hope for her, brought me around to a place where I could forgive her."

I take it in. Then I reach up and bring her lips to mine. I drink in her sorrow and pain, feeling the tingle spread over my face and into my spinal cord. I think for a moment that I might black out, but I catch my breath before Jo can kiss me again. Her hand slides under my shirt and finds my nipples already rigid with anticipation. I pull her blouse over her head and unhook her front clipping bra.

"Easy access," she quips and we both giggle as we slide down under the covers. She's so delicious with her caramel skin and round, firm breasts. I can't resist the soft down of her belly that leads like an arrow to the promised land.

Unfortunately, we don't get much further than the promise because of my brother's relentless pounding on the door. After the third time of screaming, "Go away, Ethan," we give up and get dressed. It's the closest we've come to making love, the closest I've ever come to making love to anyone. And for now, it's enough to know that she wants me as much as I want her. As she pulls her shirt down, I regret the limited time we have left. I regret that I'm leaving at all.

Ethan sticks to me like glue the entire evening, through dinner and a movie Sage picks on Netflix, while the rest of us clean up the kitchen from her completely successful, albeit messy, culinary foray. It's been a long time since he's been this sweet and affectionate with me. He reserves this kind of warmth for Sage these days, but he feels guilty about the painting and its effect on me. No matter how I reassure him, he still has that hangdog look that breaks my heart. When I come in from kissing Jo good-night, he's waiting at the door. Sage has gone upstairs to get ready for bed, but he stayed down. I wonder if maybe he's holding a grudge from their fight earlier in the day.

I wrap my arm around his waist and usher him toward the stairs. As we climb, I try again to let him off the hook. "E, you know I'm okay, right?"

He shrugs his shoulders, like he's not sure.

"You want to talk about it?" I ask after we're in his room.

He shakes his head.

"I was just in shock. Your painting brought back some bad memories. That's all. See, I'm fine now."

"Okay," he says, dipping his head to the side and turning his back to change into his pajamas. I turn away, too, to give him some privacy.

"I can leave," I offer.

"No! Don't go." He thinks it, rather than saying it.

After a minute, I turn around to watch him crawl beneath the sheets and put his thumb in his mouth. His whole body relaxes as he sucks. For just a second, I envy this release. Then my mind flashes again to the image he lives with, the image that plagues him so much that he feels compelled to paint it, and I realize how much he carries in secret. I'm not sure how much release Ethan ever experiences.

As if he's reading my mind, he rolls over to face me and extracts his thumb to talk. "It was supposed to stay a secret," he says. "I didn't want you to find it."

"I know," I say, but my mind snags on the word "secret." Maybe this is the crux of my expanding angst. "Do you keep a lot of secrets from me?" I ask cautiously.

I expect him to look wounded, get defensive. Instead, he surprises me by blushing crimson and smiling. "Some," he says with a hint of glee.

I can't help smiling too. "Tell me," I urge, moving to sit next to him on the bed.

His cheeks redden even more, and he shakes his head. "Wouldn't be secret if I tell you."

I kiss his forehead and smile, despite the million directions my mind races. "You're right," I say, "but if you ever want to tell me, I promise not to tell anyone else."

He nods and rolls over, reinserting his thumb. I'm not ready to leave him, so I busy myself straightening his room a bit more. On the floor on the far side of the bed I catch a glimpse of a sketchpad and pencil, so I circle around to pick them up. The pad looks like it was thrown there, probably during his tantrum after the fight with Sage, I reason. The spine's bent open and the pages are folded under the book, so I open it to smooth the sheets. The image on the page is familiar, Ethan's wolf tethered by a leash held by a girl.

My hand shakes as I place the drawing pad on the desk and turn slowly back around to look at my brother. No! No way it was real. E. Sage. The kisses. I look down at his sweet, innocent face, already slack with sleep. Secrets indeed!

I'm caught for an instant in the realization that I did astral project successfully, but the victory of that achievement pales in light of what I saw. I want to kill Sage! No, death would be too good for her. She needs to suffer! I struggle to my feet, shaking with anger. I make my way into the bathroom and fish my fairy from my pocket. I sit braced in the corner behind the door, take a deep breath and puncture the vein that pulses on the top of my foot. I follow the line of the vein until the blood, thick and dark like paint, gushes over onto the tile. I close my eyes and feel nothing except the deep satisfaction of knowing that I've left the door unlocked, and Sage will be the one to find me.

℅ 5 ℆

NOW THAT I AM LEAVING

Now that I am leaving
Can't find the word good-bye
I thought I knew what you wanted
I thought I knew just why
But I'm still standing here
You've long since turned away
So why am I still waiting here
Waiting to hear you say
Stay
　　　"Waiting Here" - Luna Rayne, 1997

I wake up with my feet stuck in dried blood and the taste of iron in my mouth. I wouldn't bother to clean it up, but I don't want Ethan to see. The sun's fighting to come through and winning, so when I'm done, I get in the shower. Sage isn't in her bed when I head into our room to get clothes, but I find her downstairs in the kitchen, watching through the screen door with a cup of coffee in hand as Ethan swims.

She doesn't turn around to look at me. I pour a cup and rummage around the fridge for some half and half. "It's gonna hurt like shit to put on shoes today, " she says. I smile with the satisfaction of knowing she saw.

"You kiss my brother with that mouth?" I ask.

"Excuse me?" Sage spins around, nearly spilling her coffee.

"You heard me," I say with less fervor than I'd planned. I lean against the counter for support. My head's beginning to hum with the stress of the coming confrontation, and I suddenly wish I hadn't started poking this tiger.

"What're you talking about?" She doesn't give me a chance to answer. "Does this have something to do with your martyr act in the bathroom last night?"

Now she's just pissing me off. "Nuh-uh! You do not get to turn this back on me, Sage. You know what you did, and you know it's wrong."

"The question is, how do you know?" She glances out the door. "Did he tell you?"

She's giving me an out. I could easily nod, but that would be throwing my brother under the bus.

"I saw you," I say simply. "You're still deflecting, by the way. How I know is of far less consequence than the fact that you did it." My turn to cut her off. "What're you thinking, Sage? You can't keep leading him on, making him think there's a chance."

Sage hangs her head for a couple of seconds, marshalling a response. "Elena, you don't get it at all."

"You got that right."

She doesn't even hear me. "The pull I feel toward Ethan is epic and magnetic. Like it was there before we ever met. I know this sounds crazy, but I feel like he and I are kind of destined in some weird way."

"Destined! Really? This is Ethan you're talking about. He's not destined to be with anyone. He's a child. And even if he weren't, what about Finn? Are you destined to be with him, too?" I want to slap her, wake her from this absurd delusion.

"I'm not sure how Finn fits, to tell you the truth. I just know there's something about Ethan, something familiar." She seems genuinely perplexed.

"Then getting Ethan away from you is the best thing I can do for him, isn't it? Your confusion isn't going to be of any use to him when you break what's left of his heart into a million pieces."

"Maybe you're right, Elena. But consider for one minute, what if you're wrong? What if this is Ethan's chance, a life with me? What if you rob him of that kind of love forever and he just goes on his whole life, stuck in time like a little kid?"

"You can justify it to yourself any way you want, Sage, but wrong is wrong and what you're doing is capital wrong. Jeez, sometimes I wish we'd never met you."

Sage turns back toward the door, her entire attention riveted on my boy. "I never wish that, Elena," she mumbles, and I wonder if she's going to cry. I don't wait for it, though. I push through the door and intercept Ethan getting out of the pool.

I pick up his robe from the back of the chair where he hung it and wrap it around him. He leans into me and whispers a sweet good-morning through chattering teeth. I ruffle his wet hair and he smiles. By the time we get inside, Sage is no longer in the kitchen. I pour a glass of orange juice for Ethan and sit with him at the table.

"Hey, E, I was thinking we should have a dinner with Grandmother this week. It might be the last time we see her for a while."

Ethan frowns. I know he's worried she'll somehow find out he was the one who burned down her garage, not Finn. He's afraid she'll find a way to send him to an institution. He thinks she hates him and I'm pretty sure he'd hate her if he was capable of such an emotion. I move to make my case. "I think she'd be proud of all the stuff you're accomplishing. I can just see the look on her face as you pull the car up the driveway."

Ethan's frown dissolves as he works over that image in his head. "I'd need to be really careful. No accidents. No thumb."

"We'll bring lollipops, and you can wear a diaper."

Ethan shakes his head with exasperation. "No, Lanie! No more diapers, except at night."

I remember what Jo said about me controlling Ethan. "Okay, pal, that's your call."

He nods with satisfaction. "I can do it."

I get up and kiss him on the forehead. "I believe you can. I'll give her a call. Go on up and get ready. We have a lot of packing to do today."

At the mention of the move, Ethan's mood sours. "I'm not packing anything! I don't want to go to Florida to that stupid PSI place." He rises abruptly. At the archway he turns back and mumbles just loud enough for me to hear, "Place of Stupid Idiots."

"Hey! Not nice!" I shoot back, but as soon as he's pounding up the stairs, I dissolve in giggles. Jamie will love that one. I almost text him, but he might think I'm flirting and maybe he'd be right. Too confusing, best not to go there. I text Jo instead.

The night of our farewell family dinner Sage and I are in the kitchen, waiting for Jo to arrive and Ethan to come down. I know he's really nervous about seeing Grandmother again, but I resist the urge to go up and try to calm him. Instead, I fill my purse with Dum Dums and hope he can keep it together for a couple of hours.

"He's gonna be fine, Elena," Sage says out of nowhere.

I let a quick smile slip through the tight line of my lips. "You reading my mind now?" I ask.

"Don't have to. You really need to trust him more. He's not the helpless, hopeless child you think he is."

"Uh-huh." I'm not having this conversation right now.

Sage takes the hint and changes the subject. "So, you invited Jo."

"Yep. Why wouldn't I? Lily loves Jo."

"I don't know. Things with you and Jo are — different now, more — you know."

I look her up and down, waiting for her to spit out whatever she's trying to say.

Sage shakes her head. "Fine, I'll just ask. Are you, like, coming out to your gran tonight?"

I feel like a bucket of cold water has been dumped over my head. "What? No! Why would you — "

"It's just, if there are going to be fireworks, Ethan should know ahead of time." She looks like she swallowed a fish.

"Right. Ethan should know ahead of time." I shake my head. "Sage, you're unbelievably transparent. And the answer is no. I'm not coming out to my grandmother. Jeez, can you imagine?" I'm laughing when Jo opens the door.

"Glad to see you all in such good spirits," she says, hugging Sage. When she makes her way to me and our lips touch, I realize she must have been talking to Sage about us. The thought warms me deep inside and I kiss her again more deeply.

"Whoa, nice greeting," she whispers in my ear.

We all turn when Ethan enters the room. He looks like an angel in his khakis and white, button-down shirt. His curls are tamed back from his face with gel and his gray eyes are sparkling with anticipation. He hands Sage a roll of duct tape with skulls on it. Jo and I watch as she wraps his thumbs. When she's done, he shoves his hands in his pockets and looks from me to Jo.

"We ready now?" I ask.

Ethan looks at Jo expectantly, and she nods and holds out her hand to him. Then Ethan takes a step toward her, extracts one hand from his pocket and places his palm in hers. I gasp.

Jo lets out her breath slowly and holds up her other hand to stop me from severing their connection. "It's okay, Lane."

Ethan smiles brightly and says, "Yep, ready to go now." He and Jo walk hand in hand to the car. Following behind them, I enjoy the complicated play of emotions over Sage's features. I'd swear she was jealous. She is, after all, the only person Ethan has ever been able to touch, aside from me. Maybe the success of this experiment isn't as sweet as she'd imagined it would be. For me, the thought of Ethan able to be out in the world without fear of accidentally brushing against a stranger and flipping consciousness with them is nothing short of miraculous. I can almost feel the sky opening and flooding his world with sunlight. I'm grinning so wide my cheeks hurt.

"You, my little brother, are just full of surprises these days!" I gush.

He grins back at me with pride and — could it be? — Confidence. Amazing.

At the car, Sage tosses Ethan the keys, and he slides into the driver's seat. Sage rides shotgun, leaving Jo and me to cuddle in the backseat. The weight I've been carrying feels several pounds lighter. At the same time, a hole that threatens to swallow me is opening in my chest.

Sage texts Lily to meet us outside, so she's standing in the driveway when we pull up. It's only been a couple of months since I last saw her, but I almost don't recognize her. She seems thin and wraith-like in the backlight of the kitchen. She'd always been larger than life to me; now she appears human, breakable like me, like E.

Ethan turns the key off and pulls the emergency brake quickly, like he can't wait to jump out. When Grandmother comes to the passenger side first, his face falls. She hugs Sage with a sort of stiff gusto. Like the rest of us, Lily is all about Sage. Then she greets me with slightly less enthusiasm. Her arms feel like bird wings fluttering around me, bony and reluctant.

"Your hair's getting long. Did you color it?" Her tone is accusatory, but I don't take the bait.

"Grandma, I was in Florida for three weeks. The sun bleached it." I smile warmly at her, and she relents with a grunt.

"Hello, Jo, darling," she says, taking Jo's hand, but foregoing the hug. Ethan hasn't moved from beside the driver's side door, but he's turned to follow her with his eyes, waiting for his turn. Finally, Grandmother makes her way over to him. She stops about arm's reach from him and examines him critically. Ethan manages to keep his eyes on hers, but he fidgets under her scrutiny. When her gaze lands on his taped thumbs, he quickly shoves his hands into his pockets. Then she takes a deep breath. "Well, boy, it's good to see you're learning some useful skills. I hope your sister and Sage are getting some of the more basic social niceties through to you, too." Ethan looks down for a moment, unable to hold that unnerving stare. I swear if she looked at me that way, I'd pee my pants, too.

Instead of falling apart, though, Ethan reaches into his back pocket and pulls out a folded paper. He holds it out to her and cautiously she takes it, without touching him. As she unfolds it, I realize it's his chart from the refrigerator. I grab Sage's arm. She gives me a look that says she's as surprised by this as I am. Grandmother takes in the meaning of the document and raises an eyebrow.

To my utter shock, she bestows on Ethan a rare smile. "Much better," she says, and just in case we missed it the first time, she repeats the phrase again. Ethan lifts his chin with pride and relief, then takes a step toward her. She balks, backing away, but Sage has come around behind her.

"It's all right, Lily," Sage says.

Ethan steps forward again. Awkwardly and tentatively, he places a hand on her arm as he leans in to kiss her cheek. Lily blanches at first and closes her eyes in anticipation of the usual agony that accompanies Ethan's touch, but when it doesn't come, she stands up taller, which makes Ethan scramble back a step. Lily's cheeks suddenly burn red and she waves us all inside, like a befuddled pigeon. I come up behind Ethan and whisper in his ear. "Nice job, Bro. I think you broke our grandma." Ethan giggles, and we follow the rest of them in.

The meal is my favorite, pad Thai with shrimp. The conversation's lively and enthusiastic. Under the table, Jo holds my hand. Listening to Ethan describe his success at the gallery and his interactions with Sage's math prof, I begin to see for myself what Sage has been trying to tell me. We talk about everything: school, work at the cafe and tutoring center, running, music, Rachel and Jesse's baby, and the weather. We talk about everything except the Initiative and the move. It's the elephant in the room.

Before dessert, Ethan's alarm on his watch goes off and he excuses himself from the table. Grandmother looks impressed. Sage suggests adjourning to the living room for dessert. I stay behind to help Grandmother bring in peach pie and ice cream, Ethan's favorite.

I'm pulling down the plates when she corners me. "He's doing really well, isn't he?"

"Most of the time," I say.

"Elena, do you really think moving him away from Sage is the best thing for him right now?"

I freeze in my tracks, try counting to ten, get to three and explode.

"Goddamn it! What about me? Doesn't anyone give a damn about what's best for me?"

"Watch your language, young lady!" Grandmother is in no way prepared for my outburst, and why would she be? What could she know about the collective lobbying that's been happening? Suddenly a light bulb goes on.

"So, when did she call you?" I ask, my voice teetering toward hysteria.

Grandmother looks away nervously as Sage enters the kitchen. "You bitch!" I level my gaze at Sage. "Is there anyone you haven't turned against me?" I don't wait for an answer. I push past my grandmother and out the kitchen door. In the cool darkness at the far side of the pool, I pace until I can breathe again. Then I sit and put my hand in the warm water. The door bangs, and I can see Jo's outline for an instant before she joins me in the dark.

"Lane? You okay, baby?"

I nod, but I doubt she can see me. I don't trust my voice. She comes and sits beside me.

"No one's ganging up on you, sweetie." Her voice is like blue velvet.

"Doesn't feel that way, Jo." I won't look at her. She's a part of this, too. I can see her feet firmly planted in the Ethan-needs-Sage-and-his-needs-trump-Elena's camp. We sit in silence while my resentment builds to volcanic proportions and spills over again. "All my life it's been all about him. Finally, I'm doing something for me, and I don't think I should have to apologize to the world for that!"

"I think you're overreacting, Lane. This is just all so sudden, so quick. We all were there when you guys moved to the university six months ago, and Ethan cried for, like, three days and didn't speak to anyone but Sage for a week after that. We're just concerned about how he's going to handle moving four states away, without Sage to lean on."

"I can take care of my brother, Jo. I took care of him for thirteen years after my parents — and before Sage came along. Besides, the Initiative will be good for him. He'll learn how to manage his abilities and interact with other people."

"We all hope you're right. That's all. We just want to make sure you've thought this through. You might not get a redo with that boy. He's kind of fragile, in case you hadn't noticed."

I put my head in my arms, and let the guilt that's digging a hole through my gut pour out of my eyes. The hot tears drop onto my sleeve and soak in, turning icy cold in the night air. I try to concentrate on the tactile sensation, so I don't have to think about the what-ifs that could paralyze me. Jo slides over and puts her arm around me. I let my body relax against her, trying hard to absorb her unwavering strength.

"We should go back in," she says after I've stopped sniffling. "We're missing your grandmother's peach pie."

Jo gets up and offers me her hands. I stand on my own and follow her through the empty kitchen into the living room.

"It's a matter of principle," Gran is saying when we come in.

"Really, Lily?" Sage replies, her voice edging north of neutral. "You rebuilt the garage; the insurance covered the whole thing and no one was hurt. No harm, no foul, right?" She smiles.

"Do you know where that boy is, Sage? Are you in contact with him?" Now Grandmother's on her feet, but only for a second. She doesn't even make it to her full height before sinking down again.

"Of course not, Lily! I just think that holding onto this grudge and continuing to push this investigation is wearing you down. Maybe it's time to forgive and forget." Sage has gone to Gran and is squatting beside her, holding her hand. Damn, she's good.

I glance at Ethan. He's literally squirming, bringing his hand to his mouth every few seconds, like he's forgotten about the tape on his thumbs. I cross the room and gently shove him over so we're sharing the chair. I offer him a lollypop from my pocket. He rips off the paper, slips it in his mouth and lets out a long sigh. After a few seconds, he relaxes against my shoulder.

"This is not up for debate, Sage," Gran says quietly. "When a man commits a crime, he should pay. It's that simple."

"They don't know for sure who did it, Lily." Sage gets up and goes back to the couch. She cuts another piece of pie and hands it to Jo on a plate. Her hands are shaking. She offers me a piece with her eyes. I decline.

"Well, someone runs from the law, they might as well confess. He did it, all right."

Sage shakes her head sadly and takes another scoop of ice cream.

Gran shoos us out before nine o'clock, looking like she might drop where she stands. I've never seen her so tired in my life. We take the leftovers with us and make a promise to stop by before I head out of town with Ethan. She hugs us all, except Ethan, who has withdrawn to some private, little hell. Nonetheless, Sage offers him the keys. He declines and crawls into the backseat, where he rips the tape from his right thumb and begins sucking almost desperately with his knees pulled up, his feet on the seat and head against the window. I get in on the other side next to him. When I reach over to hold his free hand, he pulls away. I try to open my mind to his, but he shuts me out. Sage and Jo chat quietly in the front seat and sing along with the radio to songs that remind them of their shared youth. I lean my forehead against the cool window on my side of the backseat and let my mind drift into the infinite darkness above the power lines and treetops.

At home, I let Jo drive away without a huge goodbye scene, while Sage and I sink back to an uncomfortable, mutual silence. I keep myself between her and Ethan as much as possible to prevent any further "magic." Neither of them is happy about me running interference, though. Ethan stomps up the stairs and closes his door in my face. I go to my own room, sit on my bed and wait. Like clockwork, he calls for me once he's in bed. I open his door and stick my head in.

"Can I come in?" I ask.

He nods.

I pick up his discarded clothes on the way to the bed and drape them over his desk chair.

"You did great tonight, E," I say, sitting next to him on the bed.

"You didn't," he says.

"Excuse me." I almost laugh, but the disappointment in his tone kind of shocks me. "What are you talking about?"

"You didn't even let us talk about it like you were supposed to. You threw a big fit and went outside like a baby." Halfway through the accusation he sits up, ready to do battle.

"Really? What was supposed to happen, E?"

"We were supposed to talk about it, all of us, and you were supposed to listen."

"I see," I say quietly. "And who planned this intervention?"

He looks down at his hands. "Everyone. . . me and Sage and Jo and Grandmother."

My eyebrows go up higher with each name he ticks off. "Guess that's everyone, all right." For a couple of minutes, I can't speak. "Is that why you were mad before we went home?"

"It wasn't supposed to end like that." His voice quavers on the last word.

"Let me guess. It was supposed to end with me being convinced to stay here."

He nods sadly.

"Did you really think that would happen?" I ask.

"No," he mumbles. His eyes are shining when they meet mine. "I know exactly what's going to happen. I just hoped that maybe — " He doesn't bother to finish. He slides down under the covers and turns to face the wall. I lean over and kiss his wet cheek.

Susan Michalski

ॐ 6 ॐ

I'LL BE STRONG

We're chipping away at the underside
Dust and stone and sweat
Breaking away one night at a time
Barely hanging on.
Hear the groan
Cracks digging in
Those ghostly fingers
Tearing it down
Tearing it down
You tell me I'll be strong
"Rock Slide" - Luna Rayne, 2014

Two days later, I'm sitting on a plane, preparing to descend into Orlando, going over the conversation I had with Sage before I left. I hope against hope that she heard me when I told her not to fuck around with Ethan's head or any other part of his body while I'm away. She promised solemnly to keep her hands and lips to herself, but I still don't trust her, not about this, not right now. Hell, I don't even understand it. How could she even look at him that way?

Saying goodbye to Ethan was even worse than the last time. He told me to stay away forever, slammed the door in my face and locked it. Through the hollow wood, I told him I loved him and promised to make everything perfect for him in Florida. My words echoed back as I listened to him cry and bang his head against the door. No amount of silent cajoling could break through his pain. Jo finally dragged me out to the car. I had a plane to catch, after all.

She dropped me off at the airport four hours ago. We were running late and barely had time for a quick kiss. Jamie's picking me up less than an hour from now, the significance of which does nothing to slow my racing thoughts. I try to picture his easy smile and playful gaze unsuccessfully, but when I close my eyes, I can taste his lips. My cheeks burn with confusion and the memory.

The unusually tall businessman beside me offers me a stick of cinnamon gum for the landing. I'm suddenly sweaty-palms, dry-mouth nervous. The guy looks at my bouncing knee, so I look away, embarrassed, without accepting his offer. Maybe this wasn't such a good idea after all. Without permission, my mind makes a list of all the ways this whole thing could go badly wrong. I suddenly want to cry, but I think the suit next to me might lose his mind if I fall apart. I push down on my knee with my hand and close my eyes. I picture my chakras all faded and out of alignment. I try to imagine my heart chakra, green and glowing, pulling the others into place like an electromagnet. The jolt of the wheels hitting the runway pitches me forward, and I catch myself.

"I hate landings, too," the suit says, smiling wryly. I manage to smile back somehow.

Jamie's standing in front of the baggage claim carousel. I see him before he sees me. I stop at the top of the stairs, and the crowd coming up from behind swirls around me like a river current around a rock. He's pacing nervously, bumping into passengers and mumbling apologies. His brow's knit in a series of wrinkles that look like the forehead of our neighbor's boxer puppy. I smile despite my hammering heart and mentally call out to him. I'm shocked when he looks up at that exact moment and catches my eye. I hurry down the escalator, ready to throw myself into his arms, but my common sense engages at the last moment, and I pull up short, accidentally invading his personal space, but not making physical contact. He must think I'm ridiculous, but he doesn't move away. Instead, he lifts the backpack off my shoulder and places it on his own.

"Good to see you, Elena," he says a little too formally.

I step away. "You too, Jamie. You looked a little worried from up there. Did you think I was going to blow you off?"

"The thought might've crossed my mind."

"It crossed mine, too, at 35,000 feet without a parachute," I confess.

He smiles and relaxes a couple of degrees. "You ready to get to work?" he asks with a genuine smile.

I shrug my shoulders, but something about his puppy dog eyes puts a stupid grin on my face, too.

Jamie insists on carrying my bags to the car. "Is this all you're bringing?" he quips as he struggles beneath the weight of all my luggage.

"These were all the suitcases I had. I pared back to what I could fit in these," I say.

"This is pared back?" he asks, incredulous.

He flips a bunch of levers and flops over the seats to make enough room in the Honda Fit for all my stuff.

"You can take me to the same hotel I stayed in last time," I offer as he fastens his seat belt. I've texted Rachel to meet me for supper at the diner across the street. I used our code word "purple", so she knows to send Finn instead of coming herself. Stupid code word, I know, but it had to be common enough that it wouldn't send up any red flags to law enforcement who might be watching us, uncommon enough that we don't use it accidentally, and it had to have nothing to do with Finn. Jesse's word is "golden."

"Why would you be staying at a hotel?" Jamie asks. His eyebrows look like little smiles when he's confused. I giggle inappropriately.

"Where else would I stay? I haven't found a place for me and Ethan yet. I did look a little online, though."

Jamie shifts away from me. "Didn't you read the contract? Housing is provided. We have a place set up for you."

I feel like an idiot. Guess I should have read that thing through at some point. I try to cover. "Oh yeah, I read that. I didn't know you had it set up already, though."

"We do." Jamie's tone is suddenly cooler, and I feel his professional wall come down between us, so I get out my phone and text Rachel that my plans have changed.

"Oh, you were planning on seeing your friend again?" Jamie says.

I nod.

His hands move nervously over the steering wheel, like he can't quite figure out where to put them. "I'm sorry, that'll have to wait. You're going to be pretty busy for the next few days," he says.

"That's okay. I can see her whenever." I finish the message and text Ethan and Sage that I made it to Florida in one piece. I return the phone to my purse without waiting for replies.

Jamie flashes me a fleeting smile. It's odd; you'd think he was the one about to start the new job. I smile back but turn away quickly to watch the scenery fly by the window. We're on the road for about twenty minutes when I realize we aren't headed to the PSI facility I worked at before. That facility was only about fifteen minutes from the Orlando airport, in a dingy generic warehouse complex just outside the city.

"Where're you taking me?" I ask.

"To our Southern facility." He looks accusingly at me. "You never read the contract, did you?"

I'm so embarrassed. He must think I'm the biggest idiot. "Well, sorta kind of. . . Okay, not really."

He shakes his head and purses his lips. "Well, put on your seat belt, Elena. You're in for a bit of ride."

I look down, then realize he's being metaphoric. "Wanna clue me in a little?"

He shakes his head. "It'll be better if you just take it as it comes. I wouldn't want to scare you away at this point."

I can't tell if he's serious or joking. "That bad? Really?"

He points out the driver's side window at a glass building rising in the distance. It has spires that glint like diamonds in the sunlight and a stone wall like a medieval fortress. The green, rolling fields around the crystal palace are reflected on the building's surface. "The Emerald City!" I mumble, not really meaning it for his ears.

Jamie cracks up. I look at him, amazed, but he can't stop laughing. Finally, he chokes out, "We're off to see the wizard."

"The wonderful wizard of Oz," I sing.

Jamie touches my cheek. "You are so damn cute sometimes!"

The look on my face makes him withdraw. "I am not cute!" I say, annoyed by the accusation.

Jamie looks at me helplessly. "I'm sorry, Elena." He pauses a beat and adds, "but you are so; you really are." And another round of giggles consumes him.

He manages to look sober as we pull up to the guardhouse in front of the ten-foot, spike-topped gates. Jamie flashes a badge and an official-looking paper. Then the guard steps up to a scanner on the side of the guardhouse. A red light flashes over his eye, and the guardhouse door opens. He punches something into a computer inside, exits the guardhouse, places his hand on a pad beside the gate, and the doors swing slowly open.

As we drive through, I can't help turning in my seat to watch the guards. When the one at the palm scanner turns, I catch the glint of metal off the gun in his shoulder holster. "Damn, that's a lot of security for a science facility," I say, turning back.

Jamie looks like he's about to say something. Several emotions cross his face, from frustration to regret. When he finally responds a few beats too late, he says, "Science, or parascience in this case, is big money." Then he shrugs.

I've already forgotten the guards. Directly ahead of us, up at the end of an elegant, tree-lined lane, is the glittering building. It's enormous, and I have to lean against the windshield to see to the top. What I'd thought were windows are actually mostly some reflective metallic substance. In keeping with the intense security, only a few windows pepper the walls, until about ten floors up. As the car approaches the building, Jamie presses a button, and the wall in front of us rises to give us access to an underground tunnel. I can't help myself. I giggle with glee and exclaim, "Holy bat cave, Robin!"

Jamie looks intentionally bored, raises one eyebrow and says indignantly, "I am not Robin. Not in this universe or any other!"

"Sorry. You're right. You'd be the Joker! Clearly, the Joker!"

He laughs maniacally in response and goes on. "Now that you've guessed my devious disguise, I'll monologue about my evil plan. Then I'll attempt to eliminate you. Wa ha ha ha ha!"

"Oh no. Help. Help. Someone save me." I bring the back of my hand to my forehead and make my voice as unemotional as possible. Jamie's smile reaches his eyes, and they crinkle around his glasses in the most adorable way.

His smile fades away, though, as he pulls into a parking space. I don't miss the cameras that record the car's location from every angle. Jamie comes around to open my car door, and I get out slowly. "Smile, you're on *Candid Camera*," I whisper.

Jamie nods. "Time to put on your game face."

I follow him through the parking garage, with its white-washed floors, walls, and ceiling lit by a black light, to a double-paned glass door. Jamie steps up to a retinal scanner and states his name and an eight-digit code. A series of clicks follows, admitting us into a sort of antechamber, the kind you might see in a space ship or submarine. "Stand still," Jamie commands. The lights in the room dim slightly, and a high-pitched whirring noise comes from the walls. If Jamie wasn't standing here next to me, I'd be terrified. I resist the urge to grab his hand. I feel like we're standing in the scanner for an hour, but in reality, only a couple of minutes pass before a guard opens the inner door. It occurs to me suddenly that getting out of this place would be as difficult as getting in. Jamie puts his hand on my shoulder and ushers me through the doors. "You'll be processed for access this afternoon," he whispers in my ear. I can feel the tightness in my chest loosen a little.

Jamie thanks the guard, and we head down a long, gleaming white hallway. It must be fifty yards long, half the school's football field, without a single door to break the icy flow of energy. At the end of the hall is an elevator and to the right lies an alcove that holds a door with a sign indicating a stairwell. Beside the elevator is another retinal scanner. Jamie steps up to it, and a second later the elevator opens to reveal more reflective white surfacing. I step in and press myself into the corner, half-expecting the floor to open and drop me into a pit of alligators. Before I can convince myself otherwise, the door closes noiselessly in front of us. The first thing I notice is that there's no keypad to identify what floor we want to stop on. I jump when Jamie speaks. "Jamie Fleming, 37724598, main level." Then he turns to me and says quietly, "State your name and say 'unprocessed' afterward."

I clear my throat and try to keep my voice from shaking. "Elena Paige, unprocessed."

An androgynous voice fills the space. "Access to main level granted." Then the elevator moves like it's on greased rails. No noise, no shaking, no lurching. Almost instantly the doors open, and we're deposited into another world. Warm, polished wood floors with bright, plush Persian rugs hold dozens of people who are laughing, talking, moving about their important and apparently enjoyable business. In the middle of the softly lit room is a large, round, mahogany reception desk manned by beautifully manicured and fashionably dressed young women with bright eyes and brighter smiles. Instantly, I feel inadequate and shabby. Then a tall blond beckons us over and greets me warmly.

"You must be Elena Paige! I'm Nora. We're so pleased you're here!" She comes out from behind the desk to shake my hand. The other girls turn and smile, too. I wave nervously and try to match their friendliness. Meanwhile, Nora has taken Jamie a couple of feet to the side. He's handing her the car keys, and they're talking in whispers. She slips back around the desk and passes him a manila envelope. My name and a number are written on the back. Jamie looks at Nora with an expression that says you're-kidding-me-right? Nora shrugs, then turns to me.

"We'll have your luggage delivered to your room, Elena," Nora says brightly.

"Okay, thanks," I say, but I'm totally confused. I turn to Jamie, "I'm staying here? I thought Ethan and I would get an apartment nearby."

A look of frustration rises in Jamie's eyes, but his voice remains patient. "Elena, there aren't any apartments — or houses for that matter — near here. The contract states that you'll be housed free of charge at the facility. Meals are provided, too, and snacks. Whatever you like, we can get for you."

"Chocolate truffles?"

"Done."

"Pad Tai with extra nuts?"

"Give them an hour."

"Guava sorbet with pistachios?"

"Served it last night for dessert." Jamie doesn't even crack a smile.

"I think I could get fat here," I say.

"Let's hope not," he says, his eyes crinkling sweetly. He points down a hallway on the other side of the information desk. The walls are paneled partway up, and the top's painted a soothing shade of blue that reminds me of Ethan's room in our grandmother's house where we grew up, or at least I did. Ugh, Ethan. I feel sick trying to imagine him navigating the gauntlet I just passed through to get here. Hopefully, our room will be nice, and he'll feel at home enough to forget about the rest of this. I'm imagining blue walls and a fireplace maybe, when we get to another set of elevators. We get in and follow the same drill. "Level 17," Jamie says.

I expect to feel the elevator rise, but instead I have the sensation of dropping deep into the earth. "We're going down," I say. Jamie nods but offers no other information.

The doors open to a hotel hallway, a nice hotel. Polished, wide plank floors, replicas of paintings I remember from Sage's art history book framed in coordinating colors, a chair rail. The hall stretches left and right with doors at regular intervals. I follow Jamie left. Each room we pass is alive with conversation, music and laughter. The doors are all open, so I peek in. Girls populate the rooms. Their ages range from maybe twelve to twenty-one or so. They stare back at me with curiosity and something else I can't put my finger on, exactly.

"Where'd all the boys go?" I ask.

"Other side of the elevator," he says, deadpan. "They aren't allowed over here."

As if on cue, a wiry boy of maybe fourteen tears around the corner ahead, laughing and shrieking past us at breakneck speed. A moment later, a much older girl follows. Her eyes are ablaze and when she yells, the walls shake. "Give it the fuck back, you little fuckhead!" Her hair's streaked with blue, and she wears more black eye makeup than Marilyn Manson.

When she gets to us, she turns to Jamie and says, "Put a leash on that dog or I'm gonna kill his ass and eat him." My eyes widen as I realize she's in no way speaking metaphorically. The girl's tall and strong, and the angry heat coming off of her is intense. She eyes me. "What the hell are you lookin' at, bitch?" I take a step back, my mouth agape. Then she turns on her heel and storms back the way she came.

Jamie looks at his feet and wrings his hands. "Sorry about that. Sometimes the natives get restless. I'll talk to Cayde and Logan. We usually keep the fireworks down here to a minimum. Sorry."

"You said that twice," I say, touching his arm.

He pulls away a little too abruptly. I must look confused because he says it again.

"So, if girls are on one side and boys are on the other, where are you putting me and Ethan?" I haven't finished the question when it dawns on me what the housing arrangement is to be. I stop dead in my tracks. "No way, Jamie!" I start walking back toward the elevators. "This is not going to happen. You don't understand. Ethan can't — He needs me — to take care of him. He can't —"

At the elevators, Jamie puts his hand on my shoulder to calm me, but I shake him off. "I didn't agree to this," I almost yell.

He looks at his feet again and mumbles, "You kind of did. You signed the contract."

My heart stops, and I forget how to breathe. He's right, of course.

I have no choice. I signed the contract. Shit. I signed the contract. What have I done? I can hear Ethan crying behind the door this morning, begging and begging me not to get on that plane, but I did, and now it's done. And Ethan can't stay with Sage, and he can't go back to Grandmother, and Jesse wouldn't have him, and I am here bound by my own hand. The tears well up in my eyes, and my knees get weak.

Jamie's voice comes from far away. "Elena, everything's going to be okay. Ethan will be fine. I won't let anything bad happen to you guys." I feel the weight of his hand on my shoulder again, but this time I don't duck away. I look up into his eyes and am surprised to find them sparkling with tears that mirror mine. He looks away, swallows them back quickly. For some reason I feel a little better. I sit in one of the overstuffed chairs across from the elevator doors. Jamie takes the other.

"Jamie, I don't think you understand about Ethan. He has problems."

Jamie keeps his hand on my knee. "Elena, I know all about Ethan. He has PTSD with regressive symptoms that include but aren't limited to social anxiety, withdrawal, panic attacks, agoraphobia, nocturnal and diurnal enuresis, night terrors, nightmares and thumb-sucking. Did I miss anything significant?"

I'm stunned. I never told Jamie anything about Ethan except that he was messed up by what happened with our mom. I shake it off. Of course, they would check us out before bringing us here. "Well, then you know he's not going to be able to live in a dorm situation with a stranger. You'd be asking for a train wreck."

"Elena, your brother is nineteen years old. He'll be able to manage better than you think. And you'll be close by if he needs you. Besides, most of the kids here have issues of one kind or another."

I fight the feeling of passive acceptance that wants to creep in. "Really, Jamie, how many of them wet the bed?"

Jamie raises an eyebrow. "You'd be surprised."

Despite my frustration, I smile. Maybe Jamie's right. I'll be just down the hall, after all, and Ethan has been doing much better, at least with staying dry during the day. I almost give in to another wave of panic, triggered by the thought of Ethan having an accident in that beautiful lobby in front of all those perfect people, but the emotion passes through me, and I let it go.

"You ready to go see your room now?" he asks gently.

I wipe my palms on my jeans and get up. Jamie slides his hand into my mine as we make our way back down the hallway. I like the way it feels, warm and large and protective. I could hold his hand for the rest of my life. At the last door in the long hall, Jamie stops and knocks. It's the only door that's closed. An abrasive voice comes from inside. "Come in, if you must. But don't expect me to get up."

Jamie types a number into the keypad that was hidden behind a nearly invisible wall panel. The door clicks, and I push it open.

The girl with the dark eye makeup is sitting crisscross on the bed in the far corner of the room with headphones over her ears and a magazine open in her lap. The wall beside the bed is painted black, and all kinds of strange images and expressions are etched into the paint. I can't tear my eyes from it.

"Don't stare at my shit, bitch," the girl says, without looking up at me.

I turn to Jamie and whisper, "Really? I'm going to live with her?"

"Logan, I want you to meet Elena. Elena, Logan."

"Charmed, I'm sure," I say loud enough for her to hear through the music.

Logan looks me up and down like a piece of rotten meat, her nose wrinkled in disgust. "That's all you got?" She shakes her head and looks back at her magazine.

"Okay then," Jamie says. "I need to get a few things done before we can do your security processing. Why don't you get settled, and I'll come back in an hour or so."

I follow him to the door, but something in the set of his shoulders keeps me from going with him into the hall. I have no choice but to make this work somehow. I leave the door open in case I need to beat a hasty exit and turn slowly, afraid any sudden moves might provoke Logan. She isn't looking at me anymore, so I take in the rest of the room. There are no windows — obviously, since we're underground — but a couple of large mirrors with lattice made to appear window-like are hung side by side on one wall. My suitcases are stacked in the corner beside the bed, positioned as far from Logan's as possible. At the end of the bed are white cotton sheets, a soft yellow blanket, and a quilt with geometric patterns that matches the quilt on Logan's bed. I start there. After the bed's made, I empty my shirts, pants, pajamas, underwear, and socks into the dresser.

When I open the closet on my side of the room to hang up the rest of my clothes, I find a large package wrapped in bright paper with a bow. The tag says it's for me, from Jamie. I bring it out and put it on my bed.

"Someone's got a boyfriend," Logan sings softly, without looking up.

"What are you? Ten?" I say.

"Just saying," she comes back.

"I play for the other team," I say, hoping it will shut her up.

"Well, isn't that interesting." She rolls her eyes, like she doesn't believe me or doesn't care.

I turn my back to her and sit down on the bed next to the box. For a while, I stare through it, trying to imagine what Jamie might've gotten me. Not a single possibility comes to mind.

"For the love of Satan, open the damn thing already!" Logan screams. I'm so shocked by her aggression that I rip the paper and throw it aside. The box is plain white, not a clue on the outside, so I tear at the sides until the top flops back. Then I start laughing, and I can't stop. Inside is a note that says, "Sorry about your roommate"; under it is a canopy that attaches to the ceiling, with drapes that fall around the bed; an mp3 player with a pair of earbuds; a bag full of glow-in-the-dark stars; and a poster of a super nova taken with the Hubble telescope with the caption, "Stars are not the limit - aim further!"

I slip the note out of the box before Logan can see it. "You are not putting any of that shit up in my room," Logan says with a snarl.

I do my best to look tough and snarl back, "Our room, not yours. And I'll put up whatever I want to put up." I'm relieved that my voice stays low and doesn't break.

Logan smiles. The effect does nothing to ameliorate her menace. "Ooo, the mouse roars. I'll give you this one. Your shit on your side. Understand?"

I nod without smiling.

"Some rules in this room are non-negotiable. No talking to me unless I talk to you first. No food in here, ever. Though from the looks of you, you probably never eat. And most importantly, this is not a fucking hotel; if you want to get your freak on, do it someplace else. Are we clear?"

"Whatever," I say, turning my back to her.

"As long as we're talking rules," she continues as if I hadn't given her my back, "I've been tasked with teaching you the rules of the asylum. And you're in great fucking luck because no one knows them better than this inmate."

I stop what I'm doing, sigh and sit down on the bed. "What are you talking about?"

"Number one: no outside communication. That means no Internet, no television, no radio, no cell phones or pagers." I must look like I've been punched because her grin widens. "And you thought I was joking about the inmate thing."

Without really thinking about it, I find myself reaching for my phone.

"Your handler will collect that from you when he comes back to process your security clearance and take you to be shrunk." Her words sound rehearsed.

I look at the phone. I can't decide if she's serious or yanking my chain for her perverse pleasure. Jamie didn't say anything about seeing a shrink. "Is that it?" I ask quietly. I wonder if all this was in the contract I never read.

"Not exactly. You'll be escorted to and from your research sessions on the upper levels. Your access at PSI extends to this floor, the main level, the cafeteria and infirmary on level three, and the gym and pool on level five."

I'm so excited they have a pool for Ethan that the rest hardly matters. "There's a pool here?" I pull the picture of Ethan, me, and Sage from the front pocket of my suitcase and run my finger over Ethan's face.

"I think I just said that. Are you deaf or just stupid?" she asks as she snatches the picture from my hands. "What do we have here?"

I try to grab it back, but she holds it out of my reach. Suddenly she stops and brings it down to eye level. I step back, surprised. "Who's this?" she asks, pointing to Ethan. Her voice goes wonky, and her face turns white for an instant. Then she plays it off and goes on like nothing happened. "Not your boyfriend. Must be a brother." She points to Sage. "That his girlfriend or yours?"

"Neither." I catch myself just as I finish the word. "None of your damn business." I rip the picture out of her hand.

"Well, I could definitely do some damage to that boy. Yummy." Her words are salacious, but her voice quavers and falls like she's masking some other emotion, maybe fear.

"Ick!" I say. "You aren't getting anywhere near my brother. Ick!"

She doesn't pursue it. She goes back to her bed and puts the headphones on.

When I think she's absorbed in her magazine, I take the phone I use to contact Rachel out of my purse, and my mother's earring out of my pocket. I slip the earring into the back of the phone cover and lift the mattress. I place it on top of the box spring near the center of the bed and lower the mattress over it. When I'm done, I turn around.

Logan's staring at me with narrowed eyes. "Well, well, well! I guess even little angels have their dark sides."

"What's that supposed to mean?"

"Little Miss Perfect is already breaking the rules. I saw your phone, all bright pink and shit. I gotta assume the black one you just hid is some kind of burn phone. Don't get your panties in a twist. I won't tell. It almost makes me wish you'd last more than a month."

I want to ask her what she means by that, but she's exhausting and I'm pretty sure I wouldn't like her answer anyway. Right now, my main concern is figuring out how to get Ethan down here without freaking him out completely, the sooner, the better. I pick up my real phone to call Sage, but of course this far underground I'm getting zero bars. Without my phone, there's only one possible way to know what's happening at home. Ignoring Logan, I lie down on my bed and begin deep breathing. I've never astral projected beyond the next room, but in theory the principle is the same no matter what the physical distance is.

I work my way down from my crown to my toes, relaxing each muscle to ground my body. I get to my calves when Logan rudely interrupts. "What the hell do think you're doing?" I don't answer, but she's already broken my concentration. I go back to deep breathing.

"You think you can astral project?" She laughs cruelly, like it's a big joke.

I sit up. "For your information, I can and have successfully projected out of my body and into a different place." I leave out that the place was the next room.

"You're full of shit!" Her voice rises with anger.

"What do you care? Just leave me alone so I can do this." I keep my voice as calm as I can.

"Do what exactly?"

"I'm trying to check on my brother. Okay?"

A strong emotion passes through her eyes at the mention of him again. This time I'm fairly certain I'm not imagining things. "Ha!" It comes out harsh and bitter. "Every idiot who passes through here thinks they've got a lock on astral projection. Do you know how many of you losers can actually do it?"

I shake my head, dumbfounded by her tirade.

"Maybe one percent! That's one in a hundred, in case you can't do the math. Do you know how many inmates are here?"

I shake my head again.

"Maybe fifty at any given moment. That means less than one person among all these fucking freaks has what it fucking takes, and that freak is me? Got it."

I'm about to tell her that she's going to have to redo the math, but I think better of it and mumble, "Okay." I wait until she turns away from me then lie back on the bed and start over. This time she leaves me alone.

I'm able to rise out of my body like I did at home, and this time I'm ready for the vibration, so it doesn't freak me out as much. I breathe through it and step out of my body, as easy as getting off a bed. I move into the hall without looking back. I desperately need to find a way home to see how Ethan's managing. I imagine being on the main level of the building and find myself beside the elevator looking at the reception desk. Nora's there, talking with the other girls.

I need to stay focused. Physically getting out of this building would be impossible, but I center myself, close my eyes, and push my thoughts to the guard gate. When I open them, I see two young guards smoking cigarettes. They're about my age, maybe younger. After a few seconds, I can hear their conversation. It's muffled, like they're talking behind a wall. The blond one's going on about some female character in a video game. Their talk is dirty and pathetic. I take a moment to be thankful I'm gay.

I'm at a loss now. How do I get home? I think about Ethan and our house. I imagine walking in the front door, but when I try to open my eyes, I suddenly feel shaky and weird, like a figure flickering on a television with bad reception. My breath catches in my throat, and I begin to panic. I reach out, grasping, grasping for something. What am I trying to grab? The silver cord. Where's the damn silver cord? I spin around and around, searching for it, and my mind slips backward until I feel like I'm falling. Down and down and down I fall, until I land with a crash back into my body. And though I'm lying in a relatively soft bed, it feels more like I've fallen onto a tennis court that's been soaking up a hundred degrees of the sun's rays for the last eight hours. I can't sit up. I can barely open my eyes. My breathing's shallow and labored. I concentrate on bringing it back to a normal depth and rate. When I can, I turn my head to see if Logan noticed. She's staring at me through slitted eyes, snake-like.

"You stupid bitch. You have no idea what you're fucking with, do you? The astral plane is not at all spatially related to the physical plane. You're never going to get very far that way."

She crosses her arms over her chest and shakes her head.

"I thought you said I couldn't do it at all." My voice comes out raspy and weak.

"Duh! Obviously, you can't." She turns away but steals glances in my direction that tell me she knows she's wrong. I wonder who died and left her the queen of the astral plane, but I have no intention of asking.

By the time I come back from the bathroom we share with the girls living next door, Jamie's there, waiting to take me for my security processing. He's frowning and grinding his teeth. Logan's smirking, like the kid who tacked the teacher's chair. Jamie hurries me out before I can ask what's going on.

The first stop is the security level. A whole level for security. That kind of blows me away. The elevator opens into a high-tech office, and I'm immediately ushered to a room with iridescent white walls, a target in the middle of the floor, and some kind of machine that will scan my bones, fingerprints, and god knows what else. A female agent escorts me to a little curtained area behind the main room and instructs me to change into a sort of hospital gown. When I come out, I watch her eyes travel over my exposed flesh, taking in the scars. I feel naked and ashamed and disgusted with myself, but she's a professional; her lack of reaction reminds me to push my own emotions down into my gut. When she places me in the center of the target, I feel a little sick, wondering if someone's going to shoot me. My escort instructs me to stay still until she returns.

During the time it takes to run the scan, about five minutes, I push the image of myself as a duck in a shooting gallery to the side and try to imagine how this is going to go with Ethan. The first issue is going to be having to deal with all the strangers. Ethan has definitely improved in this area, but the anxiety he's going to feel with all of these people touching him and telling him what to do and undressing him and scanning him — He's going to fall apart before they can even induct him into this place. Hell, I'm barely holding it together. Tears begin to well up as I remember his cries behind the door the morning I left. This morning. It feels so long ago. I should've listened to him.

When I come out, Jamie knows I'm upset. He looks at me with a question in his eyes, but he doesn't ask. On the way into the room where they're going to take my blood, he puts his hand on my back. The warmth he transfers to me in those couple of seconds reaches all the way to my toes. The guy who pricks my finger warns me that it's going to hurt. He stares at me when I don't jump. After he draws the blood into the straw, I put my finger in my mouth and suck. The acrid iron on my tongue relaxes me. Next, he puts my face against a pair of binocular-looking things that scan my retinas; I don't even tear up. It's just security procedures, after all. When it's over, a different guy hands me a card with a number on it and tells me to commit it to memory. I'm not allowed to leave until I can punch it into the keypad and repeat it aloud without error a dozen times each.

The next stop is the medical lab. This time when we get into the elevator, I state my name and number, just like Jamie. I have to suppress a giggle. I feel like an actor in a science fiction flick. At the medical lab, I have to undress again. This time my scars are examined and photographed. It's beyond humiliating. I imagine this is how Ethan must feel when he wets himself in public. All of my weakness exposed and in the spotlight. At least Jamie hasn't been allowed with me in the exam room. I stare into the florescent lights and try to think about Jo while the doctor and nurse poke and prod each and every orifice and take every imaginable sample of bodily tissue and fluids known to mankind. By the time it's over I feel like I've been violated, numb and detached from my physical self, and in desperate need of a hot shower. Jamie's smile is forced when I'm deposited back into his hands.

"Last stop of the day," he says in front of a door down the hall from the infirmary. "After you talk to Dr. Robineau, we'll get some dinner."

I'm not hungry. "Who's Dr. Robineau?" I ask through clenched teeth. The thought of another doctor picking at me makes me want to crumple up in a fetal position.

"You'll like her. She's just going to do a quick psych intake. You'll see her for longer tomorrow."

I think I'm going to throw up. I've seen more shrinks in my life than anyone should, and only one of them ever made me feel better about anything. Rachel. I'm willing to bet this Dr. Robineau is a ball-breaker with half a heart, if I'm lucky. I groan and press my forehead to the cool wall.

Jamie laughs lightly and gently massages my neck. "Really. You'll like her. You'll see. Buck up, Elena, you're almost done." He opens the door.

I take a deep breath, stand up straight, and tell myself to be strong.

Dr. Robineau's office is a cool mint green. There appear to be three separate rooms in her suite: a waiting room with a bright, purple, modern-looking couch, and a plethora of art pieces, paintings, sculptures, drawings and multi-media pieces; another room hidden behind a midnight blue door; and a bathroom. Ethan will love this space. The thought does much to defray my nerves. I hear pop music coming from behind the blue door to the left. Someone inside the room is singing enthusiastically off-key. To the right is a large, luxurious bathroom replete with copper fixtures, thick Turkish towels, crown moldings and a claw-foot tub. In the waiting room, the magazines on the kidney bean-shaped glass table include *Architecture Digest* and *Spin*. I think Jamie might be right, after all.

Jamie sits down and picks up a copy of *Spin*. I move closer to the wall to inspect the artwork. I turn back around to make a comment about one of the paintings to find him dead asleep, his head lolling on the sofa back. A moment later the music ceases and the blue door opens.

The woman who emerges is much taller than I am, and she gives the impression of beauty, even though her features aren't particularly pretty. Charisma and confidence without arrogance flow through her warm smile and open stance. Her clothes manage to be both stylish and comfortable. I can't help but like her. She glances at Jamie and shakes her head good-naturedly. "Poor thing, the first day is almost as hard on the handlers as it is on the inductees."

"Almost," I agree.

"Come on in." She gestures to her office. "We'll let Jamie catch some z's."

I go in ahead of her and take in the ambiance of the office. The softest, plushest sofa in the most beautiful shade of emerald green I've ever seen takes up the wall to the left. The only other furniture is a formidable glass desk covered with papers and clutter, with a typical office chair and an overstuffed easy chair covered in honey-yellow chenille that Dr. Robineau melts into before I've turned around. The walls are decorated with outrageous tapestries woven in wool, cotton and, I'd swear, silk. There's no particular pattern, color, style, theme, or other commonality between them, which leaves me slightly off-balance. I prefer when things make sense.

"What are you thinking about?" Dr. Robineau asks.

"The tapestries," I answer truthfully, forgetting to keep my guard up. She motions for me to sit on the sofa, and I do, immediately.

"Do you like them?" she asks.

I nod.

"But…" She starts the sentence for me.

I can't keep from smiling at her. "It's nothing. They're all so different from each other. That's all."

She smiles back. "True. But they do have one thing in common."

I relax into the comfort of the sofa and let out a small sigh. "What's that?"

"They were all gifts —" I sit up a little, not surprised but impressed maybe. "— from patients."

"Oh." I wonder if I'll feel compelled one day in a market in Kathmandu to buy a tapestry for Dr. Robineau to hang in her office.

It could happen.

A short silence provides a segue into the purpose for our meeting. "I'm going to ask you a few questions now, and I'd like for you be as honest with me and yourself as possible. Can you do that?"

Complete honesty isn't really my gig, but I nod, and I mean it. Disappointing Dr. Robineau would be. . . well. . . disappointing to me, too, for some reason.

"Good. Let's start with the top ten, oldies but goodies."

I smile. She asks me about my sleep, appetite, interests, relationships, energy, concentration, outlook, self-image, mood and substance abuse. I keep the answers short and to the point. It's not like I haven't done thirty of these intakes since the age of four. Then she hands me a ream of pages to fill out for "homework." Family History, Medical History, Psychiatric History, Suicide and Violence Risk Assessment, Social History, and my favorite, the Mental Status Exam. The pages are only the instructions. The actual questionnaires are on the PSI intranet. After she tells me I need to complete as much as possible before I see her tomorrow, she moves toward the door, and I get up to follow, but she turns quickly to face me before we reach the exit. "One more thing, Elena. Before you leave here, I need you to give me your tool."

My breath catches in my throat, like someone punched my Adam's apple. "Come again," I say, taking a step back.

Her tone is neutral now. All the friendliness is gone, but without a hint of anger or aggression. The emotional void of her request makes it all the more invasive. "Your tool, the thing you use to cut. I need you to hand it over to me now."

"I don't know what you're talking about." I take another step back and put the chair between us.

She doesn't approach me. Instead, she goes to the desk and types something into the computer. She swings the screen, so I can see that she has called up video footage. I watch as she scrolls through my entire day, including trips to the restroom. In several instances my hand goes to my pocket. Never once do I take out the object that comforts me. I'm waiting for the scene in my room to come up, the one where I hide my burn phone and the earring, but that frame is conspicuously blacked out. Dr. Robineau taps the screen with her long, well-manicured nail. "Jamie!" she yells, without betraying any temper.

In an instant he's in the doorway, rubbing his eyes and smoothing his hair. "What happened to the feed from the dorm?" Jamie stares blankly at the black screen.

"Must be Logan again," he says weakly. I'm almost certain he's lying, but I can't fathom why he'd throw her under the bus.

"See that she's put on restriction again. This time take her entertainment modules, music and print media. Make her understand the next time this happens, we paint the wall."

Jamie nods somberly and signals me over to him, but Dr. Robineau blocks my way. She holds out her hand. "I'm not going to ask again, Elena." For a moment I'm lost. There's no way I'd turn over my mother's earring to her or anyone, but I have to give her something. I take the earrings from my ears and drop them into her palm. They're earrings, after all, and an earring is my tool of choice, I reason silently. She looks through my eyes and then closes her hand as though she's satisfied. Jamie signals for me to come with him, so I slip past Dr. Robineau, through the office door, into the waiting room.

Dr. Robineau's voice has returned to its sweet, comforting timbre. "Elena, do the best you can with those questions tonight. Jamie, see that Elena is relieved of all her earrings." He nods.

By the time Jamie has hurried me into the hall, I'm hyperventilating and sweating. "What just happened in there?" I ask breathlessly.

"Relax. Dr. Robineau's trying to help you. She just wants you to stop hurting yourself. We all do. Some of the stuff you'll be doing here is pretty intense, and you can't use that. . . "

"NOT THAT!" I scream, spit flying. "Why am I starring in my own reality show?"

"That," Jamie says, shrinking to the size of a garden gnome, "is just a simple fact of life here. It's in — "

"—the fucking contract?" I shriek.

Jamie nods helplessly as he shoves his hands in his pockets. He takes a deep breath and looks at the ground. "I think we'll both feel better after a good dinner." He motions with his head toward the elevators, and I walk ahead of him, fuming. I spit out my name and number while Jamie shakes his head and stifles a laugh. "You really are cute, you know."

"I hate you," I say, but he knows I'm lying.

The cafeteria is nothing short of mind boggling. Dishes for every palette, preference, and dietary constraint: kosher, gluten-free, vegan, and caveman. Even Ethan won't be able to say there's nothing to eat. I have no idea what to choose, so I get a salad and an apple. Jamie looks crestfallen. "All this food and you're eating that?!"

"You're the one who said you didn't want me to get fat," I say.

"I was being ironic. I wasn't really worried, you know," he comes back.

After dinner, Jamie insists on a walk around the grounds. I try hard to beg off. I know he's as exhausted as I am. Besides, it's already dark out. Jamie's insistent, though, and I ultimately give in just to avoid the fight. After we pass though the five levels of security, the night air hits me like a revelation. I can suddenly breathe again. We follow a path that takes us through a well-tended arboretum. Jamie walks silently beside me, and I've been through too much today to formulate a single, coherent thought. Once we're as far away from the building as the path goes, Jamie heads off the trail, behind a row of benches and through a dense hedgerow. My arms are all scraped up by the time we emerge onto another, wilder path that veers into the untended greenbelt. The path takes us deep into a ravine with a stream running through it. Boulders border the water's edge. In the silvery glow of the moon Jamie finds the spot he's looking for and climbs between two boulders. I follow him into a little grotto, barely large enough for the two of us to sit.

"Are you going to ask me to go steady, or do you just want to make out?" I ask nervously.

Jamie smiles a tired smile. "Call your brother and Sage and anyone else you need to talk to. When we get back, I have to take your phone."

I look into his gentle eyes and know this is a huge breach of protocol. He has risked a great deal to give me this. I don't know how to thank him, but there's more at stake here.

"What about Ethan?" I hesitate, not wanting to hurt Jamie or get him in any trouble. "I don't want him to come here." I feel guilty saying it aloud.

Jamie pauses, like he's mustering some last reserve of strength. Then he says, "Ethan will be fine here, Elena. You both will. I know today was tough, but really, it's all just formalities, nothing more sinister than that. You guys are going to discover so much about yourselves and your abilities here. Nothing will be the same. "

"Then why all the subterfuge? The hike? This hiding place?"

"They take their formalities pretty seriously; that's all."

"You do this for all your. . . handlees?"

Jamie grins fleetingly and lowers his eyes. "You and Ethan are special."

I take his hand. "Thanks."

"How do you want to play this?" he asks.

I think hard about it. Ethan cannot get on a plane alone. I'm not sure he can even get on a plane with Sage. "Sage will need to drive him down. I can meet him at a hotel, get him prepared. You can pick us up at the hotel. Can we do it that way?"

Jamie turns it over in his head. "That's going to be tough. Can Sage just bring him here?"

"She'll never leave him here. She'll freak out before she makes it past the guardhouse."

He nods. "Okay, I think I can make that happen. It won't be easy, but it's doable as long as we do it soon. Can she get him here in three days?"

I nod.

"Make your calls," he says, and he leaves me there alone, giving me the privacy to call Jo, Sage, and Ethan. The last call I make is to Rachel to make good on a promise I made Finn. It's the only way I have to thank him for saving Ethan from being institutionalized. It's the least I can do, even though I know it will break my brother's heart.

Susan Michalski

∞ 7 ∞

BECAUSE IT BURNS

Your desire turned to flame
Leaving you cold and blue
Can't have what's haunting
You let it burn too hot too bright
Without a warming touch
Because it burn burns, it burns, it burns
And god, it aches so much
                    "Passion Burn" - Luna Rayne, 2001

Jamie has been gone about an hour when I hear the motorcycle in the parking lot. A strange flash of nausea washes over me. Over half a decade has passed since Finn hurt me, and even though I have no memory of what happened in my head, my body remembers somehow. He's here because I owe him. I dread the time we'll spend together now, waiting for Sage and Ethan to arrive, but I dread their arrival even more. Sage will fall into Finn's waiting arms, Ethan's heart will shatter like glass, and it will be my fault. I dig my nails into my hands, hoping for a little transfer of pain from my heart to my skin.

A few seconds later, the knock comes, strong, insistent, and full of anticipation. I open the door to the Finn of my past. His cheeks are flushed, betraying the emotion he hides behind the slouched shoulders, cocked head, and wayfarers. He pushes past me without a hello.

"They aren't here yet," I say. "Sage says they're probably at least four or five hours out." The trip's taken longer than Sage and I thought it would. On the phone she wouldn't talk about how it was going, but I can imagine how taxing a road trip with Ethan might be. There would be anxiety over food choices, strangers, weather conditions and other drivers. That would be the tip of the iceberg. I don't even want to think about making it or not making it to the next rest area or the angst of staying in a hotel with him overnight. But that becomes my problem tonight. When I checked into the room, I told the guy at the desk that my brother would be joining me and that we'd need a waterproof mattress pad and extra sheets. Ethan will be furious that I told them, but what choice do I have?

Finn puts his helmet and sunglasses on the dresser, picks up the TV remote, and stretches out on one of the beds without removing his boots. "Mind if I watch something?" he asks.

I do, but I say, "Knock yourself out."

He flips through the channels while I pace in front of the windows. His presence makes me jittery, so I get the ice bucket and some change and head outside. I take my Coke and the ice down to the pool and sit in one of the filthy deck chairs by the murky water. I told the guy at the desk to balance the chemicals so Ethan could swim in the morning, but I doubt he even heard me.

The sun's fading from the sky in streaks of orange and hot pink that remind me of Ethan's paintings. I don't think they'll be letting him paint at PSI, but I could be wrong about that. I checked out PSI's pool. Its fifty meters of salt water are the perfect temperature for lap swimming. Jamie said he got Ethan special permission to use it at six in the morning, so at least he'll have that to keep him sane.

A shadow falls across my chair, and I look up. Finn's standing over me.

"There's nothing on the tube," he explains, pulling a chair over.

"A hundred and two channels and you can't find a single thing to occupy you for a couple of hours?" I really don't want to share the air with him.

"I could pay for the porn channel," he says without cracking a smile. "Have at it," I reply, and I'm sincerely hoping he'll take me up on it, but he stays planted on the vinyl strips.

I lay my head back and close my eyes, trying to find someplace within a mile of my center. The last three days have spun me up like a web of cotton candy. At PSI, I practiced telepathy with a kid named Kai, astral projected, meditated on chakra alignment, and took classes in brain chemistry and genetic predisposition. I must have read nearly a hundred case studies of paranormal manifestations by people around the globe. Jamie had me believing that Ethan would arrive and thrive. Now, in the reality of these moments, anticipating his transition to PSI, I realize how naïve Jamie's optimism is.

"I think about it sometimes," Finn says, apropos of nothing. When I respond with a blank stare, he goes on. "This probably isn't the best time to get into this, but it weighs on me, you know."

I suck air and get to my feet. "Yeah, not the time, not the place." I can hardly believe that after all these years, he's suddenly decided to open this can of worms.

He looks at his feet. "I hate what happened to you."

I turn and stare him down with as much venom as I can muster under my panic, hoping it will be enough to shut him up.

He looks away and goes on. "I know you don't want to talk about this, but I have to explain. You need to know—" He runs out of words — my cue to bolt. I fly across the parking lot and up the stairs. The door clicks behind me, and I lean my back against it. I can't deal with this conversation, not now.

After a couple of minutes, nothing happens, so I sit warily on the bed, watching the door, but Finn doesn't knock. Finally, I get up and go to the window. He's still sitting on the chair by the pool. His back is bent over, and his head's in his hands. If I didn't know better, I'd think he was crying. I watch him sit up and run his hands through his overgrown, black hair in a gesture of inner torture. My heart almost goes out to him, but he's set my memories. Images of the morning I woke up bleeding from my rectum, vagina, and mouth fill my head till

I see red. I want him to suffer, to bleed, to know what it feels like to be betrayed physically and emotionally. Cry, Finn, I think. And maybe it will fill you with emptiness, the way you filled me.

I move away from the window and hate myself for being so heartless, hate myself for being so weak. I don't give myself the luxury of tears, though. I turn on the television to drown out my thoughts. After thirty minutes of *American Idol*, I'm able open the door when he knocks, and I don't even want to kick him in the balls.

He comes in and leans against wall, letting out a deep sigh.

"No," I say. "We are NOT doing this, Finn. I forgive you already. Just let it go. PLEASE!"

He lowers his head, and I think he's going to give me this one, but when he looks up, he starts shaking his head slowly back and forth. "There are things you don't know about what happened that night. Things you need to know before you take your brother into that lab, and they start experimenting on y'all."

"What does Ethan have to do with that night?" I yell. "He wasn't even there."

Finn's silent for a couple beats. "He was there, afterward. And he did something to you that made you forget. I promised if he helped you, I'd never tell, but now I think you need to know — all of it. My part, too."

I turn over the implications of what Finn's saying. Ethan took my memories away. It's ridiculous. I feel like I'm going to be sick, so I go into the bathroom and shut the door. I pace in front of the mirror, watching myself until the nausea passes. Then I reach into my pocket and pull out my mother's earring. I run it lightly up the inside of my arm, leaving a long, white scratch. I take a deep breath and put it back. More than anything I need to do this now, but Jamie warned me that if I did anything to my body, the scans would pick it up.

The genie's out of the bottle now anyway, and the memories are busting through whatever hocus pocus Ethan may or may not have wrought. I might as well hear the rest of it. I open the door slowly. Finn's standing right where I left him. He's flicking his lighter open and closed. I stifle a laugh. The more things change, the more they stay the same. He looks up when I sit on the bed.

"I'm really sorry about this — about everything." He pauses long enough to inhale deeply like a free-diver about to go down. "I never meant for you to get hurt. I just wanted to — you know — do it. All the other guys had gone all the way, or at least they claimed they had, but I hadn't. I had done stuff — with you — but that was all." He turns away, runs his hand through his hair again.

Bile rises in my throat. "So, you raped me because you didn't want to be a virgin anymore? Really?" I want to kick his junk into next week, but I stay seated on the bed. "And I need to know this now why?"

He turns back, his blue eyes filled with exasperation and torment. "I didn't rape you." His voice is quiet and measured. "Jared Meyers and Robert Baxter —" He doesn't finish the sentence. He doesn't need to. I can feel the knowledge screaming deep in my groin.

"The pictures that hit the Internet, Finn. They were of you, not those guys."

"The pictures were of all of us from the back, except the one of me dressing you, not undressing you, like everyone assumed. I was leaning over you to pick you up, not to —"

"Bullshit!" I yell. "If you didn't do anything, then why not tell me all of this years ago?"

He lowers his voice, shrinks a little in his skin. "I said I didn't rape you, not that I wasn't responsible. I did something, something maybe worse than that." He sits down on the other bed, head bowed, shoulders hunched miserably. The plastic pad crinkles. Time slows as my brain swells.

Stop, I think. Just shut the hell up already. My mouth won't move, though, and my throat's paralyzed. I can't even swallow.

"Hell, I can't fucking say it," he mumbles into his chest.

Then don't, I think. My mind's flitting against my will, back to that night, to the smell of rotting pine needles and dirt. To the feeling of fabric stretched across my skin, cutting into my legs, and the sound of it tearing. I start rocking to try to bring myself back to the hotel room.

The memory of the Internet pictures follows. Pictures of me on the ground without a shirt, and Finn standing over me, shirtless. The others are fuzzy - guys with no shirts and pants around their ankles. I assumed they were all Finn, but maybe they weren't. The thing I remember most, though, were the comments under the pictures. People I didn't even know calling me a ho and a slut. Even my friends, Jenny and Leah, didn't want to be associated with me after that night. A reputation is a hard thing to shake in the ninth grade.

Finn starts rambling again, but I can barely hear him over the din of memory. "I couldn't do it. I pretended to join in," he says. "I told them I was going to take you somewhere private for my turn. Then I dressed you and carried you out of there."

"So, you were a fucking hero, then! That's what I need to know? Why? So, I can applaud when you take Sage away from Ethan? You ass!" I get up and make a move for the door, but he steps in front of me and blocks my righteous exit.

"Damn it, Elena! It was my fault. Shit!" He backs away from me. "I — there was all this trash talk. I told my boys I was going to — They wanted in. I thought it was all talk. We were high and shit. Then after I dosed you — It got out of control so fast. I didn't know how to stop it." Now he's the one rocking. He wraps his arms around himself and looks at the wall. Then the tears start. His shoulders shake, and he sinks in slow motion to his knees. "I couldn't stop them. I'm so, so sorry," he sobs. I watch from a great distance as the mighty Finn becomes a child as lost and broken as Ethan. I hear the ache of years of regret and self-flagellation. I smell the pain coming off him, so familiar and disgusting.

Nausea washes over me again and I clutch my gut to make it pass. I look away from him. What can I say? I'm not going to grant him absolution, but I want to know what happened next. It's my story, after all. I have the right to know how it unfolded.

I go to where Finn's crumpled on the floor and stand over him. The urge to spit on him comes, but I let it pass. "Get up," I say, far less harshly than I intend. He shakes his head. "You stupid prick! You had your pity party. Get up and finish the damn story." Now I'm getting going. "You have no right to wallow. You weren't the one who got raped!" I kick him in the leg, not hard, but hard enough to engage his fight response and come out of his head. I step back and turn around, give him some room to pull it together.

After a while, he takes a long shaking sigh and clears his throat. "I carried you home. Five miles. I couldn't find my fucking bike. Probably too stoned to drive anyway. You were crying and screaming the whole time. It's a miracle no one called the cops. I broke the window in the garage apartment and took you in there." He shows me the scar across his knuckles. "I didn't know what to do, so I threw rocks at your brother's window until he came down."

I stifle a laugh. The thought of Finn throwing stones and begging Ethan to come down is absurd.

When we got back to where I'd left you, you were asleep. I told your brother what happened. I don't know why. I was out of my mind. He didn't freak, though. He just held you and stroked your hair the whole time. Then he said he could make it better for you. He said if I stayed away forever, he could make you forget. Then I watched him do his freaky mind-meld deal and that was that. He distracted your grandmother while I carried you up to your room. Then I beat it. I didn't believe it would work. I thought he was crazy and shit, but it did work. You need to know it really worked, and I know that's important somehow." He's flushed and panting, like he just ran a 5K.

I'm stunned. I think back on all the stuff I've forgotten over the years. I consider Rachel's theory about me and how I bury painful memories. Maybe I'm not the one who's doing the digging. Why would Ethan do this to me? Or for me? Finn is right about one thing – this is important. I have to wonder what else Ethan's capable of. I have to wonder if PSI was even interested in me. Maybe somehow they knew about Ethan. I stop myself there. Paranoia is a wicked and slippery slope that I cannot afford to ski at the moment.

When I look up, Finn's gone. He's taken his helmet and his keys. I imagine he's going to get his own room. He won't want to share with me and Ethan; he'll want to be alone with Sage. Sage. I wonder about Ethan and his connection to Sage. She says she doesn't understand it. Maybe he. . . I can't go there. My head is whirling like a Cuisinart gone rogue. I lay down on the bed that doesn't crinkle and curl into a ball, hugging the pillow. I can and will hold all the pieces together. I repeat this to myself a hundred or so times until my mind slows and my eyes grow as heavy as my heart.

I jump when a knock echoes through the darkened room. I forget for a second where I am, then remember and flip on the light. When I open the door, I totally expect to see Sage and Ethan, but Finn's standing there with a pizza and two Cokes. "Can I come in?"

"What time is it?" I ask without stepping aside.

"A little after ten," he says. "I thought you might be hungry."

"Is that Finnish for you feel so bad about earlier that you thought you'd try to bribe your way back into my good graces with Coke and a crappy-ass pizza?"

"Actually, it smells delicious and came totally recommended by the night-desk girl."

"I'm sure it did." I let him in. He's had a shower and changed into cleaner jeans and a white t-shirt. I'm sure I look as horrible as I feel.

Finn opens his mouth to talk, but I put up my hand, and he rolls it back, giving me the floor. "Look, Finn, I'm done here. No more. Okay? Can you just give me that?'

"I was just going to say I'm getting a little worried. It's been four hours." He cracks open the pizza box and hands me a Coke.

"Relax, cowboy," I say, managing a little smile. My mouth feels tight, like the muscles have forgotten how to do that. "Sage said four or five hours out, but it could be more, depending on how Ethan's faring." I take a piece and notice he's ordered my favorite kind, or at least what it was in middle school.

"I bet traveling with that head case has to be a fuckin' nightmare. No offense." He waves his hands, like he wants to wipe away what he just said.

"None taken. I know how you feel about Ethan. I was actually thinking the same thing, minus the meanness of course."

We eat in silence for a couple of minutes, sitting on separate beds. Then Finn lowers his piece and gets a faraway look.

"How do you think this is gonna go down?" he asks.

"You think she won't be happy to see you?"

"What should I think? I haven't seen or heard from her in a year and a half. The last time I saw her, she chose your brother over me."

"Come on, Finn! It wasn't like that."

He cuts me off. "It was exactly like that, Elena!"

"I know one thing, Finn." I say. "If you go out there guns blazing, all confrontational, Sage will run for cover. You won't get another chance. I should know."

"How should I go out there?"

I think about it for a minute. What I know that he doesn't is that the only reason Sage hasn't contacted him is that she's terrified that the cops will find him if she does. She's so wrapped up in keeping Finn safe and free that she's been willing to put aside her feelings. She's going to want to throw herself into his arms when she sees him, but she won't. That's just not Sage.

"First," I say, "You're going to stay up here and keep cool because all of this will be for nothing if for some reason the cops have decided to follow her. So just wait for her to come up. Okay?"

He nods. "I'll try."

"Try hard," I say. "Second, she's going to be an emotional wreck. She's furious with me for rocking her little world, and she's grieving her loss of Ethan, though two days on the road with him might have her ready to say good riddance to that albatross. I doubt it, though." My mind flashes on the image of them kissing on Ethan's bed, and I shake my head to chase it away.

"Is there a third?" he asks.

I nod. "Please, please, please, whatever you need to do with her or say to her, do it in private. Spare Ethan the reunion. Sage is all he has, and I'm taking that away from him. He's lost enough."

"Then he and I are in the same boat."

I stare him down.

"Okay. Okay. I promise. I'll spare the little freak's feelings."

"Nice, Finn. You're such a prick." I throw the crust of my pizza at him.

Finn clicks on the television and settles in to watch some cheesy western. I shake my head and curl up on the other bed to try to get a little more sleep. I have a feeling the next couple of days might be sleep-limited. I stare at the wall and fight the pull of anxiety. Why is it always easier to imagine the worst? I try to picture the car pulling up with Ethan driving and Sage sitting calmly beside him. I imagine them coming up the stairs and into the hotel room. I see Sage and Finn leaving without any drama or breakdown from Ethan. I almost laugh. I want to cry. Somewhere in the middle, the wall falls out of focus and the sounds of cars on the highway lull me into darkness.

I'm pulled back by a rough shove and Finn's voice almost high-pitched with excitement. "They're here. Sage just texted you. They just pulled off the exit." He's at the window. I look at the clock — 11:48. I pull myself to standing, but my head's as fuzzy as a caterpillar. I'm not ready to do this yet. The putt-putt of the old Volvo in the parking lot sends a needed shot of adrenaline into my bloodstream. My heart pounds in my ears. I realize suddenly how much I've missed my twin and how relieved I am to have him safely back in my orbit. As I race through the door, Finn tries to follow, but I shove him back into the room.

"We had a deal!" I say. He takes a step back. He's shaking. I'm a little horrified to see him this worked up, so I add more gently, "I'll let her know you're up here. Okay?" He nods and moves back inside, by the window. I hurry down the stairs as Sage pulls the car into the space directly in front of the stairwell. She looks exhausted. Ethan's curled up in the reclined passenger seat, sound asleep, with his thumb in his mouth and his arms around a big, soft, cream-colored teddy bear. When Sage opens the driver's side door, his eyes flutter open for a moment, but he doesn't sit up. I go to Sage, wrap my arms around her, and she melts into me. I absorb her anxiety, sorrow, and frustration into my pores. The heat travels through my skin, deep into my bones and makes me shiver. The smell of pee wafts from the open car door, and I release her.

"Thanks, I so needed that," Sage says, noticeably more relaxed

"Rough trip?" I ask.

She laughs ironically. "You have no clue."

"Is he okay?" I need to know what I'm in for.

"Probably wet and definitely hungry. He's been sleeping for the last three hours or so, and the last rest stop was a couple hours before that. I think the only thing he ate today was an apple and a smoothie. He did better when he was driving."

"Are you okay?" I ask, and she nods, but she's not with me anymore. Her eyes are drilled on the stairwell behind me.

"Holy shit," she mumbles under her breath.

I turn around. Finn's halfway down, looking over the railing of the landing. Sage moves toward him like she's steel and he's a magnet. He starts down the next flight, and she meets him halfway. For a couple of seconds, they look at each other, like they're sizing up an opponent boxer.

He asked me how this would go down, and I thought I had a lock on what it would look like, but Finn's full of surprises. I never would've called this. Tears are pouring down his face, and as Sage wraps her arms around his neck, he lowers his head to her shoulder, like he did that night when they said good-bye. Sage is crying, too. Then Finn pulls back to kiss her, but she stops him mid-pucker. At the exact same time, she and I both turn to see Ethan staring out the windshield, eyes wide open.

I hurry around to the passenger side of the car, open the door and squat down to his level. Sage is saying something to Finn on the stairs, but she's put some space between them.

"Why is HE here?" Ethan demands.

I have no satisfactory answer for him. So, I say, "Come on, E, let's just go upstairs, get you in the shower and go to bed." He stretches out and extracts himself from the car. I'm relieved that Sage had the sense to make him wear a diaper, so I don't have to clean her car tonight. I step back to give him some room, but he reaches out and crumples into my arms, still hugging the bear. "Why's he here?" he whimpers softly.

"Come on," I say, and he takes my hand. We head up the stairs as Sage and Finn circle around the car and start unloading the luggage. Sage follows us up with Ethan's overnight bag, but I usher him into the restroom, so she can't make the damage any worse with promises she won't be able to keep. I turn on the shower to drown out whatever she might think to yell, then turn to my brother, whose face is a map of misery.

"Who's this?" I ask, gently taking the bear from his arms.

"His name's Red," Ethan mumbles. I must look confused because he adds, "He had a red bow when Sage gave him to me, but I lost it."

"He's soft," I say, stroking the bear's fur. Ethan doesn't respond. I put Red on the shelf by the sink and watch as Ethan takes off his shirt and sweatpants, so he's wearing only the diaper. He hesitates then and looks at me.

"You can go now, you know," he says. "I'm not a baby. I can take care of myself."

Despite the irony, he's right, of course, so I slip out the door, smack into Sage.

"Can I talk to him? Just for a second, please." She tries to smile, but her lips twitch a little, and I know she's dying to be next door.

"He's in the shower, Sage. You should go be with Finn."

She makes a move toward the door but turns around. "Tell Ethan I love him, and I'll see him in the morning before you guys go. Will you do that?"

"Sure." I nod.

She puts her hand on the handle and says, "You set this up. Didn't you?"

"Uh-huh." I just want her to go.

"Why, Elena? Because you hate the thought of me and Ethan so much? Or is it because you want me to forgive you for leaving?"

"No and no. I did it for Finn."

"You hate Finn," she reminds me.

"I owe him," I remind her.

She leaves, smiling a little sadly, but I know that in the next minute that sadness will dissolve to joy, and even though I did it for Finn, it's her gift, too.

I wait forty minutes for Ethan to come out of the shower before going in to check on him. I use the pretext of bringing him clothes. When I open the door, the steam rolls over me like a fog. Through the curtain, I can see Ethan sitting with his knees up and his arms around his legs. The water, cold as ice now, pounds on his back and head. His chest is rising and falling with deep, silent sobs. I feel like a boulder has been placed over my ribs, and at any moment it will crush them to dust. I reach behind the curtain and turn off the faucet. Then I pull the curtain back and wrap a towel over Ethan's shivering shoulders. With another towel, I dry his short curls. Sage must've cut his hair in the last couple of days. I forgot to do it before I left. I offer him a hand to help him out of the tub, and after a couple of second's hesitation, he accepts it. I wrap a towel around his waist.

"I brought your clothes," I say, pointing to where they lie on the closed toilet seat.

"Help me, Lanie," he whines, and though I know he means that he wants me to dress him like I used to, I wonder if it's a more general plea to ease his pain.

"You're not a baby, E," I remind him gently.

He nods and begins to dress before I've slipped out the door.

I take off my shorts and slip out of my bra. I'll sleep in my t-shirt and underwear. I can shower in the morning before we leave. I lay on top of the bed and close my eyes. Next door, I can hear Sage and Finn talking and laughing. The sound is muffled, so the words are garbled, but their happiness penetrates the thin walls. I wonder if I'll ever feel that kind of synchronous connection with another human. And I miss

Jo so much that I can feel the hole opening in my sixth chakra.

Ethan pulls me out of my impending meltdown by joining me in the room. He's hugging his bear to his chest, like he's afraid it's going to be taken away. He pulls down the covers on the other bed and crawls beneath the sheets. I'm hoping his mind is too occupied to call me out for blabbing his problems to the hotel staff. No such luck. He sits up suddenly. "Lanie!"

"What?" I ask, still kind of hoping.

"You told!" he yells.

"Ethan." I shake my head. "I have to tell them. It's the rule."

"I hate you."

"What do you care? You'll never see any of these people again."

"I hate you!"

"Did you go to the bathroom before you got in bed?"

"Shut up!"

"Did you put a diaper on?"

"I said, shut up, Grandmother!"

"Well played, Brother." I sit up, laughing. Ethan joins in after a minute. I get out of bed and sit with him on his bed. "I missed you so much!" I run my hand across his cheek, and he leans into me like a cat. "Tell me about the trip?"

"Oh!" he says, tossing me his bear as he leaps out of bed and runs over to his bag. He digs through and pulls out a piece of paper that he thrusts at me excitedly. I unfold it carefully and look up in shock.

"You got your license. I was gone for, like, two days and you got your license."

He's grinning proudly. "Yeah. Sage said you'd never take me for the test, so she got a friend to get me an appointment early."

"Wow! E, this is amazing. Good for you. She cut your hair, too."

He shakes his head "Jo. She stayed the night before we left. She cut my hair and did Sage's nails, and we watched movies. I miss Jo."

"Me too, pal. Me too."

A sudden peal of laughter rings from the room next door. Ethan's smile drops. He puts the temporary license on the dresser and slides into bed. He curls up and pulls the covers over himself. I kiss him on the cheek, lay the bear in his arms and return to my bed. "Sweet dreams, little brother," I say, just before turning out the light, but he doesn't say it back. I manage to fall asleep by singing songs in my head to drown out the talking and laughing. At least they aren't having loud sex, I think as I drift off.

I'm dreaming about Jo. I'm kissing her slowly in the dark, inhaling her warm breath, tasting raspberry wine and cloves. My hand grazes her curves and stops to fondle her nipple until it's hard and excited. She groans with pleasure; it makes me smile. We lie side by side, touching at a zillion points. I can feel her skin on mine, smooth and soft and feminine. I want to purr. Then under my hand, her skin changes. The pillow softness of her abdomen becomes sinewy and hard. Her breasts melt away and a light carpet of hair covers her chest and forms an arrow that takes me down. I gasp when I find boy junk where I expected girl parts, but I don't stop touching and exploring. This time the moan's low and guttural, more animal and aggressive, more masculine. I don't need to look to know it's Jamie. My eyes pop open.

For a couple of seconds there's nothing but silence and darkness broken only by the street light coming in around the curtain. Then I hear the squeaking of the bed on the other side of the wall and the sounds coming from Sage and Finn, muffled and subdued, like they're trying hard to be quiet. I look over, hoping that Ethan's sleeping through the show, but he's not. He's sitting up crisscross, facing the wall. One hand is pressed against the stucco and his head's bowed. His breathing is heavy and rhythmic.

"Ethan!" I yell. "What the hell?"

He jumps about a mile and crosses his arms. I can't see his face because he's turned away from me.

"Ew! Yuck!" I continue. "If you have to do that, please go in the bathroom."

"I wasn't..." Ethan says weakly, his voice gravelly and quavering. He turns toward me, and I can see the tracks of his tears. He's been crying.

"Oh, E." I go over to his bed and take him in my arms. He lays his head on my shoulder and rests like a stone there for a long time. The aftershock of his sobs shake him from time to time. He gets heavier and heavier until I realize he's asleep. I lay him down and pick up Red from where he's fallen between the beds. I stay rubbing Ethan's back in circles until I'm sure he's out. Then I get back in my own bed. The noise from the other room has ceased, so sleep comes quickly.

The next time I wake up it's to the sound of shouting. Sage is yelling at Finn, screaming, really. A door slams. Another one opens and closes. Suddenly, there's pounding on our door. Ethan sits up, clutching his bear. Finn's voice comes from outside. "Elena! Elena! Wake up! Something's wrong with Sage. Something really weird's happening." By the time he's done, I've got the door open. His eyes are frantic.

"What's going on?"

"It's Sage. She just woke up and started freaking out. She was crazy, yelling that I shouldn't be in her bed. She's screaming for him." He turns and points at Ethan, whose eyes are shining like street lights, eerie and haloed.

I turn around to get some clothes, but Finn grabs my upper arm and drags me out the door. He fumbles with the key card several times. Finally, I take it from his shaking hand, slip it in the slot and get a green light. The room looks like a tornado hit it. Clothes are everywhere. The bed has had all the blankets pulled off and the pillows are scattered around the floor, like they were in the way.

I can hear Sage pounding around in the bathroom. She's talking to herself. I stand by the door and listen for a few seconds, but I can't make sense of what she's saying. I knock softly. "Sage, it's Elena. You okay in there?"

For a couple of seconds there's dead silence. Then Sage says, "Is that really you, Elena?"

"Yeah, Sage. It's me. Can you let me in?"

"Just you. Okay?" She unlocks the door and pulls me inside. Then she locks it again. Her hair's a mess, and she keeps trying to comb through it with her fingers. She's pacing and nervous, like she's about to take a pregnancy test or something. I put my hand on her arm. Her agitation and anxiety sweep through my body like a seizure, sharp and out of control. I can barely keep from yelping. I never felt anything like that before, but my touch has the desired effect. Sage stops fidgeting immediately and sinks onto the edge of the tub. I wait for her to tell me what's happening.

"Elena," she begins. "I think I might be going crazy." I give her a look, like, you were crazy when we met. "Not like woo-hoo-fun-time crazy, but like needles-and-straightjackets crazy."

"I doubt that, Sage. Just tell me what happened."

"You aren't going to like it." She drops her head to her chest and shakes it back and forth.

"Okay. But I think you should tell me anyway. I promise if I'm mad, I won't wig out. Okay?"

"You will. I guess I don't really have a choice though. Do I?"

"Guess not."

"Well, I brought Ethan here to meet you to go to PSI tomorrow, like we planned. But we got here so late, and you were asleep, so we just got a room."

"What're you talking about, Sage?"

"I'm sorry. I knew you'd be annoyed, but I didn't plan for it to happen like this."

"Like what, Sage?"

"OMG, how do I put this? There was only one bed and Ethan was so upset about saying goodbye. I guess I was, too. We just started kissing and one thing led to another. I'm not sorry it happened. I think we've been heading in this direction for a long time."

"You what? You had sex with Ethan? In this room? Tonight?"

"I know you're mad, but just hear me out."

"Sage —" She won't let me say a thing.

"Okay, here's the crazy part. We fell asleep and when I woke up to go to the bathroom, Ethan was gone and Finn was in my bed, grinning like a fox. What did he do to Ethan? How did he even find us? OMG, this is so fucked up!"

"More than you know, Sage," I say. I play the whole thing down in my mind, and coupled with what Finn told me about Ethan and how I found him in the middle of the night, I'm pretty sure I know what's happening. I just hope Finn hasn't figured it out.

"I'll go find out what happened to Ethan. You just stay put. Okay?" She nods, poised to lock the door again after I leave.

The minute I come out, Finn's in my face. Clearly, he'd been listening. "Your freak of a brother did this? He fucked with her mind, didn't he? How the hell did he do that? He didn't even touch her."

"I don't know!" I scream. "Back off and let me think!"

"I'm gonna kill that freak!" Finn grabs my room key off the dresser, where I dropped it on the way in.

By the time I follow, he's got Ethan by the front of the shirt and he's slamming him against the wall. Ethan's eyes are shut tightly against the assault, and he's trying to cover his head with his arms. I insert myself between them and press my hands to Finn's chest. He jumps back out of reach, releasing Ethan in the process.

"No way, Elena! He's gonna pay! This time he's gone way too far!"

Behind me, Ethan's sliding down the wall. His eyes are wide open now, full of questions.

"Stop it, Finn! If you kill him, then Sage is going to go to her grave thinking Ethan's her lover, and you're the piece of crap your dad said you were."

Finn looks like I sucker punched him in the nose. He turns around to gather his thoughts. Before I can relax, he spins back around and shoves me hard into the wall with one hand. With the other, he grabs the front of Ethan's t-shirt and hauls him to his feet. Before I can regain my balance, he's dragged Ethan out the door. For a minute I think he's going to throw him over the railing. I don't think the two-story fall would kill him, but you never know. Instead, Finn drags him into his room and slams him into the bathroom door. "Fix her, freak! Fix her right now, or I'm going to kill you! Understand?"

Ethan falls on the floor in a heap and in a way I'm grateful he's not fighting back. First of all, it means he didn't do this on purpose, and second, I don't have to deal with Finn suffering memory damage, too.

I hurry between them again. "Back off, Finn! Now! Let me take care of it. Go take your feet and fists for a long walk! I said, NOW!"

Unbelievably, he listens. He grabs his helmet and keys, along with the room card, and slams the door on the way out. A few seconds later, I hear the roar of the motorcycle engine coming to life, then zooming away. When the noise is a memory, I turn to my brother, who's lying in a heap at my feet.

"What did you do, Ethan? What in the name of god did you do?"

The lock on the bathroom door turns, and Ethan scrambles to standing. Sage peeks out. "Is Finn gone?"

"For the moment," I say.

She emerges and sees Ethan standing beside me, head down, arms crossed.

"OMG! Ethan! Did Finn hurt you? What did he do -" She heads toward him, and he turns toward her, too, but I'm faster. I plant myself in the middle, shoving Ethan, so he stumbles back a couple of steps.

"What the hell, Elena! Don't you think he's been through enough?" Sage is incensed, but Ethan has the sense to be embarrassed about this fiction he created for her.

"Memory is a tricky thing sometimes, Sage. And this is one of those times. Isn't it, Ethan?" I say a little too loudly. He nods, without facing her.

"What the hell are you going on about? Ethan? What's she talking about?" Sage asks.

He shakes his head and looks at me, as his eyes fill with tears. "I didn't know. I swear I didn't know what I was doing. I was just — Lanie, I've done it lots of times before, and it didn't do anything to Sage."

Sage's face contorts as she tries to make sense of this mess. I move toward her, take her hand, and lead her to the bed. "Sit down and take a deep breath," I begin.

"Please, Lanie, don't tell," Ethan whines.

I throw him my most exasperated look. Sage's confusion travels up my arm and into my spine, where it explodes in my head. I fight the dizziness. "Okay. Just lie back and relax," I say.

"Not until you guys tell me what you're talking about." she says without much conviction. Ethan sidles around to the other side of the bed. I throw him a look that stops him in his tracks.

"I have to touch her," he explains silently. "She needs to think of the memory."

I'm not happy about this, but I nod. Ethan slides into the bed beside her and gently pulls her into an embrace, with her head resting on his chest. Sage is obviously comfortable with it. Ethan's breathing is shallow and labored, like he's fighting a war inside. I remind him that fixing this isn't optional. He closes his eyes.

I place my hand on her back. "Okay, Sage, take deep breaths and think about what happened since you got here. Replay tonight over and over in your mind." Ethan nods to me. When I've drained away all of Sage's tension and she's nearly asleep, I back away and sit on the other bed. I watch Ethan's face contort as he tries to fix what he broke. I'm horrified by what he can do, and fascinated, too. I wonder how many of my memories have been replaced and why Ethan does this. The thought makes my skin crawl and my head burn. I get up and sneak outside.

The night's clear and if it weren't for the well-lit parking lot, the stars would be a map against the sky. I try to follow their blurred and faded lines, find a path out of this increasingly dense forest of confusion. It seems like Ethan's abilities are changing, growing. If I believe that he didn't know what he was doing to her, then he must be as terrified of himself as I am. Finn's right about one thing. Somehow, he accomplished this insanity without touching her. I wonder if I might be able to do the same thing. The answers seem as far as the points of light in the sea of midnight blue above. I feel like this all may end in some cataclysmic vortex. My stomach flip-flops, and I check my watch. Thirty or so minutes have passed, so I slip back inside. Ethan looks up, then slides out of Sage's embrace. He sits with his back to us both. His shoulders are shaking, either from the effort involved in replacing the truth or from what he lost in doing so.

Before I make it across the room, the key card clicks in the lock and Finn comes through the door. Ethan and I turn to watch him enter. Sage sits up, too. I hold my breath, waiting to see if Ethan's hocus pocus worked.

"Hey, Finn," Sage says sleepily. She rises, and they fall together in a soft, intimate embrace. Ethan makes his way around them, head lowered, eyes to the floor. "I'm so glad to see you, baby," Sage croons in Finn's ear. "Seventeen months is a hell of a long time." I inhale sharply, and Finn throws me a murderous look over her shoulder. Ethan stops moving and looks up. He waits until Finn's gaze swings round to him. Then the slightest hint of a smile plays at the right corner of his mouth and his eyes blaze like molten silver. But it all passes in an instant and by the time Ethan and I are behind the wall of our own room, I doubt I really saw it.

Ethan lowers himself onto the bed, bending to scoop his bear off the floor. Then he curls into a tight ball and closes his eyes.

"E, we need to talk about this," I say gently, lying beside him and spooning him lightly. He's still shaking, though I don't think he's crying. "Please, E, something really strange is happening, and I have a feeling this might not be your first rodeo." The shaking stops suddenly as he tenses up, then continues more violently, like spasms. "I'm not mad, E. I just need to understand." He shakes his head and silently tells me he doesn't understand any more than I do. He tells me he's scared, and I know it's true. I pull him in closer, tell him it's okay to be scared, but we still need to talk. He says he just wants to sleep, that whatever it is he did leaves him exhausted. I get that, too. Healing someone else's emotions wears me out more than a five-mile run. I stop pushing and hold him until the shaking stops, and his breathing becomes deep and regular.

On the other side of the wall, I can hear Sage and Finn taking up where they left off or reuniting for the first time again. For some reason, it makes me happy and unbearably sad. I spend the next hour or so until daylight mulling over the many reasons why.

At around seven, I hear the housekeeping staff hitting the emptying rooms. I get up and hang the DO NOT DISTURB sign outside the door. Finn and Sage have done the same. Jamie won't be here to pick us up until eleven, so I let Ethan sleep. I climb back in bed and the next thing I know a knock's waking me — 9:30. "Check out isn't until eleven," I yell.

"It's me, Elena," Sage's yells. Ethan doesn't sit up, but his eyes flicker when I walk past his bed. I open the door, but Sage doesn't come in. Finn's standing behind her with his arms around her waist, like she belongs to him. "We're going for breakfast to the IHOP up the road. You guys wanna join?" I glance over at Ethan. He shakes his head.

"I think we'll take a pass," I say. "Can you bring back coffee for me and pancakes for E?"

They look relieved, and I must admit that putting Ethan in the same room with Sage, or Finn for that matter, seems an unnecessary risk when I'm this close to getting him someplace where they can help us sort all of this out. Anyway, I need some time to prepare him for what will happen when he gets to PSI this afternoon.

I start moving around the room, packing stuff up and getting out my outfit. "Hey, E, I'm gonna grab a shower, unless you want to beat me to it." He doesn't answer. His eyes are open and he's staring blankly at the wall, curled up on his side, clutching the bear to his chest and sucking his thumb absently. This is going to be harder than I thought. I go over and sit on the edge of the bed. "Come on, little brother," I tease. "You can't lie there for the rest of your life."

"Why not?" he mumbles.

"Well, for one thing, Jamie will be here to pick us up in, like, a little over an hour. For another, housekeeping will be here to get the sheets off this bed any minute. Finally, most importantly, I need you to be WITH me here, in it together, like always. Please, E."

He glances at me and looks away, his eyes misting over.

"Okay, have it your way. I'll take the hot water and leave you with the cold shower." He shrugs a little.

When I come out, I expect Ethan to be ready to get cleaned up, but he's lying in the same position. My stomach falls. I have less than an hour until Jamie arrives to transport us to our new life.

"Your turn, pal. Step on the gas. Jamie will be here to pick us up soon." I keep my voice light and breezy.

He glances up, then closes his eyes.

"Come on, E, housekeeping will be here any minute." I pull the bear out of his arms, and he sits up to lunge for it. I toss it onto the other bed. He throws me the look of death, his gray eyes as cold as a day in February. "Get up!" I say in my best drill sergeant voice.

"What if I don't? What if I just stay here and never move off this bed again?"

"Eventually you'll float away, and shortly after that you'll die of dehydration," I say, acknowledging to myself that this is like conversing with a four-year-old. "Now get out of bed." I pull the sheets and blankets back and out of his reach. He instinctively pulls his knees to his chest. There's a wide dark circle around him. His cheeks burn red with anger now.

"I hate you! I hate you so much!" he yells, jumping off the bed and making a beeline for the bathroom. Good, I think. Hate me if it keeps you going. Just don't lie down and drown in your desire and loss.

After the shower's running, I sneak into the bathroom and bag up his soiled clothes. The Initiative will get him new things if he needs them. By the time he comes out, wrapped in a towel, I have all of our stuff packed and ready to go. He dresses in the clothes I've put out for him, a pair of baggy, gray, ripcord shorts and a teal polo. He leaves the diaper on the table. I get a clean towel from the shelf in the bathroom and his hairbrush from his bag. He's sitting by the window in a big chair, with his sketchpad in his lap, when I get back. When I try to dry his hair, he pulls away. "Come on, E, don't be like that," I plead.

Ethan pretends to be absorbed in drawing, but his breathing's labored. I rub his shoulders for a few seconds, hoping it will soothe him. I take Red over to him and he hugs the bear as he rocks back and forth. In my head, I can hear him repeating over and over, "I wanna go home. I wanna go home." By the twentieth or so repetition, I admit to myself that he's freaking me out a little.

"E, you need to calm down, baby." I pull another chair over, so we're facing each other. "Please. I need to tell you about what's going to happen today. Can you listen?" He takes a deep breath and nods, but he doesn't stop rocking. I'll take what I can get. "Jamie's going to pick us up and take us to a huge, glass building that has floors above and below ground, and a big wall all around it like a castle. Guards will let us in, and we'll park inside the building, underneath, like the Bat Cave." I smile, but Ethan doesn't respond. "Then they'll do some scans and take some blood, and you'll get a physical and talk to the therapist there, Dr. Robineau."

Ethan's attention snaps to when I say the word 'therapist.' He shakes his head vehemently. "No. I won't talk to him. No doctors, Lanie. You know that!"

"Her," I correct. "Dr. Robineau is a woman. It's okay, E. I promise I'll stay with you the whole time. I won't let anything bad happen. I promise. Okay?"

He nods, but I can tell he's not convinced. I make a move to get up, but he grabs my hand. "Please, Lanie. I just wanna go home." I look away as a thousand miniature daggers penetrate my heart. I reach across the table and hand him the diaper.

"E, I think you should wear it just for today. Things might get a little stressful, and it would be embarrassing if you have an accident the first day."

"Embarrassing for who?" he asks, pulling away. "For me or for you?"

He's right, or course. "Both of us," I answer honestly.

"No," he says flatly. "I said no more diapers except at night. I mean it. I won't wet my pants."

"I hope you're right," I say, but I know he will. Still, I can't afford to get him any more upset, so I drop the argument. "There's one more thing, E. We're actually going to live in the PSI castle building on one of the lower levels. It's really cool. They have a cafeteria with every kind of food you could ever want, and no one has to cook or do the dishes. And there's a swimming pool, as long as in the Olympics. It's got salt water, so it will be just like swimming in the ocean, without the jellyfish and sharks. You'll love it."

"If we're living in that building, where do we sleep?" he asks anxiously.

I knew I'd have to broach this, and I know he won't like it. "They have lots of rooms for all the kids like us that are part of the research. You'll have a room like you do at home and my room's down the hall. I have a really mean roommate, but the boy you're rooming with is really nice."

Jamie and I had spent an hour or so with Cayde the day before, explaining about Ethan and what he could expect. I must admit, the boy had been very sweet and compassionate about all of it. He told me he knew how Ethan felt since he'd wet the bed until he was ten. At fourteen, Cayde's still small, like Ethan, but wiry and lively to an extreme. I have high hopes that he might be able to bring Ethan out of his shell a bit. Ethan's having none of it, though.

"I'm staying with you. You said they would give us a house together. I'm staying with you, Lanie." The pitch of his voice rises dangerously, and his hands are trembling. "Lanie?"

"I. . . I misunderstood the deal. We won't be far apart, though. And if you need me, you can just call out in your head, and I'll be there in half a second. I promise, it'll be okay. Cayde's nice and funny, and he'll be your friend."

"He'll hate me and make fun of me and call me a baby. I'm not going! I'm not going with you, Lanie!" He jumps up from the chair and before I can get my hands around his arm, he's pulled away and locked himself in the bathroom. I can hear him sobbing, unable to catch his breath, in total meltdown mode.

I want to bang my head against the wall until it splits open, and my brains spill out. Instead, I sit down with my back against the bathroom door and take my mom's earring out of my pocket. I trace the vein all the way up my inner arm, scratching just hard enough to leave a white line that turns red after a couple of seconds. I want so much to dig in, to taste the salt and iron in the back of my throat, but Jamie's warning keeps me in check.

I jump when the knock sounds. Finally, coffee! I throw open the door. Jamie runs a hand through his hair, then returns it to the deep pocket it came from. "Sorry, I'm a little early. We have a lot to get through today. You guys ready?" He looks around the room nervously. "Where's your brother?" Ethan's sobs echo through the wall, and I point sheepishly at the door.

"Oh," Jamie says. "Oh, shit."

"That about covers it," I say.

"How long has he been like this?" Jamie asks.

"Half an hour, give or take," I say.

"How long can he keep this up, usually?"

"You might want to get lunch and come back tomorrow."

"That long? Really?"

"Really."

"Hmm. We don't have that much time. What happened?"

"Before or after he altered Sage's memory?" I ask.

"He what? Okay. Maybe you should start at the beginning but make it quick; the clock's ticking."

I'm in the middle of giving him the hundred-word run down of last night when a loud truck rumbles through the parking lot. The sound pulls me to the window. It's a tan pickup covered in mud and as generic as a vehicle can be, but the sight of it makes my heart pound in my neck, and suddenly I feel like I'm breathing sand. An image flashes in my head of a tall man with a lined face, and me running outside to stand in the driveway moments before he pulls in, as dusk settles over the street in front of a house that burned to the ground long ago.

Jamie must think I've lost my mind, but I bolt out the door and down the stairs just in time to watch the truck park. The door opens and without even looking at the face of the driver, I throw myself into his arms and hold on for dear life. At first, his arms flail around behind my back, like I've knocked him off-balance. Then he hugs me back tentatively, and finally with as much passion as I pour into him. A woman gets out of the other side of the vehicle. Her brow's furrowed, but in a few seconds, it smooths and her mouth stretches into a wide grin.

"Rachel!" I squeal, pushing Jesse out of the way to collide with her in a tangle of arms. "Am I glad to see you!"

"I thought you might need some help, based on what Sage said and didn't say when she called this morning." Rachel's still smiling, but her eyes dart up to the room with the door hanging open.

"Yeah, that's Sage all right, saying more with what she won't say." I laugh with relief and take Rachel up the stairs by the hand. Jamie stands in the doorway, shuffling his feet, his hands deep in his pockets.

"Rachel, Jesse, this is Jamie, my mentor at PSI."

"Ma'am," Jamie says, shaking her hand. "Sir," he says, looking up into my father's eyes. He invites them into the room by stepping back.

"Elena, where's your brother?" Rachel asks, looking around the empty room.

I point to the bathroom. "I can go," Jesse says, misunderstanding the situation.

"It's not on your account," I say.

"It's on mine," Jamie says wryly. "He's less than enthusiastic about joining us at the Initiative, I'm afraid."

"Not unexpected," Rachel says. "You're talking about moving an agoraphobic recluse halfway across the country and into a dormitory."

I look up quickly. "How do you know about that?"

She pulls her cell phone out of her pocket and shows me a text from Ethan. "Why don't you guys go load the car? I'll see what I can do."

Jamie, Jesse, and I pick up the luggage and take it down to Jamie's car. "Good thing your brother travels lighter than you do," Jamie teases, throwing everything in the back. "Or we'd have to leave him here anyway."

I smack him hard in the arm. "So funny!"

I reach around him and retrieve Red. I toss the bear into the backseat.

"So, what do y'all do at this PSI place of yours?" Jesse asks, addressing Jamie more than me.

"Well, sir," Jamie drawls, "I could tell you, but then you'd have to kill me."

Jesse cracks a big smile and stifles a laugh. I punch Jamie again.

"We study paranormal phenomenon. Try to capture how and why some people like your son and daughter seem to be able to do things other people can't."

"Sound's reasonable," Jesse says, "but I'm guessing you're sugar coating it a little."

Jamie's smile fades for a moment. "Purely academic. I can assure you," he says.

"So, what amazing things can my twins do that your purely academic organization wants to study to the tune of sixty large a year?"

I don't like the tone this conversation's taking. "Jesse?" I put my hand on his arm. "Dad? No one's forcing us to do anything. Coming here was my choice." I feel his suspicions and worry trickle through my hand, up my arm and into my shoulder like a cold faucet. I shiver. Jamie's eyes are focused on my point of contact. He knows what I'm doing.

Jesse sighs deeply and holds out his hand to Jamie. "No hard feelings. Just looking out for my little girl."

"No hard feelings," Jamie echoes a little hollowly.

Rachel comes down the stairs, looking a frazzled. "Soooo, that went well." My stomach rolls. "He wouldn't let me in unless I promised to take him home. I couldn't do that; could I?"

"Shit!" I say. "Where's Sage? We need Sage."

We're all quiet for a few seconds. Then Jamie says, "Let me try."

"Not a good idea. He's not so keen on strangers," I say.

"Believe it or not," Jamie says softly, "Ethan and I have more in common than you think."

"Sure," I say, smirking. "Such as?"

Jamie hesitates, looking at the three of us assembled like a panel of judges. "Not so long ago, I suffered from agoraphobia, too. For different reasons maybe, but I know how he feels."

My jaw hits the pavement. I'm not sure whether I'm more disturbed thinking he's lying or thinking he's telling the truth. I pass him the key card and flourish my hand toward the stairs. "Have at it," I finally manage to say.

While he's upstairs, I text Sage. She texts back that they're on their way. If anyone can get Ethan into Jamie's car, it's Sage.

Rachel asks about my first few days at PSI, and I tell her about the security protocols and Dr. Robineau. "Have you ever heard of her?" I ask, hoping Rachel will allay some of my misgivings.

Rachel shakes her head. "I'll ask around," she promises.

I tell her about Logan and how cold and controlling she is. I try to describe Logan's "wall." Rachel's interested, but she really wants to know about Cayde, Ethan's roommate. "He's mischievous and sweet. He never stops moving," I say. "ADHD in the extreme and up for anything, anytime. I really like him," I say. "I think he'll be good for Ethan. He won't judge."

"Good," Rachel says, and she nods toward the stairs. Ethan and Jamie are coming down. Ethan's eyes are red and swollen. He looks exhausted, spent, defeated. I move to go to him, but Rachel puts a hand on my arm and shakes her head. "Let him do this on his own," she whispers. I step back. Ethan gives Rachel a hug and eyes Jesse suspiciously. Then he opens the passenger side back door of Jamie's Fit and gets in.

Jesse and Jamie shake hands, and Jesse says, "Take care of them."

Jamie nods, "I will. I promise." His eyes meet mine, and I feel an almost electrical pulse. I know he means it. I hug my father as hard and long as I dare, and Rachel, too.

Unfortunately, just as Jamie and I are about to open the doors and get in the car, Finn's motorcycle roars through the parking lot. There's nothing I can do. Ethan's out of the car and wrapped around Sage before she can even get the helmet off her head. I can't hear him, but

I know he's begging her to take him home, and he's crying again. Finn fumes, kicking at the dirt and circling them like a jungle cat, but he doesn't interfere.

I can't watch this anymore. I push past Finn and grab Ethan by the bicep. "We need to go, E." I say. "NOW!" He lets me pull him back to the car, and he gets in on his own. Sage follows, wiping tears from her cheeks. Jesse has a hand on Finn's shoulder, either comforting him or holding him back. I can't tell which. Sage puts her hand on the glass by Ethan's face, and he brings his up to meet hers. I think I might be sick. Jamie and I get in fast. When Jamie turns over the engine, Sage takes a step back, and Rachel puts an arm around her.

As we pull away, I wonder if Ethan sees the same symmetry that I see. The perfect square that Jesse and Rachel and Sage and Finn form. There's no place for us in that little world, I think. We'll never fit there. I turn around to look at Ethan. He's found the bear that I left on the seat for him and he's holding it tightly to his chest, which heaves with silent sobs. I close my eyes, lay my head back and say a silent prayer to make it through this day.

The forty-five minutes it takes to get to PSI are painful. I make Jamie stop for the coffee I never got, but I can't convince Ethan to eat or drink anything. I get in the backseat with him, and he lays his head in my lap and curls up across the seat. I rub his back and promise him that I'll help him through this. I tell him he can hold my hand the whole time. I remind him that we're never further away from each other than a thought. Gradually, he unclenches, and his breathing comes without gasps and tremors.

As we head up the long, tree-lined drive, Ethan sits up to take in the architectural beauty of the building and grounds. He even manages a smile when the base of the bottom floor opens, and we drive into the lower level.

As we're exiting the car, I notice a group of people approaching from the far side of the garage, past the double glass doors. I recognize Maureen, Logan's handler. She's only a little taller than I am, but she's thick at the waist, with muscular arms that might be good at shot-put or archery. I'm about to greet her when she motions to the men with her, and they circle around behind us. I tighten my grip on Ethan's hand and turn to Jamie, my heart hammering in my ears. He steps away to make room for the large men Maureen commands. "I'm sorry, Elena," he says, right before one of the guys grabs me by both arms, yanking me away from Ethan.

Ethan screams and lunges toward me, but another guy's on him in an instant. I watch a second group, led by Dr. Robineau, pour out of the glass doors with a stretcher. Before I can even yell, she's plunging a syringe into Ethan's arm. My guy drags me away as my brother collapses, and his guy swings him up and onto the stretcher, like a ragdoll. Red falls from Ethan's arms. Jamie stoops to pick up the bear. He gives me one last, pained look and follows as Dr. Robineau's entourage wheels my brother away from me through the glass doors.

I fight with every ounce of strength to get free, but there's no use. In the periphery, I hear Maureen telling me to calm down. She's holding a syringe, like the one Dr. Robineau used on Ethan, in front of my face. Finally, I understand that it's a threat. She doesn't want to use it on me. I stop fighting. The Neanderthal relaxes his grip, and I rip free. Ethan's just inside the glass doors. I scream and pound until the inner doors slide open and he's taken down the long corridor. Then I collapse onto the pristine, white, concrete floor, bury my face in my knees and weep for what I've done.

Susan Michalski

ᏚᏬ 8 ᏟᎡ

PLAYING TRICKS

Match between your fingers, gun under the bed
Ready for the anything that happens in your head
Trust is an illusion only for the blind
They're playing tricks; you always say
They're playing with your mind
So, keep the curtains drawn, knife is close at hand
Hide until they go away; they'd never understand
"Illusions" - Luna Rayne, 2010

I'm escorted rather forcefully through a different entrance and the PSI labyrinth to my room. The muscle stands outside the door while Maureen walks me in. I'm done with tears at this point. Now I'm ready to light the entire place on fire and watch it burn. Maureen stands in the doorway while I pace back and forth. Logan ignores my presence, as usual.

"Elena, you need to calm down. I can still administer this sedative," she threatens, holding up the needle.

"You abducted my brother!" I scream.

Logan removes her headphones. "And you!" I yell at her. "You could've warned me! What the hell is this place? Fucking Hotel California?"

Logan laughs harshly. "Good one, pipsqueak," she says.

"You aren't helping," Maureen says to her. "No one has been abducted, Elena. Ethan's fine. You'll see him at dinner with any luck."

"You're lying!" I shriek. "I would know if he was okay. I would feel him. Even when we were thousands of miles away, I could feel him here." I point to my temple. "Now, I've got nothing! For the first time in my life, he's not there!" The tears start again, and I can't catch my breath. Logan steps forward to catch me, but I push her away.

"Fuck you, too, bitch," she snarls.

"Gerald!" Maureen calls, and the guard comes in from the hall. "Hold her down."

"No! No!" I scream, jumping onto the bed and away from him. "I'll stop! I'll stop!" I hold out my arms to ward them off while I take several gasping breaths. The three of them stare at me, ready to pounce. I know how the lion in the circus feels and trust me, it's not good. Gradually, everyone relaxes, and Gerald goes back out to the hall. I squat, then sit on Logan's bed.

"Are you ready to listen?" Maureen asks.

I nod once.

"Ethan has been given a sedative that contains a neurotransmitter inhibiter. It dulls his abilities. That's why you don't 'feel' him right now."

"Why?" I ask.

"I think you know the answer to that, Elena. You even expressed your fears about bringing him here to Dr. Robineau. Remember?"

I nod, but I don't, not exactly.

"Okay. I'm going to go check on your brother now. I'll be back to get you girls for dinner."

"Take me to him!" I jump off the bed and block her exit. "If he's all right, you can just take me to him now!" I pause for emphasis. "Please!"

"That's not going to happen, Elena. I suggest you enjoy some music or read a book, maybe take a nap or a shower. I'll see you in four or five hours." She gently pushes me out of the way as she closes the door. Then I hear her punching numbers into the keypad. After a few seconds, I try the door. As expected, it's locked.

"That's bullshit!" I yell into the camera in the corner of the room.

Logan's sitting on her bed, staring at me. "Guessing now that you're not a tourist here for the twin studies."

"I don't even know what you're talking about half the time," I snap.

"Raaarh!" she says and swipes at me, like her hand's a cat claw.

"I gotta get out of here. Ethan needs me. I know it," I say, pacing again.

She's shaking her head at me. "Idiot. How have you been checking on him for the past week?"

I rush her, grab her face and kiss her on the lips. "You're a genius!"

"Ew, get your slimy, lesbo lips off me," she says, but she's fighting a grin, maybe the first I've seen from her.

I lie on the bed and take several deep breaths, but my mind's racing with all the adrenaline that's been pumping in my blood for the last hour or so. I sit up again. "I can't do this," I say. "I'm too wired."

"You're hopeless!" Logan says, rolling her eyes. "You need to forget all the shit Jamie told you about relaxing your body and grounding yourself. Think of it like this. The astral plane is like a subway line. You just need to get on the train and get off at the right stop."

"Sure. It's that simple."

"Actually, it is. All the other crap is like waiting in the lousy, smelly station."

"Nice. I may never be able to astral project again. Thanks."

"You want to check on your brother? Stop yammering and get your ass on the train already."

"Okay," I say. But I'm totally unclear on the concept. I picture the astral plane and the train running through. It goes by a couple of times before I realize it isn't going to stop for me. I need to just jump on. The next time it goes by, I separate from my body with a sudden jolt, and it feels exactly like I've leapt onto a moving train. For a moment, I hang suspended in the air, clawing for the platform, desperately grabbing for anything to keep me from falling back. Then I experience a moment that can only be described as a rush, when I realize I've made it and I'm on the train.

Getting off is the next challenge. I have no idea where they've taken Ethan, so I need to focus on his energy, not the physical location of his body in the facility. As Logan pointed out, the astral plane is in no way connected to the physical plane. I think about my twin lying on the gurney. I search for his consciousness. Even with the drugs that dull his telepathy with me, there must be a trace of it that I can find.

Suddenly, I feel him faintly. I push toward that feeling and find myself standing in the infirmary. Ethan's lying strapped to a hospital bed. He's dressed in pale blue scrubs. I wonder what they did with his clothes. He starts to stir, and the nurse who's monitoring his vitals motions to someone on the other side of the curtain. Dr. Robineau comes in. She lays one hand gently on his shoulder, and with the other she strokes his forehead.

He's moaning and struggling to come up from the sedative. He keeps tugging at the restraints holding his arms down, and I realize he can't suck his thumb. "Lanie. Lanie?" he calls for me in his fog, and I hurry to his side.

"I'm right here, E!" I think as loudly as I can, but the tears are already coming down the sides of his face.

"You killed her," he mumbles. "She's gone."

Dr. Robineau shushes him softly. "It's okay, little one. Hush. Hush. She's fine. I promise. It's okay, little mouse. Your sister is safe and sound in her room downstairs."

"I can't feel her!" he whines miserably. "I can always feel her."

I know exactly what he means. I try again to communicate telepathically. "E! I'm here. Listen harder. Don't cry, E. Please, don't cry."

"We gave you a neurotransmitter inhibiter. It turns the volume on your abilities way down. Everything will be okay."

I wish like crazy she would stop touching him. He hates to be touched. But I watch him calm under her caresses and crooning, and he stops struggling against the restraints. I can hardly believe my eyes. After a couple of minutes, she frees his right hand, and he brings his thumb to his mouth. Then he quells the impulse and lowers his hand to his stomach. Dr. Robineau looks surprised.

"I'm Caroline Robineau," she says. "I run things around here."

"Let me go, please," Ethan says. "I need to go."

"I need to keep you in the restraints for just a few more minutes. When the sedative's completely worn off, I can allow you to get up. I wouldn't want you to fall and hurt yourself."

I hope he doesn't mean that he needs to 'go' because by the time this conversation is over, he'll have already wet himself. The look on his face tells me she's about to be sorry she didn't take off the restraints. Now, he brings his thumb up and his jaw works as he fights the tears that are nonetheless coming down.

Dr. Robineau doesn't seem surprised or particularly concerned. I would swear that she wanted him to have an accident. She wants him to feel weak, I realize. Why?

"Shhh. Shhh," she says, caressing his shoulder.

"I wet myself," Ethan confesses through his tears.

"It's okay, Ethan. Cindy can help you get cleaned up. Do you know where you are?"

"The glass castle," he says, taking his thumb out of his mouth. "Why did you take Lanie away?" I admire his near belligerence in the face of being shackled to a wet bed.

Dr. Robineau smiles. "We thought it might be easier to get you processed without her around."

"Then why did you sedate me?" Ethan's voice has a sharp edge.

The doctor's smile falters. "We didn't want you to be traumatized by all the tests we had to do."

"But you didn't mind traumatizing me by grabbing my sister and hurting her in front of me?" His voice is low, and he doesn't meet her gaze, but there's no mistaking which of them has the upper hand in this little battle of wills.

"My turn, Ethan. Tell me about the things you and your sister can do."

"Why don't you ask her? She's the one who brought us here to be studied." He almost spits the last word.

"Because I'm asking you, Ethan." Her sweet facade cracks infinitesimally, but enough for Ethan to see.

"I'm awake now. Please let me go." It's not a request. The way he says it is no longer polite, despite the 'please.'

Dr. Robineau nods to the young woman who has been busying herself on the other side of the room. The woman unbuckles Ethan's feet and his left wrist. He sits up to assess the damage and blushes crimson when the nurse's eyes meet his. For a second, I think he's going to start crying again, but he stares through Cindy, and she goes to the cabinet behind the bed, and pulls out another set of light blue scrubs for him.

Dr. Robineau places a hand on his arm, holding him on the edge of the bed. She pulls a diaper from the closet and offers it to him. "Until you can prove yourself able to stay reliably dry, you'll wear protection. Do you understand?" Ethan pulls away and gets off the bed. He stares her down for several seconds, but she doesn't budge. Then he takes a step back, shakes his head as if confused and lowers his gaze. Like a beaten dog, he takes the diaper from her and heads into the adjacent bathroom.

"Jamie, will you please accompany Mr. Paige, in case he requires assistance." Robineau's voice borders on triumphant.

Ethan spins around. "I don't require assistance!"

Jamie comes from around the curtain and hesitates briefly before following Ethan into the bathroom.

Dr. Robineau types into a tablet furiously, her brows knit in concentration.

When Ethan comes back out, he's fuming. "Take me to my sister now," he says.

"In good time, little mouse," she says sweetly, her facade back in place.

"Don't call me that." His jaw's working through the anger bubbling up.

"I thought you liked that nickname." Dr. Robineau moves toward the door, but Ethan doesn't follow. She turns back around. "Come along, Ethan. We have a few more details to take care of to get you settled in here."

Ethan stands his ground. "I'm not doing anything until I see Lanie."

If they weren't both so hell-bent, I'd laugh at this Mexican stand-off. "Good boy," I think. "Stand up to her."

Dr. Robineau walks toward Ethan and stares him down, their faces only a couple of inches apart. It's like before. Something almost tangible, like a red energy, passes between them for a few seconds. Then Ethan lowers his eyes and looks away. Robineau moves toward the door again. This time, Jamie puts his hand lightly on Ethan's back and they follow her. When Ethan slips his thumb into his mouth, his hand shakes.

"E!" I scream. "I'm here! It'll be okay. I'll get you out of here!"

I'm wondering where they're taking him when Logan's voice pulls me back by the silver rubber band. So much for the return trip by train, I think when I open my eyes. My head feels like it's traveled through a concrete block.

"Get the hell out of here, you stupid teek!" Logan's yelling.

"They shot him up!" Cayde's saying, jumping from foot to foot. "Hugo saw it on the monitors. They took him in the hard way!"

"Shut up already!" Logan yells, tossing a look my way.

"Oh, hi. You're back! What did you see?" Cayde asks excitedly.

"Hi, yourself. Can you guys keep it down?" I sit up, rubbing my temples. "How did you get in here?" I ask, looking at the door.

Cayde and Logan exchange a knowing look. Logan shakes her head. "Don't, Cayde."

"Come on, Logan. This is proof they aren't tourists! They should know the score."

"You're going to get us all put down," she says.

Cayde sticks out his tongue at her, and she jumps to her feet like she's going to pound him, but he jumps away like a puppy, obviously enjoying getting a rise out of her.

"What's a tourist?" I ask.

"A short-timer," Logan says. "Kids who come in for something stupid like twin studies and end up getting sent home in a few weeks."

"Why would they send someone home?" I ask.

"Duh!" Cayde says, "No powers, no paycheck." Cayde spins around in a circle, like a dancer.

"So, to get Ethan out of here, we just need to play dead?" I ask.

"Too late for you now. They'd know you're faking it," Cayde says, hopping across the room on one foot.

"You just astral projected into that lab, and your energy's gonna show up on their scans," Logan adds.

"Not to mention the way they brought your brother in. You guys are gonna be here a long time. Maybe forever, like us." Cayde leaps onto Logan's bed and tries to put an arm around her. She shoves him hard with her elbow, and he flips over the bed onto his back. I gasp, but Cayde pops back up, apparently unhurt.

His words make my heart flutter. "What're you saying?" I ask, not really sure I want to know.

"There're only two others that they sedated to bring them in," Cayde says, and he throws a look at Logan.

"Who was the other?" I ask.

Cayde smiles broadly.

"Jeezus, idiot! It's nothing to be proud of." Logan rolls her eyes.

"Why did they sedate you?" I ask.

Logan sighs. "Fear. They're afraid of what we can do."

"But they don't even know Ethan. I didn't tell them anything about his abilities beyond our telepathy."

Logan looks away, and Cayde dances nervously around the door, like he's thinking of bolting. Logan finally says, "You don't remember telling them anything; that doesn't mean you didn't." Her voice is flat, like she's reciting from a script.

I search my mind for places where the holes reside, but predictably come up blank. "What can you do that they're so afraid of?"

"We're not supposed to talk about it," Cayde says, looking at the camera that we all know is watching us.

"This is the prime fucking directive. It was in the contract you signed," Logan says, deadpan.

"I hate that contract."

Logan gets off the bed and goes to the wall. She picks up an awl from her bedside table and starts scratching symbols I don't comprehend into a corner of the black paint. I've seen her do this before, but never in the middle of a conversation.

"What is she –"

Cayde shushes me with a finger to his lips. For several seconds Logan faces the wall. Then she turns around slowly.

"We have two minutes at most," she says.

"Telekinesis, teek," Cayde says excitedly, pointing to himself. "Nana thought we had ghosts. Poltergeists. Then she thought I was possessed. Then she brought me here. I was nine."

"Show me," I say.

Logan laughs. "He's got some control issues."

Cayde pouts in her general direction. "Meany!"

"What about you?" I ask Logan.

She shakes her head. "You first."

"She sees dead people," Cayde says, unable to contain himself. Logan leaps over the bed and tackles him to the floor. She holds his arms down with her knees and tickles him until he's screeching. "You're gonna make me pee! You're making me pee!"

Logan jumps off him. "You better not piss in my room!"

Cayde jumps up. "Works every time!" He dances out of her reach.

"What does that mean? You see dead people? Aside from being a line from a cheesy, predictable movie."

"It means I walk the astral plane. You ride the train through, but I take the long road through the countryside. And I meet the inhabitants, who happen to be dead, mostly." She turns to Cayde. "You're a dickweed."

"Takes one to know one, Haley Joel!"

"Shut up, twerp, or I'm gonna end you!" She menaces him with her fist, but he doesn't stop grinning. "Time's up," Logan says, sitting back on the bed placidly, like the last two minutes didn't happen.

I must look confused because Cayde whispers in my ear, "The dead people muck up the camera sometimes if she asks real nice."

"Oh," I say, but I really don't. "So, this is like the X-men school or something, and Dr. Robineau is like Dr. Xavier?"

"Idiot," Logan says, shaking her head. "This isn't a fucking movie." Even Cayde deflates and looks beaten down for a moment. I feel like an idiot.

"Cayde, how did you get in here?" I ask again, changing the subject.

"Keypads are a specialty of mine," he says, the grin returning to his face. "Kid stuff!"

He makes me smile, too. "What about the guard?"

"What guard?" he asks.

"Guess he got bored and left," I say.

Logan gives me the idiot look again. "Scram, loser!" Logan says to Cayde.

"Aye-aye, captain," he needles, making an L on his forehead with his hand.

"Get out of my room NOW!" Logan roars. Cayde just about tumbles out the door.

A second later he pokes his head back in. "You're pretty," he says to me. "A lot prettier than her." Logan launches a box of tissues across the room, hitting the door exactly where Cayde's head had been the instant before.

"I think he's got a crush on you," Logan says a little bitterly.

"I think he's got a crush on you!" I throw back.

"Moron," Logan says, fighting a smile.

"I'm going back in," I say, laying down. Logan doesn't respond. She's already got her headphones on.

This time I make it to Ethan more easily. The sedative's mostly worn off, so our telepathy is returning, too. I can feel him calling for me. He's in Dr. Robineau's office. He's curled into the corner of the sofa amid the myriad tapestries. He looks miserable and angry and so very small. Jamie sits beside him, and Dr. Robineau's across from him in her big chair, taking notes.

"Okay, Ethan. Why don't you tell me about some of the things you like to do?"

He looks up at her but remains defiantly silent. Jamie fidgets, as though the sofa's made of concrete blocks, and he can't get comfortable.

"Your sister tells me you like to swim. If you answer a few of my questions, I'll take you to see the pool we have here. I've authorized a pass for you to use the pool at six in the morning, so you can swim alone. You see, Ethan, I'm not your enemy. Working together, we have a lot to offer each other."

"Just talk to her, E. It's okay to just talk," I think.

Ethan sits up suddenly and looks around. "Lanie, where are you? How can you see me?" he asks silently.

"Jamie will teach you. It's called astral projection," I tell him.

He looks at Dr. Robineau. "She knows you're here," he thinks.

My heart skips a beat. "Talk to her, E."

"I like to paint and draw," he says very quietly.

"Now that wasn't so hard, was it?" she says. "What do you like to paint?"

"I don't know. Wolves and people and trees, I guess."

"Good, Ethan. Let's try something a little harder. Okay?"

Ethan shrugs.

"Tell me about the scar on your arm."

Ethan tries to hide his scar by wrapping his arm in his shirt. He brings his knees up and shakes his head. "I don't want to talk about that. Please." His breathing comes heavy and hard, like he's running.

Dr. Robineau shakes her head at Jamie, and he touches Ethan's knee. "You don't have to answer that, pal. It's okay. We won't talk about it anymore. Okay?"

Ethan's breathing returns to normal almost immediately. He sits up again and nods. I'm nothing less than astonished. Once Ethan goes off, getting him back is never that easy.

"E, what's going on?" I ask.

"I'm okay," he thinks, and he is.

"Can we talk about your specialness? The things you can do?"

Ethan looks at Jamie, who nods slowly.

"What can you tell me about Jamie?" Dr. Robineau asks.

Jamie looks like he might throw up. Panic flashes in his eyes, and I can't help thinking he's got some huge secrets.

"Jamie hates his father. Maybe more than I hate mine." Ethan's voice is quiet and childlike. He hates doing this. I hate that she's making him.

Jamie shakes his head at Ethan. He's asking him to stop, but Ethan's on a roll.

"When Jamie was six, his father took him away one day and left him on a road far away. Jamie's mom thought he was dead. The police found him, but Jamie wanted to die."

Dr. Robineau looks at Jamie with sudden interest. "Is this true?"

Jamie nods and looks down.

"So, you're good with the past, Ethan. Tell me about Mr. Fleming's future now."

Ethan's eyes get wide. "It doesn't work like that," Ethan protests. "I'm not a gypsy or something. I don't want to talk. I want to see my sister now." He starts to tear up again. Jamie puts a hand on his arm.

Dr. Robineau motions Jamie out into the waiting room, then follows him. When the door's closed, she practically hisses at him. "I'm disappointed in you!"

"He's strong-willed. I'm doing the best I can." Jamie wrings his hands and looks at his feet.

"He's a stubborn, spoiled child. Try harder." She opens the door to the office. Ethan stops sucking his thumb when they come in.

Robineau studies him for a few seconds. "Why do you suck your thumb?" she asks.

Ethan's about to protest again. I can hear it in his thoughts. Jamie touches him and smiles encouragingly.

"I like it. It makes me feel better, calmer," Ethan says, abandoning his initial negative reaction.

"But you stopped when we came back in. Are you embarrassed?"

"It's babyish. I'm not supposed to." Ethan's cheeks go pink.

"But you do it anyway."

Ethan doesn't reply. He draws his knees up again. "I want to see Lanie."

Jamie looks beseechingly at Dr. Robineau.

She sighs heavily. She jots something down and hands Jamie the sheet of paper. I read it over his shoulder. "Take him next door and complete the intake paperwork. Then you can take him to his room. Do not allow him to see his sister tonight."

I can't believe it! That bitch! She doesn't even have the decency to tell him. For an instant Jamie's eyes flash with the same anger I'm feeling, but he fights it down. For some reason that one moment means more than all the betrayal I attributed to him today. He's on our side after all, I think.

"What does the note say?" Ethan demands in his head.

"She wants Jamie to do some stuff with you on the computer." I try to keep the next part from slipping into my mind but fail.

"They have to let me see you, Lanie. I can't do this all alone." He's already falling apart in his own mind.

"Jamie will figure out a way for you to see me. I promise I'll be with you before you fall asleep." He wipes his eyes quickly and puts his thumb back in his mouth. This time he leaves it there.

"Come on, Ethan. We're gonna let Dr. Robineau get some other work done." Ethan doesn't argue. He hurries out ahead of Jamie. Dr. Robineau presses a small, black box into Jamie's hand.

Jamie starts to open the box, but the doctor puts her hand over his to stop him.

"There are two syringes," Dr. Robineau says, patting his hand.

Jamie smiles a little, like she has just given him a wonderful gift, but the smile's fleeting and apologetic. He pockets the box and moves into the hall with Ethan.

I stay with them in the small computer lab as they work through the

Medical History form. Then Logan shakes me back to my body with a painful jolt.

"Owwwy! Couldn't you just text me that I need to come home or something?" I say.

Maureen walks in, and I give Logan what I hope she understands is a look of gratitude.

"Did I wake you?" Maureen asks suspiciously.

"All the cloak and dagger wore me out," I say sarcastically.

"I hope it made you hungry, too. Dinner time, girls." Maureen gestures toward the door.

"Don't have to tell me twice. The food's the only good thing about this joint," Logan mumbles behind Maureen's back.

"I can hear you, Logan." Maureen shakes her head, but she's smiling, and I'm shocked to realize she likes Logan, and the feeling's obviously mutual.

Despite what I heard and saw, I keep expecting Jamie to lead Ethan through the door any minute. I think I'm still only half-convinced that astral projection is real. I try to eat, but I want to get back to Ethan and Jamie. I want to wrap my arms around my brother and convince him that I had no idea it would be like this. Maureen takes her sweet time talking to some of the other handlers. She won't let me leave unsupervised, and none of them will take me back to my room. I hate them all.

By the time I'm boarding the train through the astral plain again, night has arrived and my anxiety's peaking. I find Jamie and Ethan in the boys' hall, less than a hundred yards from me. Cayde and Ethan's room is open when they get there. I'm surprised to see that their room's nearly double the size of mine and Logan's. A foosball table sits in the center of a room that also has two beds, two dressers and two desks, as well as a trampoline, a nerf basketball hoop and a giant yoga ball. Aside from the obvious, there's one more really odd thing about the room. There's nothing on any horizontal surface, not a brush or a toy or a bottle of hand sanitizer. Nothing. Ethan enters slowly, taking in the room and avoiding eye contact with Cayde, who's jumping up and down on the trampoline in time to the rap that he's singing at the top of his lungs.

"Cayde, take a break," Jamie yells, drowning him out.

Cayde bounces one more time and launches himself across the room to land directly in front of Ethan.

"Hey, man. 'Sup? I'm Cayde. You must be Ethan. Dude, your sister is a major fox."

Ethan takes a step back and mumbles, "Hi."

"Hey, how old are you? I'm fifteen, or at least I will be in a few more weeks. We gotta have, like, a total party."

"Nineteen," Ethan says. "I'm nineteen."

"Cool. You look a lot younger. I bet you get that a lot. No offense or anything. Hey, do you know how to drive?"

Ethan smiles broadly. "Yeah. I just got my license before I got here."

"That's so dope," Cayde says.

Ethan wanders over to his area to inspect his belongings. His bags are in the closet, along with a huge present. Ethan reads the tag that says it's from Jamie and rips the paper off to reveal an easel, several canvases in a variety of sizes and shapes, brushes, pallets, acrylic paints, solvents and glazes. He comes out smiling.

Jamie's shuffling his feet on the other side of the room when Ethan hurries to him and wraps his arms around Jamie's waist. I have to blink twice to be sure I'm really seeing this. He holds Jamie like that, tightly, for at least five seconds before letting go and stepping back.

"Thank you," Ethan says, picking up Red, who's been lying on the pillows. He hugs Red to his chest contentedly.

"Come on, Ethan, I'll show you where you can find things," Jamie says hurriedly, like he wants to get out of there.

In the bathroom, Jamie points out the sheets, mattress pads and plastic bags. It's hard to tell which of them is more embarrassed. He gives Ethan instructions for morning clean-up if the bedding's soiled, and they go back into the bedroom, equally relieved to be done with that bit. It's almost comical.

"Take me to Lanie now," Ethan demands quietly. Here we go, I think.

Jamie places a hand on Ethan's shoulder. "You'll be fine without her tonight. Tomorrow morning you can see her first thing. Okay?" It's strange the way he says it, almost like he's planting a post-hypnotic suggestion or something, rather than trying to comfort a distraught child. Even more shocking is the fact that Ethan doesn't protest. He doesn't agree to anything, but he doesn't throw a fit either.

"I really need her tonight." Ethan emphasizes the last word, but his tone is vague and unconvincing.

"It's okay, E." I think hard. "I'll be there as soon as Jamie leaves."

"Hey, man, you know how to play?" Cayde asks, twirling a set of guys on the foosball table.

Ethan shakes his head as if confused, and not about the game.

"I've been waiting a long time for an opponent. Come on, I'll teach you," Cayde says.

Ethan goes slowly over to the table, like he's forgotten why he's there in that room. Jamie nods to Cayde, and Cayde shrugs before turning his attention to Ethan to teach him the game.

"I'll be back in the morning at six to get you for swimming, Ethan. Okay?" Jamie moves toward the door, like he's making a calculated escape.

"Okay," Ethan says absently.

Instead of watching Ethan, I follow Jamie out. After he punches a code into the panel by the door, his hand goes to the pocket where he put the black box earlier. He hurries to the elevator and states his code and level 2100. A couple of seconds after the elevator starts, he suddenly says, "Elevator halt-authorization alpha sigma omega 01121." His voice breaks on the last sequence of numbers, but the elevator stops moving. Then Jamie turns away from the camera and leans into the wall with one arm. For a moment I think he might be getting sick or he's maybe laughing. His shoulders spasm and shake. Then a loud sob escapes his throat, and I can see he's barely able to remain on his feet, he's so overcome. My heart lurches in my chest and without thinking I reach out my hand to touch his arm. I expect a jolt as his emotion washes over me, but nothing happens because only my consciousness is with him, not my body. After a few seconds, he catches his breath, clears his throat, wipes his eyes and turns back around.

"Elevator resume – authorization alpha sigma omega 01121," and a couple of seconds later the doors open. He goes down a hallway to the end, where he enters a code and opens a door leading to a staircase that climbs up another level. The stairs open into a room about the same size as the one Ethan and Cayde share. At this point, my connection begins to fail. Everything fades until it's ghost-like and transparent. The walls, ceiling and floor of the room are covered with an insulating material and heavy, black curtains. Even the windows are blacked out. Jamie turns on a low, incandescent lamp, maybe 25 or 30 watts.

OMG! I think. My handler is a vampire! I turn from inspecting the room to see that Jamie has stripped to a pair of boxers. He's painfully thin without his clothes. In the back of my mind, I realize I should be embarrassed to spy on him like this, but it doesn't stop me, doesn't even give me pause. He picks up his pants from off of the floor and pulls the black box from the pocket before dropping them again. Then he sits on the edge of the bed. His hands shake as he removes one of the syringes. With his teeth he tears open an alcohol wipe that he takes from the bedside table, and he rubs a place on his thigh. Then he braces his leg against the running board and injects himself. His expressions pass from pain through relief to something like ecstasy. He lets the syringe fall from his hand as he curls up on the bed on his side. Then he rolls onto his back, his eyes open, and a smile spreads across his usually tight features.

A click snaps me back to my own body in my own bed, and more than ever before I wonder if what I saw was real or just a dream. When I open my eyes, I see Cayde in the entrance of the room.

"I brought something that belongs to you," he quips, smiling.

Ethan steps from behind Cayde and throws himself into my waiting arms.

"Out!" Logan screams. "This is a penis-free zone! GET OUT!"

Cayde nearly falls over, laughing. He bounces over, punches Ethan in the arm and says, "She said 'penis!'"

To my surprise, Ethan starts giggling, too. I roll my eyes at Logan, but their laughter's contagious and I have to cover my mouth to hide my smile.

"Whatever," Logan says. "You're going to get us all in trouble, moron!"

"Chillax, baby," Cayde says, sidling over to her. "Hugo's flipping the feed for us. We got all the time in the world."

"You'll keep your scrawny bones on that side of the room, if you know what's good for you," Logan threatens.

Cayde takes a step back, but his smile never fades.

"Who's Hugo?" I ask.

"His keeper," Logan says with disdain.

"He must be pretty nice to set this up for us." I'm smiling ear to ear, and Ethan's arm is wrapped around my waist. His mind's running a mile a minute, filling me in on all the events of the day. I was there, I was there, I keep reminding him, but he's having a hard time grasping the concept, and we both end up giggling.

"See?" Cayde says to Logan. "They're doing the twin thing. Guys! Guys! We told you ours. Your turn."

"Yeah," Logan says, suddenly interested.

Ethan and I look at each other in confusion.

"Your superpower! What's your superpower?" Cayde asks, jumping up and down, his voice hitting an octave above mine. Suddenly a box of tissues flies across the room and bounces off Logan's message wall. Ethan's eyes are huge, but Logan's annoyed rather than alarmed. "Take it down a notch or two, loser! You break any of my shit, I'm gonna break you." Cayde sits down on the floor and starts taking deep breaths with his eyes closed. After about ten of them, he stands up.

"All good now!" he says smiling. "It happens when I get going, you know. I just gotta take a chill, and I got it all under control."

"You did that?" Ethan asks a bit breathlessly.

"Oh yeah. Telekinesis. It's not all it's cracked up to be," Cayde says. The corners of his mouth turn down for a second, and a furrow in his brow reveals some of his pain.

"Yeah, well, it would be if you could control it, dorkass!" Logan's tone is bitter and maybe a little jealous.

Both of them turn their eyes on us now, and I feel like I'm in a spotlight. I'm surprised when Ethan speaks first. "Lanie can heal people."

"Mostly just emotions, really," I add, not wanting to give any false impressions.

"Whoa!" Cayde says and he looks at Logan to see her reaction.

"No shit?" she says. "Damn." She's shaking her head, and Cayde's bouncing again. This time my pillow flies into the door. Cayde sits down to breathe.

"It's not really that big of a deal, guys. I'm not like a faith healer or anything like that." I'm not really sure why they think my thing is such a big deal.

"Oh yeah," Logan says. "No biggie. Girl, you are one clueless lab rat."

Cayde interrupts his breathing exercise to add, "It ain't her fault she don't know. We were here almost a year before we figured it out."

"Shut up, nimrod," Logan snaps, and Cayde closes his eyes to continue.

"If I'm clueless, then give me a clue, Logan. What is it that I'm supposed to have figured out by now?"

Logan shakes her head. "Nah. You're better off not knowing, really."

"Really?" I ask. She can be infuriating.

"Don't take a tone with me, girlfriend! I'm doing you a fucking favor," she throws back.

Cayde pops up between us. "Ethan, what's your power?" he asks a little too eagerly.

Ethan looks at me. He's not going to talk about it. He never does.

Ethan can't think of his abilities as powers because he's always seen them as liabilities. I answer instead. "He can see people's pasts and sometimes the future, too." I don't think either of us want them to know the other part about how he can also manipulate memories.

Cayde's eyes widen. "That's why they wanted him," he says to Logan. "He's got both sides already. He can prove the whole thing!" He's astounded, and he looks Ethan up and down, like he might be the second coming or the chosen one or something.

"Shut up! Damn it, Cayde!"

"But, Logan, did you hear?"

Logan doesn't look surprised at all, but she does look pissed. Well, she always looks pissed, but now she looks double mad. And even more interesting is my realization that since Ethan walked into the room, she has not once looked at him. It's almost like she's afraid of him. I decide to test my theory. "I'm sorry, Logan. Where are my manners? I didn't introduce you to my brother." I pull him to his feet and over to her bed. "Ethan, this is my roommate, Logan. She sees dead people on the astral plane," I say to him. "Logan, meet Ethan," I say to her.

Ethan tentatively holds out his hand to shake hers, but she recoils and turns away from him. "Whatever. Hi. Now get the hell out of my room. I'm tired."

Ethan pulls his hand into his body, like she scratched him, and I feel bad, but I proved a point. Now I need to figure out why she's so weird about him.

"I'm gonna go with Ethan and Cayde," I say.

"Suit yourself. Just don't get caught," she says, lying down with her back to us. I look at Cayde for an explanation, but he just shrugs.

"Where do the handlers live?" I ask.

"Top floor," Cayde says. "Everyone knows that."

"2100?" I ask.

"Either leave or shut up," Logan barks.

"Yeah, 2100, I think. I ain't never been up there though," Cayde says in a voice that edges toward uncomfortable.

"What do you know about Jamie? Or Maureen? Or Hugo?" I ask.

Logan rolls over and sits up as loudly as one possibly can.

"Aren't they supposed to be graduate students or something?" I continue.

Logan actually snorts. "Man, you really are as dumb as you look, girl. You haven't noticed a single thing, have you? I wasn't here five minutes before I knew this one."

"Knew what?" I ask, looking to Cayde.

"The inmates are running this asylum, man," Cayde says somberly as he walks out the door ahead of us. He repeats it again and again as we hurry down the hallway to his room.

Susan Michalski

ℬ 9 ℛ

GETTING OLDER, TOO

Children chasing shadows, playing after dark
Practicing for lives they might not lead.
Don't step on the cracks, you'll break your mama's back
If that was all it took, we'd do it all with ease
But up you grow and down you forget
The shadows get darker each day
And you no longer want to play
Yes, you're getting older, too
Too old, too old, too old, too old for childish games.
"Chasing Shadows"- Luna Rayne, 1995

When we get back to the room, we find a tray of cookies and milk, with a note from Hugo welcoming Ethan. Normally, I'd nix the idea of Ethan drinking anything before bed, but it's a gift and it's only about four ounces. Cayde says Hugo is always doing sweet things like that. I camp out in Ethan's closet, away from the camera's prying eye, with his quilt and blanket. He crashes hard, almost immediately, before I can sing him a song. It's been a crazy, long four days for him, so I'm not surprised. After some initial silliness, Cayde passes out, too.

Alone, I'm left to ponder all the questions that are now burning a hole through my skull. Why is Logan so weird about Ethan? Why is Jamie working here if he isn't a graduate student? Is he a drug addict, and is Dr. Robineau his supplier? What exactly does it mean that the inmates are running the asylum? Do the handlers have abilities, too? Were Ethan and I recruited in some way? Why? What are they researching here? Why?

Despite all the questions, a nagging optimism sort of reigns. I like Cayde, and he's good for Ethan. Even Logan has a certain kind of charm, and for the first time in my life, I feel special. I wait for hours for Ethan to awaken with a nightmare, but the more I fight sleep, the heavier my eyelids become, and before I know it, Jamie's standing over me, and Ethan's no longer in his bed.

"You shouldn't be here, Elena," Jamie says. His hands are on his hips, his brow is furrowed, and his lips are pressed tightly together. He looks clear-eyed and well-rested, not hungover, like I'd expect.

"Well, you shouldn't have tried to keep us apart," I say. "Where's my brother?"

He points toward the bathroom, then motions Cayde over and says, "Juice."

Cayde nods, like he understands something I don't, but I think it has something to do with diverting the surveillance. Then the camera light goes dark. "That was quick," I say, pointing to the ceiling. Jamie and Cayde exchange confused glances.

"Go!" Jamie says urgently.

"What about Ethan?" I ask.

"I'm taking him to the pool. I'll come get you in your room." I think about it for a second while we all stare at the camera light. Finally, I scoot out the door and run as fast as I can to my room.

When I get to my door, I panic for a second. I don't know the code. I knock and hope Logan hasn't plugged in yet. She takes her time opening it. I almost give up on her.

"Well, look what the cat dragged in," she says. "Dead meat should be buried in the yard, not let inside."

"Stop," I say. "Ellen DeGeneres just texted me. She's afraid you might take her job."

"Now who's the comedian, shrimpo." She lets me in, closes the door and starts her morning routine.

I wait for her to shower first, then lock her out of the bathroom. The truth is, for all my bravado, I'm still a little afraid of her. When I get out, she's gone, probably to get breakfast. I'm starving, and I contemplate not waiting for Jamie, but the door's locked, and I still don't have the code. I try my own code, Jamie's — which I memorized the first day — and Ethan's. I try the authorization code Jamie used to halt the elevator, but no love. Finally, I lie down on the bed to check out on the astral express.

I find Ethan in the pool, swimming laps. My focus is on him executing a flip turn at the shallow end, so I'm surprised when I hear another splash from the deep end of the pool. The person swims a little way up the lane, then returns to the wall. Ethan stops at the wall, too.

"Good morning, Ethan," Dr. Robineau says cheerfully. "Did you sleep well?"

Ethan nods tentatively.

"Is it okay if I join you?" she asks sincerely.

He nods again, and they both push off the wall. I expect Ethan to leave her eating his wake, but she matches him stroke for stroke. He'll take her on the turn, I think. She won't be able to keep that pace, not for long anyway. He goes into the turn a stroke ahead of her, but when they surface after pushing off, she's about half a body length ahead. She knows what she's doing.

"Don't let her beat you!" I think to Ethan, but he doesn't need my prompting to turn on the competitive juice. He immediately picks up his kick, which launches him past her. She makes no obvious attempt to catch him, but she lags by less than a body length, and Ethan never seems to extend that lead. "She's riding his wake!" I say, though it's only in my mind. "She's letting him tire out while she relaxes. He's going to lose!" The thought makes me furious for some reason, and I try as hard as I can to communicate what's happening to Ethan.

His pace doesn't change until the next turn. This time he falls behind her on purpose by holding back a little when he pushes off.

"Yes!" I cheer. Since the race wasn't really planned or discussed, they play this little strategy game, trying something new on every turn, until they both begin to slow. Then the race turns into a war of attrition. Whoever's energy or resolve depletes first, loses. Ethan has had a rough couple of days, and despite last night's miraculous, nightmare-free, marathon sleep, I doubt he has much fire left by lap eight. I know my brother, though, and he won't stop on an odd number even if he's dying. On the tenth lap, he pulls into the wall at the shallow end, heaving for air with bright red cheeks and, to my intense shock, an ear-to-ear grin that goes all the way to his eyes. Dr. Robineau has just pushed off from her flip turn, but she doesn't finish her victory lap. Instead, she comes back and shakes Ethan's hand.

"You ready to go yet?" Jamie's voice retracts my consciousness into my body with a violent twang, like a guitar sting plucked too hard. I swear I feel the vibration for a full five minutes.

"Where've you been?" I ask, trying to play it off, like I was napping.

"You aren't fooling anyone," Jamie says. "I know you were watching him at the pool, but more importantly, so does Dr. Robineau."

I shrug. "The question is, where've you been? I'm starving."

"I've been preparing a little surprise for you. Get your purse." Jamie grins, changing his tune. "We're getting out of here today. There's someone I've been wanting you to meet."

"This outing better include coffee and a meal, or I can guarantee your friend won't want to meet me."

Jamie smirks. "I know just the greasy diner to appeal to a palette as delicately honed as yours."

"Harumph!" I say, grinning back. "Can you wait in the hall for a quick minute? I want to get changed."

"You look fine. Let's go."

"James!" I say with mock annoyance. "I said, give me a minute."

He blushes to the tips of his ears and nods wildly. "'K. One minute."

The second the door clicks, I flip up the mattress and slip the burn phone inside my boot. Then I follow.

"That was qui- Uh. You didn't change."

"I changed my mind," I say with the emphasis on the last word. Then I breeze past him toward the elevator. "A woman's prerogative. Ya know!"

"Oh," Jamie says, confused, but not suspicious.

Somehow Jamie managed to procure a convertible for this outing. It's a sweet, cherry red, Mini Cooper Sport that flies over the road. I feel like I can breathe again after a long, smothering winter indoors, even though it's only been twenty-four or so hours since I was last out of the Initiative, and it's a balmy eight-five degrees and has been since I got to Florida.

"Where'd you get the sweet ride?" I gush.

"You'd never believe me if I told you," Jamie yells over the roar of the wind.

"Try me," I yell back.

"It belongs to Caroline."

"Dr. Robineau?"

"Yup." He looks at me with an eyebrow raised.

"You're right. I don't believe you," I say, frowning.

"She isn't the enemy, Elena," Jamie says. His eyes suddenly stop laughing, and his smile lines smooth into seriousness.

"I don't want to talk about her." I say. "I just want to enjoy this moment. Okay?"

"Super okay!" Jamie smiles, and the lines return.

At the diner we order, and I excuse myself to use the restroom. I lock the stall before extracting my phone. I hesitate before dialing, though I'm not sure why. I've been jonesing to hear her voice for five — is that all it's been? — days.

"Hey, Jo Jo!"

"Hey yourself! They treating you little mice okay?"

"Rats! We're lab rats, not mice. Paleeze!" We both giggle, even though it wasn't really funny. "So, how are you getting along without me?" I want her to say that nothing's the same, and she misses me like chocolate ice cream.

"Same old, same old. Lots of practice, only to be screamed at that I'm not 'feeling' the music yet. Let me tell you, I'm feeling something, something a lot like rage and a little like despair, but it has nothing to do with Rachmaninoff or his concerto. I hate that old battleax, professor Weismueller." She says the name with a German accent, and it makes me smile. "What about you, baby?"

I want to break down and cry, tell her about the locked doors and the sedatives and the mysteries that seem to creep up around every corner, but I don't. Instead, I say, "Things are great. My roommate's a little Goth, but Ethan's is sweet and funny. And E's doing great."

"Well, that's good because Sage said the trip down was a vacation straight out of Dante's *Inferno*, and Ethan was a mess when you guys took off from the hotel."

"Did she say anything else?"

"Actually, she did mention something about a weird dream and forgetting something important. I couldn't make much sense of it, except that she was a little freaked out about Ethan and Finn." She pauses, waiting for me to chime in with a logical explanation, but I change the subject.

"Have you checked on Gran for me?"

"Yeah, but you know how she is. She hurried me out."

"I have a weird feeling about her right now. Keep an eye on her, please. Don't let her push you away. 'K?"

"You bet! Now what are you up to in that secret underground lair?" She wants details.

"I'm on my way to meet someone today. I don't know who. It's all hush hush, top secret, ya know." I force a laugh and hope it sounds half-real. Her long pause tells me it doesn't.

"You'd tell me if you were in trouble, right?"

I try to say "right," but nothing comes out, and I have to swallow a couple of times. "Yes," I croak. "It's all good. I swear."

"Okay, sweetie." She sounds doubtful.

"Hey, babe, I gotta go now. My breakfast is getting cold. I miss you."

"Me too. Take care of yourself and that angel-bro of yours."

"Always. Don't miss me too much."

"Too late."

We hang up at the same time, and my throat closes as the tears come down my cheeks, without the permission of my mind. I can't go back to the table looking like I've been bawling. Jamie will have a thousand questions. I wash my face and put on lip gloss.

"Good talk?" Jamie asks when I slide over the vinyl into the seat across from his.

"Excuse me?" I ask.

"Did you fart?" he tosses back, desperately suppressing a giggle.

"Did you stutter?"

He cracks up. "Elena Elena Elena. You think you're so stealth, but you're completely obvious."

I stick to my guns. "I have no idea what you're going on about."

"Okay, fine, but just remember who taught you your little tricks." He pauses, and the smile fades away. "And by the way, just so you know, you leave footprints on the astral plane." He looks sad, almost broken for a couple of seconds.

I nod to show him I understand, but there's nothing I can say.

"You don't have to lie to me," Jamie adds quietly.

But you have to lie to me, I think, and I hope he can't read my thoughts.

An hour later, we pull up to a military compound with soldiers in full gear with packs, running in formation, and drill sergeants screaming orders and obscenities at a group of shell-shocked kids, who are my age or younger, even. Everywhere I look, men and women in uniform hurry on their missions. They don't even stop to ogle the car.

Jamie parks in front of the largest building and leads me through the halls to a tiny office tucked in the back corner. Aside from the soldier at the gate who buzzed us in, no one stops us. Then, just as we're about to enter the office with *Dr. Meriwether* etched in the glass, a bass voice bellows down the hall. "Lieutenant Fleming, state your business on this base!" Jamie spins around, comes to attention and salutes the large man. "Permission to enter Dr. Meriwether's office with my trainee, SIR."

The man closes in on us and comes nose to nose with Jamie. Then they both bust out laughing. "How've you been, Captain Fox?" Jamie asks.

"Not as good as you," he says, looking at me and smiling.

Jamie's ears turn red. "This is my trainee from PSI, Elena Paige. Elena, Captain Fox, my CO from a long time ago."

"Nice to meet you," I say, holding out my hand. I turn to Jamie. "I didn't know you were in the military."

He cringes. "I never saw action."

"Why are you bringing your PSI kid here?" He looks me up and down with a combination of fear and curiosity.

"I. . . Dr. Meriwether thinks Elena might be able to help."

The officer grunts and nods. "Good to see you looking so well, Jamie."

Jamie salutes again and Fox returns the gesture before heading back from where he came.

"I sense a story," I joke, touching Jamie's arm lightly.

"Later." He opens the door and holds it for me.

Dr. Meriwether stands up when we enter and hurries forward to welcome us in. She's a tall woman, taller than Jamie, even, and she looks strong, despite the fact that she must be nearing seventy. There's barely enough room for the three of us to stand, so after hugging Jamie soundly, she sits back down in the chair behind her desk. The only other seating is a leather loveseat behind the door. Jamie and I sit so close I can almost feel the pulse in his leg.

"Elena, I'm so happy you could join us. Jamie has been telling me about you. We think you might be able to really help around here." She smiles so warmly that I have no doubt of her sincerity, but I have no clue about how I can help or with what.

Jamie pipes up. "I haven't briefed Elena about your work, Dr. Meriwether." His voice is a little tight, and the formality feels contrived, like this is not how these two people usually interact. Dr. Meriwether isn't put off at all by his announcement.

"No problem," she says. "Let's just show her. It's probably better anyway."

She grabs her purse and leads us out of the building and to her car. We drive maybe ten minutes away to a strip mall office park, where we enter a door emblazoned with only the number 211C. This office is somewhat like Dr. Robineau's, with a waiting room, bathroom and two inner offices. The furnishings are designed more for comfort than style and they have a hodge-podge, garage sale feel that reminds me of Sage and Rachel's apartment at my grandmother's house before Ethan burned it down. Dr. Meriwether explains that she shares this space with two social workers and another psychotherapist.

"I treat soldiers returning from deployment or before they go out," she explains, glancing at Jamie, who keeps his head down, like he's avoiding her gaze.

"But you have an office on base," I say. "Why did we come here?"

She looks at Jamie again and says, "It's easier for soldiers to seek help off-base, away from the eyes and tongues."

It makes sense. "So why am I here?" I address the question to Jamie, who looks up after a beat when he realizes I'm talking to him.

"Oh. Well. I — we thought you could sit in on the sessions. Maybe, if it was appropriate, you might use your ability to — you know — help."

I look at Dr. Meriwether. She smiles patiently. "Jamie says you're able to help people who are struggling with emotions."

"Oh!" I say, finally catching on. This is it. All of a sudden, I'm going to be helping people like I planned. A surge of pride and importance fills my chest and I suppress the huge smile that wants to spread across my face.

A little bell rings as the door in the antechamber opens and closes, admitting a young man in fatigues. He takes his hat off and sits down in one of the overstuffed chairs. Jamie excuses himself to the waiting room and sends the young man in. I take a seat in a chair in the corner of the room.

"Ryan, it's good to see you." Dr. Meriwether waits until he's seated to make the introductions. "This is Elena Paige, the young woman I said was going to be working with me for a few weeks. Is it still okay for her to join us today?"

Ryan looks me over carefully. His eyes are a piercing, dark brown. They're deep set in a kind face, with a strong, square jaw and close-cropped hair. He's a little older than I am, maybe twenty-five or so. I meet his gaze directly, but I don't smile. We aren't going to be friends, but I'm asking him to trust me with maybe his darkest secrets. The weight of that hits me full on, and I suddenly doubt my ability to help him. Still, he nods and shifts his gaze back to Dr. Meriwether.

"So, how's your week been going?" she asks, like they're having afternoon tea or something.

"Not so great," he begins.

Little by little, his story unfolds. He returned from deployment six months ago and almost immediately got married. At first, everything was great. Then little things began to bother him: the hum of the hair dryer, being cut off in traffic, and the smell of onions cooking. He admits that his reactions are out of proportion to the events. In fact, he's completely flipped out a few times. He punched a hole in the wall of the kitchen, smashed the hair dryer, and chased another car fifteen miles out of his way to scream at the driver. He doesn't understand why he feels so angry and on edge all the time. His wife has become frightened of him and that's breaking his heart. He moved back in with his parents to try to reconnect with the gentleness he'd known and practiced growing up.

I don't see the anger. All I see is guilt and the weight of memory. When he starts talking about leaving his wife, he breaks down. He wraps his arms around himself and rocks forward on the edge of the couch, like he wants to escape from the emotion. Dr. Meriwether looks at me and nods toward the soldier. As light as a moth, I reach over and place my hand on his bicep.

The weight of his pain nails me hard in the chest and feels like liquid lead running through my arteries as it travels up into my head and throughout my extremities. I try hard not to gasp from the pressure, but it's almost more than I can bear. The seconds tick by loudly in my ears, and I fight to keep my eyes in focus as gradually Ryan stops crying and sits up. I become heavier with each passing second as I watch him become lighter. I feel like I should say something, but I can't engage my vocal cords.

Dr. Meriwether's voice comes from beside me, too loud and echoing with reverb. "It'll get easier, I think, Ryan. Keep track of the things that set you off and write them down before you react. Also write down the things that make you feel better. It's good for you to reconnect with who you used to be. Just don't run away from who you are now."

They keep talking like this, but long after my hand has fallen away from the man, I can feel his skin on me and in me and I can't concentrate on words anymore. If I had the strength, I'd run from the room. Instead, I sink into the chair and watch the train coming across a great expanse. I brace myself and resist the urge to jump out of my body and onto the astral express. I don't hear Ryan leave, but Dr. Meriwether's smiling benignly at me when I'm able to open my eyes. Jamie's there, too, wearing that worried, weary expression that's becoming familiar.

By the time the next patient comes in thirty minutes later, I can hold a conversation, and the pulse in my head is a dull ache. Angela's tough and pretty, like Jo. She talks about how hard it is to feel close to people, how she feels like her life here lacks meaning. Her real issues are with her husband and children. She's having trouble with intimacy. She says she only feels alive when she's with her unit. She's attracted to one of the guys she was deployed with, but she knows that giving in to that attraction would be like setting off a landmine in the middle of her life. It's easy for me to lay a hand on her knee and absorb her passion and frustration little by little as she talks. This time I'm not so shaken after she leaves, but my head aches, and Jamie insists I've had enough. Dr. Meriwether drives us back to the base, and we head back to the

Initiative immediately.

When Jamie wakes me, I expect to find us in the underground garage, but instead I find us parked on a small hill overlooking the ocean. Jamie comes around and opens the car door. He helps me out. My hand lingers on his a couple of seconds too long, and his body's so close I can feel his warmth.

He doesn't move away from me to talk. "Why don't you go for a walk and make the other calls you need to make."

This time I don't bother to deny it. I wrap my arms around his neck and pull him into a slow, lingering hug. He presses his face against mine, and I can hear his heart rate increase. I wonder if he'll finally kiss me, but he pulls away. "We only have twenty minutes, so make it fast."

I take the phone from my purse and head down the beach, close to the surf.

"Oh my god! Elena! I've been trying and trying to reach you. We all thought something was wrong!"

Finn's in the background calling out, "You never write; you never call; you never text; you just don't love us anymore – ugh!" Sage must have silenced his diatribe with a sharp elbow somewhere soft.

"For real, girl, are you alright?"

"I'm fine. Relax. Most of the complex is underground, so reception's for shit. Not a big deal." There's no way I'll tell her they confiscated our phones. I hear a door close, and Sage drops her voice, so I can barely hear her.

"Can I talk to E? I've been so worried about him."

"He's not with me right now. I only have a few minutes, so tell me what's happening with you and the asshole. And please don't use the words *dreamy, electric,* or *love.*"

"Can I say 'hot sex?'"

"Ew! Yuck! No, you cannot say those words, at least not together." Sage laughs. "Well, then I have nothing to say on the subject."

"Too much information." A part of me is happy for her; a part of me wants to find Finn, rip off his package and mail it to him in a plastic bag.

She pauses for a couple of seconds and sighs. "He wants me to stay here with him."

I nearly drop the phone into the surf. "And?"

"I can't stay here! I have school and a job and an apartment and friends and a life. There's nothing here for me but Finn."

"And Rachel and Jesse and your new sibling," I add.

"Yeah," she says. "They're kind of gross. I mean it's cute and all, but they're all about each other. No one else really exists for them right now."

"Oh," I say. What I hear is that my dad and my therapist don't care about me or my brother.

"I didn't mean it that way, Elena. We're all worried about you and E. How is he?"

"It's been, like, one day. He's fine. I mean, for Ethan, he's fine."

"Whatever went down in the hotel was messed up." She doesn't ask the question, but it's implied. I don't want to throw my brother under the bus, but I don't want to lie to Sage either, so I don't say anything. "Do you know what happened, Elena? Finn won't tell me anything. He just keeps saying that Ethan's dangerous. That's ridiculous! Right?"

"Finn's just jealous," I say. "Hey, Sage, I have to go. Can you tell my dad I love him, and I'll be by to see him and Rachel as soon as I can?"

"Sure. But when can I talk to E?"

"Give him some time to get used to being without you. Can you do that?" I say.

"I'm not sure. I can't stop thinking about him. I miss him."

"I'll tell him you said hi and that you love him. Okay?"

"Fine, but if he can just call..."

"We'll see, Sage. I really have to go."

"Well, bye then. Call again as soon as you can. I love you, girl."

"Back at you."

The line goes quiet, and I feel oddly empty, like I just threw up or finished crying. I need to get back to check on Ethan. He's been on his own without me or Sage for the whole day. That hasn't happened since — the fire, and that didn't work out so well for anyone. The guilt starts clawing at my mind. How could I have agreed to this? And who's looking after my brother?

I run up the beach back to the car. Jamie's sitting in the driver's seat with the door open, listening to the radio with his eyes closed. He jumps when I get in.

"Thanks," I say. "Let's go back now."

The drive takes far too long. I work myself into a state of controlled panic, imagining Ethan sitting in a corner in a wet diaper, rocking, crying, and sucking his thumb. When I open the door to his room, I'm shocked to see the complete opposite. He's in mid-air, jumping from the trampoline to the bed. He tucks at the last second and rolls over the bed and off the mattress, where he lands more or less on top of Cayde. They're screaming and laughing like little kids. They both pop up when they see me in the doorway.

"Come on, Lanie, you gotta try this. It's so much fun!" Ethan runs over, grabs my hand and pulls me toward the trampoline. I'm so shocked I can barely move.

"Lanie, stop looking at me like that! We've talked about this," he scolds half-jokingly. "Okay, so all you have to do is jump up and down a couple of times to get your momentum built up. Then, push off toward the bed, calculating your trajectory to land here." He points to the edge, where he landed. "Tuck your head and do a somersault."

"What he said, but careful you don't overshoot, or you'll be in a world of hurt," Cayde adds, rubbing the back of his neck and patting the wall behind him.

"I said that," Ethan says, shaking his head.

"Yeah. Yeah. Whatevster, E-man." Cayde bumps Ethan hard with his hip, and they both almost fall over, cracking up again.

Okay. I now know what age Ethan is. Cayde's like a really immature fourteen, so that would put them both at around twelve.

"That's okay, E. I think I'll take a pass." He shrugs and goes back to the bouncing and flying and laughing. I lie on Ethan's bed and watch them until dinner time.

That night we all eat dinner together: Logan and Maureen, Hugo and Cayde, and Ethan, Jamie and me. Then we go back to the boys' room for foosball. We even convince Logan to play, but she'll only play on my team. After cookies and milk, everyone else leaves, and I help Ethan get ready for bed. I tuck him in with Red in his arms.

"You don't have to stay here tonight," he says. His eyes are already heavy with sleep. I kiss him on the forehead.

"You sure?"

He nods. "But you have to sing."

So, I do. When I finish my favorite Luna Rayne song, Ethan's asleep, but Cayde mumbles, "You better watch out Lanie-girl. There are some mighty jealous angels up there. Mm-hmm!"

On the way back to my room, I smile. Coming here was so right. My chest opens up, and I feel like I can breathe.

The next three weeks, we fall into a pattern. Ethan swims with Dr. Robineau at dawn. After breakfast, Ethan and I work together on telepathy exercises with Jamie in one of the observation labs. He tells us that no other set of fraternal twins has demonstrated a connection anywhere near as strong as ours. Then we split up until dinner. I go with Jamie to work with Dr. Meriwether three days a week, while Ethan works with Dr. Robineau. He won't tell me what they work on, but it doesn't seem to disturb him, so I don't worry about it. The other two days, Ethan works with Jamie on astral projection and precognition stuff. On those days, I work with Dr. Robineau on using biofeedback to concentrate my healing abilities, and analytical psychotherapy to try to determine the source of my power.

After dinner, our time's our own. We play games, we hang out, I listen to music, and Ethan paints. Before bed, I sing the boys to sleep. Ethan stays dry all day and has no nightmares at night, and I stop digging my mother's earring out from under the mattress in the cover of darkness, all of which seems like a miracle. I find it oddly easy to sweep to the side Cayde and Logan's darker speculations, Jamie's strange mood swings, Logan's bizarreness around Ethan and my own exhaustion from being pushed to the limit to heal the wounds of so many suffering soldiers. In fact, my pride and confidence in my abilities grow exponentially as Ryan returns home to his wife, and Angela begins to enjoy her family again.

At the Initiative, life begins to feel like some kind of normal. Cayde flirts endlessly with me, refusing to accept that I play for the other team, and at the same time works desperately to get a rise out of Logan. Maureen and Hugo watch Jamie's every move, like they want to peel his grapefruit. Ethan and I agree that Hugo's a brother, but we argue about Jamie's intentions toward me. Ethan and Cayde approach every day like it's an opportunity for mischief, and nothing makes them more gleeful than getting caught. No one makes a big deal about Ethan's bedwetting. We have something here that I thought Ethan and I might never experience – friendship, along with all the joy that entails. I feel nothing short of invincible, with my decision vindicated. Until the day they rip it all away.

Friday transpires like all our days, but instead of heading back to PSI after working with Dr. Meriwether, Jamie takes me to the beach again, like he did on that first day. After I've called Jo, who seems a million miles away from me, despite the fact that she says all the things I long to hear from her, and Sage, who has returned home and can do nothing but lament her loneliness for Ethan and Finn (and even me perhaps), he pulls a picnic basket out of the hatch.

"For me?" I ask.

"For us," he says, shuffling his feet with the kind of sweet nervousness that I find so endearing. "I just wanted to spend some time with you, alone, away from there, before —"

He leaves the word hanging. My mind screams above the crashing and the howling wind, 'Before what?' But I don't ask aloud. Everything's so perfect; I don't want any bad news. I let the flutter of panic spin away, like a feather in the breeze.

Jamie spreads a blanket on the warm sand, and I drop to my knees beside him. We unpack the food in silence. Jamie watches me like a man who has never seen a woman do this, and who might never see it again.

"What is it, James?" I ask in the gentle voice I normally reserve for Ethan.

He looks down. "I was just admiring your —" he pauses, shaking his head and grinning his embarrassment.

"What?" I say. "Admiring what?"

"Nothing." His voice is small.

"Come on, how embarrassing can it be? I mean, unless you were going to say my boobs."

He laughs out loud, a belly laugh that takes me by surprise. "Oh god, no! That's not what I was going to say."

"Then what?" I reach over and put my hand over his. "I don't really get admired too often, so I'd like to know."

I lift my eyes, and they meet his. For once, neither of us looks away. "Your grace," he says so quietly the seagulls almost drown him out. "Your grace."

I take it in for a second, and a small creature in my soul stirs. No one ever accused me of having grace, at least not to my face. My brain clouds along with my eyes and without thinking, I lean over the chicken and baked beans to kiss him on the lips. I fight the creature for control and push back, ready to apologize, but his hand's cradling my head, bringing my lips back to his. I close my eyes, so I can take in the mildly annoying brush of his stubble on my cheek, the urgent press of his mouth, and the smell of salt and coleslaw. He sighs as we separate, and I leave my eyes closed for an extra second to hold it in.

Finn never kissed me. I loved him from the age of twelve until fifteen and he forced me to service him in so many ways, but he never kissed me until the night he took away my innocence, my soul. Or didn't.

I've kissed Sage with my heart, but hers is so vague and untouchable, it was more like kissing a ghost. Then there's Jo and the hundreds of kisses we've shared, like an old married couple who kiss out of habit, rather than passion most of the time. Jamie's lips are not as soft as Jo's, but his soul is so, so — present. I feel like I've lost a small piece of myself in the exchange, but I've taken a bit of him to keep with me, too. I need that second to put it someplace it won't get lost. Ever.

When I open my eyes, Jamie's smiling at me. Crinkles form in the corners of his eyes and mouth. He looks almost happy. We eat and navigate the conversation around the threat he hung over our heads as we got out of the car, but once the food is put away, he broaches the subject again.

"I didn't really bring you here to kiss you." He looks down, trying hard not to grin. "I brought you here to prepare you, I guess."

"I'm not going to like this. Am I?"

"Probably not, but I think it'll be easier if you know about it before it starts."

"Okay. Give it to me straight." I almost crack up at my pun. That is, after all, the only way Jamie could give it to me. He misses the joke.

"Things have been pretty easy so far for you and Ethan, and you guys are doing exceptionally well at PSI, but they don't pay you all that money for things to be easy. The program is about to become more —" He searches his mind for the right word. "— challenging, a lot more challenging."

"I see," I say, looking out at the ocean where a boat far from shore is bumping up against the horizon. "So, the honeymoon's over."

"That's one way to put it." He follows my gaze, unable to look at me.

"What exactly does challenging look like?" I ask.

"No more milk and cookies, for starters."

It takes me a couple of minutes to grind through what he means, but the light bulb comes on eventually. Three weeks of milk and cookies and no nightmares. They've been sedating Ethan at night. A knot begins to tighten in my gut. "What else?"

"No more twin stuff."

The knot pulls tighter. "They're going to separate us."

"As much as they can." He digs his feet into the sand and rotates them back and forth.

"Why?" I ask.

"They want to push your abilities to the next level."

"Because we're doing so well."

"You've both plateaued." He lifts his eyes to meet mine, but the angry darts I can't keep from shooting force him to look away again. I fume silently, digging my fingernails into my palms as I picture Ethan falling apart in the many lovely ways he does. I taste the salt and iron in my mouth as the creature, so briefly free, goes back into hiding.

"Say something, Elena," Jamie says sadly.

"Can't they just do whatever it is to me? Leave Ethan alone? Can't they let him feel good for a while longer?" I know I sound pitiful, like I'm begging, and I am. Mad as I feel, I'm begging for my brother to be spared any more trauma.

Jamie shakes his head. "I don't make the decisions. I'm just the messenger boy here. I'm not really even supposed to be telling you, but I — I like you and Ethan. I don't want you to hate me."

He sounds so torn. "Jamie, I couldn't hate you," I say. "I know you're taking care of us." He hangs his head, then looks hard at me, like he's figuring out if it's true.

I'm shocked when he says, "You say that now, but you'll hate me." His voice is tight, like he's fighting back more emotion than he can hold. He stands up and starts gathering up the picnic paraphernalia. I can't take seeing him like this. I stand up, too, and slip under his arms, pulling him into a hug. The emotional energy that spills from his skin into my nerve endings is complex and confusing. I find my fingers and toes tingling, and my ears ringing with a sort of feedback loop. What I don't feel is the moment of release when the person's emotion sort of explodes in my brain. I feel blocked, like with Ethan.

Jamie pulls gently away from me. "We have to get back now. Ethan's going to need you."

I spend the drive stewing about what Dr. Robineau's doing to Ethan and nervous about the state I'm going to find him in. I rush through the security protocols and leave Jamie in the elevator to run down the hall to Ethan and Cayde's room.

At first I think no one's there. Then I hear a small noise coming from the closet. When I open the closet door, I hear a sharp intake of breath as I peer into the darkness.

"E? Are you in here?" I know he is because I can smell urine. My eyes adjust and I make him out, crouching in the far corner behind the suitcases.

"Lanie?" His voice is high and tight, like he's being strangled.

"It's me, E. Why are you hiding?"

"I'm scared." He doesn't elaborate.

"Come on out. I'll protect you."

He shakes his head.

"It's okay, E. I'm the only one here."

"They'll find me," he whispers.

"Dr. Robineau?" I ask.

"And the others," he adds in a shaky voice. "I did something bad."

"What did you do?"

He shakes his head and buries his face in his knees as he hyperventilates.

I'm getting nowhere, so I leave him there and go into the bathroom to get what I need to clean him up. Then I return to the closet. This time I crawl all the way inside, until I can touch him.

I squat next to him. "What happened?" I ask, placing my hand on his arm. He relaxes a bit.

"I wet my pants," he confesses, without the usual tearful meltdown.

"Before that, sweetie." I stand up and offer him my hands. He allows me to pull him shakily to his feet. I undo the string on his pants and slip them down. He catches on to my agenda and removes his underwear, socks and shirt.

"Really, E?" I say. "Everything?" I hand him the wipes.

"Less than ideal trajectory," he says sheepishly, and I laugh a little at the inside joke, but Ethan isn't even a little amused. "That's why they call it an accident, ya know. I didn't exactly have time to prepare."

I take the sarcasm as a good sign, and it reminds me of what Sage said about Ethan's sense of humor.

He takes the diaper without an argument and sits back down to put it on. "What happened, E?" I ask again. He makes a choking noise in his throat and shakes his head, unable to speak.

I decide to ask something easier. "Where's Cayde?" This time I get a whimper. I sit down across from him and take both my brother's hands in mine. In a flash, I see the entire scene unfold from Ethan's memory and I'm struck by how strong our telepathy has become in just three weeks.

I feel like I am Ethan, reliving the memory. I'm in the elevator on the way to lunch. Cayde and Hugo are with me, and we're singing "99 Bottles of Beer" in a three part round. The object of the game is to mess the others up so you're the only one left singing. I sing louder and ignore the ridiculous faces that Cayde's making, and the outlandish poses Hugo's attempting. We pile out of the elevator and a couple of girls who are there for twin studies, Nina and Nora, give Cayde dirty looks. They smile at me, like I'm a piece of chocolate. I shrug. Then Cayde flips over and starts walking on his hands while he sings, trying to show off for them. Suddenly, I get a weird feeling that something's going to go very wrong. As we step through the double doors into the cafeteria, I pull down his legs to flip him back upright. He stumbles into a worker carrying a flaming pan warmer. I see Cayde bump the guy's arm, and in slow motion the heating element falls to the floor and rolls under a table, where it ignites the tablecloth. Without a thought, Cayde dives under the table to retrieve it as Hugo yells, "No, Cayde, use your telekinesis!"

At that instant, a flame shoots up toward the ceiling. Hugo looks at me, like it's my fault. I wet myself. Just before I dart out of the sea of faces witnessing my humiliation, Logan shakes her head at me and mutters, "Impressive." It's the first time she has ever spoken directly to me.

Maureen puts out the fire with an extinguisher, and Cayde rolls out from under the table, screaming in pain. I turn to bolt, but I'm blocked by Nina and Nora, who tear their eyes from Cayde to look at me and the puddle on the floor with the usual mixture of horror and disgust. I push past them and end up here.

Back inside my own mind, I feel Ethan's guilt and fear of repercussion, as well as his wish that everyone would just forget that it happened, forget his public humiliation, forget that he caused the accident that hurt Cayde, but more than all of that, I feel his terror about Cayde's injury and his conviction that it was his fault.

When the memory's played out, he's crying with anger and frustration. Now I hear the words the way I normally do with our telepathy, and it's like déjà vu. "I wanna go home. I wanna go home. I just wanna go home." He stands up to pull on his pants. I get up, too, and go to his dresser to find a shirt. He follows me back into the room. As I'm pulling his shirt down around his waist, I stop and hold him there. "It wasn't your fault, E. It wasn't your fault Cayde got hurt." He crumples against me and mumbles, "I should've known. I don't know how I didn't know sooner." I have no idea what he's talking about.

Suddenly, the door to the room opens. Cayde's riding on Hugo's back.. His arms and the side of his face are bandaged, and his eyes are glassy. He moans when Hugo lays him gently on the bed. Jamie, Logan, and Maureen follow them in. Everyone turns to look at Ethan, who rushes back into the closet and shuts the door.

"It's not your fault, Ethan," Hugo says to the door.

There's no response from inside. Cayde's as pale as his bedsheet and tears are seeping from his eyes. "Can't they give him something for the pain?" I ask Jamie, who stands as far from Cayde and Ethan as one can get in the room.

"They have," he says through gritted teeth.

Logan has moved to the side of the bed, where she squats to get eye to eye with Cayde. "Nice going, retard. Way to hog all the attention." Her tone is in direct opposition to the harshness of her words. Cayde tries to smile, but it looks more like a grimace.

Hugo's still trying to coax Ethan out of the closet when Maureen pipes up. "Okay, guys, doesn't look like there's going to be a foosball tourney tonight. Let's give Cayde a little peace and quiet, so he can sleep." She ushers Logan to the door and motions for me to join them. I shake my head and point to the closet. Hugo joins the others by the door.

"Elena." Cayde's voice is small and shaky as he calls me over. I kneel down on the floor next to him. "Sing — please," he rasps out between clenched teeth. My eyes fill up with tears. It's awful seeing him like this. He reaches down to hold my hand. As I sing a Luna Rayne song, I close my eyes and concentrate on siphoning off the mental anguish that must be accompanying Cayde's physical pain. I feel the familiar rush of blood, elevated heart rate and crush against my spinal column before the explosion in my brain. I wish I could do more, heal his actual wounds somehow. In my mind, I erase the burn from his face and the seared flesh on his arms.

My voice falters and stops along with my heart. My eyes open wide from the sudden sensation that every nerve ending in my body has been struck like a match and flared into flame. I try to scream, but my vocal cords seem paralyzed. I can't pull my hand from Cayde's weak grip, either. In slow motion, I turn my eyes to the others, who are still by the door. Logan's trying to get to me to help, but Jamie holds her back. Maureen and Hugo are looking away. Tears are coursing down the big man's cheeks. Finally, just before it all goes black, I see Ethan dart from behind the closet door. I feel him sever the physical connection between me and Cayde.

Time is a vortex in the next place. There is no atmosphere. Color does not exist. I don't mean that things are gray; I mean that there is no color. Sound, likewise, has lost all importance. I'm wondering if this is the astral plane, when I realize I'm not alone. My mother is here close to me, reaching out, not in a physical way, because the physical is irrelevant here. Suddenly, Logan is with me too. Deep in the animal part of my brain, I realize I shouldn't be on this plane. My mother's presence moves closer to me, so comforting and full that I long to fall into it, like a feather bed. Logan silently compels me to go with her. Her frenetic, living energy is electric and undeniable in this realm. I'm pulled toward it like a magnet. For an instant, I feel torn nearly in two. Logan's energy reminds me of all I have in the other place: Ethan, Jo, Sage, Rachel, my dad, the baby. I let go of my mother and follow Logan. Again, coming and going are not as you might think, even at the outer reaches of your imagination.

I open my eyes as Jamie leans in to kiss me. A chorus of voices hollers at once and Jamie pulls back. 'That was rude!' I think. 'Why can't we kiss?' On my right, Ethan's wringing my hand and crying with an absurd abandon that makes me want to ask who died. But my voice doesn't respond to my mind's messages. I look up and see Cayde sleeping soundly in the bed. It takes only two beats for all of it to rush back with a vengeance. I sit up, violently pushing everyone away. Breathe. Breathe. Breathe, I tell myself until the adrenaline runs its course, and my heart rate approaches something like normal.

"What. . .?"

Jamie sits back on his heels and wipes at his eyes. His breathing seems almost as labored as mine. I realize that he was performing artificial respiration on me. I shiver and take a brief inventory of people in the room. Logan's gone, and only Cayde looks peaceful and pain-free in his sleep.

"I think that's enough excitement for one night," Maureen says, attempting her normal bossiness and missing the mark.

Hugo can't stop staring at Cayde. He makes a move to cross the room, but Maureen grabs his arm and ushers him out instead. "Good night, y'all," Hugo offers as they exit.

I try to stand, but immediately sink back to the ground. Ethan surprises me by scooping me into his arms effortlessly. He and Jamie head toward my room. Girls are running around the hallway in their pajamas, giggling. Up ahead, the twins who had been crushing on Ethan before his unfortunate accident are suddenly directly in our path. Ethan tries to turn around, but with me in his arms there's no graceful way to navigate. He looks at me, conveying a boatload of trepidation and embarrassment. They stop when they realize it's Ethan and we both cringe a little, anticipating looks of disgust at worst and dismay at best. Instead, they smile with genuine sweetness and say in harmonized unison, "Hi, Ethan."

"H... h. . . hi." He looks at me as though I have an explanation.

When we get back to my room, Ethan sits beside me on my bed. Logan's on the floor beside her astral communication wall. She doesn't acknowledge our entrance as she writes frenetically. Ethan settles on one side of me, and Jamie on the other. We watch her for a while without talking. I take the time to turn the day over and over in my mind. I try to decide how to frame the questions I have for Jamie, but with Logan in her zone, I don't want to speak.

Finally, she drops the awl and rests her forehead against the stucco. Slowly, she turns toward us.

She exhales heavily as though relieved. "Oh, good. You made it back. I pissed off a lot of people up there, chasing you down like that. I guess 'people' isn't really the right term, but you know what I mean; you were there."

"Thanks," I say. She nods.

Jamie gets up. "I'm gonna go now, I think, if you're okay?"

"I'll live," I quip.

"Not funny," he sighs with his shoulders sagging, like a tired old man. "You coming, Ethan?" It's not really a question. E isn't allowed to stay here with me, and Logan would blow a gasket if he tried.

Ethan nods, then nuzzles close to me for a couple of seconds. He throws a few plaintive glances at Logan, and I know he wants to say something that will do damage control, something that will erase her image of him standing in his own pee.

Logan does not like being looked at. "What do YOU want?" she asks from the floor.

"I. . . I. . . it's just that. . . I was burned. . . in a fire." He holds up his arm in explanation.

"Duh! Everyone can see that. Why do I care?"

I decide to give my brother a hand. "Jeez, Logan, can't you try to be nice? He's trying to explain why what happened, happened. You know, so you understand it was just the situation."

"What the heck are you talking about? What happened to your brother? Cayde was the one who got burned. Ethan bailed before anything went down. So what?" She shakes her head in confusion.

This time when Ethan's eyes connect with mine, he's not confused; he's astounded. "I made them forget," he screams inside our heads. "Like Sage. I didn't touch them, but I changed their memories. All of them!" He's swelling with power and pride, but he doesn't verbalize it. Instead, he soaks it in and splashes it into the air.

As he and Jamie make their way back to their rooms, an icy foreboding slithers up my legs, slips down my throat and comes to rest in my heart. Nothing good will come of this, I think as I fall into a dark, restless sleep.

℘ 10 ℞

BLINDED FOOL

Sorry excuse for vision
The lines blur again and again
Lovin' like it's my mission
With lines that converge
In the distance
Can't trust my ears
A love song's all they hear
Poison perfume
When love draws near
Leave me a blinded fool
A blinded fool for you
Your blinded fool
    "Blinded Fool" - Luna Rayne, 2014

When the world returns to me, my awareness begins with a desire to stretch out — and the frustration of that desire being impeded. A familiar scritch-scratching, like a small animal trying to get in or out, is magnified by my ears, but I can't place it, exactly. Though my eyes are closed, I know the lights are on because of the shards that intrude around the edges. That fact is the one that finally pulls me into consciousness.

Ethan sits at the end of my bed, drawing in his sketchbook. For a second, I wonder if it's the middle of the night, but he's presentable in black shorts and a green baseball shirt. I turn over to see if Logan's here; she's not. I clear the sleep from my throat.

"Hey, E. What ya doing?" I ask.

"Waiting for you to wake up." He stops sketching to smile down at me, and for a split second I see the angel that others see when they look at him. "Are you better? You scared me last night." His brow creases a little as if to prove he's been worried.

"I'm okay, E. What time is it?" I ask. One of the more frustrating things about living underground is never having a sense of what time it is.

"Like, one or so. I brought back some lunch for you." He points to a tray on top of the dresser. "A salad and a bagel with butter. Oh yeah, and some of the chocolate pudding you like."

"Nice. I can't believe it's that late. Hey, how's Cayde?" I have only a vague recollection of last night's insanity. Cayde was hurt, and I tried to heal him. That's the sum total. Oh, yeah, and Ethan's memory-altering, power-revelation celebration. Ugh!

"He's been sleeping all day, like you, so I don't know. You wanna go see?" He asks the question, but he doesn't move from his place by my feet. I sit up to see what he's sketching. It looks like random scribbling, but really familiar random scribbles. My eyes follow his across the room. A little eruption happens in my brain.

"E, why are you drawing Logan's wacky wall?" I try to keep my voice steady.

Ethan stops and looks at me, like I'm a child who isn't grasping a simple concept. "Don't you see it?"

I see this wall every day, and it makes no sense to me. All I know is that Logan uses it to communicate with souls on the astral plane. The strange symbols mean nothing to me. "There's nothing to see, at least not that I can understand," I say.

"It's a pattern, like a code. I'm gonna figure it out."

I'm shaking my head, about to say Logan wouldn't like that, when she barrels through the door.

She's vibrating with rage, and her face is as red as her bloody nail polish.

"You obnoxious little moron!" She bears down on Ethan but doesn't get close enough to physically harm him. He recoils, nonetheless. "Don't you ever, ever fuck with MY head!" She pauses to take a breath and glances at the page of his sketchbook, which is spread out on his lap. "What the hell is this?"

She surprises him by ripping the book right out of his hands.

"Hey!" Ethan yells, jumping down onto the floor.

"You have no right to invade my privacy! You aren't even supposed to be here!" she shrieks and the strangest question flits through my mind, like a shadow. He isn't supposed to be here in this room or here on this plane? Maybe Ethan and I were supposed to die in the fire with our mom. As I get tangled up in this idea, time slows down. I only had an instant with my mom on the astral plane, but I got the sense that she was waiting for me, for us. Suddenly, I feel certain that Logan's oddness with Ethan is connected somehow with her wall and my mother and the astral plane. The knot in my stomach twists a bit tighter.

Ethan takes a step toward Logan, reaching for her arm, ostensibly to get the sketchpad back, but I know what he really wants to do. Though she tries to dodge him, Ethan's much quicker. The instant their skin makes contact, an electric charge fills the room. Logan screeches and tries to pull free, but Ethan's got a death grip on her wrist, and he's not about to let go until he finds what he wants. I try to get up to pull them apart, but the minute my feet hit the floor, I collapse under the weight of whatever my body went through last night.

"ETHAN!" I yell as loudly as I can from where I've fallen. He swings his head around, and Logan breaks free. When he turns back, she nails him with a sucker punch to the chin. He goes down, but he doesn't stay there, like I expect. He pulls himself up, and, holding his chin, squares off with her.

He's not savvy enough to put up his guard, but it doesn't matter because Jamie and Maureen rush in like a SWAT team. Maureen places herself between them, facing Logan with her palms out. In one hand she's holding a syringe, but she doesn't touch Logan. Jamie swings Ethan around and grabs him by the shoulders. Almost instantly, Ethan's eyes go from blazing to calm, and a shiver runs up Jamie's spine. It's eerie. Logan sits on her own bed and rolls up her sleeve. Maureen injects her. In a few seconds, Logan's eyes glass over, and she curls into a ball by her pillow, her face a picture of emptiness. It makes my heart hurt.

Jamie drops his hands and his head, and lowers himself onto my bed, next to and above where I'm half-sprawled on the floor. Ethan drops on the other side of me, rubbing his jaw as tears fill his eyes. I expect a complete meltdown, but the spark returns almost immediately. He leans in to whisper in my ear, "Logan knows her! She knows our mom! How is that possible? How can she have memories of OUR mother?"

Jamie answers before I even inhale. "How are you able to see a stranger's past or know the future? How's your sister able to heal people?"

Ethan, never the one to accept an easy answer, wrinkles his nose and sniffs. "Memories are real. Healing is real. Ghosts aren't!"

"How do you know?" Jamie comes back, his eyes dark and angry.

Ethan backs down, though he still shakes his head. He turns to me. "It hurts," he whines as he rubs his chin.

A light knock draws all our attention. Maureen opens the door.

"Cayde!" We all exclaim in unison, like he's Norm in an episode of *Cheers*. He's riding piggyback on Hugo, like he was last night, but he dismounts by rolling over Hugo's bent head and lands on his feet, hands high above his head in the parody of a gymnast.

"Perfect ten from the Russian judge!" Hugo quips. "And the crowd goes wild!" He makes a roar, but Maureen shushes him. He sits on the floor next to Ethan. "What's happening?"

"Don't ask," Jamie says, rubbing his temples.

I stare at Cayde's face. Last night, pus was seeping through the bandage on his left cheek. Now it looks like he might have gotten a little sunburn. My eyes move to his arm, which was much more damaged than his face. The gauze has been replaced by a square Band-Aid. He shows no signs of the pain that wracked him less than twenty-four hours ago. He smiles at me and comes over. "Thanks, Lanie, ya know, for what you did for me." He leans in and gives me an awkward hug. I have no idea what to say. I can't begin to take credit for what he says I did. It's just too much. My heart begins to beat in my throat and a tremor in my hands is spreading up my arms. I push him away and rise shakily to my feet. "I need some air."

I'm not talking to Jamie in particular, but in an instant he's beside me, not crowding me like everyone else, but, like always, being exactly what I need. "Let's go for a walk," he says.

"I can take the boys swimming," Hugo offers quickly. Then he looks at Cayde and whispers, "Zip line," behind his hand.

"No!" Maureen says sharply. "Those are for us, not them!"

"You've taken Logan," Hugo says.

"Come on," Cayde begs. "I nearly died. I deserve to live!"

"That doesn't even make sense," Maureen says.

Maureen looks at Cayde's and Ethan's hopeful faces. I have to do a double take. I can't imagine Ethan wanting to participate in such an adrenaline-packed activity, but there he is, mumbling, "Please, please, please," beside Cayde.

Maureen relents with a nod and a roll of her eyes. The three boys whoop it up.

Just before they bolt out the door, Ethan tugs on Hugo's arm and whispers in his ear. Hugo nods and stares concertedly at Logan's wall for a few seconds. "I've got it," he says to Ethan, and Ethan asks if he's sure. Hugo shakes his head good-naturedly and shoves Ethan and Cayde through the door. "Last one to the roof eats the green Jell-o with shredded veggie guts at dinner," he shouts.

Maureen rolls her eyes one more time for good measure. "I'm gonna stay with Logan until she wakes up."

I grab some clothes and head into the bathroom to make myself presentable. With the water off, I can hear Jamie and Maureen talking in hushed tones.

"Why do you think Logan freaked?" Jamie asks.

"Who knows? It went better than we thought it would. I don't get what's going on with her. Can you get a read?"

"That's never easy with her, but if I had to guess, I'd say guilt. I think she's getting involved," Jamie says.

"And what about you, Zero?" Maureen asks.

"What about me?" Jamie raises his voice.

"Are you getting involved?"

"Is that what Robineau thinks?" he asks, biting off her name.

"Just asking, man. They're precious. I'd understand if you were." Maureen says.

"Well, I'm not," Jamie's voice is as hard as an iron bar.

"Fine," Maureen says.

"Stop worrying about me and get your girl under control. That was just round one," Jamie says.

They stop talking, so I turn on the water to brush my teeth. My mind is bouncing around like a laser light show. Why did she call him Zero? What does that even mean? Jamie's little preparation speech is gnawing at me, too. What if the whole accident was staged for some reason? Maybe Cayde wasn't even hurt. I shake my head to clear that thought. I know what I felt when I wanted to heal him. I know that was real. What are they playing at in this place? The suspicion in my mind tightens the knot in my belly again. It's threatening to strangle me from within.

Jamie would never hurt us. I feel sure of this. I focus on the picnics at the beach and the memory of his gentle eyes. I can trust Jamie. He must be stringing Maureen and Dr. Robineau along, pretending to play their game.

By the time we get out of the building, I'm winded and tired. Jamie leads me to a bench in the garden. All the things I need to ask him hammer against the inside of my skull, but when he puts his arm around me and I lean into his chest, where I can hear the gentle thud of his heart, they melt away, leaving only the peace of this moment, with the wind rustling the leaves of the trees, the squirrels chattering high above, the smell of Jamie's soap and the warmth of his body touching mine at numerous points. If I were a cat, I'd purr.

"You were amazing last night," Jamie says. "I've never seen anything like that."

I'm glad he can't see my face. "Surely you've seen things here —" My voice trails off. I realize I don't want to know what he's seen. I don't even want to know what I've seen. "Can we not talk about it? I'm not sure what I did or why or how, and I really don't want to know."

He turns me around. "Elena, you can't turn away from it. You need to explore it, develop it, be proud of it. I've been here a long time and no one we've tested has come close to doing anything like what you did. Think of the possibilities!" His face flushes with fervor as he talks, and his eyes are almost envious.

My stomach flips over and the taste of bile rises in my mouth. I look down. "Jamie, it almost killed me. I don't ever want to do that again." I pull away from him and start walking. I can't look at his face.

I hear his footsteps behind me, but he doesn't talk for a long time. "What was it like?" he finally asks.

I don't turn around. "What?" I'm pretty sure he's not talking about healing.

He's silent for a couple of beats, but his desire to know wins out over his fear of saying the word aloud. "Death."

I stop walking and turn to face him. "Why would you ask me that?"

He drops his eyes and shakes his head. "I don't know."

Instead of telling him, I say, "There comes a point where the pain can be so bad, when the hole gets so deep, that the only peace imaginable is an end of some kind. But some other kind of end might be what you really need; not the ultimate end to all of it."

He looks so tired, beyond even tears. I put my hand on the side of his face, and he leans into it, kissing my palm.

"It won't work, Elena. You know it won't work on me."

I think back on all the times I tried to help him. "So, what's your superpower, Jamie?" I whisper.

He walks away. He's not going to break the rules for me, not now at least. I know he has an ability now, and I'd bet my last nickel Hugo and Maureen do, too.

When I get back, Logan's awake. She and Maureen are painting Logan's wall with black chalkboard paint. A huge box of chalk and two erasers sit on Logan's dresser. They don't acknowledge my presence, so I take a page out of Logan's book and stick my earbuds in and close my eyes.

That night I lay awake, tracing a path through the stars on my ceiling, identifying the constellations Jamie placed there for me to find and loving that he did that for me. I want to go to Jamie now on the astral train, but I'm restrained by the knowledge that he'll somehow see the footprints I leave. Instead, I decide to try to contact my mother. I assumed that the reason I felt her was that I was dead or dying, but what if having access to the astral plane gives me access to her? I have to try.

Riding the train is getting easier. I can leave my physical body behind within seconds. Once I'm out, though, I have no idea how to go about finding her. I'm moving through the astral plane, and she's here somewhere on it. I reject that concept; it's too limiting. The astral plane is spiritual, not physical. I concentrate my energy on the memories I have of her. I hear her singing to us when we were little. She was always singing. I like to think she passed that gift to me, and when I sing, I'm somehow channeling her. The feeling of the music in my throat and mouth moves my heart toward her. I remember her smell, like almond and cream. I see her gray eyes every time I look at my brother's and the echoes of her face appear each time I look in a mirror. Pangs of loss and loneliness for her pierce my chest and make my stomach and throat ache.

Then, suddenly, she's there. I can't see her, but I feel her presence, at once calming and enervating. "Mama," I call into the void.

"Lanie Lou, how I love you," comes back. She was the only one who ever called me that. Her essence surrounds me, more completely than a hug. I could drown in her, stay forever. But far away I hear another voice, a physical voice, and he's weeping, distraught, torn and broken. Ethan. I don't want to leave. He'll be fine. He'll be fine. My mother's singing in my head, creating a warm sensation that starts in the center of my chest and spreads outward, down to my toes and up through the top of my head. My mind's numbing over.

"Lanie. Lanie. Please wake up!"

I fight against the pull of the living. Death might not be so bad if this is what it is.

"Lanie!" Ethan's cries are so close; I can't bear hearing them. How could I be so selfish? I untangle myself from the dream, thread by thread. Somehow, I find myself again and return to the physical.

Ethan's in my bed, curled up facing me, with his thumb in his mouth. His cheeks are streaked with the tracks of tears, and his breath comes ragged and hard. He opens his eyes moments after I open mine. This is the old Ethan, four-year-old Ethan. I haven't seen him like this in a long time.

"Nightmare?" I ask, sitting up and brushing sun-streaked curls from his face. He needs a haircut again.

He nods, his eyes growing wide with the memory of a dream he won't share. "Can I sleep with you?" he asks. When I hesitate, he adds, "My bed's all wet."

I look over at Logan. Her back is to us. Her breathing's heavy and regular. "How did you get in?" I whisper.

"Cayde helped me." He takes his thumb out to answer the question. "Please, Lanie." His voice trembles. I nod and lay back down beside him. He takes a deep breath, and I can feel tremors move through his body as he exhales.

"That must have been some dream."

"Not a dream," he mumbles. When I don't respond, he opens his eyes.

I know it's against our unwritten code, but I have a feeling it's time for me to face this, whatever it is. "What does that mean?" I ask.

He sits up crisscross and puts his hands on his knees. I sit up facing him and take his hands in mine. I close my eyes and lean in, until our foreheads are nearly touching.

I feel the door to his mind open slowly. "Dr. Robineau is using us," he begins.

"Of course, she is." I'm not an entire idiot. I try to keep the snarkiness out of my thoughts, but I can't help feeling a little condescended to.

"No, Lanie. You don't know!" I'm surprised by his anger. "She hurt Cayde on purpose. She did it to push you. To make you heal him."

I have no response. I know he's right. It fits with Jamie and Maureen's conversation. "What about you? What you did last night."

He pulls away, slams the door. I open my eyes and he's staring at me. "There's more coming," he says. "They aren't nightmares. It's gonna get bad, Lanie. Really bad." His eyes fill up and the trembling starts again.

"It's going to be okay, E. Jamie's watching out for us. I promise it'll be okay. It's a science lab. How bad can it be, baby?" A small whine of frustration comes from his throat before he looks away. He wipes his eyes with the backs of his hands and lays down. I lay down, too, watching him suck his thumb furiously as he fights the tears. Finally, he rolls over. I do, too, so we're lying back to back, attached like we were in the womb.

"Sweet dreams, little bro," I whisper.

"Sweet dreams, littler sis," he tosses back in his ragged voice. I'm glad he's not stuck at four any more, but I'm terrified that he might be right about the road we're on. Still, for some reason it's easier to sleep with Ethan there beside me.

The next morning isn't pretty. Logan's standing over the bed. At first it looks like she's watching Ethan sleep. Her face is all soft and her expression borders on tenderness. But it must be my imagination because I barely have time to inhale before she's pelting us with chalkboard erasers and chalk. Then the yelling starts.

"Get your disgusting, scrawny, diaper-wearing ass OUT OF MY ROOM!" Ethan pretty much falls out of the bed, onto the floor at her feet. Logan jumps back, like touching him is going to give her Ebola, as Ethan scrambles backward, crab-style, toward the door. He reaches up to open the door and realizes he can't; he doesn't know the code. A look of unparalleled terror crosses his face, and I'm supremely relieved that his scrawny ass is wearing a diaper at the moment. Logan screams 78892114 at the top of her voice, and the lock clicks. Ethan pulls himself to his feet and bolts from the room, like it's about to explode.

I wait for Logan's breathing to return to human. Then I ask quietly, "Why do you hate Ethan so much?"

She spins around, like I just challenged her to a fight. "I thought we were clear. Boys aren't allowed in this room."

"He had a nightmare. He needed me. Why are you so weirded out by him?"

"I don't like him, and for the record, I don't like you either."

"Yeah," I say. "That's why you chased me down on the astral plane and pissed off all the ghosts by dragging me back."

"Whatever," she says.

Maureen breaks it up by walking in. "Breakfast time, chickies. You're with us this morning, Elena." Logan makes a face at me, but I smile sweetly back. Maybe that's it, I think. Maybe she doesn't hate Ethan. Maybe she likes him and is trying to hide it. Hmm.

I plan to test out my theory at breakfast, but Ethan doesn't show up. I try hard not to panic, but I have a really bad feeling because I can't "hear" him either. Maureen walks me back to the room after we eat, then heads out with Logan, locking me in.

It takes me about seven seconds to hit the astral express. I try to concentrate on Ethan, but the silence from his end is deafening. Panic begins to overtake me. I yell for him in my mind and scramble from physical location to physical location. He's not at the pool or in his room. I even check the closet. I'm so desperate I risk going into Dr. Robineau's office, but it's empty. Sobs threaten to wrack my body and pull me back into the physical plane, but I fight them off, deciding to find Jamie instead. I'm off-balance now, and I can't tear my mind from the search for my brother. It's finally the memory of Jamie's smell that leads me to him, and I find him standing right outside my door, punching in the code to enter. I memorize it: 78892114. By the time he steps through the door, I'm back in my body with my eyes open.

"You ready to go?" Jamie asks.

"Go where?" I ask as calmly as I can.

"We're working with Dr. Meriwether today, at her office on base." He smiles, like this is just another day.

"I need to give my brother something. Can we stop by his room?" I keep my voice honey-sweet.

Jamie looks me up and down. "Did he leave something here last night?" The last two words are hard and unyielding.

"Jamie, he was scared. He needed me."

"You know the rules and so does he. He broke the rules." Jamie looks over my head with eyes of ice. "We need to leave now, or we're going to be late."

"What did you do to him? Where is he?" My throat's getting tight and blood's pounding in my ears. "You might as well tell me because I'm not going until you do." I sit down on the edge of the bed, with my arms crossed over my chest.

Jamie looks down at me and starts laughing. "Really, Elena? How old are you? Like, four?" He reaches for my hand, but his words sting, and I don't move.

"I can't feel him, and I need to know he's okay!"

Jamie's smile dissolves. He squats in front of me and puts a hand on my knee, like he's talking to a small child. "I'm sorry. I shouldn't have made light. He's all right. Dr. Robineau's working with him in a controlled lab several floors below this one. She probably gave him something that's blocking his telepathy with you. He's fine. I just saw him thirty minutes ago."

I want to believe him. "What's going to happen to him? For breaking the rules, I mean."

"Dr Robineau and I talked to him during breakfast. We're going to start a behavior modification program to reward him for staying in his room at night. Of course, there will be consequences if he doesn't."

"What does that mean? What kind of consequences?" I demand.

Jamie looks confused. "We aren't going to beat him or anything. I think Dr. Robineau settled on restricting his swimming."

"What's she doing to him in that lab?" I fight to hold onto my conviction, despite the calm that's inexplicably creeping over me, covering me like a fuzzy blanket.

"We have observation rooms down there for more controlled experiments. Nothing sinister, I promise." He smiles again and dips his head apologetically. "Can we go now? Please."

I have no more fight left, so I take his hand when he offers it and let him lead me to the car.

Today we meet in Dr. Meriwether's office on base. She greets us with her usual warmth and offers me peppermint tea, my favorite. After we get settled in the tiny space, Jamie doesn't leave like he usually does. I have a bad feeling about that.

The first patient comes in on crutches. She's a young recruit in basic training. Lydia's frustrated about being held back from participating with her unit because of a sprained ankle. Dr. Meriwether lets her talk and talk about how angry the injury makes her. She and Jamie keep looking at me, waiting for me to offer my "talent" to help her, and a part of me wants to. I know a sprained ankle is nothing like third degree burns, but logic doesn't stand a chance against the terror of the memory of the last time I healed someone's physical ills. When the fifty therapeutic minutes are up, Lydia leaves no better off than when she arrived. I shake my hands to try to relieve the strange tingling that started in them halfway through the session.

Two hours pass painfully as two more young soldiers come in with angst and minor injuries. My throat and eyes start to burn from holding in my emotion. When the second one leaves, I excuse myself, too. Hard as it is to hear their stories and see their physical discomfort, it would be harder still to open myself up to this thing inside me. I go to the bathroom to splash my face and rinse my hands, to quell the tingling I feel.

I stare myself down in the mirror, trying desperately to understand what Jamie sees when he looks at me. Sadly, even I can see the fear shining out of my eyes today. Surely Jamie and Dr. Meriwether must understand.

Jamie's waiting in the hall when I come out. "What do you think you're doing, Elena?" Jamie asks, barely concealing his frustration.

"Nothing," I say, putting up my guard.

"Exactly! You're doing nothing. Are you really that much of a coward?"

I hate that word coming from his mouth. I hang my head. "I guess so."

He looks up at the ceiling in exasperation. "There's nothing to be afraid of."

"Really?" He's starting to piss me off.

"Elena, you've been doing this for weeks now. Nothing has changed. Nothing."

"You don't understand," I say. "How could you possibly understand anything about this?" I push past him.

He grabs my upper arm and whispers in my ear, "There are few people on this planet that could understand better than I. Fear and I are old friends. The only way to deal with that demon is to take it by the balls and tell it where to get off."

I shake free. "You just said 'balls.' How am I supposed to take this seriously when you say things like that?"

He hangs his head. "I suck at this, don't I?"

"Kind of," I say. "But you don't exactly have the easiest of mentorees, or whatever they call us."

"True," he says without smiling.

"Hey! You aren't supposed to agree." I punch his arm hard.

"Ouch! You got a mean right hook there, Ali."

"Sorry." Now I'm smiling, and I feel suddenly like I can do anything.

"You ready to go back in there and show our friend, Fear, that fighting spirit?" he asks.

I shake my head. "Could you be a little dorkier? Yeah. Didn't think so." I lead the way back to Dr. Meriwether's office. I don't need to turn around to know Jamie's smiling. I can feel it behind my back.

The next boy who comes in is a little trickier. He's small and shy like Ethan. He's there because he got beat up by some other guys in his squadron. They claimed they were punishing him for being slow and weak, for bringing the whole squad down. I don't need to ask to know the real reason. I'm not sure I would even be tolerated on this base if they knew about me and Jo. What I don't get is why this boy joined the military, of all things. A big part of me wants to help him escape through the kitchen and out the back door, but being here is a lot like being at PSI; once you sign that contract, only an act of God or nature can get you out clean.

He walks into the room slowly and pauses to make eye contact with each of us, smiling wanly and holding out his bandaged hand. His left eye is several shades of blue, yellow, and purple, and his lip is sliced in two places. Other, less spectacular bruises are visible on his arms and face. When he sits down, he holds his gut and winces.

"How are you feeling today, Ash?" Dr. Meriwether asks kindly.

"I moved back into the barracks last night," he says, instead of answering the question.

"How did that go?" she asks.

Ash looks away and his glasses slip down his nose a little. He doesn't bother to push them up. "I just don't understand what I did to make these guys hate me. I'm faster than Fat Freddy, and I climb the goddamn ropes and barricades now. They act like my presence is a personal affront to their manhood. Fucking idiots!" He glances up, like he suddenly remembers I'm in the room. "Pardon my French, Miss."

I smile and wave my hand. "My French is much more colorful, trust me."

Ash attempts a real smile, but his split lip prevents it from stretching across his face. He leans closer to me. "I sincerely doubt that."

"I think I knew those guys in high school," I say. "They were the ones who felt sure one kiss from their very special lips would be enough to convince me to play for their team."

Ash's eyes light up. "Finally, someone I can really talk to." For a second, I think he might cry. "You aren't military, are you?"

I shake my head. "But I know what it feels like to be alone in a crowd of people who are all bigger and meaner than I am."

He takes in my stature and smiles.

I get up and move to the seat next to his.

"What're you going to do?" I ask, opening my hands and offering them to the boy. He takes them immediately and almost instantly the walls blush a deep red. I allow his anger to seep through my pores and electrify my spinal cord. His anger gives way to frustration and, finally, self-loathing. He relaxes under my touch as his emotions are released and relieved. I feel them filter through my skin and nerve endings in a comforting, normal-for-me way.

I'm almost done, but I can't let go of the thought that I can take away his physical pain, too. I feel a strange vibration, sort of like the one that happens when I astral project, but slower and steady, at a lower frequency. I want to let go, but I can't somehow. The vibration picks up in speed and intensity. Suddenly, my hands and face begin to ache. A sharp stab to my ribs makes me gasp. Ash doesn't notice. He has no idea what's happening, but I do, and I can't stop it. The pain doubles me over as the vibration becomes a high-pitched hum in my ears. I try to call out to Jamie, but I can't speak. My field of vision suddenly narrows to black and all I can hear is the deafening hum of white noise. I'm slipping from this plane.

I concentrate on the only real world sense I have left: the nauseatingly cloying scent of the eucalyptus that Dr. Meriwether keeps on the window sill. I count to twenty, imagining the numbers as pins tacking me to this plane. Eventually, the sounds from the hallway come back into focus. Ash's bandaged hand rests heavily in my own sweaty palm. Gradually, the light from the window pierces the darkness, and I feel the weight of my spirit inhabiting my body again.

Ash's consciousness returns at the same time as mine. He pulls away awkwardly, and his cheeks flush. "Sorry," he says. "I guess I zoned out there for a minute. What was I saying?"

I shrug and slump back into the chair with my eyes closed. I could sleep for a hundred years. Ash's voice close to my ear opens my eyes. "Thank you." He leans back a little. "I guess talking to someone who really understands helps more than I thought it would."

I can't speak or move my jaw. His lip and black eye are completely healed. No one would ever suspect he'd been in a fight. I shift my gaze to Jamie, whose expression likely mirrors my own. Dr. Meriwether is glancing from me to Ash and writing furiously in a notebook. A smile plays at the corners of her lips.

A wave of nausea hits me like a tsunami, and I bolt into the hall and lose my breakfast in a trashcan. I press my forehead to the cool, concrete block wall and concentrate on breathing. I hear the door click and feel a warm hand on my back. "Amazing!" he whispers in my ear. I can't speak. I let him help me back into Dr. Meriwether's office, where I collapse onto the tiny sofa and curl into a ball. I can barely keep my eyes open, but I fight to hear what's happening.

"Ash, I think you should go back with Jamie and Elena to PSI, so the doctors there can check you out." Ash is holding a mirror up, examining his face.

"Uh — okay. You think they might be able to tell me what the hell that girl just did to me?"

"They might," Dr. Meriwether says, but there's a laugh in her voice, like this might be little inside joke. My eyes fall shut, and the world begins to fall away.

"Hey, is she alright?" Ash's voice.

"She just needs some rest," Jamie returns.

A few seconds or minutes later, I feel strong arms lifting me up and carrying me like a child, for a long, or maybe not so long, time. Then there's a gentle hum and swaying movement. Finally, Jamie's shaking me gently. "Elena, wake up. We're home."

"Sage will be so surprised. I hope you called ahead so Jo will be here," I mumble in my fog.

"PSI, Elena. We're at PSI. Come on, wakey wakey. Can you walk?"

"Don't be ridiculous! Of course, I can walk," I slur, but I have no idea if I really can. I feel weak, like maybe I've been beaten up or very sick for days. I manage to pull myself to sitting and swing my legs out of the car. Jamie takes my hand to help me out, and I come to standing, albeit precariously. When I take my first step, I stumble, but a nice boy catches me. His eyes are so very blue, like the sky, and he smiles, though his brow's furrowed. His John Lennon glasses slip down his nose. I swear I know him from somewhere.

Suddenly, Jamie's grabbing me by the arm and bending down. A second later, I'm flipping upside down, and I realize he's carrying me like a sack of potatoes over his shoulder. "Remind me never to get you drunk, Paige," he mumbles through clenched teeth.

"OMG! Put me down right now, Mr. freaking Fleming. This is uncomfortable and undignified, and my face is in your very cute butt. Oh, shit, did I say that out loud? Did you get me drunk?"

The nerdy boy's giggling. "Bet she's fun at parties," he says.

"I wouldn't know," Jamie says wryly.

"I don't play for that team," I say. Then I remember who the boy is and why we're all here like this. I want to scream at him to run, but it's too late. The first set of glass doors has closed behind us and Jamie's reciting his security protocol. I go limp over Jamie's back, defeated by the thought of having dragged another innocent boy into this nightmare.

As my mind works its way over what they might possibly do to Ash, I have a devastating realization. Ash has been brought here to be worked over by Ethan. If my powers are being pushed — and they are — then the same must be happening to my brother. Robineau is using us both for some warped agenda. I resolve to get to the bottom of all of this, but no sooner does this determination cross my mind than it evaporates like smoke, replaced by a strange, warm fantasy of what Jamie's sweet butt might look like, sans the army fatigues. Nothing could possibly be wrong here. What was I thinking? And while I'm at it, what team am I playing for again?

Finally, Jamie puts me down in a chair in the lobby. Ash sits beside me while Jamie goes to the reception desk to powwow with the pretty people. "What is this place?" he asks.

"I'm not really sure how to answer that," I say, awash in the glow of my first impressions again. Another, much darker thought is creeping over my shoulder, and it nearly makes it into my head, but Jamie returns, and poof, all's well again. I resist the urge to throw my arms around his neck.

Jamie's voice brings me back to earth. "Elena, Maureen is coming to help you back to your room. I'm going to take Ash to meet Dr. Robineau. I'll catch up with you at dinner, okay?" I nod, but it isn't okay at all. I need Jamie to bring me to Ethan. The minute I think about him, my mind reaches out on its own to connect, but just like this morning, I come up empty. As the physical distance from Jamie grows, so does my certainty that something is horribly, desperately wrong.

Susan Michalski

℘ 11 ℘

HEADED FOR A BREAKDOWN

Baseball bat comes swinging
Shatters bone like ice
Breaks through my defenses
Through all that kind advice
Dig my heals in too slowly
The ground is made of rock
Losing hold so quickly
Are you ready for the shock?
Nothin' to do, nothin' to say
Can't hold it together anyway
Headed for a breakdown
Shards flying all around
"Broken" - Luna Rayne - 2013

By the time we get into the elevator, I'm halfway to hysterical. Maureen keeps telling me to calm down. Her assurances that Ethan is fine are hollow and unconvincing. The only thing that keeps me from flying apart at the seams is the knowledge that somewhere in her possession is a syringe that will put me down for hours. Hours I could be using to figure out this mess and find my brother. I know she's sent out an SOS to Jamie, but I doubt he'll be here anytime soon. I'm sure Dr. Robineau will need a thorough report. Maureen keys in the code to open the room. I try desperately to see what digits she's typing, but no dice. Logan's sprawled out on the floor doing crunches when we walk in.

"Are you alright?" she asks.

"Fucking peachy, considering that my brother's probably dead or unconscious, and the only thing anyone will tell me is to calm down." I drop down on the bed. A push of adrenaline hits up against the exhaustion that's still heavy in my bones.

Logan stops mid-crunch to consider me, with one eyebrow raised.

Maureen exchanges glances with her.

"I'm fine!" I scream. "Just get the hell out of my damn prison cell!" I pull my pillow into my lap and wrap my arms around it. Tears of frustration burn against my lids, but I will not give these bitches the satisfaction.

Maureen crouches down in front of me, so we're eye to eye. She puts a hand on my arm. "Elena, I promise you that Ethan isn't dead or dying. Dr. Robineau won't let anything happen to either of you. You and Ethan are more important to her than you know, to all of us here. If you want me to give you something to make this easier, I can."

I shift my gaze to Logan. She nods, encouraging me to take what Maureen's offering.

"I said, I'm fine." I stare Logan down.

Maureen nods, puts a bottle of water on the dresser, hands another to Logan and leaves. The pillow I throw hits the door just before it clicks closed, locking me in.

"Temper. Temper. You should've taken the drugs," Logan says, opening the water bottle and taking two long draws.

"Bite me, bitch!" I say before I can consider the consequences, but the moment the words are out, I remember I'm locked in here with Logan, a girl almost twice my size, with a giant chip of mean on her shoulder. I want to suck the words back in, but Logan just goes back to her crunches, without even tossing me a glance.

I watch her for a few minutes, letting the steam from my frustration dissipate. As I watch, it occurs to me that being locked in with her might be just what I need right now.

"What're you staring at?" Logan's voice startles me.

"I was just wondering what they do to you."

She shakes her head, glancing almost imperceptibly at the camera. "What do they do to you?"

Shit! Why do I always forget about that damn camera? I'd climb on the chair and disable it, but I'd never be able to reach it, being as vertically challenged as I am. I shrug my shoulders, weighing the possible punishment against my need for information. Even if I tell her, there's no guarantee she'll give me anything. On the other hand, she saved my life. It cost her in some way, but she did it anyway. Maybe she's more on my side than I think. I wonder why she doesn't disable the damn thing. I know she can, or at least she can get her "friends" to.

I motion toward the closet. "You wanna see the new stuff I got?"

She gets up off the floor. "Jamie takes you shopping? Are you blowing him?"

"No! And gross! That's just nasty!" We both start giggling like junior high girls. She gets what I have in mind. We go into the closet, and I rattle the hangers.

I talk fast in a whisper. "They take me to the army base near here. I work with a therapist named Meriwether. At first, I was just supposed to heal the emotional stuff, like I do. You know? Now, because of Cayde, they want more. I healed a kid that got beat up by his platoon. Then they brought him here."

I can't read her expression in the half-dark. "Well, I'm no fashionista or anything, but that's about the ugliest dress I've ever seen. Jamie pick it out or you?" Her voice is loud enough for the camera's microphone to pick it up.

"Thanks," I say with less sarcasm than might be expected.

"Let's just say you got it easy, girl. The rest of us, Cayde, me, and your brother" — she won't say his name — "They take us to the labs. Pump us up with steroids for the brain and god knows what else to see what we can do." She's whispering so low I barely catch it all.

"Does it hurt?" I'm not sure why, but it's the first thing that pops into my head.

Logan steps back. "The only thing uglier than that dress is those shoes. Have you lost your mind?" Her voice drops to a whisper "Sometimes." Her eyes are soft, and they don't break from mine. She doesn't ask me back because she knows what it does to me.

"Where is it, the lab?" It's the last question I'll get as we move back into the room.

She shrugs. She doesn't know, but she can get there because she has no need of trains or psychic twin connections. I take the bottle of water off the dresser and open it. I'm so thirsty, hungry, and tired, I could cry.

"I guess I need some serious help!" I whine, hoping she catches my meaning.

"You're asking for my help?" Logan's nothing if not quick. I hope whoever's watching us isn't.

"It's not like there's any choice," I say.

"Sure, there is. There's always a choice." Logan watches closely as I gulp the water. Then she looks away from me. "You better be damn sure you make the right one because redemption's a long time coming in a place like this."

I wonder if she's talking about her decision to save me, or something else she wants to be redeemed from. I glance up at her wall. It's nearly whitewashed with chalk erasures, so her friends are still in contact. I miss the cacophony of symbols that used to remain etched in the paint. I wonder if Ethan ever figured out what they meant, and if he'll ever get a chance to tell me. I wonder if Logan has "talked" to our mother, and if she knows what's happening to him. I wonder if she watches us, protects us, or even cares. What if her spirit is as crazy in death as it was in life and all she wants is for us to join her? I shudder a little.

"Well, I might not make the best fashion choices on the planet, but I'm pretty sure they're the right ones for me," I say, offering her a drink from my water.

Logan shakes her head and smiles a kind of half-smirk. "It always feels that way, doesn't it? You never realize your mistakes until you take them home and try them on in the light of day."

I still don't know if she's onboard. Truth be told, I'm not even sure what her help would look like anyway. I lie back on my pillows and stare up at the stars. Time for an astral trip. Stellar idea, I tell myself and giggle a little. I'm feeling sort of dizzy, and the stars seem to be moving closer and closer, like the ceiling's coming down to crush me or I'm floating up toward it. I choose to focus on the second option. Much less morose. I giggle again. Then I float up, up, and away.

I wake up to large, wet lips pressed against mine. "What the —!"

Cayde falls backward into a sort of somersault that fails halfway through, so he ends up in a giggling heap. "Sleeping Beauty awakens to her prince's kiss," he quips in something approximating a British accent.

Logan tries hard not to smile. "You ever try that with me, you'll be walking with a cane for the rest of your pitiful life."

"Noted," he says to her. Then he turns to me. "Arise, fair maiden, and come into my —"

"Stop right there!" I say. "No one's coming into anything. And yuck and yuck and yuck again."

Cayde's smile drops. "Aw, now you're just being mean."

I look around the room. "Where's Ethan?"

Cayde looks at Logan.

"Cayde, I asked you the question. Why are you looking at her?"

He turns back to me, but he doesn't speak.

"Come on, you guys. Tell me what you know. Please. He's not exactly special forces. He's like a little kid. He needs me."

Cayde looks at Logan again, then up at the camera. He closes his eyes, and the room's silent for a long ten seconds. Then he opens his eyes. "I'm gonna do it; I gotta," he says to Logan.

"Don't be an idiot!" Logan comes back, sitting up straighter.

"Um," I clear my throat loudly and look up at the camera.

"He disabled it," Logan says. "Telekinesis."

"It works better on small stuff, sometimes. Today anyway." Cayde turns to Logan again and adds, "Like computers."

"You're both gonna get caught, and then all bets are off." Logan crosses her arms over her chest for emphasis.

"Not if you don't narc us out," Cayde says. "I can do this clean. No one will ever know."

"You always say that, and you always fuck up. You really want to take your little girlfriend down that rabbit hole with you?"

Cayde puffs himself up. "She deserves to know. I can do this. All you need to do is keep your big mouth shut."

I'm a little stunned by the way Cayde's standing up to Logan, but I'm even more surprised when she backs down.

"Have it your way, but don't come crying to me."

"Wouldn't dream of it," Cayde says. Then he turns back to me and pulls an iPad from under the back of his pants and shirt, like he's doing a magic trick.

"What? How?" I stammer as he grins widely.

"If I told you, I'd have to kiss you," he quips leaning in.

I pull back, and he shrugs, plopping down on the floor with his back against my bed. I watch from above as he boots up and handily hacks the intranet. He types in something that makes no sense to me, closes his eyes and waits. At first, it seems like nothing's happening. The white curser just blinks at the end of the line of characters on the black screen. Then the thing goes nuts. Pages and pages of code scroll by so fast I can't read a single character. Then the black box closes itself and a video program like YouTube on steroids pops open, their camera system. Cayde selects one of the squares.

Ethan's on the screen, dressed only in gray drawstring scrub pants. He's in a small sterile white cell with a bed, a couple of chairs, some cabinets, and a sink, like a doctor's office or a hospital room. A time stamp at the top of the screen shows that the video was taken hours ago. He's hiding behind one of the chairs, peering out and glancing furtively over his shoulder every few seconds. My heart lurches in my chest. He must be terrified by whatever's happening in there to be hiding like that. The camera pans in, and the sound comes on.

"Just wait," he says to no one behind him. "He'll be here." There's no tremor in his voice. "He's coming. Now!" he says and breaks from behind the chair. He runs across the room as far as the limited space will take him.

"What's he doing?" I ask Cayde. He shrugs, his eyes wide with confusion. Logan has come around behind the bed. She's leaning over, watching as raptly as Cayde. I force my eyes back to the screen when Ethan's voice rings out again.

"Hurry, Lanie! Hurry!" He leaps onto the chair and climbs up onto the arms, and then the back. He's poised precariously there, reaching back down beside him for someone he can see, but we can't. "Take my hand. I'll pull you up." His voice is urgent and higher pitched now.

"He's hallucinating!" I say. "What the hell are they giving him? PCP?"

Logan and Cayde both shake their heads.

"Not hallucinating," Cayde mumbles, almost awestruck.

"Are you watching the same thing I am?" I nearly screech.

Logan puts a hand on my shoulder. "He's not awake. Look at the monitor."

In the background beside the bed is a monitor with three kinds of colored lines spiking up and down and scrolling left at a steady rate. "What's it measuring?" I ask.

"Brain waves," she says. "See the blue lines? Those are delta waves. They happen when someone's in a deep sleep." She's talking to me, but her focus never wavers from the screen.

Now Ethan has climbed back down off the chair, and he's crouching on the ground. "There's no time for that, Lanie! He can make it. Finn, get up! You can make it! Come on!" He reaches down and struggles with an imaginary Finn. "Just climb over the wall, please." His desperation plays out in the delicate features of his face, and beads of sweat trickle down his naked chest and back. His breathing gets more and more labored as he climbs slowly back up onto the chair.

"So, this is a dream?" I can't wrap my head around this. "That makes no sense. He doesn't sleepwalk. This can't be a dream!"

"Yeah. Not exactly a dream," Cayde mumbles. "Flip-side of every superpower."

"What?!"

Logan touches me again. "He messes with people's memories, sees the past when he touches you. Right?"

"How do you know that?"

"This is Ethan's flip side. He's seeing the future." Her tone's quiet and patient, not Logan-like at all.

I feel distinctly like I've stepped into some warped, parallel universe. In a minute, I'm going to wake up next to Sage and say, "I just had the weirdest dream." I press my palms to my lids and concentrate on waking up. Ethan's voice screaming my name pulls me back into the nightmare that seems to be my reality for the moment.

"Lanie!" He's reaching down, groping like he can't catch something that's falling away from him. Suddenly, the chair topples over, and he crashes to the concrete floor. A line of crimson opens on his forehead, and I jump up, like there's something I can do from here.

The nurse, Cindy, from the first day, rushes in along with a guy I've never seen, who scoops Ethan up and deposits him on the bed. Ethan's hand goes to the cut, and he smears the blood across his face. I suck in air and swallow a sob rising in my throat. Cindy gently moves his hand, cleans off the smear and dabs at the wound. She gets up and goes to the cabinet. Ethan rolls onto his side and sucks his thumb. He's whimpering softly. I'm relieved he's not unconscious. Cindy goes around to the other side of the bed and works on his head, talking to him low and sweet until his whimpering stops. When she's done, she brushes the curls from his face in a gesture of pure affection.

The feed flickers, and another one comes up. It's Cayde this time. Same type of room, but with differently colored walls and chairs. I expect him to work his magic and change the feed again, but I think he's forgotten that Logan and I are in the room. On the screen, Cayde's sitting in a chair with his feet flat on the floor and his hands on the armrests. Dr. Robineau stands sentinel-like beside him. An array of objects lies on the floor around the room: a beach ball, a balsa wood plane, jacks and playing cards. Cayde's staring intently at the ball. As we watch, the ball rises into the air slowly.

"Good, Cayde," Dr. Robineau says. "Now move it toward the door." The ball moves in fits and starts in that general direction. Cayde's face is set and serious, completely devoid of its usual animation. "Now, bounce three times, then suspend it from the ceiling." One. Two. Three. Four. Five. And up to the ceiling the ball goes.

"Okay," Dr. Robineau says wryly. "We clearly need to work on your math skills." A slight smile plays on Cayde's lips. "Now, keep the ball there and send the jacks to me one at a time." All of the jacks rise at once and begin moving randomly around the room. They pick up velocity, and their movement becomes more erratic. Then the ball begins to bounce, hard, like someone's slamming it into the ground. The red waves on the monitor behind Cayde's chair begin to spike at random intervals.

"Cayde! Stop this now." Dr. Robineau's voice is stern, but not panicked. She slowly extracts a syringe from the pocket of her lab coat and holds it poised. "Cayde, stop. If you don't stop, someone will get hurt." Her voice is ice.

The playing cards join the jacks in their free-for-all. Cayde's shaking as he tries to control the objects. The ball flies into the doctor, beaning her on the side of her face. Behind me, Logan stifles a laugh. In the next second, Robineau's jabbing the needle into Cayde's neck. The jacks fly wildly, embedding themselves in the walls all around the room. Everything else falls to the floor in the same instant and for several seconds the only thing moving is the beach ball as it bounces to its inevitable conclusion. Then Cayde slumps forward in the chair and Dr. Robineau leaves the room. The screen goes black.

"Shit," I say, looking at Cayde with new eyes. He's still staring at the screen. "You okay? I ask.

He nods. "Man, that's so fucked up. I didn't realize until just now how jacked up they got me down there."

I put a hand on his shoulder and take the iPad from him

Suddenly, the feed blinks back on. Ethan's dressed in purple scrubs now. He's sitting on a chair across from Dr. Robineau. The time stamp is only a couple of hours ago. Ethan's legs are drawn up in front of him on the chair, and he's rocking back and forth. His forehead rests on his knees.

"Ethan, all you need to do is adjust one small memory in Private Lake's mind. It should be very simple for you. You've done it before. If you do this, Ethan, I'll take you to see Elena. Okay?"

Ethan's head shoots up when she says my name. I expect him to accept her reasonable offer, but he shakes his head. "No! You bring Elena here NOW. I'm not doing that until I talk to her." He drops his head again. I have to blink back the tears of pride and fear for my twin. It takes a second to sink in that Lake is Ash's last name.

"Ethan," Dr. Robineau says in her frigid tone. "If you don't do it, you won't see her again for a very, very long time. Do you understand me? You need to do this to protect her."

"Bullshit! You can't send her away. You need her here," Ethan mumbles.

Dr. Robineau's face changes then, as the heat of anger creeps into her cheeks. She slides forward in her chair, then reaches over and forces Ethan's chin up so they are eye to eye, no more than a couple of inches apart. He tries to pull away from her, but her grip's strong. The skin on either side of his mouth is white where her fingers dig in. Tears well up in his eyes.

"Don't test me, little boy," Robineau says. "Do as you're told or suffer the consequences." Ethan looks away, and the tears spill over. She releases him, and he puts his thumb in his mouth. She stands up and hovers over him threateningly. "Remember, Mr. Paige, anything you divulge about PSI puts this young man in danger. Just do your job and don't be foolish!"

"He's ready now," she says to someone beyond the camera lens.

"Bring in the soldier."

The nurse, Cindy, leads Ash in gently and indicates that he should sit in the chair that Dr. Robineau has just vacated. He watches Ethan with a furrowed brow. Cindy and Dr. Robineau leave them alone. For a long time, the two boys sit in silence. Ethan doesn't acknowledge Ash's presence.

Finally, Ash speaks. "Hey, man, are you okay?"

Ethan unclenches a little and takes his thumb out of his mouth. He puts his knees down and wipes his eyes with the backs of his hands. He nods.

"I'm Ashton Lake," Ash says, holding out his hand. "Private First Class, Ashton Lake, United States Army." He smiles.

Ethan leaves him hanging. I know why, but poor Ash has no idea what touching Ethan could do to him. "I'm Ethan," Ethan mumbles.

Ash pulls his hand back and asks again, "You sure you're okay?"

Ethan doesn't bother to nod this time. It's obvious he's nowhere near the neighborhood of okay. "Did they tell you why you're here?" Ethan asks quietly.

"Um, well, they just wanted me to meet you for some reason."

"I'm sorry," Ethan says, and he looks away as more tears roll over his cheeks.

"Hey, it's okay," Ash says, and he leans in to put a hand on Ethan's arm. Ethan pulls away sharply.

"Don't touch me!"

"Okay. Okay." Ash pushes his chair back several inches. Ethan relaxes again.

Ash stares at Ethan, wide-eyed and on alert for a long time. Gradually, he relaxes, too, and casts around for something to talk about. "Hey, man. I met this girl today from here. I wonder if you know her. Pretty, like an angel. She did something you'll never believe."

Ethan looks up. "She heals people." His voice breaks, and he starts to shake.

"Yeah," Ash says. "I was beat up bad, and this girl — she, like, holds my hands and bam! I'm totally fixed up, no more pain or bruises or anything. A freaking miracle. Unbelievable, huh?"

"She's my twin." Ethan's voice is choked.

"No shit." Ash's eyes are huge. "Yeah, I can see that now. Same hair, same mouth. Your eyes are different, though. How does she do that?"

Ethan regards him carefully, his wheels turning over all the things Dr. Robineau said. "What do you think would happen if you went back to your unit and told them what Elena did?" he asks.

"Well, first off, they'd never believe me. Except, look at me. Right as rain. This morning, I could barely roll off the cot without feeling like I'd been in a knife fight with a herd of ninjas. Now, no pain." He bends this way and that to prove his point.

Ethan stares at him. "What if they did believe you? What if everyone found out what Elena can do?"

Ash freezes and stares back at Ethan. Ethan breaks eye contact. "Oh," Ash says. "I see your point."

Ethan slides his chair forward and brings his eyes up to meet Ash's. "Tell me exactly what happened when you met my sister." Ash opens his mouth to speak, but no words come out. His eyes, though trained on Ethan's, are blank and empty. A panoply of emotion plays over Ethan's features and his respiration becomes labored. His hands clench the arms of the chair, like he might fly apart if he lets go. The whole thing takes maybe three or four minutes, a far shorter time than it took for me to heal Ash. Ethan simply looks away and Ash returns.

"Hi, I'm Ash, Ashton Lake." He holds out his hand to shake Ethan's. Like before, Ethan leaves him hanging. He draws his legs up and buries his head in his knees. "Hey, man, are you okay?" Ash asks nervously.

Dr. Robineau comes into the room. "Private Lake." Her voice is full of authority. "I've been instructed to escort you to your new assignment." He gets up and salutes her, and they leave. Cindy comes in and helps Ethan into the bed. He puts up no resistance, but when she moves to inject his right arm, Ethan intercepts her hand. "She said I could see my sister." His voice is as hard as diamonds. "If I did what she wanted, she said I could see Elena."

"You will, Ethan. I promise. First, you need to rest. I promise." For a couple of seconds, they remain poised like that. Then Ethan lets go and puts his thumb in his mouth. Cindy injects him, pulls the covers up to his waist and leaves the room. The feed remains on as Ethan sleeps.

My chest feels like the breastbone has been crushed like a saltine. Logan goes back to her own bed, where she stretches out, opens her laptop and puts on her headphones. Cayde hands me the computer with the feed still running. He doesn't get up to leave, though. He just sits there, like he's waiting for something.

Suddenly, the door opens and in comes the entire goon squad: Hugo, Maureen, Jamie, Dr. Robineau, and a couple of the thugs. Cayde tries to roll under my bed, but Hugo hauls him out by one foot. At the same time, Jamie takes the tablet out of my hands. He passes it to Dr. Robineau, with it still open. She shakes her head.

"Cayde Jackson. Explain yourself." She doesn't yell, which is somehow worse.

"He didn't do anything," I say. "I did it myself."

Dr. Robineau laughs. It's not a pleasant sound. "That was unexpected and completely ineffective."

Cayde looks at the floor. "I . . . I just wanted to . . . help."

"Look at her. Look at Elena. Does it look like watching all of that helped her?"

Cayde glances at me. I try to smile at him. Total fail.

"No, ma'am," he says.

"Hugo, please take Cayde back to his room." Dr. Robineau never takes her eyes from me. "Now, what am I going to do about you, Miss Paige?"

"You could stop drugging me, for one thing," I say with a lot more confidence than I actually feel.

Dr. Robineau's eyebrow goes up. It's not a good look on her. "Jamie, I think you should take Elena to see her brother now. I made a promise, and despite her behavior, I intend to keep it."

Jamie helps me get up off the bed. I take the water bottle from the dresser and empty what's left of it onto the floor in front of Maureen. She's smart enough to understand that I know she dosed the water. I hand her the empty bottle and follow Jamie without looking back.

Jamie takes me down in the elevator to a floor a couple of levels above the lobby. He leads me through a labyrinth of corridors to a room that looks like a monk's cell. A futon for sitting or sleeping is against one wall. Beside it is a small table that might serve as a desk. Above that is a window that's permanently closed, but it looks out over the back of the building, where the stream that Jamie and I sit by flows. The desk is covered with art supplies. Next to it is an easel with a canvas bathed in various shades of blue, with the dark outline of trees crisscrossing threateningly over tiny figures nearly hidden in the colors. Ethan's there, too, curled into himself, sketching something that requires all of his concentration. After a few seconds, he looks up.

"Lanie!" He flings the pad and pencil away in his rush to throw himself into my arms. "What did they do to you? Where did you go?" His words are jumbled and desperate, like we won't have enough time to say everything we need to. "Are you okay?"

"I'm fine, E. What about you?" I push him back to inspect the bruise and cut on his forehead.

He looks down. "I fell."

"I know," I say. "I saw it on a video feed."

Ethan's eyes get wide.

"I'll leave you guys to it, then," Jamie says, shuffling his feet nervously. "I'll be back to get you soon, Elena." The emphasis on the word 'soon' sets me on edge, but he's gone before I can ask.

I wander over to pick up the discarded sketch pad. Ethan tries to grab it away from me, but I manage to keep it. As I flip it open, Ethan turns away. The sketch is stunning in its detail, like all of Ethan's work. I can almost taste the mango ice that Sage says I remind her of. In the sketch, she's lying on her stomach, with her chin resting on the backs of her hands. I turn the page. In this one, she's reading a book. In the next one, her hair's slicked back, like she's just showered or swam. In the next one, she's taking a selfie. I go to the bed and sit next to my brother. I hand him the sketchbook. "Oh, E. I'm so sorry. With all that's been happening, I completely forgot how much you must be missing Sage."

"She's never going to talk to me again." He says it in his head. I can barely hear him.

"It's only one year, E. The contract is only for a year." I take his hand, but he pulls away.

"We can't stay here a year. We have to get out of here, Elena. Things are going to happen, bad things." He's almost screaming in my mind. "Please, please listen to me. Don't treat me like a child!"

"I know, E. I saw what happened to you. Cayde and Logan said it wasn't a dream. Something about brainwaves."

Ethan doesn't say anything. He shakes his head, like he can't believe it.

"Is that what you see?" I ask. "In the nightmares that aren't nightmares? The future? You see the future?" I wait for his reaction.

He turns slowly, his gray eyes piercing mine. "Yes." He pauses for a reaction. "You believe me?" I nod. His eyes turn to liquid. "How are we getting out of here?" he asks in his head.

"I'm not sure. I'll figure it out, though. I promise." He curls up with his head in my lap. I brush his hair away from his face and resist the urge to pull his thumb from his mouth.

"About Sage," he thinks. "I wasn't talking about us being here and her there."

I knew what he meant, but I hoped he'd let that go. "She'll forget." I try to comfort him.

"Only if I make her." I hear the bitterness.

"Like Ash," I say. "Like me," I add quietly.

Silence settles between us. I expect tears that never come.

As Ethan relaxes, I look across the room at the canvases lined up along the wall and on the easel. "It was nice of them to let you paint, bring you all this stuff."

Ethan tenses up like a porcupine. "Dr. Robineau wants me to paint what I see. You know, the future."

"You aren't doing it, are you?" I ask.

"I can't." I don't know if he means that he's not able to or that he won't, but I don't press. "She isn't stupid. She's going to figure out that I'm lying, sooner or later," he thinks.

"Well, let's hope it's later, and we're long gone," I think.

He rolls over and looks up at me. "We need to call Jesse and Rachel," he thinks.

I'm a little insulted, and I feel chastised. After all, Rachel and Jesse both warned me against coming here, but I wouldn't listen. What would it look like if I came crying to them now? "E, I got us into this, and I can get us out. I think I know someone who might help."

Ethan sits up and backs away from me. "Whooo? Jaaamie? He's not going to help us. He's playing you."

"Ethan Michael Paige! That's just mean!" I'm screaming so loudly in my own head that it echoes.

"Truth hurts sometimes, little sister." He's baiting me now, and I take it. I push him as hard as I can, and he falls back onto the pillows at one end of the futon. I watch him register the weapons now at his disposal. A devious smile spreads across his face. I jump up and search for cover. I'm too slow. One, two, three, the missiles hit me faster than I can react. When he's out of ammo, I turn the pillows back on him. But he knocks every shot away with his right arm, catching the last in his left hand. He's just about to launch it, and I'm bracing to duck, when the door opens. Sweaty and laughing, we turn as one.

Jamie and Maureen stand there with game faces on. Ethan goes white and drops the pillow at his feet. Instinctively, we move closer together.

Maureen's the one to deliver the bad news. "It's time to go, Elena."

"No!" we say in unison. "I just got here! We didn't even have an hour," I add.

"Sorry," she says, but she doesn't look sorry.

I turn to plead my case to Jamie. He looks sorry enough for the both of them, but he doesn't contradict her. Ethan slides his hand into mine and holds on tightly. Then he steps slightly in front of me, like he's protecting me. I'm completely blown away.

"Come on, Elena, don't make this difficult," Jamie says quietly. "I'll stay here with Ethan."

"Jamie, please. Thirty more minutes. Please!" I beg.

Maureen steps forward. "It's not going to happen Elena. Ethan, say goodbye. You two may not see each other for a while."

That's the straw that breaks it. Ethan steps forward, reaching for Maureen's arm, but she pulls away too quickly. I don't know why he doesn't just make her forget why she's here like he did with Sage and Ash. He didn't need to touch them. Jamie easily subdues Ethan by twisting his arm behind his back. Maureen injects him with her trusty needle. I scream, but no one cares.

Without further discussion, Maureen drags me from the room by the arm. Her grip's tight, and it hurts. She's so damn strong. I hate her, and I want to hurt her. I want her to feel the pain she's causing me and Ethan by keeping us apart. We make it maybe a dozen steps from the room when she suddenly lets go of me and doubles over, clutching her stomach.

I don't run. "What's wrong with you?" I ask.

"I don't know," she says through gritted teeth. "Cramps or something."

I swallow hard and think, no. No way I'm doing this.

After a few seconds, she stands up, shaking it off. "There's someone here to see you, Elena. We didn't want to upset Ethan."

"Who?"

"A therapist who claims to have treated you."

I can hardly believe our luck. Rachel's here. Now with the opportunity for help practically falling from heaven, I have to admit that Ethan's absolutely right. I'll tell her everything that's happening. She and Jesse will get us out of here and maybe shut the whole operation down in the process.

Maureen takes me to Dr. Robineau's antechamber, tells me to wait there and leaves. I pace the room, desperately trying to organize my racing thoughts. My heart's beating in my throat, and my stomach's flipping around like a fish on a dock. I'm not sure I can speak without losing my lunch, and I have to make this count.

Dr. Robineau comes out of her office and invites me in. I expect to see Rachel there waiting for me, but we're alone. "Maureen said someone came to see me," I say heavily, after scanning the room.

"Before I take you to see Ms. Evans, we need to review the agreement you signed before joining us. Please sit down, Elena."

My stomach lurches. I perch on the edge of the sofa. Dr. Robineau takes a sheaf of papers from her desk and sits across from me. She holds up the packet. "Do you know what this is?" she asks, like she's talking to a dull child.

"It's the contract." I sound like I have a mouth full of cotton.

"Yes. The contract you signed, in fact." She shows me my initials at the bottom of every page. "There's one part in particular that we need to review, dear." There's nothing affectionate about the way her voice hovers over the last word. "Please read the highlighted sections," she instructs as she passes me the papers. My hands tremble, so I can barely focus on the words. After a minute or so, she starts talking again. "The general gist is this. If you disclose to your former therapist ANYTHING about our work or practices here, you can and will be prosecuted for treason against the United States government."

My blood turns to sludge and time moves in slow motion. "Treason?" I say. "What does any of this have to do with treason?" My head's spinning like a carousel.

Dr. Robineau rolls her eyes. "You aren't the brightest bulb on the tree, are you, dear? It's a shame I'm not having this discussion with your brother. He's so much quicker on the uptake, but so inconceivably fragile. It's a shame, really. Pay attention, darling. This laboratory is owned by the US government, the military, actually. The work is highly classified. Disclosing what we do here is a breach of security that could endanger our country. Are you with me so far?"

I don't know whether to feel more insulted or stunned by this revelation. I nod.

"This is the critical part, Elena. Treason is punishable by death, or a lifetime in prison. Do you understand?" I nod again. She gets up, then, and crosses the room to her computer. She clicks around and points to the ceiling camera. The light is now off. She comes back and sits again.

"Why did you —?"

"Elena," she interrupts. "I know you're thinking that if you tell Rachel, someone will come to your rescue and any consequences will be acceptable because you'll have saved your brother. I can assure you that this is not true. If you say one word, and I mean one word against PSI, not only will you be sent to prison and possibly death row, but so will your brother. In addition, your stepmother and anyone she talks to will also be prosecuted by Uncle Sam, with unpleasant repercussions. So, when you look into that sweet, pregnant lady's eyes, and you long to unburden yourself, stop and imagine pretty, fragile, pitiful Ethan at the hands of lifers in a federal penitentiary." She pauses to let the threats sink in.

I feel the hope I had moments ago circle the drain. Maybe there's no escape after all. And the weight of being utterly alone in this labyrinth settles squarely onto my shoulders. It bows my neck and back until I feel like I'm being suffocated from within.

"Are you ready to greet your guest, my dear?"

I stand up slowly, painfully.

"Smiles, darling. We wouldn't want Rachel to think anything's amiss, would we?"

I shake my head. Then I clear my throat and ask, "What about Ethan? Aren't you going to let him see Rachel? She's here for both of us, I'm sure."

Dr. Robineau shakes her head. "Your brother is far too unpredictable and dangerous to expose to civilians at this point. Besides, he's indisposed at the moment and probably won't awaken for several hours."

The hatred I felt for Maureen is nothing compared to the loathing that rises up from the darkest reaches of my soul now. In the elevator

I imagine Dr. Robineau clutching at her head as an aneurism explodes in her brain, shattering all life functions and leaving her a writhing, drooling mess on the floor. I wish for it so hard my entire body trembles.

Then the door opens and we're in the teeming lobby. Rachel rises from a seat far across the room and hurries in our direction. In the final seconds before I'm wrapped in her maternal warmth, Dr. Robineau puts a hand on my shoulder and whispers in my ear, "While it's nice to see you finally embracing the darker side of your gift, it's useless on me. Your brother has been trying his luck for days, and his powers are far stronger than yours. You'd be wise to conserve your strength. You may need it."

෩ 12 ൚

THE PASSAGE BACK

How did we end up here
Barely recollect the path
Bright lights beckon, a sign
Smell of honeydew
Do you remember the before time
Since we drank the milk
Do you remember that fine line
Or the passage back
Did they promise us paradise?
Think I remember that
"Milk of Paradise" - Luna Rayne 1996

Dr. Robineau leaves me alone with Rachel in a conference room on the main level. I don't bother scanning for the cameras that I know I'll find. It wouldn't matter if they weren't here; I'll be as good as gold because I have no choice.

After the pleasantries and the news about Jesse, Sage, and Finn, which go in one ear and out the other, I get to hear about the baby. It's a girl, they think, though the view on the sonogram wasn't definitive. Rachel and Jesse decided against the amnio testing, even though Rachel's age makes the pregnancy high-risk. I concentrate hard on watching her lips and keeping my tears in check.

"So, where's Ethan? I really wanted to see how he's managing here." Her tone's upbeat, nonchalant, but it fails to conceal the anxiety in her eyes and body language.

"He's great," I say, forcing a smile. "They put him through the paces this morning, though. I'm afraid he was sleeping when you got here."

"Oh," Rachel says quietly. "Well, this isn't really a social call. It took me two weeks and about a thousand forms and interviews to get in here to see you. I think we should have 'them' wake Ethan up. It really is important."

Dissuading Rachel from her mission would only make her suspicious. I think Dr. Robineau should be made to handle this set of lies. "Okay," I say. "I'll call Dr. Robineau and tell her." I pull over the phone that sits in the center of the conference table and punch in the number for the main desk. One of the mannequins answers. I tell her I need to talk to Dr. Robineau. Instead of patching me through, she tells me she'll send the doctor in. It doesn't matter to me. Either way, Rachel won't be seeing Ethan.

A moment later, Dr. Robineau appears and puts on a performance that not so long ago would have taken me in completely. They talk in shrink-speak that I catch only part of and couldn't care less about. In the end, Rachel concedes and Robineau leaves us alone again.

Rachel rings her hands and paces a couple of steps away and back. "Well, Elena, I'm sorry to have to put this on you. I really wanted to tell Ethan myself, but as usual it's going to fall to you, honey."

The drastic change in her demeanor snaps me out of my dark reverie. "What are you putting on me, Rachel?" I physically retreat now and brace myself, like I'm about to do battle.

"We've been trying and trying to reach you. Sage and Jo are beside themselves with worry. They say they haven't talked to you or had a text in weeks. Is that true?"

I can't remember the last time I called or texted. I have no frame of reference for time here. Every day is like the one before and after. I shrug. "They keep us pretty busy."

"It's about Lily," she blurts.

My hand goes to my mouth as I picture her the night we said goodbye. She was so thin and tired. She barely ate. The tears are on my cheeks before I can make an effort to control them. "No!"

"She's holding on, but barely. We moved her to hospice last weekend. You and Ethan need to come home and say your goodbyes NOW."

I feel a vague hope creep up my spine. Surely, in the face of losing the only mother we've known, PSI will allow us to go home and have closure. I cover my face with my hands, so Rachel won't see the smile tugging at the corner of my mouth. I sit down, and Rachel sits in the chair beside mine. I let her hold me while I sob and hope.

"Why didn't she tell us she was sick before we left?" I ask.

"Because she didn't want to hold the two of you back. She trusts you to do the right thing always, and especially for Ethan."

I cry harder. I don't want her to know how monumentally I fucked this up. I don't want her to see what a mess I made of everything, but I don't want her to die without thanking her for taking care of us. It couldn't have been easy, and she gave up so much. I have to see her before she goes.

I've barely pulled myself back together when Robineau comes in to break up the reunion. Rachel steps up to the plate and throws the pitch. "If it's not too much trouble, I'd like to take Ethan and Elena with me in the morning. Their paternal grandmother, the woman who raised them, is in the final stages of pancreatic cancer. I have all of the affidavits proving the details of the situation to be true." She hands a large folder of papers to Dr. Robineau, who places it gingerly on the table, like it might contain anthrax.

"When I heard you were coming, I suspected something like this might be in play." Dr. Robineau looks directly into Rachel's eyes. Her voice remains soft and friendly. "While I certainly sympathize with the gravity of the situation, and I in no way doubt your word, I cannot release the twins from their contract, which clearly states that they agree to remain here in the PSI facility for a period of three hundred sixty-five days. Surely you understand that the work we're doing here is extremely sensitive and complicated. Allowing the twins to leave would jeopardize all that we've accomplished in the past couple months."

Rachel doesn't flinch. "I understand the importance of your work and the binding nature of the contract Elena signed for herself and on behalf of her brother, but surely you can understand the uniquely tragic nature of this situation for these young people, who have already suffered so much loss in their short lives. I'm certain that allowing them to have closure with their grandmother before she passes will make both Ethan and Elena better able to participate in the work they're doing here. I'm only asking for a day or two away, so they can say goodbye. Surely, you can reasonably allow that." Rachel's smile is open and almost genuine. I want to hug her. I hold my breath as Robineau processes.

Suddenly, she turns and steps outside. A moment later, Jamie stands in the doorway. He motions for me to come with him. I shake my head. There's no way in hell I'm leaving this room with anyone but Rachel.

"Elena, my dear," Dr. Robineau says in her fake genuine voice, coming up behind Jamie. He moves aside to let her back in the room. "Jamie needs to brief you on your assignment for tomorrow. Please go with him now." Rachel steps forward, ready to have her say, but Robineau stands her ground and calmly says, "Ms. Evans, I think we're done here."

Two security guards flank Jamie in the doorway. I want to push past them, run like hell to the elevators and down that long white hallway. I would dive through the glass on both sides of the processing chamber. Being cut to ribbons would be nothing compared to the way I'm being sliced open inside right now. Jamie steps in the room and puts a hand gently on my arm. I turn away from him, throw my arms around Rachel and bury my head in her neck. In my head I'm screaming, "Get us the hell out of here!" But with my voice I say, "Tell Gran how much I love her and appreciate everything she did for us. Tell her I'll be with her in spirit when she crosses over. Tell her —" I can't go on because I'm bawling like a baby. My shoulders heave and my stomach clenches. I can't catch my breath. The next thing I feel is Jamie's strength flowing through his hands and into me as he pulls me from the room with a force that has nothing to do with muscles. I pull away from him for a second and try to stand on my own, but the grief and hopelessness that begin to run through my veins paralyze me. I opt for holding his hand. I grip a bit too tightly, but he lets me.

By the time we get to my room, I know Rachel's long gone, and my chance for a graceful departure has slipped through my fingers. I made a promise to Ethan, though, and now I have a deadline to meet. We have to get out of here before Gran dies.

Back in the room, Logan has been a busy little bee. Her wall is beyond full of symbols and patterns, crisscrossing chaotically over each other. She's plugged in, so she doesn't hear us enter. We both stop in the doorway to watch her. Her hair's wild and sweat's dripping down the center of her back. She mumbles to herself, or whoever she's communing with. It's obvious she's in distress. Jamie and I exchange a look of expectation for the other to step in. I shake my head. Jamie leads me to my bed and faces me away from her. He's not willing to interfere either. Coward.

"Do you want to talk about what happened with your friend, Rachel?" he asks, rubbing my arm.

I do. I want to fall into his arms and tell him everything, but Ethan planted that seed of doubt, and just now it's poking at me like a tiny pea from under a hundred comfortable mattresses. I shake my head.

"She's the one you visited before when you were here, isn't she?"

I nod, avoiding his eyes.

"I wish they'd let you go home with her," he says. I check his expression and body language for sincerity. Jamie always seems so sincere that I'm not sure I'd know what a lie looks like on his face. I want so much to trust him. Hell, I need to trust him. There's no other way out of this rat maze.

"Unfortunately, there's no time to sit around crying about how unfair it all is. We have another assignment, a new way to push you further," he says. I swear I hear a tinge of bitterness in his tone, but it could be nothing more than wishful thinking.

"No," I say. "I'm not doing anything unless they let me and E go see our gran." It's all I can come up with. If we make ourselves useless, then they'll cut us loose. Cayde said as much the first week we were here. Rachel said we'd be better able to work if we had closure. I can do her one better. We won't work unless we have closure. Jamie stares at me without surprise.

"That isn't going to work, you know."

"Why not?" I ask.

"Dr. Robineau has a sure way to make you do anything she wants."

"Whose side are you on?" I ask.

"Just saying," Jamie says, glancing down.

"How exactly is she going to control me? I can stand a whole lot of pain, remember?"

Jamie smiles sadly and mumbles, "But Ethan can't."

My mouth drops open, and my eyes begin to burn. Jamie touches my arm, like he wants to comfort me. I jerk away. "You should go now," I say between clenched teeth.

Jamie doesn't move. "I can't. I need to brief you about tomorrow's assignment."

"I told you; I'm not doing another assignment." My voice quavers. Even I know my words are mere bravado.

"You will because you love your brother, and you want to see him again. She won't let him see you until she thinks you're fully onboard with fulfilling the terms of your contract." Coming out of Jamie's mouth, the words don't sound like a threat, but I'd be an idiot to not see Robineau's hand up his back, like a creepy dummy in a vaudeville parody. My choices are dwindling.

"Whatever," I say, looking at the door.

"We leave before breakfast. Set your alarm for six. We're going to a hospital about an hour and a half away. Dr. Meriwether will meet us there and brief us further."

"Fine," I say. "Six in the morning, drive to hospital, meet

Meriwether. Got it. You can go NOW."

Jamie gets up and heads toward the door.

"Wait!" I call out. "Can you ask Robineau to let him swim? I'll do what she wants, but she needs to let him swim. Can you pass that on?"

"I'll do what I can, Elena, but that particular privilege depends on him too."

Not exactly a promise, but I've got nothing here. No power to choose or demand a thing. I lie down and curl into myself. Hope is the thinnest, weakest thread a spider can weave. A gentle breeze could blow through it right now. I need a plan and a partner. I roll over and look at Logan. She's still oblivious to my presence in the room. I watch her and wonder where she'll stand when I tear it all down. If I believed in any god, I'd pray that she'd stand beside me.

After ten minutes or so, Logan suddenly rips the headphones off and throws her iPod down on the bed. "Damn it! You stare louder than most people are able to fucking scream! What the hell is your problem, bitch?"

I don't sit up or smile or anything. I can't figure out if she's joking, pissed off or merely annoyed. I'm beyond caring at the moment. I avert my eyes.

"Oh shit. That bad?" She sits on the end of her bed and leans forward. "It's okay. My friends took the cameras down. What happened?"

I clear my throat to tell her about Rachel coming and Gran dying, and how they're controlling me by threatening to hurt Ethan, but when I open my mouth, nothing comes out except a kind of strangled squeak. Tears run sideways out of my eyes and over the bridge of my nose.

Logan comes over and sits on the floor next to the bed. For several seconds she just sits close to me while I cry in silence. "Elena," she finally whispers, "I want to help."

It's all the prompting I need. I glance up at the camera, just to be sure. Then I sit up and spill the whole story between sobs. I finish with the burning question: "What am I going to do? How the hell am I going to get out of here?"

Logan thinks about it for a couple of minutes while she draws circles with her finger on the floor. When she looks up, her eyes are glistening with excitement. "It's not really that hard, if you think about it. I mean, you get out of here nearly every day. All you need to do is just walk away, disappear into a bathroom or a broom closet or onto a city bus and - boom - you're free."

"What happens to Ethan, then? Don't you think Robineau will take her anger out on him? No. I need to get him out first."

"I can tell you that ain't never gonna happen. If he ever made it past the garden gate, you'd be on lockdown, the likes of which you've yet to imagine."

"Then we have to get out together somehow," I say, frustration creeping into my voice.

"I don't think you'll have that chance. The goon squad is going to keep you two apart for a while. Robineau's all over that one."

"Fuck! What do you suggest, then?"

"You need to get out at the same time, but not necessarily together. Robineau will never see that coming in a gazillion years." Logan's smile is contagious for a second.

My hope wavers again. "How is Ethan going to get out of the compound on his own?"

"We'll figure it out," she says reassuringly.

I throw my arms around her and find myself fighting tears again, but a different kind entirely. Suddenly, the light on the camera blinks on again. Her eyes follow mine up, and she moves away from me, almost embarrassed, I think. We need to make plans now, but the cameras are going to make it impossible. I want to scream.

The alarm to wake up goes off moments after I'm finally able to close my eyes. All night long I tried to imagine a scenario where Ethan could get out of the complex on his own. Even if I could come up with a plan, I have no idea how I'd communicate it to him since he's locked away. The only way to reach him is telepathically or via astral projection. The second option is useless without the first, since the sensory input seems to be primarily one-way. Logan thinks she can bridge to the physical realm. Apparently, she's been working toward this goal for years, so if I fail, she promised to step up. I don't see how that's even possible. How can a projection of your consciousness move something physical? No way! Hopefully, when I get back today, we'll have something brilliant to pass on to Ethan.

". . .on the third floor?" Jamie finishes his question at the same time I tune in.

"Sure," I say, pretending to have half a clue.

"Wrong answer. Were you even listening?" If he wasn't driving, he'd put his hands on his hips about now.

"Not so much," I say and turn back to the window to tune out again.

"Obviously, something's on your mind. You want to talk about it?" He doesn't even sound cheesy saying it; he's that damn sincere.

"My grandmother's dying, and I'm never going to see her again. Yes! Something's on my mind." I don't mean to be so prickly, but my anger's justified and has the added benefit of providing a smoke screen for what's really filling my headspace.

"I'm sorry." Jamie hangs his head a little. "You have every right to be upset. I wish I could change things. I really do."

I barely hear his apology. We're pulling into the hospital drive, and I have no idea what tricks I'll be called upon to perform today. If I were small enough, I'd crawl under the seat and refuse to come out. That's how badly my spidey-sense is tingling right now. I am in no way up for this challenge. This I know with a certainty I can't explain.

The hospital smell assaults my senses immediately. The sounds of crinkling plastic, rubber-soled shoes and hushed, urgent voices make my stomach go wonky. Ethan has a pathological fear of hospitals. He nearly had a nervous breakdown a couple of years ago when Sage had to be taken to the ER. My feelings aren't quite that debilitating, I think, right before the floor rises up to meet my knees and then my face.

Suddenly, I'm four again. I'm on a gurney that moments ago had been in a fast moving van with sirens and lights. I keep my eyes closed tightly because I want everyone to think I'm unconscious. I smell the disinfectant and body smells that mean hospital. I hear the crinkling of plastic and the squeal and crunch of the wheels punctuated by the scuffling and squeaking of the shoes the nurses, doctors, and paramedics are wearing. Every part of my body hurts from the shattered glass that rained down on me, and the rough hands that pulled me from the fire and tossed me around like a ragdoll until I landed on this cart. More intense than those injuries is the scalding, burning feeling on my skin from sitting in water that was far too hot for too long. The echoes of my mother's and brother's screams and the roar of the fire won't leave my head. Tears leak from my eyes, but I don't brush them away because if they know I'm awake, they'll make me talk and I can't. I just can't.

The memory's shattered by the sharp smell of ammonia. My mind is suddenly alert. Someone's waving a capsule-like thing in my face, and Jamie's hovering above my field of vision. "You fainted! Are you okay?" His eyes are creased with worry lines, and his mouth is turned down in a pout that I really want to kiss for some reason. Of course, I don't. I push myself to sitting as a gurney arrives. I wave the orderlies and nurses away. "I'm fine," I mumble. "Low blood sugar." A nurse hands me a chocolate bar that she has thoughtfully unwrapped partway.

I take a small bite. Jamie helps me to my feet, and the crowd magically disperses.

"What happened, Elena?" He won't let go of my arm, despite my relative steadiness.

"Nothing. Can we just forget about it and find Dr. Meriwether, so I can do my stupid people tricks and get the hell out of here?" I say. It takes an act of will to block out the sounds and smells so I don't hurl as a follow up to my first act of humiliation. I hand him the chocolate and clutch my gut as he steers me onto the elevator. We get off on the top floor. It's a little better here. Not so much activity, at least. We move quickly down the hall past several doors. Finally, we stop and Jamie knocks. A male voice invites us in. Dr. Meriwether is sitting in one of the four empty chairs. A handsome, youngish doctor with tired eyes and an easy smile is behind the desk.

"Hello, Ms. Paige. I'm Dr. Murdock, Trey. I've been looking forward to meeting you," the man says, stepping from behind the desk to shake my hand. His smile reaches his eyes, and they crinkle in the corners. I like him immediately.

"Hi," I say, sitting next to Dr. Meriwether.

"Sorry we're late." Jamie makes the apologies. What else is new? "Elena wasn't feeling well." He downplays what just happened. I'm not sure if I should be grateful or angry.

"I'm fine now," I say, despite the lingering queasiness.

"Good," Dr. Meriwether says. "We have a lot of work to do today."

I look at them, waiting for the hammer to fall. "I'm a pediatric oncologist," Dr. Murdock begins.

It's the last thing I hear. My mind takes off like a rogue rocket. They brought me here to heal kids with cancer. OMG! What exactly is that going to do to me? I suddenly feel weak and cowardly and ready to cry.

"Do you have any questions?" Dr. Murdock asks after a long speech that sounds like the teacher from a Charlie Brown cartoon. I reach for Jamie's hand and find it waiting for me.

Instead of answering the doctor, I turn to Jamie. He leans in so I can whisper in his ear. My panic makes it more like a stage whisper. "I can't do this." My hand's shaking in his, and I'm starting to hyperventilate.

"Ms. Paige? Elena? Are you okay?" Dr. Murdock has come from around his desk and squats in front of me. I imagine that he's an awesome kid doctor. If I were a child, I'd crawl into his arms and entrust him with my life in a heartbeat. But he isn't here to help me. Like everyone else, all he wants is to use me. He has no idea what this will do to me, and he probably doesn't really care as long as I cure his patients.

"I… I don't want to die," I mumble like an idiot.

The kind doctor looks at the others for an explanation. Jamie fields the question that hangs in the air.

"The first time she… she did this, her heart stopped beating. I did CPR." Jamie swallows a couple of times. "Why would that happen?"

Dr. Merriwether looks shocked, like this is news to her, maybe. Clearly, she has no answers, so I look at Dr. Murdock.

He looks even more flummoxed than she does, perhaps because he doesn't really believe yet, but he offers an explanation. "I couldn't say for sure, but I imagine exerting the kind of force it would take to heal damaged cells must take a terrible toll on the nervous system, like getting an electric shock maybe. Just a guess." He smiles reassuringly. "We'll check you out completely first, just to be sure that your body can handle the shock. Okay?"

When I don't respond, he adds, "No one's going to die on my watch today. I promise."

I nod.

We leave Jamie and Dr. Meriwether behind in his office, and he takes me into an exam room where a nurse instructs me to dress in a hospital gown. About this time, I start wishing I'd been listening to his words instead of my panic, but I'm not about to start asking questions now. I decide to just go with it. It's not like I have a choice. I hold onto the thought that by now Logan has hatched a plan that will have us out of Florida and back home in a matter of days.

I wait on the edge of the exam table, trying to force the gown under my legs for a modicum of relief from the refrigeration, when Dr. Murdock comes back in with the nurse.

"Good, you're ready. We're going to start by taking some samples. Then we'll look at your heart, lungs, and the rest of you. Any questions?"

I shake my head and resign myself to whatever poking, prodding, and probing might be required. The next hour is a haze of needles and pee cups and scans and exams. I feel like I've been abducted by aliens that look almost human on the outside. Finally, my clothing's returned, and I'm left blissfully alone for several minutes.

Not only am I left alone, but I'm left alone in a room with any number of sharp implements that could instantly relieve my anxiety. Out of habit, I scan the room for cameras. Finding none, I choose a little thing called a lancet. Normally, it pops out of a tube, striking once like a snake, to draw blood from a fingertip or toe. It can easily be rigged to stay open, though, and it serves beautifully to slice perfect parallel arrows in the soft flesh of my left calf. I close my eyes and revel in the sting of air on the open wound and the tickle of the blood droplets chasing each other down my leg. I can feel the air in my lungs again as I take a deep breath. I ignore the knocks on the door, sending away the nurse a couple of times. Time's up, so I slap on a couple of bandages and take a quick look around the room to ensure that all evidence is gone. I pocket a few of the lancets and unlock the door. I can do this now.

Jamie and Dr. Meriwether are pacing in the hallway. "Jeezus, Elena. What took so long?" Jamie asks, rushing over.

"We were starting to worry," Dr. Meriwether adds in a much kinder, calmer tone.

"Nothing to worry about," I say lightly, riding the euphoria wave. Jamie's eyes tell me he's not convinced. Takes an addict to know one, I think. "Let's get some lunch. I'm famished!" I stretch my mouth into a smile and take Jamie's hand.

"Good idea," Dr. Meriwether says. "Once your baselines are back, we can get started, but until then, time is ours. I hear the grilled cheese and tomato soup in the cafeteria are actually edible."

Before my lunch has time to digest, I'm back with Dr. Murdoch, and he's introducing me to the three young cancer patients I'm supposed to work my magic on. The first is a little boy, Tucker, eight years old, lanky and tow-headed. He's just been diagnosed with a rare form of leukemia. He tells me all about it, statistics for having that type, what it's doing to his blood, the trajectory of the disease and the options for treatment. He's logical, taciturn and brave. Before we leave his room, he asks if I'm his nurse. He's sad when I say no. He tells me it's probably for the best, though, because if I was his nurse, he'd never want to get better. The endorphins from the cuts are beginning to wear off.

The second girl, Riley, is twelve. She's still got the round, apple cheeks of childhood, but her curves are becoming visible too. She's wearing a hot pink wig. The cancer she has isn't particularly aggressive, but it's tough to kill. She could live another decade like this, a couple rounds of chemo and radiation each year. Eventually, before she has a chance at a real life, it will take her. Logan would like this kid. She's cynical and wise, with both a darkness and light that come from prolonged suffering. She tells me I'm pretty in one breath and in the next asks me if I could be more stupid. She tells me being funny makes up for a lack of intelligence every time. I'm not sure if I should be insulted or flattered. I want to be her friend, but I don't think I should tell her this. My buzz is dead now, and I haven't healed a single child.

The last kid, Amelia, is five. She's a mouthy, demanding ginger, which I know only by her temper, and her mom and dad's coloring. She wants me to draw her a picture. I tell her I'm not a good artist, but my twin brother is. Then all she wants to talk about is what it feels like to be a twin. She wants to know if Ethan looks like me and if we like to eat the same foods and wear the same styles of clothes. She asks if he's my best friend, and I have a hard time not crying. Then she insists on that picture. I draw a sunny day with flowers, and a pond with a paper boat and ducklings floating side by side. She giggles and hugs me. I'm glad I get to see her again.

Next, Dr. Murdoch takes me to a room that's been set up like a playroom. A tiny table with paper and crayons, and a chair, occupies one corner. The floor's covered with a padded puzzle. I choose to sit on the floor. If I pass out from the pain, it will be less frightening for the kids. Dr. Meriwether comes in. "How are you feeling, Elena?"

My heart's racing, and I want to find a quiet corner to carve several more arrows into my calves, but I don't want to disappoint her. "Fine."

"Good. I'm going to inject you with the same neurotransmitter booster that you were given at PSI before you healed Cayde. It's going to be a lot stronger because it's going right into your bloodstream. If you start to feel strange, raise your arm and wiggle your fingers. I'll come right in and shut this down. Dr. Murdoch's going to hook you up to some monitors so we can observe your blood pressure, brain waves and oxygen stats. If we notice anything from our side that's off, we'll come in and call it. Okay?'

I nod and attempt a smile. I'm sure it comes out all wrong. The truth is that her assurances make me feel a little less like I'm about to jump off a bridge without a bungee cord. Still, I have to wonder about the security of the harness she's giving me. She rubs my arm with an alcohol pad and jabs the needle in quickly. I don't think she likes this part any more than I do.

Mere seconds later, I feel the tingling in my hands, and my mind feels like it's been split open by a rainbow sword. The colors in the room grow blindingly bright, and I can hear the thoughts of the people walking down the halls of the hospital. The din is deafening. I put my hands over my ears, but it doesn't help.

I have no idea if seconds or hours pass before Dr. Murdoch comes in. He thinks about how pretty and young I am. He doubts that I can do anything at all to help these kids. He hopes I can't because if I do cure them, my life's over. People from all over the world will follow me; scientists will want to study me. He thinks about his pregnant wife at home and the fight they had last night about his long hours. He wonders if his baby will ever get cancer and how he couldn't handle that. I feel sorry for him, so I touch his arm. His mind clears and he smiles as I'm hooked up to EKG, EEG, and biofeedback devices. He has no idea what I've just done for him.

As for me, I feel like a science experiment. I guess I am. When the doctor asks if I need anything to get ready, I ask him to send Jamie in.

Jamie comes in before Murdoch leaves. I guess they must be watching from the next room. He squats down so we're eye to eye. I can feel raw energy pouring out of me, but Jamie's presence isn't like Murdoch's. I don't hear any of his thoughts; in fact, what I hear is something akin to white noise or rushing water. What I feel is different, too. Murdoch felt like a vessel I could fill. Jamie feels like a current of energy, like me. If we touched, we might bring the entire hospital down around us. He doesn't touch me, so I'm left to wonder if he feels the same way.

"What do you need, Elena? The kids are ready." His voice is echo-y and far away.

"I don't think I can do this." I can hardly hear my own voice. "I feel really strange."

"It's the neurotransmitters. They turn up the volume on your abilities, make you stronger." He looks at me sideways. I can't hear him thinking, but I know he's wondering if I can do what they're asking of me.

"I'm afraid. It's going to be horrible and painful, and I don't want to do this." My throat's raw from the terror that's building inside me.

"Elena, think about the kids. Think about what it would mean to them not to be sick anymore. What it would mean for them to have a future. Focus on that. Okay?"

His words are righteous, but what he means is that I need to find a way to get on with it. People are waiting. People are counting on me. Riley, Amelia, and Tucker are counting on me. I nod in slow motion. Jamie leaves me with a fake smile. Inside, I groan and writhe. They give me no time to dwell, however.

Amelia's first. She dashes over to me but stops short of throwing her arms around my neck. There are too many wires in the way.

"'Lena! Are you sick, too?" Her voice is so full of worry and concern that it makes my heart hurt.

"No. No. The doctors are just watching to make sure I don't get sick." I manage a smile for her sake.

"Oh. That's good." She wraps her arms through the cords and snuggles into my lap. Almost immediately, a sharp pain shoots up through my spinal cord. I push her away, gasping for breath. "'Lena! Are you getting sick now?" She touches my arm, and I wince. She looks around the room, searching for someone to help. "Should I get the doctors and nurses?" I shake my head and pat the ground across from me.

"Amelia, let's play a little game. Okay? I think if we play a game, I'll feel much better." The words sound disjointed and strange even to me, like I'm speaking in another language, but Amelia smiles and sits where I indicated.

"Tell me something you love. Something that makes you very happy," I say.

She doesn't hesitate. "Marshmallows."

"Really?" I say. "Marshmallows? Why?" I force a smile.

"They taste like camping at the lake with my grandpa and brothers. We have guns that shoot them, and they stick to the walls of the cabin. Plus, they're sweet and gooey. You just can't beat that."

"Lots of great reasons. Now think of something you hate, something you wish you could make go away forever."

"Centipedes. I hate them! My brother, Jake, put one in my bed once, and it almost crawled in my ear. I want to smash everyone in the whole world!"

"Wow. That's horrible and a good thing to hate. What good do centipedes do in this world, anyway?" This time the smile comes a bit easier.

"None! I can tell you, not one!" she says, quite seriously.

We both giggle. "Okay, Amelia, now for the best part of the game. Lay down and close your eyes. I'm going to lie right next to you and we're going to hold hands. I want you to imagine the sickness in your body is a bunch of centipedes."

"How many?" she asks.

"I don't know. How about 10?"

"Ew! That's a lot."

"It's okay because I'm going to kill all of them and flush them down the toilet."

"Hooray!" she yells, throwing her arms up in the air.

"Now for the great part. After the icky centipedes get flushed away, we're going to fill you up with marshmallows. Special, magical marshmallows that make you strong and happy.

"Yummy. I can eat a lot more than ten!"

"You can eat as many as you want. Are you ready?"

Amelia nods enthusiastically and lies down. I lie beside her and give her a wink as we join hands. Then she turns away and closes her eyes. Her breathing changes after a couple of seconds, and I know she sees the centipedes because I see them, too. I hurry through the hallways and rooms of her mind, stomping on them with thick-soled boots. I count the carcasses as I scoop them into a dust pan. My legs feel like lead and sweat pours off of me from the effort. It takes a long time to find all the bugs because they hide under furniture and on the ceiling and under doorjambs, but finally I have ten bodies that I drop into the toilet. I hear Amelia giggle as we watch them swirl down and away. Then the marshmallows arrive, a mountain of them that one by one fill the house from floor to rafter until I'm forced outside. Amelia sighs with pleasure at the sight of them. After some time, we open our eyes simultaneously. Her smile makes the pain coursing like poison arrows through my extremities worth it. I try hard to smile back, but a wave of nausea washes over me. I turn to the other side just in time. Amelia jumps up and rubs my back.

"I'll go get the doctors. Thanks for the game, 'Lena. It was fun."

I close my eyes and collapse on my side, curled in to fight the next wave. Time passes. It feels like hours because each breath is a new experience in agony. Dr. Murdoch's thoughts are loud in my head. He wants to stop now. Meriwether insists that I'm fine. Someone comes in to clean up the mess. The orderly's thoughts are chaotic and disorganized, memories of getting sick as a child and last weekend when drinking with friends. He's not interested in me or what's happening here. Then the white noise is back, and Jamie's real voice penetrates the pain.

"Elena, you're okay. You need to sit up now. Come on. Be strong. You can do this." He leaves the "you have to" implied. I open my eyes and reach a hand toward him. He shakes his head. "You don't need my help."

"But I want it," I whine. I sound like Ethan. It's enough to make me sit up on my own.

"See." He smiles a tired smile. "Let's take some deep breaths." He sits in a lotus position, and I imitate him. Together we do the chakra breathing, and he leads me back to my center. The pain flows away from me, fading with each breath.

"Riley's waiting," he says eventually.

"I know," I say. "I can feel her, hear her."

He nods. "The neurotransmitter enhancer. I don't think it will hurt so much with her."

"Thanks for saying that," I say, but I'm pretty sure he's lying. He gets up to leave. "Hey," I call out. "Why can't I hear your thoughts?"

He shrugs, looks away guiltily. "I don't know."

Another lie.

I approach Riley with the same tactic I used on Amelia, but this time we stay sitting up across from each other, holding both hands. Riley's cancer is miniature zombies; her cure is unicorns, which pierce the zombies with their horns and turn them into glitter. I use the chakra breathing and push the pain out as it comes in. It's a struggle to keep ahead of the pain, but in the end, Jamie's right. It doesn't hurt as much this time. In fact, my heart is so full by the end of the session that I cry when Riley hugs me goodbye. She cries, too, and promises to never forget me, even though she has no idea why I'm here or what we were doing. After she's gone, I cry and cry. I can't stop. I must cry for an hour or more.

Then they bring Tucker in. At first he hangs back out of habit of being careful. He thinks I'll make him sicker somehow.

"What are all those wires for?" he asks.

"What do you think they're for?" I ask.

"They're looking for what's making you sick," he says matter-of-factly.

"Kind of," I say. "I'm not sick with anything you can catch. Promise," I say.

Tucker isn't interested in my game. He won't hold my hands or concentrate. He wants to tell me about the video game he planned to make someday before the cancer. I listen while he talks about how the players would have been able to create monsters out of different animal parts and battle other people's monsters online and add parts of the monsters they kill onto their monsters. They'd score points during the battles that they could use to buy weapons, power, and secret stuff. His voice becomes musical in my ears, but his thoughts come to me like discordant notes from a broken cello. He thinks he won't live long enough to create anything. He thinks no one likes his idea or him because he's sick. He thinks he's sick because he's done something wrong, and he's a bad person who deserves to die.

I can't let him think these things! "Tucker!" I yell without meaning to. "That is the most wonderful game I've ever heard of! You're amazing, and you need to fight hard to make your dream real. How could anyone bad be so talented? You deserve to live."

He shakes his head, his eyes open wide, like saucers.

"Say it with me." I say, making my voice quiet and touching his arm. "I deserve to live." On the third round he comes in quietly. We keep saying it louder and louder. I keep my hand on his arm. Then the disease begins to trickle into me. I can't go on chanting, but he does. He goes on and on with increasing conviction as his pain fills my body, and I realize how very brave he has been. I begin to see stars, and I fight to hold on to consciousness, but I fail, and it all goes black as Tucker's voice rings in my ears.

I wake up in Jamie's car and wonder if we're still on our way to meet Dr. Meriwether and whether or not the whole day was a bad dream. But the sky's dark, my hands tingle and my mind's wide open, so I know. The car pulls up to a hotel. Jamie leaves me to get a room. I pull myself back to the world.

"Good. You're awake. I wasn't sure how I was going to carry you up to the second floor," he says, sliding back into the driver's seat.

I clear my throat. My mouth feels like a desert crawled inside and died while I slept. "You saying I'm fat?" Jamie laughs and shakes his head vehemently. "Why are we here?" I rasp.

"It's too late to go back to PSI." He pauses. "I wanted some time alone with you." He pauses again. "I wanted you to have some time away from there."

"Thank you," I say, but I wonder what strings might be attached. We park the car and make our way to the room. I feel like my limbs are made of lead, rusty lead, if lead could rust. By the time Jamie gets the door opened, I'm too tired to even make a big deal about the fact that he only got one room. I drop into the bed closest to the door, curl into a ball and close my eyes.

Jamie wakes me up a second or an hour later. "I ordered some Thai takeout and drew a bath for you. Food or soap first?" he says.

I look around. It takes a minute to remember where we are. The room's nice. White duvets and big fluffy pillows, wood floors and modern furniture. Dinner's spread out on the table.

"Bath," I say. Even though I love Thai, the thought of eating is a little scary.

Jamie produces an overnight bag and shows me the contents: light pink scrubs, a toothbrush and toothpaste, lotion and soaps, a hairbrush and comb, and a safety razor. "You planned this?" I ask.

He smiles apologetically, "Planned for this. I never know when I won't make it back, so I always bring an overnight kit or two." He grins wider.

"Good thinking." Something about the guy makes me want to kiss him. I take a step closer to accept the bag. He holds onto my hand for a couple of seconds too long.

"You should try to see Ethan before the boost wears off. Oh, and I have something else for you." He reaches into his pocket and pulls out my cell phone. I literally squeal with delight and make a grab for it. He pulls it away. "Uh-uh! All the rules still apply. Nothing about PSI. Nothing! That's the condition."

"Accepted!" I say, jumping up to try to reach the phone that he's holding just out of my reach. I crash into his chest as he brings his arm down, and he catches me up in his free arm. Our noses are almost touching. I can taste the peanut sauce on his breath. My mind stops working, and I'm kissing him without even deciding to do so. His mouth relaxes around mine, and his heart thuds against my chest as he pulls me in tighter. Gradually, we stop kissing, without moving apart. "Thank you," I breathe. After a couple of beats, he releases me, and I practically skip to the bathroom.

A steaming tub of bubbles that smells like lilacs and rosemary greets me, and I can't rip off my clothes fast enough. I melt into the porcelain and take a moment to get centered. Astral projection is child's play to me now, even without the enhancer. With it, I feel like I could go to the outer reaches of the universe and see God. I find Ethan quickly. He's in the same room I last saw him in. He's standing in front of the easel, painting in huge, wide swaths with a thick, flat brush. I've never seen him paint like this, wild and unfettered, loose and free. The bottom of the painting draws me in with a pool of crimson. I watch as a figure gradually appears, immersed in the red. Soon the red appears to flow out of the figure like blood. As I puzzle over that part of the painting, a second figure emerges above the first, like one person looking down on another.

I turn from the art to observe the artist. Ethan's eyes are glassy and pained, as though he's looking at something horrifying and distant. He paints with a feverish urgency that makes no sense given his captivity. He pauses and removes his shirt. He uses it to wipe his face and the brushes. He looks so thin and small, like he's not eating, like he's not swimming, like he's wasting away.

I turn back to the painting. A third figure has now been roughed in beside the second, looking over the prone body that's clearly bleeding. The postures of the pair that stand behind the injured form begin to come into focus. One's reaching out toward the prone person, while the other holds him or her back. Ethan lets the large brush fall from his hands and grabs a smaller brush, working in the details of the faces. I move closer and ask telepathically, "Ethan, who are these people?"

He freezes midway from the pallet to the canvas. "E? Can you hear me?" I ask as loud as my brain can yell. He looks around the room as though he's been awakened from sleepwalking.

"Lanie? Where are you?" he asks. Then his eyes light on the

painting, and a look of panic flashes over his face. "Oh shit!" he says aloud. He rummages through the jar of brushes, grabbing the largest one and spilling the rest so they roll off the table and onto the floor. The glass jar that held them falls and shatters as well. Ethan barely notices. He's opened a can of white gesso, and he's desperately trying to cover over the images he just created, but the gesso's watered down. He gets nowhere with it, so he abandons the jar and the brush unceremoniously. He squeezes a huge glob of black paint onto the pallet from a tube and picks the pallet up in his hand. He spreads black over the painting in a wild vortex, like a child who's finger painting. With each passing second, he becomes more and more desperate to cover his painting, and he continues his frenzy long after the image has been obliterated. Finally, he wears himself out and wipes the paint from his hand onto his pants.

"Was that the future?" I ask. "Is that what Robineau wants from you?"

"Don't, Lanie," Ethan thinks. "Don't ask me, please, just don't." He doesn't cry, but he's shaking. He walks to the bed and begins to sit down, but he stops because of the paint on his pants. He takes them off with trembling hands and legs and crawls between the sheets wearing just a diaper. He lies on his side, rocking himself gently as he stares blankly at the wall.

In my head, I do the only thing I can to comfort him. I sing a lullaby over and over until his body relaxes. His eyes remain open, like he's afraid to sleep. Maybe he'd been painting in his sleep. He rolls over and takes in the mess and the black canvas vortex. "Lanie, we need to get out of here. NOW. Before —" He doesn't finish the thought. Instead, he looks at the spoiled canvas, and I know. Furthermore, I believe. The sudden pounding in my veins and the rush of adrenaline bring me back to my body, lying in the now lukewarm bath in the hotel, miles from my brother's terror.

I get out and get dressed. The scrubs are huge on me, so I roll up the waist and legs. My phone vibrates suddenly, making me jump out of my skin. An incoming text! It's been so long since I texted. My heart nearly explodes; it's from Jo.

"Hey, sweetie, are you still alive? Please call."

I think about texting back, but the pull of hearing her voice is too strong. I press the phone icon instead. My hands shake, and my heart beats hard in my throat. Her voice is like chocolate syrup.

"Oh my god! I thought I'd never hear from you again!" she says.

"Oh, Jo!" It's all I can say because tears are clogging my throat.

"No, Lane, don't cry." Her voice is shaking, too.

"I won't if you won't," I say, half-laughing half-crying.

"We left things all wrong," she says. "I should've begged you to stay. I should've held onto you with both hands. I should've —"

She doesn't finish. "It's okay. Jo Jo, please don't do this. We're fine. I didn't expect grand gestures."

"You should've had one, though."

"It doesn't matter, Jo. You're a part of me, always a part of me."

She sniffles. "When are you coming home?"

I'm silent on my end. I want to say soon, sooner than you can imagine, but I don't dare.

She fills the void. "I'm sorry. I know you have to be there for a year. It's just so damn hard. Lily's dying, and Sage is crazy with worry over you and Ethan. We've been staying at your grandma's house. We were trying to take care of her, but she's in hospice now. She wants to see you. I think it's the only thing keeping her alive. Sorry I'm rambling and putting all this shit on you."

"It's okay, Jo. I already know. Tell Sage we're good. Ethan's good. He's making friends and painting. He's getting stronger, growing up. She won't recognize him. He misses her like crazy. Tell her."

"I will. What about you, baby? How are you?"

The tears come pouring down now. There's no way I can talk without her hearing the truth. I swallow hard, but I've already paused too long. "I'm fine. Good."

"What can I do?"

I can't do this anymore. It's ripping me apart from the inside out. "Hey, Jo Jo, I gotta go. I'll call again soon. Promise."

"Okay. Elena, I love you."

"Oh!" I can't say it back. "Bye, angel. Be good!" I hang up and press the phone to my forehead, wishing I could fall inside and through the wires, back into her arms. Then I remember. I drop the phone on the counter and grab my pants. I rummage through the pockets. The lancets. Where the hell are the lancets? Jamie must've found them, or they fell out when he carried me to the car. I tear the bathroom and the bag apart, looking for something I can use. The only candidate is the safety razor. I need to break the plastic off to get at the blades. I bang it on the counter with my shoe.

I don't hear the door handle click, so when Jamie's face appears behind me in the mirror, I jump out of my skin. He gently places his hands on my shoulders and turns me around to face him. Then, ever so slowly, with the utmost care, he extracts the razor from my hand and drops it in the wastebasket behind me. I don't fight. He enfolds me in his arms until I relax into him. I absorb into my skin his calm, blue aura. I feel like I've been immersed in a cool, clear pool. His hands find my face in a delicate caress that pauses to bring me forward into a soft, sweet kiss that warms me from head to toe. Then he scoops me into his arms and carries me to the bed.

A fleeting notion passes through my mind when he releases me for the briefest moment, that I wouldn't do this if I really loved Jo, but the instant we are skin to skin, the thought flutters from my head, like a puff of smoke. My hands tug his shirt over his head of their own accord, and my fingers unbutton his jeans with an adeptness I didn't know they possessed. The sight of his trim belly contracting under my touch trips the "no return" switch in my body. He's already stripped me of the loose clothing, but I feel anything but naked as he covers me in kisses.

He starts at my neck and ears, teasing me with the tip of his tongue until I moan. He stops and waits for me to meet his gaze. Then he lowers his head to kiss my lips. So soft, barely touching until I can't stand the heat, and I pull his head down into a harder kiss, slipping my tongue into his mouth, then biting his lip lightly. His arousal is palpable now, but he's not a kid, desperate to get off; he's all about me. His hands and mouth move down my body, stopping to play at my breasts and lick around my waist and down farther. As he sends my mind spiraling into the stratosphere, I look down and watch his light brown, wispy locks transform into Jo's jet curls. When he glances up, his eyes are chocolate, and his lips are thick and feminine. I don't feel the stubble when I brush his cheek with my fingertips. Oh, Jo! How long I've waited for this! And the back of my mind explodes in a hundred brilliant sensations, far stronger than when I pleasure myself.

When I open my eyes, Jamie's back, drinking deeply from the bottle of water on the table between the hotel beds. He rinses his mouth and kisses me sweetly, but he doesn't pursue his own release. "What about you?" I mumble, barely able to talk.

He smiles. "Tonight's for you, whatever you want."

I want him to feel like I do, but I don't want to go breeder, and I can't do for him what he did for me. For a heartbeat, I feel profoundly guilty, but before it can gel, it flows away, and I'm filled with gratitude and exhaustion. The moment's gone anyway, because I've paused too long. The passion has cooled to comfort. I gather my clothes and kiss him on my way to the bathroom. When I turn on the light, I see my phone blinking a text. I turn it over. "I love you, baby. I'll be waiting." The words blink at me like a warning light. I pull on the pale pink pants and roll the waistband until they don't fall off. I must've left the shirt by the bed. I open the door as quietly as I can, so I don't wake Jamie, but I needn't have worried.

He's sitting up, with his back to the bathroom. The glint of the metal needle plunging into his thigh muscle is barely visible, but his groan of pleasure as he falls back onto the pillow rivals the one I emitted when I climaxed. I stare, open-mouthed. For a couple of seconds, he's not aware that he's being watched. Then he opens his eyes, brings a hand to his forehead and mumbles, "Oh shit." He struggles to sit upright. "It's not what you think," he slurs.

"If it walks like a duck and talks like a duck —," I say, shaking my head.

"NO!"

"Jamie, you're an addict."

"No." He shakes his head. "You don't understand. It's not like that."

"I think it's exactly like that," I say, scooping up my shirt and putting it on.

Jamie runs his hand through his hair, and his eyes fill up from frustration. "Just listen."

I sit across from him on the other bed, and he turns to face me.

"It's just a blocker. You know, a neurotransmitter inhibitor. It shuts everything down, makes it quiet. I was supposed to give it to you as soon as we left the hospital, but I wanted you to see Ethan, know that he's okay."

I think about what he's saying, and Cayde's theory about our handlers. "So, what does it do to someone without abilities?" I level him with my eyes, for once confronting things head-on.

He looks away. He knows what I'm getting at. I can hear the wheels turning as he tries to decide whether or not to lie to me. I realize suddenly that I'm not hearing white noise. I'm hearing his thoughts. He has no clue.

"Nothing. It does nothing."

"What's your superpower?" I whisper, even though no one's watching or listening here.

He shakes his head. "I can't tell you."

"I'm not giving you a choice," I say sternly.

He falls back against the pillows and closes his eyes. I hear his thoughts screaming in my ears now. "She'll never understand. She's going to hate me. Oh shit! I should've just given her the shot. I wonder if the booster has worn off." He sits up with great effort and looks deeply into my eyes.

"Please, Elena, don't do this. If you do, it'll change everything! Just let me have my moment, like I gave you yours. Don't ruin this night."

I pause for a second, then nod. "Okay, I'll wait for you to tell me." I mean it. The act of letting go opens the door to a wave of fatigue that hits me like a strong wind. I pull down the covers on the bed beside Jamie's, turn off the light and curl up.

"Good night," he whispers, and I hear the sadness in his voice. He wants me to be in the bed with him, but this chasm between us cannot be bridged with physical proximity. He needs to fill it with trust before we can ever be that close again.

"Good night," I mumble back, swallowing my tears. Sleep takes me almost instantly, so there's no time to dwell or fight the urge to search Jamie's mind for the information I want. Unfortunately, as quickly as sleep comes, it goes, and I'm lying wide awake in the dark without my starry sky for comfort. I slip out of bed. I'm not worried about waking Jamie; he's long gone to the land of nod, like all good junkies.

I walk to the window and peer out into the night. The car's parked across the lot. I look down at the dresser I'm leaning against, and the keys sparkle in the reflection of the streetlights, like a sign. Logan's words come back loud and clear. "Just walk away. It's so simple." I picture myself picking up the keys, walking outside and getting in the car. I hear the engine turn over and feel the miles dissolve under the tires. I'll have hours and hours of a head start. Freedom tastes powerful and satisfying, like Thai food.

The smell of Chu Che chicken wakes me from the fantasy. I could drive all night, but I'd never get away. They have the other half of me locked in a room that I can't get to.

ဢ 13 ⭗

THE WILL OF INSTINCT

Caged birds sing
Sweet as wild birds do
For love or affection
Though they never flew
Cage birds sing
If you clip their wings
But the will of instinct
Is sure to make it sting
Better check that cage door
'for you go to sleep
'cause the will of instinct
Gonna make you weep
"Caged Birds" – Luna Rayne, 1999

I spend the next morning sulking and exhausted. Jamie looks worse than I do. We drive back in silence, but I barely notice. My head aches and every cell of my body feels like it's been sucked dry. Logan's gone when I'm returned to our cell, and she doesn't come back for hours. I try to connect with Ethan about a hundred times, but my powers are down, and I can't concentrate. I'm too tired to even dig out my mother's earring and relieve my stress. Plus, I'm not looking forward to the repercussions for my slip at the hospital. No doubt it will provide Dr. Robineau with plenty of fodder for our next session, if there is a next session. The thought makes me smile, but we still need to reach Ethan with a plan and find a way to get him out of solitary confinement. My smile falls with the thought that the clock keeps ticking toward Gran's death. My throat clenches.

By the time dinner rolls around, I'm starving. Out of desperation, I try the door, and I'm shocked to discover that I'm no longer on lockdown. I can't believe it. With each step, I expect guards to come racing down the hall to subdue me. When that doesn't happen, I head straight for Cayde and Ethan's room. If I'm free, maybe Ethan is, too.

The door to their room is open. Cayde's sitting motionless on the floor, and Hugo's perched on the edge of the bed. Before I even walk in, the heavy vibe hits me.

"Hey, guys," I say cautiously.

Hugo swipes at his eyes with his big paws. "Hey, beautiful! Where ya been?" He meets me halfway into the room and catches me up in a bear hug. For a second, I'm lost in his warmth and sadness. I try to absorb his pain, but when we finally break off, I can tell by his face that my efforts were a fail.

"What's wrong?" I ask.

Hugo's eyes fill up, and he turns away. Cayde steps up onto the bed and begins jumping like it's a trampoline. His hands are balled into tight fists. All the toys that populated the room have been removed. It looks like a dorm at the end of a semester.

"There's a saying here: 'Grow or go.' An' I'm goin'," Cayde says bitterly.

"Going where? I don't get it," I say.

"PSI has a strict policy of 'if you put out, we put you up,' but once the honeymoon's over and a kid peaks, they're done."

Hugo's explanation leaves me more lost.

Cayde bounces off the bed and lands in front of me. "It's like this. I'm not getting any stronger. In fact, the older I get, the weaker my superpowers get." He hangs his head as if ashamed.

Hugo jumps in again. "It happens with a lot of kids. They have something. Then they hit puberty, and it just goes away, like they outgrow it or something. Especially with telekinetics. I've never seen one make it past thirteen. I thought my man here was gonna go the distance, but these last couple of months —" Hugo's voice trails off sadly.

"What're you going to do? Where will you go?" I ask Cayde.

He shrugs, so I look at Hugo. "Don't know what happens to kids who 'go.' We never hear from them again. I guess their folks come and get them, or the government sends them off to military school or something."

"Fuck that!" Cayde says. "They're gonna off me. I'll bet you a million dollars I'll be shot in the back of the head and my ashes'll be mixed into concrete for the next fucking war monument. 'Course that million dollars you're gonna owe me ain't gonna be no help by then."

My eyes get big, and my mouth goes dry. Hugo isn't refuting Cayde's theory. "Why would they kill you?" I manage to croak.

Cayde gives me a look. "Secrets, girl! I know all their secrets. You think they want me going on TV or the interwebs and telling everyone and their dog all about how they drug up kids and test them for superpowers to make them into weapons or something? My damn story is worth a million bucks out there, and all I gotta do is make one phone call, and it'll be a freaking bidding war. The government ain't about to risk all that."

Cayde's more serious than I've ever seen him. Hugo nods his concurrence.

"How do you know they're cutting you loose?" I ask.

Hugo looks down. "I saw it for an instant in Dr. Robineau's office." He glances up to meet my stare and adds, "Ya know — my superpower."

I suddenly realize we're in full view of the cameras, carrying on like they aren't there. Cayde catches my panic.

"I can still do little things," Cayde says, "but even that will go away in time, and I'll never get to see my reciprocal. That's what Robineau's all about. No reciprocal, no nothing."

I table the concept of reciprocals and ask Hugo, "What's your superpower?" I barely hear his answer as my mind flashes back to Jamie just one night ago. I should've read his mind when I had the chance.

"Eidetic memory. Auditory, visual, tactile. The whole shebang, hyperthymesia. I remember every little thing that happens. No reciprocal. What would it be? Super forgetfulness?"

"Yeah. Alzheimer man! Forgetting who's in danger and how to save them. You can't miss him. He wears a yellow cape and a diaper." Cayde's laughing like a hyena at his own joke.

"What's your reciprocal, Cayde?"

His laughter stops instantly. "Don't know. Robineau never got that far with me."

"She thinks she has with Ethan, though," I say, just to confirm. Both Hugo and Cayde nod.

"Well, not for long," I say, deciding in that instant to loop Hugo in to the plan. This whole situation might just be a perfect setup or a perfect opportunity; my vote is for synchronicity. I have no reason not to trust Hugo. He's been nothing but kind, helpful, and on our side. On the other hand, he's one of "them." I shake off the negativity. I have to trust someone, or Ethan and I will be here until the contract ends or we die, whichever comes first. I take the plunge. "We aren't going to sit around here waiting to see if Cayde gets offed or sent to military school or the zoo; we're going to get him the hell out of here, and he's going to take Ethan with him."

Cayde's eyes light up like a city at dusk. Hugo nods solemnly. "Count me in, gorgeous!"

With Hugo in, things will be much easier at this end, but I'll be on my own, unless I decide to trust Jamie. Hugo lays out a plan. I'll prep Ethan tonight when I visit him from the astral plane. The plan begins with a map of the grounds and surrounding area that Hugo draws with his flawless memory. One section of the compound isn't fenced. You can get to it by wading in the creek, upstream about half a mile. From there, you have to climb a sheer rock face about twenty-five feet up and crawl through a tiny cave, a crevice really, that runs about a hundred or so yards underground until it opens out near a small lake or a big pond; take your pick. If you swim across the lake and climb through the muck, you end up a couple hundred yards from a county road outside PSI. It's complicated, but if anyone could make it physically, it's Ethan and Cayde. Hugo will point them in the right direction and remain behind to misdirect the search.

When Hugo's done explaining, I throw myself into his arms and weep my gratitude. When the plan's finally cemented, we all realize that we missed dinner.

We test our stealth skills by sneaking down to the kitchen to get a snack when the dinner crew's gone. I return to my room full of chocolate cake and a tentative certainty that I'll be free in a day or two. Logan's absorbed in her wall. I want to talk to her, but I know better than to interrupt.

I spend a long time staring up at the stars, wondering what Jamie was trying to say when he put them there. I think about the constellations and how they've guided travelers since the dawn of man, despite the fact that the stars themselves might have disappeared or exploded long ago. I wonder why humanity has so much faith in something that might not even exist anymore. I wonder if I should put my faith in a man I know almost nothing, and yet everything, about.

Ethan's asleep by the time I'm able to astral project into his room, and I have no way to wake him up. I stay with him as long as I can, watching his face contort in some horrific dream. He whimpers and talks, but I can't make out what he's saying. Eventually, he drops into a deeper, more peaceful sleep that makes him look like he's about five. Not long after that, I drift back to myself and float away on my own sea of dreams.

I don't see Jamie again until the next night. By then, I'm feeling almost back to myself, and I'm itching for another opportunity to walk away, simple as that. Hugo, Cayde, and Logan are all keeping tabs on my next "mission." As soon as I leave the grounds of PSI, Hugo will move heaven and earth to get Cayde and Ethan out of there. I'll have to find my own opportunity, wherever I can take it.

When Jamie knocks on the open door to my room, I expect he's there to brief me, so all these thoughts rush through my mind, and my heart rate hits panic level. I don't get up to greet him. He probably thinks I'm upset about what happened at the hotel, but I haven't had the headspace to even worry about all that.

"Can I come in?" he asks with his usual hangdog look.

"Sure." I say from where I'm sitting on the bed. I cross my arms over my chest and take a deep breath.

"How're you feeling?" he asks. He stands awkwardly, halfway into the room.

"Are you asking about my health, or about my abilities, or about us?" I probably sound snarkier than I mean to; Logan would approve.

He shrugs and shifts his feet. "Uh . . . any or all of the above."

"Health-wise, I'm still tired, but the headache and nausea are mostly gone. As for my abilities, if Logan came through the door and cut off your head, I'm pretty sure I could reattach it." I pause for dramatic effect. "If the urge struck me."

"I see. Jury's still out on us," he says. Then he actually looks over his shoulder to make sure Logan isn't about to come at him with a sword or ax.

I have to smile.

"What? You had me going there," he says, moving closer to the bed. I don't invite him to sit. "I wanted to thank you." He digs his hands deeper into his pockets. "You know, for respecting my request, for not prying when you have every right to." He glances toward the camera.

"Sure." I say. I have to admit, though I hate to see him squirm, I kind of love it too. A long, uncomfortable silence follows before I ask, "So, what's up next?"

"Are you sure you're ready for a next?" he asks with genuine concern.

"I told you, I'm fine." I muster as much sincerity as I can for the camera, knowing there needs to be a mission to give Ethan a fighting chance at getting out with Cayde before he's sent away.

"Okay," Jamie says. "Can I sit down?"

I wait a couple of beats, then shrug. He hedges for a few more seconds and finally decides to sit at the foot of the bed, as far from me as possible.

"Tomorrow we're back on base. Dr. Meriwether wants to talk to you about how you do it. The healing thing, you know. She's going to hypnotize you and take you back through the experience at the hospital." He gives it a minute to sink in. "Can you handle that?"

I close my eyes in resignation. It wouldn't matter if I couldn't or if I said I couldn't, so I nod. "Whatever."

"I'm sorry." He reaches out and touches my knee.

"I know," I say.

"Come on," he says, "let's go for a walk."

I'm not really in the mood. I was thinking of taking a bath and getting out my mother's earring, just for fun. I consider his offer, though.

"Please, let me do something nice for you," he says. He caresses my arm. Something about the way he touches me like that is so intimate and heated. Suddenly, I want to go with him more than anything.

I nod.

When we're away from the prying eyes of the cameras, he slips his hand in mine and pulls me close. In an instant, his arm's around my waist and his lips are on mine with a combination of sweetness and insistence. I return his kisses and run my hands over his back.

"Elena," he sighs. "I would give anything for all of this to be different."

I pull away. "Different?"

"You know, normal," he says sadly. "Someplace else. In a world where you trusted me."

My heart skips a beat. "I want to trust you, Jamie, but you —"

"I know," he says. "I'm sure it seems like I'm working for them, but I'd do anything to protect you and Ethan. Anything."

It's just what I want to hear, what I need to hear right now. The last thing I want is to go through this whole ordeal alone. I need his complicity, his blessing, maybe. I pause only a split second before I lay it bare. The whole time I'm talking, I'm wondering if this is maybe the second biggest mistake of my life, but he holds both my hands, and the peaceful green of his eyes melts any remaining reservation, like mango ice on a summer sidewalk.

When I'm done, he says, "I don't want you to go." My heart spasms. "But I'll help you if I can."

'If I can?' What's that supposed to mean? I stop short of asking. Maybe it means nothing.

He reaches out and pulls me to his chest. I relax against him and listen to the steady beat of his heart. I summon some calm and match my breathing to his.

"I think Dr. Meriwether might be able to help, too. Can I talk to her?"

I pull away and shake my head. "Uh-uh. The more people who know, the more fucked up it'll get. I just need you." A little, satisfied smile plays at his lips. "I meant to get out of here," I add, hitting him in the arm like a fifth-grade girl.

"Sure you did."

We make our way down to the creek where I check out the place Ethan and Cayde will begin their journey tomorrow. I can't see very far, but it doesn't look that daunting from here. Suddenly, I'm excited about being with Ethan again, under the same roof, where we can fight and laugh and just be around each other. I hope he'll forgive me for bringing him to this horrible place.

"You're lucky, you know," Jamie says out of the blue. "I never had that kind of relationship with anyone."

I step away and swallow. "What're you talking about?"

"What you're feeling right now. Of course, I'm guessing that it's about your brother."

"How do you — ohhh." I take some deep breaths. "So, this is your way of telling me why you're here."

He looks at the ground.

"You're an empath."

He nods. I move a step away to process what he's telling me. It explains a great deal, but not what he said in the hotel when he begged me not to read his mind. I'm not sure what to say, so after an awkward silence, I mumble, "I'm getting tired. Let's go back." I take his hand to let him know I'm okay with his big, or not so big, revelation. Still, we walk across the darkening grounds without talking.

We enter the building through the back doors, the ones Maureen took me through the day I brought Ethan here, a hundred years ago. Jamie steps into a small alcove to the right of the door and turns to face me.

"No cameras here," he says, shifting his feet. "I... uh —" He wrings his hands and fails to finish his thought. "That door over there," he points, "goes to an emergency staircase that leads up to the staff dorms. No cameras there either," he says, glancing at me sideways. After a beat, I get it.

"James! Are you asking me to come up to your room —" His eyebrows go up expectantly. "— and spend the night?"

He opens his eyes wide. "Well, if you put it like that, yes. Yes, that's what I'm doing, rather badly, I might add."

I giggle. "Now why would a girl like me, a girl who likes girls, I might add, do that?"

"Are you mocking me?" Jamie postures indignantly.

"No, teasing maybe, but definitely not mocking," I say.

He smiles for a second, but his face turns serious again. "After tomorrow, I might never see you again." His hand grazes my arm, and my skin catches fire. I can't tear my eyes from his.

Finally, I shrug like he asked if I wanted a glass of water. "Lead the way," I say. As we climb the stairs, my resolve from the hotel just a couple of nights ago returns as a passing flutter. My mind tries to grab hold of it, but it's like trying to hold a hummingbird. It flits around until he takes my hand again, and then it's just gone.

His room is exactly as I remember from my astral spying. Vampire central — dark colors, dim lighting, mysterious vibe and all. There's little here that reveals anything about the man. No photos or art work decorate the walls or surfaces. A couple of books, best sellers and classics that you read in school, lie face down on the tables with the spines broken, like several insomniacs picked them up and put them down in the dead of the night. The bedding that lies strewn sideways across the double bed is institutional, even more so than the linens in my room.

Jamie rushes around collecting towels and discarded clothing that he tosses haphazardly into the closet.

"Sorry about the mess. I didn't really plan on company. I thought —"

"Yeah. I was a little thrown the other night, but I guess I'm not really in a position to cast stones." I sit on the end of the sofa that he's just cleared, while he continues to bustle around.

"No. Yes. You are. Sorry. Let's not talk about this. Okay?"

"Sure," I say.

Now that I'm here, I think he's not sure what to do with me or maybe how to do it without seeming like he's that guy. You know, the one who will use any excuse to get laid. My resolve to keep him at a safe distance taps on my shoulder again. I've watched enough late night TV to know junkies are not to be trusted. They'll sell out their mothers for a score. Then it occurs to me that he knows I'm having doubts here, and I wonder how distressing that must be because as an empath, by definition, he'd start having doubts, too.

"Can I get you a Coke? Or water? That's all I have. Well, and potato chips." He hasn't stopped moving since we walked through the door.

"Not bad. Three of the four college food groups. You've got the caffeine, sugar, and salt groups covered. All you're missing is the alcohol group," I say.

He laughs at my joke. "They don't let us drink; it messes with our powers. Let that be a lesson to you, young lady."

"Good to know. I'll remember not to bring my flask to the hospital next time I work my mojo on a bunch of cancer kids." It's not funny, and his smile fades.

"I'm really sorry they put you through that. I hated watching what it did to you. But damn, girl, you were amazing with them. Like an angel or a goddess or something. You blew me clean away."

What do you say to something like that? My face and neck burst into flame, and all I can do is mumble, "Thanks."

"Hey," he says, crossing the room to sit with me on the sofa. "I didn't mean to embarrass you."

"I'm not —" I stop mid-sentence. "Yeah. I guess there's no point in lying to you about what I'm feeling or not feeling," I say.

"Oh no. You can lie all you want," he says. "I'll just know."

"Fabulous!"

"Isn't it?" He puts his arm around me and pulls me into a playful hug.

That's all it takes. The moment physical contact has been initiated, whatever logical arguments I have in my head about junkies and safe distances become weak and specious, buckets with holes that won't hold water, not the least of which is the fact that I don't even like boys, and this is the first time I'll be having real sex, where it's my choice. I can walk away or stay, and I'm all in without a single good reason to be.

His kisses accelerate from sweet to sexy in a matter of seconds and I can't get his body close enough to mine, despite the fact that I've pulled him down on top of me. I tear his polo shirt over his head and fumble madly with the buttons on my blouse, but my hands are shaking so badly I get nowhere. His hands take over for me, but they're shaking almost as much as mine. We both laugh with relief when I'm finally free of my top.

I pull him back down on me, skin to skin, and if what we had before was fire, this is like a pound of C4 blowing us sky high. Every place he touches me begs for more. Every kiss is deeper than the last. The few vestiges of clothing left on are intrusive and painful. I've never wanted anything more than I want him in me at this moment. Suddenly, my hands find the dexterity I need to get his jeans off, and I take a moment to thank the gods for the fact that he's chosen to go commando this day.

With all barriers to nirvana removed, the pace shifts into slow gear. Every second is stretched into a bliss-filled hour of feeling completely with and for Jamie in a way I never thought I'd be able to be with anyone, let alone a guy. I want this to never end. Counterpoint to that, deep inside, an urgency and tension are building, beginning to cry out for release. The rhythm takes on a life of its own, ebbing and growing in a heated dance that has me moaning and panting and desperate. We climax at exactly the same moment.

I let the explosion penetrate from brain to toes, absorbing the feeling into every cell. No one in the history of the world has had a first time better than this! Jamie's there inside me, in every pore. Still, it takes me a moment to realize that his shoulders are shaking and my neck's wet with his tears. I wrap my arms around his back. I can't for the life of me imagine why he'd be crying when I want to dance.

The world comes back in waves as we lie together. The sofa eventually becomes too small to accommodate us uncoupled, so Jamie gets up and goes into the bathroom. I find a box of tissues and clean up as best I can. I search through his dresser until I find a t-shirt that smells like him and put it on. Then I curl up in his bed to wait for him to come back. He returns with two glasses of water and an apology.

"I'm so sorry about that," he says, averting his eyes from mine.

"Which part?" I ask, sitting up.

He smiles. "Not the good parts. Just at the end there."

"No worries," I say. I want to ask him why, but I don't.

"Sometimes," he begins, "all the emotion coming in gets to be too much. When I was a kid, my parents thought I was crazy, like seriously crazy. I was up and down like a lunatic, depending on who I was with. The only time I could relax was when I was alone, and they were afraid to leave me alone. When I was six, I was hospitalized for being suicidal. Dr. Meriwether was a doctor at the pediatric psych hospital. She's the one who figured out what was 'wrong' with me. She was a graduate student then. Turns out her sister was there, too, as a patient. She and Dr. Robineau were working on a theory about kids with abilities back then, but they had a lot of trouble getting support from the rest of the psychiatric community. Lucky for them, the politicians were a bit easier to convince, and the boys in Washington set up the PSI lab. Unfortunately, it wasn't in time to help Sarah, Dr. Meriwether's sister. She committed suicide while out on a weekend pass. Rumor has it that Dr. Meriwether was the one who found her. When I was twelve, I was sent to a group home, where they kept me massively medicated, even though it didn't really help. Somehow, Dr. Meriwether convinced my parents to let her take me, and she brought me here."

"So you were like patient X, sort of," I say.

"I guess." He gives me a strange look. "Weird analogy, Elena." Then he goes on. "Maureen and Hugo showed up soon after, and a little later, dozens of other kids passed in and out, like a revolving door, until Logan was dragged here, kicking and screaming. Then Cayde's custody was signed over to Robineau like mine was to Meriwether."

"So, you've lived here," I gesture around the room, "for sixteen years?"

"Not here, exactly. This facility has only been around for about five years. And when I came of age, I went into the military for a while."

"So, if Robineau is such a big hero, why is she so... so evil?"

Jamie laughs. "Trust me, she's not evil. She's just driven."

I push away and sit up. "Driven? I can't believe you're defending her after what she's done to me and Ethan."

Jamie hangs his head. "I'm sorry. It's hard for me to forget the fact that she and Dr. Meriwether basically saved my life."

"Where do Ethan and I come in?" The question comes out hard.

"What do you mean?" he asks.

"How did they find us?"

Jamie smiles. "You called us. Remember?"

He's right, of course, but I still feel like a piece of this puzzle is missing somehow. I roll over, and Jamie moves in close to spoon me. Any critical thought that might have had a chance dissipates as his body presses up against me.

The next morning, he sneaks me down to my room before dawn

and goes back up to shower and get ready. Logan rolls over while I'm pulling clothes out of the drawer.

"Look who's doing the walk of shame this morning," Logan mumbles sleepily.

I shake my head and smile. "No shame here. I promise."

"You should be ashamed. While you were up there getting naked with your mentor, the dykes called, and your lesbo card has been revoked. They're thinking of bringing you up on charges of defection."

"Shut up," I say.

"Oh snap! I'm not hearing a denial." She sits up. "You did it! — with Jamie. That's unbelievably disgusting."

"Get your mind out of the gutter," I say, turning away so she can't see me smiling.

"That is so gross. I think I need a shower."

"Me first," I say, rushing into the bathroom. I have no idea how she moves so fast, but her foot's in the door before I can close it. We both push as hard as we can while we laugh hysterically. Logan finally steps back, but I don't close the door in her face. We stare at each other across the space. Her eyes go sad. She doesn't say it; she doesn't have to. I know she's thinking the same thing I am, that this is the last time we'll be playing this game. I close the door quietly and turn on the water. When I come back out, she's at the wall, lost in her world of the dead. I shiver a little. We can't say goodbye, not without tipping off the watchers, so I stay in the closet and compose a note that I slip into her shoe.

On the trip out to the base, Jamie tells me he met up with Hugo this morning and everything's a go. Ethan gave Robineau something she wanted, so she okayed Hugo's outing on the grounds after breakfast. Only a couple of hours until Ethan's free. My heart's beating so hard, I wonder if I might pass out.

"You should try to contact him now. It might be the last chance you get for a while," Jamie says.

"I guess," I say, a little confused. "But with any luck we'll be together tonight."

Jamie smiles and keeps his eyes on the road. He's having doubts about us pulling this off. He won't say it, but I can feel the vibe coming from him. I lean back in the seat and reach deep inside my psyche for a place of calm. I have a hard time getting there through the layers of emotion swirling like a tsunami in my mind, but I finally find it. Ethan's not nearly as hard to find. He's practically screaming out to me telepathically.

"Lanie! Are you here?" he calls.

"Right here, E. It's almost over now. Are you ready?" I can see him pacing around the room, searching for his left sneaker. "It's behind the canvases in the corner," I tell him.

He goes there, pulls it out and sits on the floor to put it on. He looks so small and vulnerable, I could cry. "I'm scared, Lanie," he thinks. "Something isn't right. I know it."

He used to say this all the time when he was little, whenever we had to leave the house for school or a doctor appointment or anything. He was always convinced that something would go wrong, and if we could actually get him out the door, something usually would go wrong. His anxiety created any number of disasters that ended in puddles and tears and general hysteria. The fact that he's saying this now isn't a good omen.

"Ethan, you need to be calm and just go with Cayde. Follow the route Hugo showed you. You know it, right?"

"Yes. Yes. I know the route and the plan and what to do to stay hidden from the PSI cops when they come after us. I know Rachel's phone number and how to get to Jesse's ranch. I know everything, but something's wrong!"

"Ethan, if you know all that, then nothing can go wrong. You're going to be fine. Just keep it together. Be strong. Can you do that for me?"

"I guess. But, Lanie, what about you? What if something goes wrong for you?"

I haven't allowed my head to go there. "Jamie will be with me.

Nothing can happen that he can't protect me from. Piece of pie."

"You mean cake," Ethan corrects. "I wish you could come back and come with me and Cayde."

"Me too, pal. But by tonight, we'll be comparing adventures and holding hands." Far away, back in my body, I feel the car slowing. "Ethan, I have to go now. Just be strong. You can do this. I know you can."

"You, too, Lanie. You be strong, too," he says. "Please be careful, Lanie. Please," he begs.

"Promise." Suddenly the car jerks to a stop, and I'm slammed back into my body. "Oww!" I say, reaching over and hitting Jamie in the center of his chest. "That wasn't a smooth landing!"

He smiles at me. "We're here. Are you ready?"

"I'm not even sure what I'm supposed to be ready for," I say. "So, no. But let's not jump the gun. Hugo's still a little while from getting the boys out of there."

Jamie nods. "He's gonna text me when the ball's rolling."

He comes around to the other side of the car to help me out. For a few seconds, he stands with his arms around me, so close I can feel his breath. Between the two of us, every emotion known to man is kicking up dust. For the first time I wonder what's going to happen to him and Hugo when Robineau finds Ethan and me missing.

"Don't worry," he says.

"I hate when you do that, you know," I say.

"Everyone does," he says, half-grinning. "We should go."

I suddenly notice that all the base personnel are watching our little scene, and my cheeks burn. I push him back gently. "We shouldn't keep Dr. Meriwether waiting."

She greets us warmly and offers us tea. I take it with complete trust and savor the cool minty flavor. It's all small talk while we drink, but a few seconds after I put my cup down, I realize that my hearing's fading in and out like a radio station when you're driving through the hills. I turn to Jamie in slow motion, and the room tips dangerously.

"She dosed me," I say, slurring my words.

Jamie doesn't respond, but Meriwether puts a hand on my arm. "It's okay, dear. I just need to have you relaxed so the hypnotism can work." I can't turn around to look at her because the room's spinning in the opposite direction, and I'm sucked in like it's a whirlpool.

"Jamie," I whine, reaching out for his hand. He catches my whole body and lies me out on the sofa, like he did last night. I wrap my arms around his neck and pull him into a deep kiss.

He pulls away. "No, Elena, not here," he whispers.

I giggle because his ears are turning scarlet. He steps away, and Dr. Meriwether comes into view. She pulls a chair close to the sofa.

"Okay, Elena. I want you to watch the tip of this pen. Don't take your eyes off of it. Count backward from twenty. By the time you get to zero, you'll be in a deep state of relaxation. The whole world will melt away, and all you'll perceive is my voice. Begin."

I don't want to be relaxed. I need to stay alert, ready to move when Hugo's message comes in. I try to resist, but I can't keep from counting. "Twenty, nineteen, eighteen, seventeen, sixteen, fifteen..." My own words drone in my head until I'm not even aware that I'm the one speaking them. Gradually, all color fades from the room and it transforms into a gray void, like so much static on an old school television.

Meriwether's soothing voice comes out of the void, like a mother. "Elena, can you hear me?" she asks.

I nod, because speaking takes too much effort.

"Go back to the room in the hospital from yesterday."

Immediately, the void's replaced by the brightly colored, puzzle piece floor. My heart begins to beat harder, and bile rises in my throat.

"Do you see it?" the disembodied voice asks.

I nod.

"Amelia's with you now. Tell me what you're thinking."

The little girl tries to curl into my lap, and I push her away.

"It hurts," I say. My voice echoes as if I'm in a long tunnel. "I'm scared. I don't want to do this!" I hear my pitch rising.

"It's okay, Elena," Dr. Meriwether assures me. "You're perfectly safe. Nothing's going to hurt you now. You just need to remember what you did to help Amelia."

"I don't know," I say from the inside the tunnel. In the room, Amelia watches me curiously.

"Think hard, Elena. You played a game with her. You both laid down and joined hands."

The scene shifts suddenly, and I'm on my back. Amelia's hand is burning through mine, and my spine's on fire.

"No!" I cry. "No! It hurts. Make it stop." I sit up and vomit over the side of the sofa. I'm back in Meriwether's office on the tilt-a-whirl teacup ride. Jamie's beside me, rubbing my back. I hurl over and over. Every time I think I'm done, and I just about choke it down, another spasm wracks me until I'm caught up in dry heaves that are exhausting and painful. Tears pour down my cheeks, and my whole body trembles. Finally, I'm too weak to throw up again, and I lean back against Jamie, sweaty and exhausted.

I feel his phone vibrate against my thigh. Oh shit! Not now. He rubs my arm. "I think Elena could use some air," he says to Meriwether while he offers me his hand.

"Of course," Dr. Meriwether says. I can tell she's disappointed. He laces his arm around me and practically carries me out into the hallway.

When we're a few doors down, Jamie takes the phone out of his pocket. "Show time," he says. "You gonna make it?"

"I'm okay," I say, hoping the adrenaline will propel me forward. As we make our way down the hall, Jamie fishes around in his pockets.

"No way," he says, stopping. "My keys."

"You don't have them?" It's a stupid question, since obviously he doesn't.

"Did you see where I put them?"

I close my eyes and channel Hugo. "Maybe they're on Meriwether's desk," I say. I remember him putting them there right after we walked in.

"Shit!" he says, running a hand through his hair.

"Just go back and get them," I say.

"She'll want to know why I'm there and you aren't," he says.

"No," I say, "You can't tell her. Make something up. Tell her you're taking me back to PSI or that you need to get me some medicine.

"It won't work," he says.

I lean my head against the cool, cinderblock wall. "It has to. I'm not going to make a hundred yards on foot. We need the car."

"Okay," he says. And he hurries away, back toward Meriwether's office. I turn around and lean my back against the wall. In a few seconds, I'm so tired that I slide to the ground.

Jamie suddenly grabs my hand and yanks me to my feet. He's dragging me behind him like we're being followed, but the hallway's empty. The sunlight blinds me as we burst through the doors. I hear the car beep as Jamie unlocks it across the wide lawn. We're jogging now, and Jamie keeps looking around, like he's expecting someone to pop out of the ground to grab us. In one deft move he opens the car door and slides inside. I'm several steps behind, and I barely pull my legs in before the car's rolling.

"What happened in there?" I ask in gasps.

Jamie doesn't answer. He holds up a hand. "Don't say anything," he instructs.

We pull up to the guard post at the base entrance. Jamie waves to the soldiers on duty.

"Hey," he says, rolling down his window.

Instead of raising the gate automatically, the guy comes out of the guard shack. As he walks forward, he swings the gun off his shoulder and into his hands. Before the rush of fear floods my brain, Jamie has stepped on the gas. His car shreds the wooden arm that never went up. A split second before the first bullet hits the car, Jamie's hand shoves my head down into my knees. The car's rocked by the impact.

I want to scream, "Faster! Go faster!" But I can't speak.

The second bullet hits one of the back tires. The car veers wildly but manages to keep moving forward with Jamie driving on the rim. We must be almost out of range of the bullets, I think. The third bullet hits the other back tire. Now the car's dragging its ass on the ground, monumentally impeding forward progress.

"We're going to have to make a run for it," Jamie says.

I look out the windshield. We're maybe a hundred yards from the highway. If we make it that far, someone might stop to help.

He doesn't bother braking. We both pop the doors at the same time and a fraction of a second after he rolls from the slowing vehicle, I follow suit. The ground's soft and swampy from the recent rains, so the fall doesn't hurt, but jumping from a moving car is all kinds of discombobulating to a girl who's been dosed, hypnotized, and upchucked clean in the last hour. I'm desperately trying to find my feet, when Jamie's there, hoisting me up by the arm and shoving me in front of him.

A voice from a bull horn yells, "Private Fleming, you are ordered to stop and return to base!" I jump a mile inside my skin.

Jamie turns and yells over his shoulder, "Fuck you!"

"Return the girl to base, or we'll be forced to open fire," the bullhorn voice instructs calmly.

For half a second his eyes meet mine, and a jolt of fear shoots between us like an electric shock. I want to stop this madness and go back before one of us gets dead, but Jamie holds onto my arm like he's falling from a cliff while he simultaneously picks up the pace.

Guys with bull horns and big guns don't bluff. Shots echo behind us, and Jamie goes down, skidding on his knees and dropping onto his face. He releases my arm, and I'm several steps gone before my brain realizes he's been shot. I change direction and hurry back to him. He's covered in dark brown mud. I roll him over.

"Keep going," he croaks. "Get the fuck out of here, Elena!"

I don't have time to heal him, and the guns are still going off at intervals. Tears are pouring down my cheeks as the two guards from the checkpoint approach us at a run.

Suddenly, something happens inside me. I feel a twist, like a yoga pose gone awry, inside my gut and spine. In my head, I want the men running toward us to feel their hearts stop. I want them to hurt so badly that they can't hurt us, so we have time to get away. I think these dark thoughts as my insides twist, and something like an aneurism explodes in my brain. I wonder for an instant if I've been shot, too. I close my eyes, scream and the pain's gone. I look up and the gunmen are gone, too. I see them writhing in the mud some twenty yards from where we are. Two more emerge from the guardhouse with weapons drawn. They make it only a few yards before the explosion happens in my brain again, and they go down, too.

Jamie's looking at me with eyes wide and terrified. Terrified not of the men trying to kill us, but terrified of me. Another voice suddenly pierces the thick air.

"Elena! Come with me. I'll get you out of here." Dr. Meriwether's making her way through the muck and weeds from the highway. Her hand's extended. I start to close my eyes.

Jamie grabs my hand. "No, Elena! Don't hurt her! She's here to help! Please, let her help us."

I open my eyes and the realization hits me hard. I took those men down with my thoughts. I hurt them. The reciprocal gift. Of course. I can heal, and I can harm. My stomach roils. But Meriwether's here now. I feel her arms around me. I hear her whisper, "It's over now, sweetheart. You did really well." Then I feel the needle go into my neck. I have no time to react. The bloody scene instantly flows into inky darkness.

Susan Michalski

℘ 14 ℘

SOUND OF DRUMS

Your hand's played out
You're left with Jacks
Four queens to my aces
My jokers attack
Once child's play
Don't kiss and tell
Spin the bottle
For ten minutes in hell
Tension's building
Between the lines
Sound the drums
The war has begun
Sound the drums
For a war that won't be won
        "War" - Luna Rayne, 2013

When I open my eyes, Logan's face is only a couple of inches from mine. I gasp and sit up suddenly. The field, with its dark mud and tall weeds, the smell of brine and blood, the crack of gunshots, and the nausea materialize in my memory like fragments from a nightmare.

"What the hell?" I say to Logan.

"I've been waiting for hours to talk to you!"

As I put my hand back to brace myself, I notice the unmistakable lump made by feet under a blanket. I turn slowly to see who's occupying the bed I just sprang from. "Shit!" I scream, albeit silently — because the body in the bed is mine.

"Jeezus, girl! Calm down. It's not like this is your first rodeo."

"I just thought — I'm not sure what I thought. How're we doing this if I'm not conscious? I thought it was impossible to astral project without conscious intent."

"Damned if I know." She looks down at the floor. "I brought someone to see you. Please don't be mad." I watch Logan's form fade into the wall. A moment later, Lily materializes where Logan had been.

"Gran?" I ask.

"Elena! What happened to you?" She walks over to the bed and gestures, like she's smoothing the hair from my forehead.

"Gran, what're you doing here?"

Gran turns from my body to face my projection. "Your friend said you'd understand."

Then it hits me. "No. No. No." I shake my head. "You aren't here! This is a dream. Tell me it's a dream. I need to see you, be with you before —"

"Elena, stop. It's okay. Sage was with me. I wasn't alone, and it didn't hurt. Please, don't be upset. I had a reasonable death."

"I was going to make it in time. I was going to —" I feel like a failure, like I betrayed her, but Lily would have had none of that in life, and she isn't going to let me go there in death either.

"Well, you didn't. And besides, I'm here with you now. I know how hard you tried. It was probably better this way. You and the boy didn't need to see me like that. It would've been too hard. You weren't ready for all the tubes and pills and mess. You can remember me before I was sick. That's better. It really is."

I pull myself together. "Have you seen Ethan? Like this. He can astral project, too," I say.

Gran smiles her tired smile. "I saw the boy, but he didn't see me.

You did right by him, though. You always did right by him. He's safe with Jesse and Rachel now." She pauses. "I needed to talk to you before I move on. To tell you I'm sorry."

"For what, Gran?"

"Not doing right by you and your brother sooner."

"But you did, Gran. You took us in and gave us everything we needed. You kept us together and didn't send Ethan to an institution. You were everything to us."

"God knows I tried, but I just didn't have what it took to be a mother or a father to you two. If I'd done better, you wouldn't be in this pickle."

"This mess is my doing. All mine. You rest easy, Gran."

"Always the one to make everything right. Aren't you an angel."

Now the tears come down. I feel them on my face, the one on the pillow, not the one standing here with my grandmother. I'm no angel, will never be one, not after what I've done.

She goes on. "I'm so proud of you. You're a soul pure and good, one of the few the world has in it."

"Gran, stop. You wouldn't say that if you knew what I did."

"No, Elena, you stop. Anything you think you did is not your fault. Don't let them do that to you!"

I want to believe her, but I hurt those guards, maybe killed them, and they were so young, like me, doing a job they probably never wanted. Whatever happened to them is my fault.

My grandmother reels me back in. "I left you some things in the attic room, in the trunk in the back of the armoire. There are things in there for Ethan and the Mulcahy boy, too."

"Finn? Why would you leave something for him?"

"You'll just have to get yourself home to find out. I have to go now. I don't have much time here before I have to move on."

"Will you come again?"

"I don't think so. Be strong, Elena. Fight hard and go home to Sage and Jo. Most of all, be happy. Just be happy. Help the boy find some peace, too. I love you, Elena. More than you'll ever know."

"I love you, too, Gran. So much." Then she's gone, like she was never standing in this room, like a dream designed to break my heart. I wait for Logan to come back, but she doesn't, so I find my way back into my body and fight to wake up.

The first thing I notice is the sound of someone groaning and panting. I make a tentative move to see if my limbs are intact. Every muscle in my body feels weighted down, like I landed on another planet where gravity is double Earth's. Just opening my eyes takes a concerted effort. Eventually, I manage to turn my head in the direction of the sound.

"Elena," Jamie says through clenched teeth. "Oh, thank god, you're finally awake."

"Jamie?" I pull myself to sitting to get a better look. He's pale and sweating. Blood seeps through a bandage wrapped around his shoulder. "What —?" I stop mid-question as the memory inserts itself into my consciousness. I struggle to my feet and drag myself across the room.

"Where are we?" I ask.

"Elena, help me. Please," he begs.

I think about it. I doubt in my current state I could muster the energy it would take to heal a hangnail, but something else makes me hesitate. "I can't," I say.

"You can. Just try, please." Tears of desperation threaten his eyes.

"First, tell me what happened out there," I say.

"What do you mean? They caught us. I was helping you escape." His voice wavers ever so slightly.

"You were helping me?" I ask it quietly.

"You know I was." Now his voice is insistent. "I was shot. You think I was part of this? You think I got shot on purpose? Really?"

I consider the situation. He was shot. You can't fake that, but the rest of it was wrong somehow, like we were playing out a scene staged for a B movie.

"Why did they stop us at the gate?" I ask.

"Dr. Meriwether must have been suspicious when I got the keys.

She must've called them."

"I thought she was on my side. You said she would help me. You said I could trust her. Plus, in all the time I've known you, Jamie, you've never lost or forgotten anything, but today or yesterday or whenever it all went down, you suddenly come down with a case of ADD? I don't know."

"Fuck that, Elena." His voice has risen a full octave. Under the pain, he's desperate, desperate like someone caught in a lie.

"Just admit it, Jamie, you were following orders. You set me up!" I pause before I ask the question that's burning through my brain. "Did those soldiers die?" I keep my voice as steady as I can. In the back of my head, I'm pleading with a god I never believed in to let them be alive. Please don't let me be a killer, I pray.

Jamie doesn't answer. He groans again, louder and more insistently. "I don't know. Elena, you have to help me. Why would I be in here with you if I was with them? Please believe me."

His voice is a drone now, like traffic on a highway outside a window. I have to block it out because he's getting to me. A part of me wants to heal him; a part of me wants to believe him, but a bigger part feels like all of it is somehow wrong. I turn away and shuffle into the bathroom. I sit on the toilet and put my head in my hands. What Jamie's saying makes some sense, but out there in the field, at the last instant, he told me to trust Dr. Meriwether, and she betrayed me. Or did she betray us? Is that so impossible? Could Jamie have made love to me, knowing he was throwing me to the wolves the next morning? I wish there were a way to know for sure.

I get up and splash cold water on my face. My image in the mirror is small and pinched. I look as helpless as I feel. An icy realization creeps up my spine. I'm far from helpless. Any time I want to, I can get out of here. Any time I'm ready to admit what I am and use my reciprocal gift, my curse, I can make them release me. It's going to be a long time before Meriwether or Robineau has the guts to be in a room with me. So why leave Jamie here? Aren't they worried that I'm going to hurt him? I can't wrap my head around this massive clusterfuck. I wish Logan were here.

I rip the bathroom apart for anything that can be used to relieve the pressure, but they were careful. They haven't left me so much as a pen, pencil, tongue depressor, or spork. The sharpest object I can find is the tag on the towel. I throw it down on the floor amid the rest of the crap that can't help me. I try to suppress a deep desire to scream, but I realize there's no reason not to scream. No one but Jamie will hear me anyway. So, I let it loose from the tips of my toes and up through all the chakras, until I feel like a volcano erupting ash and fire through my vocal cords. When I stop, my throat feels scorched, but my psyche feels lighter, clearer. I don't bother cleaning up the mess.

"You okay?" Jamie asks between grimaces.

"Fine," I say. I turn back toward my bed. I'm going to try to contact Ethan. I need to be sure that he made it out.

"What about me?" Jamie asks.

I don't want to turn around because I know I'll see tears in his eyes. I don't think I can bear to see him cry. "I told you; I can't help you. I'm tapped."

"You don't know that. Elena, please try." He's full on sobbing now.

Slowly, I turn around. I try to hold my ground, but I can't leave him like that, even if he did play me. If I let him suffer, then I'm just letting them turn me into a monster. I go to the side of the bed. "You have to help me," I say, squirming into the space next to him without touching him.

"Just tell me what to do," he pants.

"You know how this is going to go. I'm going to puke, and my head will spin around, and at some point, I'll pass out. Do not let me fall on the floor. Also, I think it helps if you concentrate on banishing the pain. Try to give it a face, then kick the shit out of it."

Jamie smiles somehow. "You weren't that eloquent with the kids."

"Just imagine if I had been." I smile, too, but I'm so scared I think I might pee. I have no experience with this kind of pain, unless you count Cayde, and my memories of that experience are far from fond. "By the way," I add, "If I do this and find out later you were part of this shit, I'll put a world of hurt back in your body that makes this look like a silly knee scrape."

Jamie looks away. And I know. Still, I close my eyes and snake my arm under the blankets and around his bare waist. The pain is like a fire hitting every damn dendrite in my nervous system. I scream my lungs out, then cough until I puke all over both of us. Jamie moans and thrashes, hitting me several times. My insides hurt so badly that the blows just glance off me, like insects landing on my skin. We seem locked in combat for eons, unable to complete the process. It goes on so long that I begin to wonder if one or both of us must die to be free of it. Finally, mercifully, the pain becomes too intense to bear, and my mind swirls down the drain into lovely darkness, punctuated only by the points of light in my stellar landscape.

Once I'm free from the constraints of consciousness, I navigate a celestial path through the constellations to a place of peace and freedom. Among the pictures in the stars there are no locked doors or two-way mirrors, no plotters or players, just me and the freedom of my thoughts. I travel around and through each of the chakras to restore my strength and balance. I cleanse my aura of all the negativity that has been raining down on me. I see my brother reunited with Rachel, Jesse, and Sage, safe in the arms of our family. I place myself in their midst and embrace the child who will join us as a lynchpin between the two bloodlines. The thought strikes me that it was all meant to be from the beginning. Sage was meant to be my sister, and Rachel my mother. She brought our father home and gave Ethan and me the strength to heal the scars and work toward wholeness. Light of that knowledge showers down on me and sinks into every pore. For the first time in a long, long time I feel happy.

Hours later, I wake in my own bed in the makeshift hospital room. Jamie's bed has been made and pushed into a corner. When I stir, he gets up from a table, where he's been eating.

"Are you okay?" he asks.

"I guess so." I gingerly pull myself to sitting. My body aches, but my mind's clear.

"I thought you were tapped out." He shuffles his feet and attempts a grin.

"Me too," I smile.

"Hungry?" he asks.

I shrug. I'm not sure how food will settle, but I follow him to the table. There's fruit in a basket and cinnamon rolls, eggs and bacon, too. It must be morning. I take a couple of grapes and a strawberry. When I reach for the orange juice, Jamie shakes his head almost imperceptibly. I take a glass into the bathroom and fill it from the tap. I wonder how he knows the OJ is spiked. Why wouldn't they dose all the food? These questions will have to wait, because I know with complete certainty that we're being very carefully watched.

I go back into the room and smile for the paparazzi. Then I look Jamie over from head to toe. "Guess my magic did the trick," I say.

"Well, you got the pain and infection anyway." He pulls the bandage back to reveal a much cleaner, healing wound. "The bullet's still in there, so the party is in no way over, but I'm feeling much better. Thanks for asking."

"Good. Keep that sucker clean, 'cause I'm not doing that again. Ever." I look toward the glass wall when I say the last word. I want my message to be crystal clear to Robineau, Meriwether, and whoever else is behind that glass. "So, what happens next?" I ask Jamie. "Will I be serving out my sentence in here with you? For how long? Months? Years?"

Jamie's mouth is stuffed with food, but he stops chewing and glances up at the glass. I wait for him to swallow, and he motions for me to sit down in the chair across from him. I comply.

"Elena, I have no idea what happens next, but I'll bet my sweet ass that answer depends completely on you."

I study his face and body language. Every gesture is calculated to make me feel small, like a naughty child. He wants me to do what I do best, turn the blame inward on myself, but I have to resist that faded, old pattern. I know what they did to me and what they made me do to those soldier boys. They pushed me all those months to that moment for one purpose, to expose my reciprocal gift. And now they want to put the tiger back in the cage. No fucking way. I'm not going to go down quietly, but Jamie doesn't need to know that. I don't know exactly what his part was in this, but I know he played one. Hell, I know he played me. No one likes to be played. Right now, I need a way out of this, and my mind is my best weapon. I have to keep my emotions in check.

"I see," I say reasonably. I take a few more grapes and move back toward the bathroom. "I think I need a long, hot shower." I smile benignly and slip behind the door.

Someone has cleaned up from my earlier rampage; how very considerate of them. Everything I need is here: my favorite shampoo and conditioner, my body scrub, and face wash. Even my lotions are lined up on the counter. They expect I'll be staying for a while. We'll see about that.

I turn the shower as hot as I can stand it, until the room's filled with steam. I can't see across the room, which means neither can they. I sit down on the shower floor and prop myself in the corner. Leaving my body behind is easy in the comfort of the humidity. As I move through the main room, I pause to see what Jamie's up to. He's at the window, trying to see through. He's talking to the people behind the glass. He's begging on my behalf. I'd be touched if it didn't confirm his complicity just a smidge more. Finally, he gives up and goes to a cabinet. When he opens it, I'm surprised to see a television, like the kind you'd find in a hotel room. What the hell?

I shake it off and move through the locked door. I'm in a long hallway. The door to the observation room is to the left. Perhaps half a dozen other doors line the hall to the left and right. Straight ahead at the end of the hall is an elevator. The security system gives away our location. We're at PSI. I need to figure out what floor we're on. Like the answer to a prayer, the elevator opens. Dr. Meriwether emerges. I keep my emotions level, despite a deep desire to set her hair on fire. I get great glee from picturing the scene and basking in the knowledge that I just might be able to make that happen with a thought. In the elevator, I discover that we're on negative seven, the deepest level that can be accessed from this elevator. I would wager my firstborn that there are levels below this one, though. Now that I have my bearings, I head to my real destination, Logan.

As usual, she's not hard to find. The girl must have a permanent address on the astral plane.

"Hey, Lane!"

"Logan, did you know?"

"What?"

"Were you part of all this? Did you know what they were doing to me?"

"Truth?"

"Fuck, yes!" I say

"I suspected." She pauses for a long time. "I tried to warn you. I told you not to trust loverboy."

"You should've warned harder!"

"It wouldn't matter if I had. He's got an unfair advantage," she says.

"What're you talking about?"

"Okay, Sherlock, tell me you still don't know his thing."

"Of course, I know his thing," I say defensively.

She waits for me to have some kind of aha moment that continues to elude.

Finally, she gives up. "Let me help you connect the dots. Hugo and the others call Jamie, Zero, and it has nothing to do with the fact that he's a total loser."

I heard Maureen call him that once. It takes me a second. "Like, patient zero?" No wonder he acted weird when I said that.

"She has a brain after all," Logan quips.

"What does that mean? He's the first, but the first what? We don't have a disease," I reason.

"Don't we?" she asks. "Catch a clue, already. Cayde told you what it's all about."

"Reciprocals? Yeah, trust me, I know all about that, up close and personal now."

"Jeezus, do I have to spell it out? Jamie is an empath. Strongest ever recorded. Yet, he can be around other people. Now, how is that possible? Enter Robineau's reciprocals. What exactly might the reciprocal of empathy be, you ask? You better ask him, my dear. I have no desire to be the messenger, especially not to you. Not after what they're saying you did anyway."

"Fuck you, Logan!" I say. "I don't have the time or energy for your games. I need your help." I pause for maximum effect. "You're all I have!"

Logan sort of fritzes out for a couple of seconds, but then she's back. "What do you need me to do?"

"First, do you know what happened to Hugo?"

"Yeah… You must be having a little guilt about that. Knowing your brother and Cayde made it out, safe and sound, leaving poor sweet Hugo here to bear the brunt."

"Just tell me if he's okay." She's right; the guilt's eating at me.

"Maureen thinks their buying his story for now, so you can stop beating yourself up on that score at least. Anything else you need?"

"Later we need to discuss who did what to whom and when and why. Right now, I just need to get out of here. Are you in or out?"

"In. I said I'd help, didn't I? But I swear on my mama's combat boots, if you get me killed, I'm going to haunt your ass until the end of time."

"Thanks. Right now, I need to find my brother, and I'm not really good at the long distance thing. Can you give me a boost?"

"I'll take you there."

In the time it takes for a heart to beat once, I'm on the front porch of a rustic farmstead. Ethan stands at the edge of the long, rough-hewn, plank walkway looking out over a rolling field that stretches on and on in a wide ocean of grass. The expanse is dotted with cows and sheep at odd intervals, like some osmosis experiment gone awry. His arms are crossed over his chest, containing himself in the space that's far too large to hold him together. His eyes are dark-rimmed, and his mouth is a small line, shut tight with worry. Animated voices drift through the screen-door leading inside the small house. Behind the dark grid, Rachel and Jesse wash dishes together, while Cayde charms or annoys them with his incessant chatter.

Across the yard to the right is an old, worn-out barn that looks like it might've been standing since the 1800's with a few repairs. It's wholly out of place in the Florida landscape. Leaning in the doorway is a tall man in jeans, boots, and a Stetson, with a cigarette hanging from his lips. James Dean returned from the dead, to break hearts far and wide. I do a double take before I realize it's Finn. He raises an arm to wave, and for an instant I forget I'm not really here, and I wave back. Then I realize he's waving to Ethan. Ethan doesn't return the gesture, either because he doesn't see Finn, or he just doesn't want to. I have no way of knowing which. Finn crushes out his cigarette with the heel of his boot and saunters into the barn. Ethan doesn't stand a chance with Sage.

I concentrate on communicating with my twin the way I would if he were across the room. I remind myself that distance shouldn't be a factor in this equation. Telepathy doesn't travel by satellite or fiber optic cable.

"Hey, E. I'm here. Can you hear me?"

I watch him sink slowly to the floor of the porch. He buries his face in his knees and wraps his arms around his legs. Then he thinks. "You aren't coming, are you, Lanie?"

"Not yet, Ethan."

"I knew. I knew this would happen. I knew what they'd do… what they'd make you do." He begins to sob.

"It's okay, E. I'm okay, and I'm going to get out of here. Promise, I'll be with you soon."

"Oh, Lanie, you don't understand. This isn't over yet for any of us. I don't want to go back there."

"You aren't coming back here, pal."

"You don't know, but I do. You need me to get out, and Cayde and Finn, too. But, Lane, it's going to be bad… really bad. Worse than you can imagine."

"Don't say that, E. Just sit tight. I'll figure a way out on my own. Hell, I'm a one woman loaded gun. How're they going to stop me?"

Ethan raises his head slightly.

"Okay, don't answer that," I add.

Rachel comes through the screen door. She's awkward and round. She pulls up a lawn chair and sits beside Ethan. He scootches closer to her and puts his head on her knee. She strokes his hair until his tears stop.

"Don't worry, Ethan." Rachel says. "The lawyers will get Elena out of there. She'll be home before you know it. Oh, and I just talked to Sage. Jo's handling the funeral arrangements, so Sage can be here on the first flight tomorrow. I know you miss her terribly."

Ethan's eyes fill again. Rachel must not know about what happened at the hotel, not all of it, at any rate. Poor, poor Ethan.

Suddenly, light years away, I feel my physical body trembling. I search for the impossibly thin, silver thread and follow it back to the shower, which is ice cold now. My lips are nearly blue and my teeth chatter as I slip back inside my body and return to consciousness. The hospital robe and disposable slippers do nothing to warm me, so I wrap my arms around my body.

I catch a glimpse of myself in the mirror, and I'm oddly terrified by how small I look, how helpless, like my brother. I fight tears, remind myself of what I can do to these people, what they made me into. A sense of invincibility warms me from the inside. I should feel more guilt about possibly killing those boys, but right now all I feel is powerful, resourceful and ready to beat them at their own twisted, little game. I have no faith in Rachel's lawyers, but I believe in what I can do. Game on, I think.

When I step into the room, Jamie stands up from where he's been sitting at the table and heads toward me.

I stop in the doorway. He stops, too. "What?" he asks.

"Why do they call you Zero?" I ask.

His face goes white, and he turns away from me. "Where did you hear that?" he says quietly.

"You don't get to answer my questions with questions. You owe me an explanation and so much more." My voice sounds forceful even to me.

He sits down at the table and indicates the chair across from his. "You might want to sit," he says with a kind of resignation that's somehow different from his usual apologetic air. I take the chair with my back to the window. "You hit the nail on the head the other day. I was, like, patient zero, the first one that proved Dr. Robineau's theory about the reciprocal gifts."

"What does that even mean with you? For Ethan and me, it's pretty obvious. He sees the past and future; I can heal and harm. What the hell is the opposite of empathy? Someone who feels nothing, an apath?"

"Not exactly." He glances up at the window, like someone might be coaching him from the other side. I spin around, but the glass remains opaque, expressionless and creepy. I turn back to Jamie. "Do you remember once that I told you I'm a lot like your brother? Well, I am. In fact, Ethan and I have very similar manifestations and issues. I used to have a hard time filtering all the emotions that were coming in from the outside, so, like Ethan, I developed a sort of defense mechanism."

It strikes me that I actually know very little about Ethan's gift. I know that when he sees someone else's past, he inadvertently sends them into his past. A flash of white, like a camera strobe, goes off in my head. Holy shit! Argh!

I get up so fast that the chair flips over behind me. I pace as far away from Jamie as I can in the small room. Everything that's happened to us from the beginning, from maybe before the beginning, this whole wild ride, has been a massive manipulation. I press my back into the door and wish with all my might that I could pass through the metal like a ghost. I slide down and press my palms into my eyes. I picture the first time I met Jamie, the sweet humility that pulled me in and how he made me feel special. He MADE ME FEEL whatever he wanted me to feel, whatever THEY wanted me to feel. Now all I feel is sick to my stomach. I trusted him, made love… I shake my head hard to dispel the memory. Well, at least this explains why I'd want to be with a guy. Jo will be relieved. NO! She won't ever know any of this. Another thought assaults me from the left. Ethan knew about Jamie. He tried to warn me, but I wouldn't listen. My stomach churns into a tight knot. I should've listened to my brother from the start. Why didn't I just listen to Ethan?

I hear a chair scrape across the linoleum and feet padding slowly in my direction.

"If you know what's good for you, you won't come near me," I growl, like the wounded animal I am.

He retreats to the bed. I hear it squeak as he gets in. I stay where I am, wrestling with my memories. I watch the colors fade to gray as I realize that the feelings I attach to those moments are fabrications force-fed to me. I will myself not to break down. Tears will weaken me, but the anger that gradually grows in my gut will arm me for the battle ahead. I can't let it take over, though. If I accidentally kill Jamie, then I might as well be dead, too. I need him to get out of here.

I take deep breaths and concentrate on counting slowly, like I used to when I was young and Ethan would wake me up, screaming from night terrors. Gran would tell me that the bad moments in life end just like the good ones, and all you have to do to get through them is count out the time it takes to be finished. Then it's done. So, I would count to four hundred or whatever, and Ethan would wear himself out, collapsing into a deeper sleep. Gran would ask what number I got to, nod in her matter-of-fact way and shoo me off back to bed, where I'd count until I fell back asleep.

It's not easy to keep my mind on the numbers with all of the emotion swirling through my head, but the counting helps me keep control. I make it to almost a thousand before I can pull myself from the floor. I make a silent vow not to talk to Jamie for the rest of the day, night, or afternoon. Not knowing the time of day is unbelievably disorienting. I stretch my legs and roll my neck.

Jamie turns over to look at me. His face is streaked with tears. "I'm sorry, Elena," he mumbles.

"Don't!" I hiss, breaking my promise. "Don't you dare!"

I go back to my bed, the only place I can go aside from the bathroom. I need to concentrate on making a plan. Let's start with what I have to work with. Obviously, I have no allies. Jamie is a zero. I almost smile at the joke in my head. I have my abilities. I am a walking, talking, killing machine, but they know that, too — though none of us knows how well I can control it. The first thing they're going to do is try to shut me down. The injection Meriwether gave me in the field surely contained a neurotransmitter inhibiter, but I healed Jamie, so it must've worn off. They can't risk sending anyone in to inject me again, so they're going to try to pass it through the food.

Oh my god! This majorly sucks. I can drink from the tap in the bathroom, but I can't eat anything until I get out of here. Now I'm on the clock. It's already been probably a day since I've eaten anything substantial, and the last meal I had ended up in Meriwether's trash can. Pretty soon I'll be too weak to walk my ass out of here, let alone run.

So, back to Jamie. I can't trust him, but I can sure as shit use him. If I can make the watchers on the other side of the glass believe I'm going to kill their precious Zero, maybe they'll open the doors to stop it. I also need a working code and a person to wield it to navigate the elevators and doors. Logan or Maureen? Both long shots. But maybe. And I need a ride out of here, someone from the outside to drive a get-away car, someone fearless who owes me. Finn? Once I'm out, I can worry about the Initiative coming after us and the repercussions that will definitely follow. I just need to get the hell out of this room, and soon. I need Logan.

I lay down on the bed and prepare myself to disconnect from this plane.

"I know how you heard about Zero," Jamie says, pulling me back from the brink.

I sit up to face off. "Shut the hell up! You have no talking room! Understand? You fucked me in every way one human can fuck another. There's nothing you can say that I can hear any more."

He swings his legs over the edge of the bed, like he's thinking of coming over to me. I shoot daggers from my eyes while I concentrate on not killing him. I want to so badly I can taste the blood in my mouth.

"Logan," he says. "Logan told you about all of it, didn't she?"

I turn my back to him and pray that he'll shut up.

"She played a part in this, too, you know. You think you can trust her, but she's part of it, too." His voice is desperate, like this information might redeem him in some way.

"Fuck you," I say, and I lie back down to get on with my plan.

"Ethan knows about her. Ask your brother why she was so weird with him."

I try to shut his voice out and concentrate on leaving this plane, but I can't find the station, let alone make it onto the train. Eventually, I give up trying and sink into sleep.

I wake up to Maureen hovering above me, with a needle poised over my bicep. I try to pull away, but Maureen's quicker and stronger. She puts her hand over my mouth, pressing me into the pillow.

"Just relax," she whispers ominously in my ear. I stop struggling and she transfers her free hand from my face to my arm so quickly I have no time to make a move.

"Aren't you afraid of me?" I ask between gritted teeth. I want her to be afraid of me. Instead, she laughs.

"Really?" she asks. "I guess the gossip mill isn't all it's cracked up to be."

"Must not be, or you'd be running, not walking away from me," I throw back. I keep looking at the needle suspended precariously over my skin. Maureen seems intent on talking.

"Sweetie, I've heard all about you and what you did at the army base. Truth is, I'm not scared of anything, though. You see, that's *my* thing."

I consider this. What would it be like to not be afraid of anything? And how are they controlling her if she has no fear?

"Elena, this will be much easier if you remain still." She presses down harder and looks at me, like I'm a tiny bug she's about to squash. Her grip cuts off my circulation. I know there's no hope of fighting my way out of this. My body and mind succumb, and my heart hates them both.

I gasp audibly as the needle grazes my skin. Then Maureen releases the fluid into the mattress beside me. I want to throw my arms around her neck, but all I can do is cry.

"It's just a neuro-inhibiter, Elena. We aren't going to hurt you or anything. I'll be back later to check on you." She marches out of the room like a good soldier. I roll over on my side to hide my smile.

Logan's there instantly once I'm able to disconnect. She's grinning ear to ear. It's a little scary.

"You're amazing!" I say.

"I know," she comes back. "We don't have much time before they figure out what's happening. Here's how it's going down. After they bring your next meal, pretend to eat. Then, when they come in to clear it away, attack Jamie. Either get him to act like you're killing him or make him bleed from the eyeballs. Your choice. They'll open the door; I guarantee it. Use him like a shield to get to the elevator. From there, everything has been set up. Maureen and Hugo will get you out while a bunch of the twin study losers and I make a massive distraction. Someone named Finn is playing the role of get-away driver. Easy as pie."

My first thought should be gratitude or nervousness, but instead I'm perplexed by how familiar this plan is. Like Logan read my mind or planted the ideas in my head in the first place.

"Get back there and make them buy that Maureen kryptonited you."

"Okay," I say. "And, Logan, thank you. I owe you."

"Fuck off, pipsqueak," she says, grinning again.

I open my eyes and wipe them with the backs of my hands. Jamie's lying down, facing me. I can see that he's awake. He looks miserable. I'm glad. I have no idea when the next meal might be coming in, so I'm not going to waste any time. I get out of bed and head straight for him. He sits up quickly. The terror in his eyes both enervates and unnerves me. I lean in slowly like I might kiss him. He backs up a little, hesitates, then moves forward as if to meet me halfway. Instead of kissing him, I bring my lips to his ear.

"Follow me. We need to talk."

I pull back, and he nods. I make my way slowly to the bathroom, without turning around to see if he's following. I immediately turn on the water as hot as it goes and circle around him to close the door. His face is the picture of confusion. I look directly into the camera as I strip to nothing. I don't exactly perform a strip tease, but I come close. Jamie's jaw drags on the floor, then closes suddenly when I say, "Your turn, pal. Take off your clothes." His hands shake as he pulls off his shirt and unties the scrub pants. He's not wearing anything else, same as me.

I get in the shower and crook my finger at him to follow. He gets in and I close the curtain. He looks at me with a goofy, ridiculous grin that makes me see red. I slap him as hard as I possibly can. The crack echoes off the porcelain walls and fixtures. The red imprint of my tiny hand appears clearly under the palm he holds to his face. His eyes fill with tears. Now I have his attention.

"I need to know whose side you're on. Do or die time, James. Are you going be their puppet or are you as sorry as you claim to be?"

He starts to answer, but I interrupt.

"The truth, please. The very least you owe me right now is the truth."

"Okay," he says. I watch as the anxiety of his conundrum plays through his body. He moves a couple of inches back and turns away from me. Then he looks over his shoulder and rotates slowly back around. I wait with my arms crossed over my chest, letting the steaming water stream down my back.

"We don't have all day, Jamie."

He shuffles his feet. I count to five.

"I guess I have an answer then," I say and move to get out. I guess I didn't really want to hurt him as much as I thought I did. I bite the inside of my cheek to keep from crying. I really can't do this right now. I try hard to remember all the ways he's betrayed me, but when I catch his naked image in the mirror, all I can think about is how his skin felt against mine.

"Wait," he finally says in a hoarse voice.

I wrap myself in a towel and glance at the camera, which remains engulfed in steam. I go back to the edge of the shower, where a light mist falls between us.

"I'll help you," he says. "What do you want me to do?"

I bring my lips to his ear. "Just act scared and in pain when the time comes. Can you do that convincingly?" It takes a couple of seconds for the irony of my statement to hit me. "Of course you can."

Jamie half-smiles, and I wonder if manipulating people's emotions gives him the same feeling of invincibility that hurting people gives me. I imagine it must.

I wait for him to dry off, and we go back into view of the mirrors, together and very much apart. The imprint of my hand is still pink against the white of his skin. We find clean scrubs have been left on the freshly made beds. Someone came in. I doubt they could have heard us over the water, though. The table is set, too, with fried chicken, potato salad, corn-on-the-cob, ice cream and Cokes — opened, of course. My stomach lurches with desire.

Jamie's already dressed by the time I tear my eyes and nose away from the meal. He sits down and serves a plate full of everything. My hatred for him surges again. I move to the far side of the room and dress with my back to the mirror. I'm starving, and I don't know if I can resist eating, but if I don't sit down and eat, they'll suspect I've been warned. I reluctantly join him and put some food on a plate. He raises an eyebrow. I make a big show of cutting the meat off the bones and the corn off the cob. I push the food around my plate and bring the empty fork to my mouth. I'm so tempted. If I only took a small bite, it might not matter. I bring some chicken to my lips.

"Don't even think about it, Lanie. It's too much of a risk." Ethan's voice is loud and clear in my head, like he's in the room.

I turn around and around to find him.

"Real subtle, Sis. Let them know, why don't you?" he scolds.

"Astral projection?" I ask silently.

"Duh." I can imagine him grinning.

"Wow, that's freaky weird. Can you see me?"

"Your hair's wet and tangly. You kind of look like shit. Gray really isn't your color."

"Thanks."

"Logan told you my plan, right?" he asks.

"Your plan?" Suddenly, I realize the plan was never mine or Logan's. I must have picked it up at least in part when I visited Ethan with Logan's help. "Yes, I got the message."

"Lanie, are you okay?"

"Everything's really whacked out right now, but I'll be fine once this is over."

"Do you want to hurt Jamie?" Ethan asks.

"Do you want me to?"

He doesn't answer for several seconds. Then he thinks, "It doesn't matter. That's not the way this is going to happen."

"How's it going to happen, E?"

"It's time, Lanie. We're here. Be brave."

It's weird hearing that from Ethan. It kind of shakes me. "You too," I think, but I'm pretty sure he's already gone. How strange it must be for him to already know what's going to happen. I wonder if he's ever wrong, or if in just knowing, he inadvertently changes something, so events don't play out the way he thinks they will. Maybe not, because he seems pretty sure. He must be right a lot of the time to be so sure.

Jamie has cleaned his plate. He's staring at me like I'm dessert. His eyes are half-closing, and it occurs to me that they put a sedative in the food. I try to look as drowsy as he does. After a long minute, Jamie gets up and offers me his hand. "We're all we got in here now, Elena. Please, forgive me." He nods toward the bed. As if! I'm about to stand up and get all in his face, but I realize what he's doing. He's putting us in close proximity, so I can attack him when they come in to clear the meal.

I'm still sitting, mulling all of this over. I suppose it's logical to our watchers that I'd be hesitating. My problem is that I don't really trust Jamie. If his food wasn't drugged, he'd be able to work his mojo on me again, and I'd be helpless to stop it. Maybe. In the meantime, my head might explode trying to figure out who's doing what to whom, making all of this a moot point. I just have to go with it.

I tell him yes with my eyes and follow him to the bed. We arrange ourselves on top of the narrow mattress. When I roll on my side, away from him, he turns in to spoon me. I love the way it feels, and I hate him for it. In just a few seconds, Jamie's snoring lightly against my back. Under any other circumstances, I'd let the sweet vibration lull me to sleep, but my heart's racing in desperate anticipation of whatever my brother knows is going to happen. All I can do is wait.

৪০ 15 ৫১

COWBOY KID

The way that boy leans up against the wall
The girl's already to take the fall
For his belt buckle faded jeans
Hooded eyes, I don't care
He's not what he seems
Cigarette, black boots
Can't dispute
Cowboy kid's surely got
Something more than just heat
Want to know what's under that
Want to see what's under that
Want to get under that hat.
　　　"Under That Hat"- Luna Rayne, 1996

I don't have to wait long. A nearly silent click makes me jump like a gunshot. I try to nudge Jamie awake without moving enough to alert whoever has been sent in. I pray it's Maureen; that would make this whole thing infinitely easier. Jamie groans as he fights his way out of the sedative. Every muscle in my body tightens, but the other person in the room doesn't seem to notice.

Jamie squeezes my hand to let me know he's awake. Now that it's time to do this, I'm not sure how I should begin. Do I pull Jamie out of bed like I have a gun to his head? Based on the differential in our sizes, that might provoke more mirth than terror. Should I just make a run for the door? That seems simpler. I may not need Jamie at all. I slide out of bed as silently as I can and dart on cat feet for the small opening in the door.

The loud speaker erupts with a crackle and a sharp command. "Door!"

But by the time the guy turns around I'm already there. I slip through the crack easily and spin to run. A soldier comes from a door down the hall, close to the elevators. He moves toward me purposefully. "Shit!" I say and backtrack. I stand half-in and half-out of the door to our prison room.

"I don't want to hurt these people," I yell at the glass. "But I will."

"I don't think you will, Elena." Jamie's voice comes from behind the door. He could reach around and grab me; he's that close.

"Call them off, James!" I say. This is the moment of truth; either Jamie will use his ability to take me down, or he'll play along and get me out of here. I take a deep breath, swing around the doorjamb and grab him by the wrist.

For a couple of seconds we stand there poised, looking into mirrors of fear and distrust. It takes me a moment to realize that he's as terrified of me using my power on him as I am of him using his on me. If the situation weren't so dire, I'd laugh. But suddenly Jamie winces like I've just put my hand through his chest. He clutches at his heart. I narrow my eyes and squeeze his arm hard.

"Argh!" he cries. "Elena, please."

I'm almost convinced that I'm somehow hurting him without even knowing I'm doing it.

The boy they sent to clean up is young. He's dressed in fatigues, so I guess he's military; he looks more like a gamer geek who hasn't seen the sun for weeks and eats and pisses twice a day when he can tear himself away from a crappy computer. "You!" I say with more force than I knew I had. "Come." Like a beaten dog, he sidles up to us. I point to the door. "As long as you stay in front of me and don't look back, I won't hurt you." He looks at Jamie, swallows and nods. He shuffles around me, careful not get too close, like I'm a venomous snake that might strike. He's not too far off.

The loudspeaker voice is silent as I yank Jamie out the door and shove his body in front of mine. The soldier with the tranquilizer gun takes several steps back. The hallway's narrow, so he can't circle around behind us. It occurs to me that the boy in front of us could do any number of things to turn the tables should he choose to.

I steel myself to the possibility that I'll be forced to take him down, but I'm not really sure I even know how I did it before. I'm glad no one here can read my mind.

I push Jamie's groaning form in front of me. Between us and the elevator, there are two doors, one to the left and the other to the right. The elevator lies directly ahead.

"Call off your dogs," I scream, hoping the person running this show can hear.

Jamie screams again and stumbles. His performance is flawless.

Robineau's icy alto echoes in the hall. "Stop this, Elena. You don't need to —"

Jamie falls to his knees. I roughly yank him to his feet. I'm counting on the cameras in the corners to be broadcasting into the observation room.

We're nearly past the first door when it clicks open. I jump back, pulling Jamie with me by the back of his shirt. Robineau explodes into the hallway between me and the elevator. My ticket out of here, gamer-boy soldier, is on her side.

"Jamie, are you alright?" Her face is distraught, and it shakes me to think she might really care about him. She whirls around and shouts a single word to the guards, "GO!"

The boy from the room looks at me, like I'm in charge. "Not you!" I say. I motion him back to my side, and he makes a move to obey, but Robineau grabs him by the arm and holds him steady. She stares at me, waiting for me to make some kind of move. If I don't do something, this stalemate will be over, and I may never see my brother again. I crush Jamie's arm with my fingers, and he goes down on his knees. Robineau gasps and wobbles, but she stands her ground.

"You don't have to do this. No one here was ever going to hurt you. And the work you could do with us would help people. Think of the kids you healed. The doctors are calling it a miracle. They want you to come back. And the soldiers. You helped so many of them deal with their pain and problems. That has to feel pretty good."

"You used me!" I say. "From day one, I was manipulated and lied to." I look down at Jamie and my vision clouds. A deep hatred rises from a dark place inside. "You made me kill innocent boys for nothing!" My tears run red down my face, and my hands are visibly shaking.

Suddenly, the boy Robineau is holding clutches at his throat. Down at my knees, Jamie begins to claw at my legs with one hand as he holds his throat with the other.

"Stop it!" Robineau yells, dropping to the ground beside her precious protégé. "You didn't kill those boys. You didn't kill anyone yet!"

"Liar!" I yell, stepping away from Jamie. I shove the boy who has to serve up his voice and codes to get me out of here toward the elevator before he drops, too. In my mind, I try to loosen my grip on my anger, but I can't beat it back. It's surging up in me like vomit and I can't control it.

Robineau's voice comes from behind me, tearful but strong. "Elena, you're killing him."

I whirl around. Why is she still standing? The confusion distracts long enough for the boy to regain his feet. Jamie takes a deep, shaking breath and lifts his head. His eyes are full of terror, and they scream at me, "Why?"

An electronic vibration signals that the elevator's rising to this level. Shit! More guards. My options are diminishing by the second. Jamie lets Robineau help him to his feet. I expect him to turn the tables on me. Then to my surprise and hers, he shakes her off and moves haltingly between me and the opening doors, like he means to protect me.

"Jamie?" she says. I'm curious to hear this, too, but there's no time. I press my back against the wall and try to summon the emotion that will drive the party crashers to the ground. I guess if hurting people is my only way out, I'm not above it. At this point, Robineau might be figuring out that she's immune to my "gift." It won't take her much longer to decide that she can take me down without any help.

I close my eyes and see the field, Jamie falling in front of me and the blood on my hands, already so much blood on my hands. Then someone's grabbing my hands, both of them, pulling me hard into the open elevator. My feet stumble after the rest of my body into the tiny space, which is crowded by others. The doors shut instantly behind me, and I open my eyes. Hugo! Oh, sweet, strong Hugo. I want to throw my arms around his neck, but he's holding my hands in a vice grip. The cacophony of voices pulls my mind back from the field. Ethan! Hugo releases me into Ethan's embrace. He's hugging me so hard, my feet leave the ground. Cayde bounces like a deranged pogo stick beside us. Logan and Maureen are talking at once. Suddenly, the elevator shudders to a halt, and it's like someone threw the off switch. We look around at each other in silent terror.

"No, it's all right, guys," Hugo mumbles sheepishly. "I did that." He holds up a mobile device that looks like a big cell phone. "I'm scrambling all the floors, so they don't know where the elevator's going."

"Oh," I manage. "Good thinking." Hugo looks at Ethan. My eyes follow his.

"Your plan, E?" I ask, trying not to sound too shocked. He nods and glances away.

"The fat lady ain't singin' yet, kiddos," Maureen says. "Miles to go. Stay sharp."

"What's next?" I look at Ethan.

Ethan and Logan exchange conspiratorial looks. "We split up," Logan says.

My mouth drops open.

"Ethan, Cayde and Hugo need to get to a place where they can do damage control. Maureen's going to get you out of here. A dude named Finn is set to jet you out on his bike. I'm going to generate some video interference from my room, so the left hand never knows what the right hand was doing after the fact."

"I'm not leaving Ethan here," I say. I don't like this plan at all. There are about a thousand ways this could go wrong.

Ethan looks at me with something between annoyance and plaintiveness. Logan grabs my upper arm and spins me to face her. "That's how it's going to happen. You get me?" She shoots a glance in Ethan's direction. I follow her eyes. He won't meet my incredulous stare. There's no arguing with the inevitable, so I switch my focus. "What about Jamie?" I ask.

Hugo and Maureen shake their heads in disgust, but no one answers.

Finally, Jamie speaks for himself. "I'll be staying."

Hugo crosses his arms over his chest. "No surprise there, Zero."

"What?" I'm stunned.

"What would I do out there —?" He hangs his head.

"Without your precious drugs." Logan finishes the sentence for him.

Jamie bristles. "You don't want to do this with me, Logan."

She steps forward, chest out. "Bring it, Zero."

"Fine." A wicked grin spreads over Jamie's features. "Did you tell Elena how you found them, Ghost-talker? Did you tell her how you got her dead mother to give them up?"

"Did you tell her how you lured her, Mister Manipulation?"

"Did you tell her —?"

"Stop it!" Ethan yells breathlessly, bringing his hands to his ears. "Just stop!"

Everyone's instantly silent for a couple of beats. Logan backs off to her corner.

"If Jamie stays, he can make sure that no one gets interested enough to ask questions about the Paige twins. Everyone will just be really sad about the accident that took their lives," Ethan says.

My heart jumps into my mouth as my brain does double time, leaping to conclusions. Our friends are going to kill us! I pull away abruptly when Maureen puts a hand on my arm.

"We aren't really killing you, idiot!" Logan says. "Ethan's just going to make everyone remember it that way." Something about how she says it still sounds ominous, and I wonder if Ethan can really do that to all these people.

The whole scheme takes form in my mind now. Getting out of here is only part of Ethan's plan. He wants to make it, so they won't come after us. I look at my brother with a newfound admiration. So fucking smart! "Remind me not to play chess with you anymore," I say to him.

Ethan smiles fleetingly, to humor me, I think, and the elevator door opens. "This is my stop," Logan says, pushing her way to the front. Before she gets out, she turns and wraps me in a hug that's far too tight. "I probably won't see you again. I'm sorry I sent them to you. We never should've brought you here." She doesn't give me a chance to respond. As the doors close behind her back, a million thoughts run through my mind, but the one that presses to the fore is: Logan's staying, too. Hugo puts a big paw on my shoulder.

"You're next," he says to Jamie in an icy baritone.

Jamie begins talking, fast and desperate. "Elena, I know you don't believe this, but the work we do here — there's nothing sinister about it. All the stuff you think you know, you made up in your head. You can still stop all of this now, before someone really does get hurt." His voice makes my head swim. What if he's right? What if I made all of this up in my mind? What if I overreacted, jumped to conclusions? I was helping people like I wanted to.

The elevator doors open again. Jamie steps across the threshold and holds out his hand. "Last chance. Come back with me. We can make it right."

I wobble and lean toward him, but before my hand can rise to meet his, the doors close. I take a deep breath. Ethan slips his hand in mine, and when our eyes meet, I realize he's trying to comfort me, not looking for me to comfort him. I smile and lean my head against his chest. "I'm okay," I say to reassure them all.

"Good, because we're up next," Maureen says, moving beside me.

"Just come with me, Ethan," I say.

"Only room for one on the back of Finn's bike," Ethan says. His eyes are far away.

"Don't worry, gorgeous," Hugo says. "I'll see to it that the boys make it to the highway."

"Yeah," Cayde chimes in. "We did it before; we can do it again. Nothing to it!"

"Besides, Sage will be waiting with a car and towels this time," Ethan says. "No worries, little sister." But his eyes speak nothing but worry. The image of the painting he obscured and his warning from the porch play on repeat in my head, filling me with anxiety, too. I know with some certainty that this isn't going to end well. The questions taking up my headspace are who's going to end up on the ground in a pool of blood, and who will be standing over them?

The elevator opens. Maureen puts her hand on my back and gently moves me forward. The doors close before I can so much as say goodbye. "Stay sharp," Maureen says, leading the way down the hall.

We're on a level I've never seen before. Like everywhere else at PSI, the walls are blinding white, but the lighting's different, subdued and less industrial. I expect that if I opened a door, I might find a room with a fireplace and Persian carpets. The effect slows me down, makes me long for a soft bed and a luxurious nap.

"Elena, we don't have all day! Move it!" Maureen's several paces ahead of me and moving faster every second. She knows something I don't, I realize. Gone are the homey images. Every door in the hallway takes on a sinister hue. I imagine Robineau or Meriwether popping out and ripping me back from the brink of freedom. By the time we reach the end of the hallway, I'm back on Maureen's heels. She stops in front of the retina scanner at a door. She mutters about her access possibly being revoked already. After a pause that feels way too long, the door clicks open, revealing a narrow, steep stairwell.

"Go!" she says, pushing me not so gently in front of her. The door slams shut behind us. We're incredibly vulnerable, trapped between the two doors in this tiny passage. As we climb, the space seems to narrow. The air feels thinner, like we might run out of oxygen before we get to the top. My field of vision gets smaller and darker as we approach the door leading out. Then, just a few steps from our goal, the door swings wide, and a soldier wielding a weapon fills my field of vision. I stop, and Maureen crashes into me.

"Now we know why my access card worked," Maureen says.

I have an idea, but I don't have time to explain it to her, so I throw myself in front of her and press our bodies tight against the wall. Simultaneously, I picture the bone in the soldier's leg snapping in two like a dry twig. I never have a chance to wonder if it will work because his gun clatters down the stairs just ahead of his body. His piercing screams echo around and around deafeningly in the small space.

"Shit," Maureen mumbles, looking down to where he lies crumpled at the bottom. I can't tear my eyes away until she physically twists my body forward and pushes me up and through the opening into the daylight. The man continues to cry out behind us, but the sound fades as we race across the rooftop.

"Where are we going?" I gasp.

"Zip line," she throws back over her shoulder, and I balk inwardly. At the edge of the building, we stop. Maureen bends over to pick up the lone harness.

"No way," I mumble. "Please tell me you're kidding. You couldn't have chosen something more Scooby gang, less Kim Possible?"

"You know I never kid about my zip lines," she says. "I'm just glad the boys had time to get the harness up here." I look out across the expanse that stretches below, some fifteen or twenty stories down. A wave of nausea and dizziness washes over me. From here I can see Finn sitting atop the stone wall he scaled, smoking a cigarette. His motorcycle sits on the other side, not far from the gatehouse. It seems impossibly far away. He's holding a pair of binoculars and every few seconds he brings them up to his eyes. He's looking in the wrong direction, though. He's focused on the doors.

"Let's go, girly. You're first." She's holding the harness for me to step into.

I'd take a step forward, but I'm frozen with terror.

"Elena, there's no other way down! You have to do this."

"I know," I say. "Just give me minute."

She grabs my wrist and pulls me forward. "Trust me, it'll be better if you don't think about it. At least that's what they tell me. Just step into the harness. Focus on that."

"I think I'd feel better if this was scary for you, too." I step in and Maureen cinches it.

"I can pretend if it'll help," she offers.

"I really wish I were you right now," I say, stepping onto the lip of the roof.

"Lean back to go faster, and don't lean too far forward. That's all there is to it. When you get to the ground, just stand up and slip off the harness. I have it rigged to pull it back up."

I'm shaking so hard my teeth are chattering.

Maureen's holding me in place from behind. "One more thing. As soon as you're free, run like hell for your friend's bike, there." She points, and I nod.

"What about you?" I mumble.

"I'll follow, but there's only room for one on the bike. I'll meet up with the guys and catch a ride out with this Sage chick. On three. One. Two." Three never comes.

A gentle shove, and my body falls, leaving my stomach behind. I scream silently as the ground approaches at an alarming rate.

Then a flash of movement and a glint of steel catch my eye. On the roof directly in front of me a sniper is steadying himself. In the split second that he adjusts his hat and turns in profile I recognize him. Ash! On my right, Hugo, Ethan, and Cayde are ducking into the trees, heading toward the path leading into the woods, where the stream runs. Ash spots them and takes aim. Finn has made his way down the wall and is running across the lawn, screaming at the boys to get down.

He's seen the sniper, too. I echo his scream in my mind and pray Ethan is "listening." Finn's calls catch Ash off-guard, and he turns toward the sound. With Finn in the open, Ash has a clean shot at him. I try to yell, but I can't find my vocal cords. Ash won't remember me anyway; Ethan was forced to see to that. Too fast, it's all going down way too fast. I know who's on the ground in Ethan's painting now. In just a moment, I'll be the one standing over him.

As my feet hit the earth, Ethan and Cayde burst out of the tree line toward me, heading in the wrong direction. Finn is some fifty yards beyond that, moving fast toward them. I will them all to turn around and take cover, but Cayde stops mid-stride and looks up at the building where Ash is crouched. My eyes follow his.

Suddenly a spiral of leaves and dirt swirls up from the roof around Ash, obstructing his shot. It's too localized to be caused by the wind. He curses loud enough for me to hear him on the ground. I turn back toward Finn. If Ethan gets my message, they'll see I'm safe and head back into the woods. "Please run!" I beg Ethan in my head.

I make a beeline for the crazy cowboy who seems destined to save my ass again. I promise myself I won't look back this time. He finally spots me and urges me on with wild gestures. As our paths converge, he reaches out his hand to take mine. A barely audible crack precedes the sudden contraction of Finn's body. I watch his face contort with terror as he goes down. A spot of crimson is already spreading over the back of his white t-shirt.

In the movies, people scream things like, "No!" or they call the person's name in a drawn out way, "Fiiinn!" But when you see someone shot by a high-speed rifle up close, and the next bullet whizzes by less than an inch over your shoulder, there's no time for words or feelings.

I stand over Finn only a split second. Ethan's painting flashes in my mind, and I know he's the third figure running towards us in the distance, but if I wait, Finn and I will both be dead. The adrenaline hits my bloodstream, and I yank him to his feet and slip myself under his arm. I half-drag him for several steps, but he's too heavy. I'll never get him over the wall or onto the bike. Panic rises in my chest, along with a sob that I hold down. We make it a few more yards. Then, suddenly, Ethan's on the other side, taking much of Finn's weight. At the wall, I turn to see Cayde kneeling on the ground, staring up at the building, which is now engulfed in a miniature twister. Ash is completely obscured by the debris swirling around him, which explains how we made it this far without taking any more bullets.

Ethan has scaled up the wall a few feet, and Finn's pulling himself up with one arm parallel and a bit below my brother, who reaches down to help me. With a strength I only ever see glimpses of, Ethan has me up and making my way down the other side of the wall in seconds. Then he goes back for Finn, who stalled halfway up. Miraculously, they come down beside me before I have time to worry.

"Well, that went just like you planned, genius," Finn quips.

"Shut up," Ethan says. "I need to think."

We slip our shoulders under Finn's arms again and inwardly I cringe at how sweaty gross he is. Then I realize the moisture I feel is mostly blood. I gag a little. Finn stumbles, and it occurs to me he's getting weaker by the second.

When we get to the bike, Ethan says, "Elena, you need to circle around the wall that way." He points away from the guardhouse. "When you get to the road, head east. Stay in the weeds off the shoulder, so they can't see you. About two miles up, head north on the farm road. I don't remember the number. But I think there's only one." He puts his thumb in his mouth for a couple of seconds, then goes on. "Sage is at the cross-street with that farm road and the Inter-coastal. She won't leave without me, so she'll be there. It's only about five miles. You can make it." As he's speaking, he's helping Finn onto the back of the motorcycle. I watch in horror as he climbs on the front.

"No, way! Ethan, you can barely drive a car. You're going to get yourself killed or worse! You can't do this."

"No, Lanie. I can do it. I just need to get his memories of riding. Then I can do it. That's how I learned to drive." Finn's leaning hard against Ethan's back, with his head resting on E's shoulder.

"You better not piss on my bike, Paige," Finn mumbles groggily.

"You better not bleed on my shirt, Mulcahy," Ethan says, rolling his eyes. Finn tries to pull himself up and fails. "I was kidding," Ethan says quietly. "You need to concentrate on two things, asshole. Holding on to me so you don't fall off the bike, and how you drive this thing. Can you do that?"

Finn groans his assent. I have my doubts.

"One more thing, Lanie. In case something happens, and you miss Sage, we're going to rendezvous at the hotel where we stayed when we got here. Go, Lanie!" Ethan says to me and smallest hint of a whine makes it into his voice.

I start running in the direction he pointed, but I look back to see him half-turned so his forehead's almost touching Finn's. His eyes are closed in concentration. Finally, he rotates to face front and sits up tall in the saddle. He turns the key, jumps on the pedal like a pro and the bike roars to life. The look on his face is sheer terror, but he makes a perfect arc in the road and is gone in a blaze of something akin to glory.

I can't believe this is my timid, broken brother. When did he become so strong?

There's no time to ponder. Maureen's words come back; "miles to go," literally. Stay sharp, I remind myself. I start trotting in the direction Ethan pointed, but I'm no runner. I'm concentrating on remembering the directions he rattled off and inflating my heavy lungs, so I don't notice the distant rumble of engines until they're uncomfortably close. I drop down into the ditch behind the tall grass and hold my breath, probably too late. Maybe they aren't even from the Institute, I try to convince myself. But when I gather the courage to take a look, there's no mistaking the logo on the side of the Jeeps, or the tranquilizer guns the guys in the back with the binoculars are holding. My stomach falls. I could give the drivers an aneurism with a single thought, but I'm so tired, and I don't have the stomach for any more violence today. There's no one else here to fight for or to fight for me. On my own, I suddenly have so little will to survive. I hear a shout from far away. They've spotted me, I think. It's over.

Then a high-pitched engine from the opposite direction approaches fast. In less time than I can count to two, it's screeching to a halt beside me.

"Get in!" Jamie yells. "Hurry."

I leap to my feet and scramble up the embankment and down to the road. I don't hesitate; I slide through the door Jamie holds open from the inside and slam it closed when we're already moving. It takes me a full ten seconds to realize we're heading back toward PSI. I exhale all my hope in a single breath.

"No, Jamie. Please don't do this. After everything we've been through, don't —"

The Jeeps pass us, returning to base, satisfied that their mission has been accomplished. The drivers wave to Jamie, and he waves back.

"If you take me back to PSI, my friend, Finn, will die. How's Robineau going to explain that?" I'm grasping at straws. Jamie's face is completely impassive. I bring my knees up and curl into myself as the grief and exhaustion overwhelm me. Sobs wrack my whole body. I cry for a long, long time. Much longer than it would've taken us to get back to the PSI garage. I pull myself up and glance out the side window. Nothing but fields to the left and right. I swivel around; PSI is a glimmer in the distance.

"Where am I taking you?" Jamie asks.

I throw my arms around his neck, swerving the car into the oncoming lane. He gets us back between the lines and smiles.

"Remember the hotel I stayed at before?"

"Sure."

"Is it safe?" I ask. "Do they know about it at PSI?"

"No. I was the only one you told, and I had no reason to report that information to Dr. Robineau. It's safe."

"Hurry!" I add.

We don't talk the rest of the way there. I'm preparing myself for what I'll have to do to help Finn, if he makes it that long.

When we get to the hotel, Ethan waves us into a parking space. He points to a room frantically. Jamie rushes in immediately. When I try to wrap Ethan in my arms, he pushes me away, dragging me with him. Finn's on the floor, unconscious, but still breathing. His clothes are soaked in blood. I almost gag. Ethan has stripped the linens off the bed, leaving only a plastic mattress protector. It feels like this was planned for.

"I couldn't get him on the bed," Ethan manages to pant out. He's barely holding it together.

"Help me," Jamie says, rolling Finn over and grabbing his arms. Ethan takes Finn's feet, and they swing him gently up onto the bed. Finn groans, and Jamie looks at me with the pained look of one who knows what a gunshot feels like. Finn's pale from the blood loss, and his face is wet with sweat and tears. I let my eyes travel down to his stomach to view the damage, but from this distance all I can see is a pocket of red gore. I unglue my feet from the floor and move tentatively toward the bed. Jamie has taken a knife from his pocket and is slicing open Finn's t-shirt. Then he slices down the outseam of Finn's jeans and rolls him halfway over to inspect the wound.

"Through-and-through," he says with clenched teeth. "But I think it hit his bowel and possibly something even more vital. He's lost a lot of blood, Elena. You don't have much time." He rolls Finn onto his back. I look for my brother and find him squatting in the corner, pressed up against the wall, with his thumb in his mouth and his eyes like saucers. I feel a sob of panic rising in my gut, but I beat it down. No time to think about all the history I have with this boy. The years of longing, hatred, and a deep desire for redemption.

"I'm going to go out and keep the others clear so you can concentrate. Elena? Are you with me?" Jamie says sharply.

I nod, but I barely hear his words or the click of the door. Ethan's screaming at me in my head. "Don't do this, Lanie. You can't do this. Just let him die. Please. Please. Please. Just let him die."

"What do you know?" I demand. "Is something going to happen to me if I help him?"

Ethan doesn't respond because there's a sudden commotion outside. He jumps up and somehow beats me to the door. Sage is trying to get past Jamie into the room. Cayde, Maureen, and Hugo are standing awkwardly behind them.

"Let me see him! I need to see him!" Her face is streaked with tears, but her voice is steel and ice. Then she sees me and Ethan. "Oh my god, Ethan! Are you alright?" She opens her arms, and he falls into her, like a child. "Lane, tell your boyfriend to let me through."

"Let Elena help him. He'll be fine if you just give her some space. She can save him. But there really isn't time for this drama!" Jamie must have missed the boyfriend comment because his voice is high-pitched and desperate. Sage looks at me like I'm a magician or a goddess.

"Can you do that?" she asks. "Can you really save someone who's been shot?" Jamie and I exchange glances, and I nod slowly.

"I think so," I say, barely audibly.

"No!" Ethan screams in my head. "Elena, don't. Please don't. No one will blame you."

I try to shut him out. Even if he told me that I was going to die if I tried this, I'd still do it. No choice really. Is there? I remember someone saying something like, "There's always a choice." So, maybe?

In unison, Sage and Ethan say, "Please!" and I feel split in two, like a walnut in a vise.

"I'll go get another room," Jamie says. No one notices; their eyes are riveted to me as I walk back through the door to the room where Finn lies dying because of me.

ॐ 16 ಞ

GRANTING INNOCENCE

Yesterday you came to my door
Heart in the open, hat in your hand
Yesterday you couldn't try anymore
To hold in the memories of what we'd been
We walked to the end of the road
As far as the light would take us
We looked back on where we've been
What we've done and how we've failed
So much, so much between us
But the sun was granting innocence
At the end of that road at the end of the day
"The End of the Day" – Luna Rayne, 2015

I wake up in a feather bed that smells of honey and lilacs, like my grandmother. A strip of light makes a pathway from the attic window behind my bed to the stairway, as if beckoning me back to a world below. Voices come up in waves from the kitchen, not enough that I'd recognize the people speaking, but enough that I sense the urgency of rising. The memorial is today.

For the next five or six hours, I'll have to put on a public face and swallow my guilt. Then I can come back here and be alone with my music and the stars Ethan put on the ceiling over the bed. Just six hours, that's all the time I'll give this pain that hovers like a hummingbird, sucking nectar from my heart. Here in this room, I can chase the pest away with show tunes and arias. I might even find a way to make wishes for the living and hurry my own half-life along.

The door that connects the attic to the room that's now Sage's opens, and I hear the quick pounding of her feet on the steep, wooden stairs. She pokes her head over the half-wall at the top. "You awake?"

I remember a time when she and I woke up side-by-side, a time before I was lethal. She stays on the stairs, a safe distance from my death-ray vision. Sage would find this idea funny, but I don't.

Speaking requires so much effort. "I'm awake," I rasp.

"Good. There's someone downstairs who wants to see you."

My heart beats double-time for a second or two. Then I remember the thousand ways I could hurt Jo and the thousand ways I've hurt her that she doesn't know about, and my heart stops dead. "I'll be down in a few."

Sage doesn't come up to banter. She slips silently away. I can't carry her pain, too. I'm so heavy with just my own.

I pull myself to sitting and swing my legs over the side of the bed. They feel like they're made of stone. I roll my neck to release the stiffness that makes me feel like my joints have been shrink-wrapped. Another side effect of exercising my powers, maybe, or just a symptom of the depression that's taking root in my psyche. I know exactly how Ethan has felt all these years. I'm ashamed of what I am, what I can do, and more ashamed of what I can't do.

I try to remember what happened in that hotel room after I closed the door. I wrack my brain for a sliver of memory of how I came to be back here in this house, that's as empty as I am. Ethan didn't even seem to mind when I moved up into this attic and not into my old room next to his. He has his own stuff to deal with, and he doesn't want me to mother or sister him anymore. I won't bother to ask Rachel his age again. He's all caught up, innocence lost. He proved that when he wanted Finn dead.

I silence the voices and concentrate on making myself presentable.

When I'm finally heading down the stairs, Jo appears in the doorway. She looks beautiful and strong. Her hair's longer, curling around her ears, and her eyes are bright with expectation. I freeze, torn between running away and throwing myself into her arms, like I did the last time I came home. She doesn't wait for me to decide. She climbs up to meet me. One step above her, I'm the perfect height to wrap myself around her neck in a desperate and silent embrace. She holds me tightly, breathing lightly into my hair. I bite the insides of my cheeks to keep from crying, and the urge almost passes. Then Jo's shoulders tremble a tiny bit, and I'm lost. We cry and kiss and hold each other on that ridiculous stairway for an amount of time that could never be measured in seconds or minutes.

Eventually, Jo leads me to the kitchen, where Ethan, Rachel, and Jesse are eating pastries and fruit, Rachel and Sage's attempt at brunch. I take a few strawberries and sit next to my brother, but I'll be surprised if I can eat them. These are the seats we used to occupy when we were kids. The tears well up again, and I'm surprised to feel Ethan's hand slip into mine. He isn't grieving, but he knows I have to. Jesse looks a little lost, too. Rachel reaches around her belly to grab another scone. She puts half on Jesse's plate, but in the end, she eats both halves. Rachel and Sage chat quietly, but the rest of us have nothing to say.

Ethan tries to communicate with me. "Lanie, it's not your fault. You can't blame yourself. You tried to make it. Please, Lane, don't be so sad." I'm not sure if he's saying it for my benefit or his own, so I shut him out.

Finally, we pile into cars and head to the church. I've been so self-absorbed; I haven't thought about how hard an event like this will be for Ethan for reasons that have nothing to do with death. Sage's arm is slipped through his because his hands are deep in the pockets of the crisp khakis she must've bought for him. At the door, he balks and runs his hand through his hair. His thumb is taped, and he chews around the edges.

"Do you want me to take you home?" I ask, but now that I'm here, I couldn't tear myself away. People are expecting me to say something to comfort them. Sage hands him a hard candy and he puts it in his mouth.

After a few seconds, he shakes his head and mumbles, "I can do this." I have my doubts.

We hold hands and go in together. The aisle feels endless, and I can't help thinking of some song lyrics about the long road home. I wish someone had planned some music for this part. By the time we sit in the front row, Ethan's agitated again; he keeps looking over his shoulder and bouncing his leg. Sage chatters quietly to distract him. I don't have the energy for dealing with his drama.

Jo slides in beside me, and I feel like I've been given permission to breathe. I close my eyes, rest my head on her shoulder and concentrate on the constellations behind my eyelids. Leo, Ares, Orion, Ursa Major and Minor. I picture them in the sky, tracing the lines between them, looking for some pattern that has brought me to this place in this universe. I contemplate jumping ship and drifting onto the astral plane, but the ceremony begins, and I have to step up and do what everyone expects of me one more time. I vow that it will be the last.

I'm only vaguely aware of the smattering of faces in the congregation as I speak slowly and carefully the words I memorized over the last few days in the attic room while I recovered. I keep my eyes on Jo as much as I can without seeming creepy. At the end of the service, I sing "Amazing Grace" without breaking down, somehow. Finally, it's over, and I'm shaking hands and hugging people who voice condolences and concern. Ethan manages to remain at my side, though he eschews the physical contact of these mostly strangers. They seem inclined to give him a wide berth anyway. Thankfully, that part is over quickly. We didn't plan a formal reception, but Rachel's preparing something small back at Grandmother's house for "family." I wish she weren't.

When we get home, I plant myself on the sofa next to Ethan. He's trying to sink into the upholstery. This sofa's so enormous, we must look tiny in contrast, like lost children. Suddenly, I'm overcome by a wave of memory. We were so small then, and so utterly lost. Ethan's arm was wrapped in bandages, and he was doped up on pain killers. That day I couldn't get away from the smell of smoke and ash inscribed in my nasal passages. I reached into my pocket and fingered the tiny moonstone, smooth and cold in the hands of the sharp fairy. I pierced my fingers again and again until tiny spots of blood dotted my white pinafore. Why did my grandmother dress me in white for my mother's funeral?

I reach into my pocket now and come up empty. My mother's earring was left behind at PSI. I finger the spots of blood Lily never got out of these cushions after Sage was injured in the rubble of our more recent blaze. In my head I almost blame Finn, but I pull myself up short. Not Finn's fire, Ethan's. I glance at my brother. He has one foot up on the sofa and his knee pressed to his chest. He gnaws at the tape on his left thumb and watches Sage hungrily as she crisscrosses the room, performing hostess duties. When he finally looks at me, I glance away. We don't have much to say to each other.

Sage comes over and sits down next to me. "How you holding up?"

"Okay, I guess."

After an awkward lull, she tries again. "You sang like freakin' Beyoncé! Everyone was bawling like a baby."

"Thanks," I say. She knows I couldn't care less about how much people loved my singing.

She pauses again. Third try's the charm. She gets right to it. "I need to talk to you about Finn."

"Now? Really, Sage?"

"Why not now? His name still needs to be cleared."

Ethan rises and scurries up the stairs.

"Nice going," I say.

"He needs to talk about this, too. We all do."

I shake my head. She ignores me. "Tomorrow, first thing, we're going to the cops to tell them to drop the charges. Once that happens —" She doesn't bother to finish the sentence.

"Fine," I concede. "We can go to the cops and tell them that pressing charges for the fire is no longer necessary."

Sage exhales audibly.

"Did you really think after everything that happened, I wouldn't?"

"No. I'm going to go up to talk to Ethan."

I'm not sure it's a good idea, but I don't really care to be honest. It's a relief to be alone again.

The next morning, I wake to a brief banging on the door to the attic and Sage's pounding up the stairs. Jo's asleep beside me. She rolls over to face me. "Don't go," she mumbles. A shock of dark hair falls across her forehead. I brush it aside and kiss her. "Promise," I whisper.

"Get a room!" Sage says between gagging noises.

Jo props herself up on an elbow. "If you don't like it, don't come up here." She looks at me with a conspiratorial glint and rolls her eyes. "Breeders!"

"Dykes." Sage rolls her eyes in response and pounds back down the stairs.

I can't help but smile. Jo lets my hand slip from hers as I drag myself from her warmth. I'm not looking forward to this.

When we get to the local precinct, Sage gives them the case number from the fire. We wait for a long time for the detectives assigned to the case to come and get us from the waiting area. Sage reads a year-old *People* magazine and chatters on about paparazzi and the high jinks of the Americana royals. I can't follow. I keep going back to the night of the fire, both fires. I have to stand up to shake off the tinkling of shattered glass ringing in my ears and the crush of hands around my ribs, lifting me from the near-boiling water. I pace the whole time, but as usual Sage is in her own little zone and doesn't really notice.

Finally, two familiar faces come around the corner.

"Sage Evans?" The cop's deep voice is somewhere between annoyed and surprised. "What in the name of Beelzebub brings you here to darken my fucking door?"

Sage embraces him. "Good to see you, too, DeSocio! Henderson."

"You look great, Sage," Henderson says. Then she turns and hugs me lightly. "Elena, you get prettier and prettier."

"I doubt that," I say, wondering how she hasn't noticed my greasy hair and the dark circles under my eyes.

"How's your brother?" she asks.

"So much better!" Sage says, beating me to it. "You wouldn't know him."

"That's good to hear," Henderson says.

We follow them back to an office and sit across the desk from DeSocio. He has the case folder open. "What brings you ladies to our lovely precinct?"

"Lily passed away." Sage just jumps in. I get up and look out the window.

"Sorry to hear that," he says.

"Since she's no longer here to press charges, even if the perpetrator of the fire is found, we'd like the case closed. I mean, Elena, as the executer of Lily's will, would like to do that." I turn around and try to look official.

DeSocio raises an eyebrow. "Is that so? How long have you been practicing that little speech?"

Sage narrows her eyes. "I Googled it. She can do that, and you can't stop her. No one was hurt, and the amount of property damage was too low for it to be a civil matter. Plus, it was private property."

"Let's take it down a notch, Norma Rae!" he says, putting his hands up.

Henderson puts a hand on Sage's shoulder.

"He didn't even do it!" Sage says. "Finnian Mulcahy didn't even start the fire."

She's almost in tears. I pray for her to stop now. I will her as hard as I can not to say the next thing coming out of her mouth. I will it so hard I'm afraid I might hurt her. I gasp and turn back to the window. I could hurt her. I don't want to hurt anyone anymore.

"We know," Henderson says quietly. "We knew it wasn't Mulcahy from the start."

I whirl around. "What?" My voice is shrill even in my own ears.

"Henderson liked the other boy for it," DeSocio admits.

"My brother?" I screech.

"Your grandmother never pressed any charges," Henderson says quietly, calmly.

I can't process this.

Sage is maybe even more confused than I am. "You mean all this time Finn was in the clear? There was no warrant for his arrest? No need for him to be on the run? That can't be right!"

"She told us," I mumble mostly to myself. "She told us she was going have him prosecuted. Sage asked her to drop the charges. She said —" My voice completely fails, and my throat and eyes become thick with tears. I feel like an idiot. Why am I crying? What does it matter?

"Why would she do that?" Sage asks, a little too stridently.

"I couldn't really speak to her motives," says DeSocio. He shoots Henderson another look. He won't look at me or Sage.

Henderson puts a hand on my shoulder. "Maybe she was doing it for Ethan. Maybe she was afraid of what would happen if Finn stayed in town. Lily was a good lady, selfless. She cared about you kids. I'm sure she did what she did for you."

"Right!" Sage's voice drips sarcasm.

I struggle to control the wave of emotion that threatens like a tsunami inside. I never saw this coming. I never would've believed my grandmother would lie to me, to all of us. I suspect Henderson is right, though. Knowing Lily Paige, she would've done exactly what she thought would be best for everyone, though only one person really benefited from this untruth. "Ethan," I say out loud without meaning to.

All eyes turn to me. "She did it to protect Ethan and to give him the one thing he really wanted."

"What was that?" Sage asks, a little more calmly.

"You."

Her eyes grow wide as she opens her mind to the total implication of Lily's plan. With Finn on the run, no one would have any reason to suspect Ethan and, perhaps more importantly, Finn wouldn't be able to have a relationship with Sage. Sage would, by default, stay behind with me and Ethan.

DeSocio walks us to the car, probably to make sure we're okay to drive home. On the way, I get lost in the labyrinth of revelations. And for some reason, for the first time since we've been back, I remember the talk I had with Lily just after her death. I hurry to the attic. So, Lily had her secrets, too. Time to bring everything to light.

I stand in front of the armoire, readying myself for the battle ahead. I must look a little comical with my hands gripping the handles of the door, poised but not moving. It's not like my grandmother's bones are going to fall out, I remind myself, but the image makes me shudder. I can do this. It's time to do this.

I ease the door open. No ghosts. No rattling old bones. No lightning strike from the heavens. Just the creek of the rusty hinges. Inside, I find dresses from another era, carefully preserved in plastic. Two wedding dresses with tulle, lace, and pearls. My grandmother was married twice. I knew this, but somehow it had been irrelevant. It seems less so now that she's gone. I don't think I ever really knew her as a person. I can't even picture her in a wedding dress. I unzip the plastic, run a hand over the yellowing silk and wonder. Did she miss them, her husbands? Did she ever feel hopeless about me and Ethan? Did she cry in the shower when Ethan was hospitalized, or when she found blood on the bathroom floor from my cutting? I should've helped her more. I should've sought her out at night for a cup of tea and a chat. I bury my face in my hands, ashamed of who I never was to her.

Under the dresses, the rounded top of an old trunk protrudes, scrunching the ones in the middle up a bit. I wipe my eyes and nose on my sleeve and kneel down. The trunk has handles on the sides that for some reason make me think of a magician's accoutrement. I pull it out and place it in the middle of the floor. I probably should get Sage and Ethan. What's inside is as much theirs as it is mine, but I make no move toward the stairs. Maybe Lily's still waiting on the astral plane for this moment. Maybe she's here with me now, just behind my shoulder, watching my hands shake as I undo the clasp.

I manage to get it undone just as Ethan appears on the landing. I beckon to him, and he squats next to me, in front of the now-open container. The item on top is a deed to the house. It shows that the mortgage is paid in full, and the property is in both our names. She didn't want there to be any nonsense about probate and whatnot, I imagine. Ethan tears up.

"She gave us the house. Not you, both of us," Ethan says.

"She knew you were getting better, E."

In a folder under the deed is a number of insurance papers and bank account records. Ethan calculates it quickly. Over $750, 000 in total that she put away for our educations and healthcare and whatever else we might need. A long letter in the folder outlines the uses she envisions for the money, but there are no strings; it's ours to use as we please. A business card with the name and contact information of her financial planner rounds out the gift.

The next treasure is a photo album. At first, we're perplexed by the faded photographs of the people in clothing from other eras, but gradually we piece the stories together and discover Gran's husbands, and Jesse as a baby growing up. It seems like Jesse had a sister a few years older, too, who sits or stands beside him in many of the shots until somewhere around his senior year of high school. She doesn't show up again until the wedding pictures. We're surprised to discover our dad was a swimmer and a tennis player in his youth.

After Jesse's graduation portrait, we turn the page and look into the eyes of a pretty, pixie girl. The pictures of our mother could've easily been me, except I never owned those clothes or wore my hair that way. We look for a long time at the photos of our parents holding hands and smiling and laughing.

I don't remember them being happy. My memories of them together are filled with conflict. "You look just like her," Ethan says in awe. It must have hurt Gran to look at me every single day and see the woman who ruined her son.

There are five pages of wedding pictures. One of the photographs grabs my attention, possibly because of the composition or maybe because the one just before it is missing from the book, leaving only a faded square on the page. In the photo, a young Jesse holds hands with our mom. His head is turned, gazing at her in adoration, but she's looking at the woman beside her, the one we think must have been Jesse's sister. That woman is looking at her, too, with an undeniable intensity. A man stands behind Jesse's sister. His arms encompass her almost proprietarily. The man looks vaguely familiar, with his cocky grin and the shock of black hair falling over one eye. There's something important about this photo. Ethan feels it, too. I know because his hand falls over it, covering it until the page is turned again.

Next come the baby pictures of me and Ethan. When we're around age three, the album ends. Another smaller album contains a smattering of shots that chronicle our growing up, with three times the number of shots of me as Ethan.

"I've had, like, no life, Lane," he says after we close that book.

"Your life is starting now, E. Make it count."

He sets his jaw and nods.

Then he pulls two more envelopes out of the trunk, one with his name in neat, controlled printing, and one with my name in a shakier scroll, like it was written at the very end. He puts his letter in his back pocket.

"Aren't you going to open it?" I ask.

"I know what it says."

"What?"

"It's about Sage, and what Gran did to protect me. It's about manning up."

"How do you know that?"

He gives me a look that says, "Come on, surely you get it by now."

"Oh," I say.

"You gonna read yours?" he asks.

"Not yet," I say. "If I hold onto it, it'll be like keeping her here just a bit longer."

Ethan smiles a little. "I get that."

He reaches into the very bottom of the box and pulls out two more envelopes, one with Sage's name and one with Finn's.

"What the hell?" Ethan says, standing suddenly. He drops the one with Finnian Mulcahy written across the back onto the floor. "Why did our grandmother write that degenerate a letter?"

I shake my head. "She told me she had when she visited after her death, but she didn't tell me why."

I turn the envelope over a couple of times, contemplating opening it. Ethan watches with his arms crossed over his chest. "Let's burn it," he says. "That would be fitting."

I resist the macabre urge to laugh, like a villain in a superhero movie. "No. Gran had her reasons and something important to say. Besides, what harm could come of a simple letter?"

"You might regret saying that," Ethan says ominously. Then he turns to go. "I'll take this down to Sage." He waves her letter in the air.

"I'll come with. I can give her this one, too." I pick up Finn's envelope and a photo shifts inside. I wonder if it's the one that was taken out of the book.

"Whatever you gotta do," he says, pounding down the stairs ahead of me.

Sage is in the kitchen, sitting at the table, writing in her journal. Nothing ever changes. Ethan drops the envelope over the page she's been writing on. "What's this?" she asks, turning it over like a clue. He slides into the chair next to hers.

"It's from Lily," I say, standing awkwardly in the doorway. "She left one for each of us." Ethan takes his out of his back pocket to show her. I wave mine in the air.

"Oh," she says sadly. "That was sweet of her."

"You already knew about this?" It's obvious she did.

"How did you find them?" she asks, confirming my suspicion. Ethan leans forward to see how much I'm willing to divulge.

I have nothing to hide from Sage. "Lily told me about the trunk in the armoire when she visited me on the astral plane —" I pause for dramatic effect. "— after she died."

Sage smiles and starts to laugh, then looks at Ethan, whose eyes are serious. "Oh! You're serious. Did you see her, too?" she asks Ethan.

He nods. "Not at the same time. She didn't tell me anything about the letters or the trunk."

"Okay. Wow! Yeah, okay." It's actually a little amusing to see Sage so off-balance. She looks at the envelope again. Without hesitation, she slips a finger under the tab and rips the seal open. She pulls out the letter and reads it. Ethan and I alternate between watching her and each other. Sage mists up a little, then reads the whole thing again.

"Wow," she exclaims, slipping the note back into the torn envelope.

"What did it say?" Ethan asks.

Sage looks at him warily. I hate the way they are now. It feels wrong, somehow. They used to be so in sync, so easy with each other. Now it feels like Ethan's trying too hard to get close, and Sage is trying too hard to keep a safe distance. It's unnatural.

"You don't have to tell us," I say, but I linger, waiting to see if she will.

"She says she left you the house, but I can stay here as long as I want." Sage is such a bad liar.

"She asked you to stay and take care of us," I say icily.

Sage gets up and looks out the window. "Pretty much."

Ethan sits back in his chair, turning the truth over in his head. "Don't do us any favors," he mumbles. "We don't really need to be taken care of anymore. Jeezus! That is, like, so insulting."

"It doesn't matter," I say, but I'm truthfully just as pissed, or more so, than he is.

Sage changes the subject. "She left me some money for college. I can't believe she did that."

"Good," I say. "Anything else? Does she explain the whole not-pressing-charges thing?" I ask, kind of pointedly.

"Not really," Sage says. Liar.

"So that's it, then?" I ask.

"Pretty much." She smiles a fake smile and sticks her head in the fridge. "What did she say in your letters?"

"Nothing," Ethan and I say in unison.

"You didn't read your letters, did you?" she says.

Ethan and I look at each other guiltily.

"And you wonder why she thought you needed someone to look after you?" She shakes her head.

Enough of this shit. I drop the real bomb on the table, so she can see the name on the final envelope.

She makes her way toward the table slowly, like the letter might be wired to explode. "Why the hell would Lily leave a letter for Finn?" Sage mumbles more to herself than either of us.

Ethan shrugs, but she doesn't look at him. Her eyes are glued to the envelope. "Should we open it?" Sage asks, looking at me.

"I think that should be your call," I say. "Ethan wants to burn it."

He jumps to his feet. "Hey! I never said that!"

Sage smiles at him patiently and motions for him to sit back down. "It's all right. I get it," she says. Ethan sits, crossing his arms over his chest and staring me down angrily. Sage picks up the envelope and slips her nail carefully under the seal. It pops open easily, and a photograph flutters out and onto the table. We all move closer, but none of us touches it. The photo is a classic wedding pose of a bride in front of the mirror and her maid of honor adjusting the veil. Our mother, Lana Hartman, is the bride. The other woman is Jesse's sister, Lily's daughter. This much I've figured out. Why Finn would care about this photo is beyond me.

At first glance, the picture seems normal, but upon closer inspection, you can see that the bridesmaid's crying, and in the mirror, out of focus behind the women, a man sits with his head in his hands. "I know who that is," Sage says a little too loudly. "That's Finn's mom. I saw her obituary once."

"Really?" I say. "I think that's Jesse's sister."

We don't have time to argue the point. Jesse suddenly appears in the doorway. He's already seen us standing over the photo.

"Whatcha got there?" I move back to let him in. "That's Sabine, my sister! And Lana! On our wedding day?" He picks up the faded picture.

His face is a map of emotion and confusion. "Where the hell did you kids get this?" Sage holds up the envelope with Finn's name on it. Jesse's face falls. "Oh my god! She didn't!" He sinks into the nearest chair. "Who else has seen this?" he asks, just as Rachel opens the screen door. I'm beginning to piece things together now and from the look on Sage's face, she's not far behind me.

Behind a bag of groceries, Rachel asks, "Seen what?"

Ethan, Sage, and I turn to Jesse to see what he's going to do. Rachel has already spotted the picture in his hand. "Ah, an embarrassing photo. Let me see." She puts the bag on the table and reaches out to take the photo, all smiles and playfulness, but something in the way Jesse hesitates changes her mood instantly. "What is it?" She withdraws her hand and takes a step back.

"Nothing," Jesse says. "A photo from my wedding to Lana."

"Yeah," Sage adds, faking a smile, "We were just noticing how much Elena looks like her mom." Rachel looks at each of us. Ethan puts his thumb in his mouth and brings his feet up onto the chair, and Sage and Jesse exchange furtive looks. I almost shake my head; they are so obvious.

Rachel holds out her hand to Jesse again and he passes her the photo. She studies it carefully and looks sadly at Jesse. "Who's the girl Lana's in love with?"

"It was complicated. This is complicated." He holds out a hand to Sage, and she passes Finn's envelope to him. "Lily left letters for each of her grandchildren." He holds it up so Rachel can read the name.

"That's nice, but how could Finn be considered her —" Rachel blinks a couple of times. "You had a sister. She was married to Sean Mulcahy. Oh my god." Rachel turns away, back to the door. "Now I get it. Why you were so willing to give it all up for Finn? You knew he was your nephew." She stares out past the pool. The sound of laughing male voices floats in through the screen door. I hurry to the window.

Jesse goes on. "Her name was Sabine. Lana was her best friend since grade school. I didn't know they were in love until the wedding, but it was too late by then. I was in love, too. I didn't want to share her."

Despite the anger I feel building in my second and sixth chakras, I'm gratified and comforted to know that my mother was like me in more than just our looks. I feel rumbling in the back of my mind. It's Ethan. He's rocking back and forth. No one notices his distress. By now, Rachel, Jesse, and Sage are with me at the window, riveted, watching Cayde and Finn race around and around the pool.

"I'll go talk to him," Rachel says coldly.

"No, I should do it," Jesse says and that's the end of the discussion. He takes the letter and photo and walks out the door. Rachel and Sage move together and watch him cross the patio with his head down. Ethan gets up silently and disappears upstairs. I hesitate for a second, but in the end, I follow him up to my old room, which is now his art studio.

When the door's closed, Ethan rages. "That asshole is not related to us!"

"How do you think I feel?" I ask. "Gives new meaning to 'kissing cousins' — and not in a good way," I say.

Ethan grimaces. "God, I hate that prick!" he says, pacing the length of the room with his arms crossed tightly against his chest. "I hate everything about him. I just wish he were dead." In his head, he adds, "You should've let him die. Why didn't you just —"

"Stop it!" I yell out loud. "Don't do that! Don't make this worse than it is already."

Ethan looks at me with tears in his eyes. "I wish I were you. If I could do the things you can, I would —"

"No, E! Don't say that. Please don't even think that shit." I grab his arm and spin him to face me. "We need to forget about the things we can do. If we let ourselves even consider using our gifts, the Initiative will find us. This safe, sweet life in this house with our family nearby will be over. You understand that, right?"

He flinches out of my grasp and stares down at me for half of a second like I'm batshit crazy. "Get out of here, Lane." He pulls a partially completed canvas from the closet. "Just leave me the hell alone."

I watch him squeeze crimson, gold, and cerulean onto a pallet. His hand runs over the brushes that protrude from a mason jar like a bouquet of straw. He picks one and brushes his knuckles across his eyes, but the tears still come down and drip onto the pallet. With his brush, he mixes the paint and tears, then swipes across the canvas with an abandon that has come into his art of late. I watch him lose himself in the painting for a while, wishing I could join him in that elusive escape, but I can't, so I leave him to it.

I'm struck in the moment that the door clicks shut at how alone we both are. We used to always find each other, but a wall or a gulf separates us now, and I'm not sure how to traverse it. Ironically, I wish I had Ethan's power, so I could make him forget all of this and so much more, so we could go back to how we were.

In the attic room, I can't see or hear the fallout, but I can imagine Finn's confusion, frustration, and elation at discovering he's not really alone. He has a family and a place. In my mind, I imagine him joking with Sage about being cousins. In the meantime, Ethan's feeling displaced and angry, with one more reason to hate his father. I have no idea what to feel, aside from lied to and deceived, yet closer to my mother than I ever have. I lie on the floor and look up into the rafters. How sad for her to be in love with Sabine all those years and to marry Jesse. How awful it must've been to lose Sabine and feel trapped in a loveless marriage. In my mind, I can see Jesse blaming Lana for his sister's death, hating her for loving Sabine instead of him. It ties my stomach in knots that choke me to the point of tears without the release of them.

When Jo comes back, I tell her everything, and she holds me, but the tears refuse to cleanse me, and I fall asleep, feeling my heart harden, brittle like a loaf of bread left out for days. The next day, I stay in the attic, listening to music and singing when the lyrics move me. The next day's the same, and the next and the next. Rachel, Cayde, Ethan, and Sage come up to check on me, and, satisfied that I'm not suicidal or visibly bleeding, they leave again. Sage is the most relentless, of course.

The girl never stops digging, so I tell her what's in my head, but my heart remains stale and intact. If I try to open it, the whole thing will explode into a gazillion crumbs that could never be swept together again.

Ethan tells me that Lily left the garage apartment to Finn. "We're stuck with him for life!" he laments loudly but leaves off the accusations. Rachel and Jesse have rented a house a few streets over. Cayde will stay with them, unofficially adopted for as long as he'll obey their rules and play nice as part of their family. Ethan should be over the moon about that, but instead he complains about Finn ruining Cayde. There's no point in trying to talk him down; Ethan's officially obsessed, and I don't know how to change that.

One morning, though, I wake up and realize I have a job waiting for me. I'm not sure how I forgot about it, but I did. Now that I remember, I can't stay away. I get up and shower at 5 am. Jo hasn't bothered to stay the last couple of nights, so I don't disturb her by getting up so early. I leave a note for Sage and grab the keys to the car.

Marco screams when he sees me. "Angel-face! What took you so long? We heard you were back in town, but, baby, that was days and days ago." He wraps me in his arms, and all I feel is an intense fear that I might hurt him. I pull away.

"I'm sorry. There was the memorial and getting settled and. . . you know."

"I know, angel." He looks at me sympathetically. It's kind of an odd look on him.

Myra comes sweeping in from the kitchen, like Marco might be on fire. She tucks herself under his arm and stares me down with a smile. "Well, look what the cat dragged in. Are you on leave or vacation or sabbatical or whatever they call it in that fancy-pants company you went to work at?"

I smile back and wonder what she has to be so insecure about. I don't even play for her team. Then I remember that I told Marco about Jamie. At the thought of his name, a rush of emotion threatens to bowl me over. This is literally the first time he's crossed my mind since that day. I shake it off. "Good to see you, too, Myra. Actually, I'm back for good."

"So, you're here to beg for your old job back? Well, 'Angel face,' it just doesn't —'

Marco breaks in over Myra. "No begging necessary. Grab an apron and get started on cleaning up table two." He hands me a rag, and Myra hits him hard on the arm before stomping back to the kitchen.

"Trouble in paradise?" I ask quietly.

"You mean purgatory. Trouble in purgatory," he corrects. "Nah. Nothing I can't handle, anyway."

"Thanks," I say. "I'll smooth things over with Myra before the lunch rush."

"Well, it'll take me at least until close." He laughs at his joke, but I don't. "Get to work," he says.

I spend the morning in a mindless haze of one finite task followed by three more. It's a relief to be out of my own head.

Around noon, my comfort's shattered. Sage walks in, all smiles and nerves. She waves at me from the door while I'm taking an order at table three. I wave back, but my stomach twists. I know who will walk in the door behind her, and I can't deal with him or anything about our past. And now we're blood connections. I lose the thread of the order and have to ask the woman to repeat it. She does so slowly and deliberately, as though she's talking to someone disabled or addled. I don't hold it against her. I must seem that way to the casual observer.

Sage has the decency to stand by the door and wait, rather than chasing me through the café. I go into the kitchen, somehow remember to put in the ticket and go back to the break room to retrieve the car keys. I try to pass them to Hadly, the androgynous, little, steampunk busser, but he shakes his head and indicates the number of tables that have suddenly been vacated.

I take them to Sage myself. "Sorry, I just needed to get out and do something productive," I say.

"Don't worry about it. The car belongs to both of us. I'm glad you didn't wake me up. I need to do some stuff over at the college, though." She smiles, puts a hand on my arm. I feel like I'm seeing it through some kind of portal.

"Sure," I say, offering up the keys.

"Finn can take you home." I can barely hear her words. He's standing just on the other side of the glass door. He won't make eye contact.

Marco comes up behind me. "Yeah, go home. You've done plenty for your first day back. I'll get you on the schedule. Call me later."

There's no arguing with Marco or Sage. Besides, if I keep avoiding this, it may only get worse. I nod. "Tell him I'll be out in a minute." I go to the bathroom to collect myself.

I haven't seen Finn since the day he lay dying in the hotel. I don't remember much about what happened except that somehow, we both ended up on the astral plane. Perhaps we both died and came back. I couldn't say for sure, but when we were there together with all the physical barriers gone, the truth about Finn was laid bare to me.

Everything he'd said at the hotel was true. I came to understand the way he feels about Sage and Rachel and Jesse. I was surprised by how much good he possessed, and how much anguish he still suffered over his mother and father and the way he behaved as a kid. At one point, I realized he must see me, too, and I felt naked and ashamed. We were only there for a few seconds perhaps, but I haven't been able to face him, knowing the things he must now know about me. Sure, I saved his life and all, but the reasons I did it couldn't be considered honorable, not really. The truth is, I hate Finn, and now that I know that we're blood and more than blood because of the love our mothers were denied, I wish I'd just let him die. The worst of it is that I have no clue why I feel this way. But I have to go out and pretend everything's cool.

Finn's leaning against his bike, chewing gum and fidgeting with the gas cover. He looks heavier and older. When he sees me, he lifts a hand, like he did when he saw Ethan on the porch. The gesture's neither welcoming nor off-putting.

"Hey," he says without making eye contact. He hands me the only helmet.

"I've never done this before," I say. "Anything special I should know before I get on this thing?"

"It's just like riding a bicycle, only faster and less tiring." He smiles, sort of.

"Ah, well, that helps," I say, taking a step back.

"Don't tell me you never learned to ride a bike?"

"Don't tell me you're shocked. My grandmother wasn't big on the idea of sports or freedom." It occurs to me that she was his grandmother, too.

"Well, then, just get on behind me and put your feet up here." He points to places on either side of the bike. "Don't let your leg touch that pipe, or you'll get burned. Oh, and lean into the turns with me, but not too far."

"Is that all?" Now I'm pretty sure I'm going to die.

Finn laughs suddenly. "Don't look so scared. You're not going to die, I promise. Come on, your wimpy-ass brother fucking drove this thing. Surely you can ride on it for a few minutes." He's done talking, so I pull on the helmet.

Finn gets on the bike and swivels to offer me a hand. I manage to get on without his assistance. Once I'm balanced behind him, I scoot back as far as I can, so our legs aren't touching. Still, I have no choice but to wrap my arms around his waist, unless I want this ride to end right here in the parking lot. I hesitate too long.

Finn turns to look me up and down. "Jeezus, Elena. I'm not going to bite you or rape you or kill you or whatever you're afraid of."

I look away, but I can't bring my arms up.

"What the hell is wrong with you? Did I not thank you properly for saving my sorry ass? Did I act like it was your fault I got shot any fucking way? Are you pissed because Sage is with me and not Peethan? Or are you mad we're related?"

Tears form under my helmet, and it feels like a steam bath on my face, but I don't want him to see me cry. "Just go," I say putting my hands lightly on his waist.

He takes a beat, shakes his head, and revs the bike. When it lunges forward, I fall into him, and I'm forced to wrap my arms all the way around him to stay on. The ride home is like Mr. Toad's wild ride. I've never felt such terror or exhilaration, except maybe coming down the zip line. All I can do for the first three minutes is hold on for dear life. I relax by degrees only because my muscles begin to ache.

When we finally pull into the driveway, I can't get off the thing fast enough. I nearly fall, but Finn catches me. I right myself and pull away harshly. Finn gives me a look that pierces my heart.

"Fuck this!" he mumbles. "I risked my ass to save your fucking life. Twice! And for some reason you still hate my guts. I don't get it. Is this about your creepy brother? 'Cuz if that's the problem —"

"He's your cousin, you prick!" I shove the helmet into his gut.

"Just tell me why you hate me so much, Elena." I can't see his flashing eyes or his obnoxious, self-satisfied smirk because I've already turned my back on him. Without the visual cues, his voice sounds almost plaintive. I can't imagine why he'd care how I feel about him.

The next morning, the doorbell ringing over and over wakes me up. Jo sleeps though it, but I hurry down the stairs and through Sage's room. Her bed hasn't been slept in. Across the living room, I see Ethan standing at the top of the stairs with a towel around his waist. "I'm getting it," I say, but he stays put. I open the door and stare.

For a second, Logan blanches white and steps back, but she shakes it off quickly. "I brought your shit," she says, holding out a box and attempting to sound pissed off.

"What? — How —? Why are you here?"

"Did you lose the ability to talk in complete sentences when you lost your manners?" she asks.

"Sorry. Come on in." I hold the door open and take the box from her. Ethan's partway down the stairs, still wearing only the towel. "It's Logan," I say, expecting him to beat a retreat, but he comes all the way down.

She looks him up and down with raised brows while I put the box on the coffee table. "You gonna put some clothes on, or am I gonna get a show, little worm?"

He doesn't rise to her challenge. "What's in the box?"

Logan flips open the lid and pulls out Ethan's bear. She throws it at him, and he manages to hold onto his towel with one hand and catch the bear in the other. "I think this is yours," she says.

"Red!" Ethan can't disguise the smile in his voice. "Thanks." He takes the bear and runs up the stairs.

"Thanks, Logan," I say.

"Don't worry, I didn't forget you." She puts her hand in her pocket, pulls out my mother's earring and drops it into my open palm. I close my hand around it until the post pierces my Venus mound. I feel instantly calmer.

"Your phone and clothes and the shit Jamie gave you both is in the box. After you died —" Logan pauses awkwardly. "— I got tasked with packing your stuff, and I convinced Robineau it'd be better for the family to get your effects in person rather than through the mail. Maybe prevent a lawsuit or something. Of course, that was before Jamie told me."

"Told you what?"

"Duh. That you weren't really dead, that your brother put the freak on the whole Initiative, so we remembered you dying."

I think about that for a minute. "No shit. Ethan did it. He made everyone there remember something that never happened. I guess I should've assumed that it worked when we didn't hear the dogs baying, but truth is, I've been a little lost. Out of sight, out of mind, I guess."

She looks at me like I've grown another head. "Uh, yeah. Jamie said Hugo hacked the video feeds and doctored the footage to support the fiction they concocted. Hell, I totally believed it. PSI is waiting for the other shoe to drop, lawsuit from your parents, whatever. Play your cards right, and your folks could get a chunk of change."

"Jamie," I whisper. "How's Jamie doing?"

"He's a jerk." Logan crosses her arms over her chest. "But with Maureen and Hugo AWOL, he's all I got."

"They called me the day they got out. Hugo said something about looking up their families to see if they still had families they wanted any part of. I think they'll stay together, at least for a while," I tell her.

"You know Hugo's gay, right?"

"Duh," I say, imitating her. "I didn't mean together, together."

Logan laughs.

The kitchen screen slams. Sage and Finn come through the door, hand-in-hand. "Whose car's out in front?" Sage asks. Finn hangs back, like he doesn't want to be in the same room as me, which suits me fine.

"That would be mine, but not really mine," Logan says.

Finn gives Logan a once-over.

Logan offers Finn her hand. He drops Sage's to shake hers. "You got a name?" she asks him.

Ethan comes down the stairs, in clothes this time. "Sage, check it out! Logan brought Red back." Sage crosses the room to him, but she avoids touching him. I can feel his heart lurch.

"Nice to meet you, Logan," Finn says, taking his hand back, but not offering his name.

"Are you the mystery man?" She turns away dramatically.

"Finn. His name's Finn," Ethan says coldly.

"Nice to meet you, Finn. But I already knew that anyway." Logan's flirting. I'm not sure if I want to puke or laugh.

"Did you, then?" Finn says. His ears turn a little red, and I wonder if Sage is catching this.

As if on cue, Sage moves back to Finn's side and puts a proprietary arm around his waist. "I'm Sage, but you probably knew that, too." She holds out her hand.

Logan ignores it. "No, I actually didn't. Nice to meet you, Skye."

"Sage. My name is Sage."

Logan winks at Finn, and he stifles the smirk playing around his lips.

I brace myself for a cat fight, but the screen door slams again, and Cayde comes flying into the room, like he was shot from a cannon. "E-man, E-man! Jesse's setting up the trampoline!" He slides to a halt and stares at Logan for a full five seconds before a huge smile eats his entire face, and he literally leaps at her. She throws up her arms in self-defense, but she ends up sprawled on the floor under him. "About time you fell for me," he says, but he's laughing so hard Logan has no idea he's made a joke.

"Get your disgusting, punk-ass off me," she screams. Finn steps in and easily lifts Cayde off of her by the belly. Cayde hangs like a ragdoll, pulling with all of his might to get back to Logan, to no avail.

"Whoa there, pal. That's no way to treat a lady," Finn says as he tosses Cayde onto the sofa and offers Logan a hand up. He winks at her.

She graces him with a fleeting smile. "My hero." Her tone is total sarcasm. I glance at Sage. She's actually frowning.

"You want some coffee?" I ask. I need out of this weird scene.

"Whatever." "K." "Absolutely." "No thanks." "Fo shizzle!" they all say at once.

"What's all the commotion?" Jo wanders out into the living room in her robe. She comes over to kiss me. "Oh, we have guests." She's still groggy.

"Jo, this is Logan, my roommate from the asylum."

"Well, I'll be damned; Elena really is playing for the other team. I thought it was a line. I mean, nice to meet you, Jo," Logan says.

Jo looks at Logan like she's a puzzle that needs putting together. I steer her into the kitchen with me. "That was weird," she says.

"That was Logan. She talks to dead people," I say.

"You have the strangest friends," Jo says, smiling, and she kisses me again.

"You don't know the half of it," I say, smiling back. The warmth that momentarily engulfs me dissipates instantly as Finn walks into the kitchen.

He looks at me and nods at Jo. She nods back. "I'm gonna go get myself together," she says. She's gone before I can protest.

"We need to talk," Finn says. "We're practically living in the same house. You can't avoid me all the time."

"I can and will." I busy myself making coffee.

"Please, Elena! Tell me why you hate me so much." I won't look at his face, but I don't have to. His voice conveys just the right amount of pathos to pain me.

"I don't hate you, Finn. I just hate seeing you."

"That makes no sense. You know that, right?" He takes a step toward me, but I back away.

"It's complicated. My feelings are complicated," I say. Waves of guilt push through me, guilt for blaming him for raping me all those years ago, guilt for almost letting him die, guilt for getting him shot in the first place, guilt for being jealous of his relationship with Sage. Maybe it's not so complicated, I almost admit to myself.

"All this 'news' hasn't exactly been easy for me either, you know. I lost nearly two years of my life, running from a crime I didn't commit. Add to that the fact that my mom was a dyke — no offense — who was in love with your mom, which means my dad probably did murder her, in addition to offing himself. Yeah, I've got shit to deal with, too, but I'm not blaming you."

"You're right," I say. "What can I say? You're right." I'm backed against the sink, but I make a move to get around him and away from this conversation.

"I won't tell," he says, almost too quietly for me to catch. The words stop my feet. They spin me around, and our faces are inches apart.

"What did you say?"

"I won't tell anyone about what you're capable of. The things you know I know from when we were dead, or nearly dead." My mouth must be hanging open because he adds, "Just saying, you can relax. I'd never tell. Who would believe me anyway? Your angelic reputation is intact, so please give it a rest. Okay?"

I want to scream and pound his chest until he weeps. I want him to hurt. Suddenly, Finn groans and grabs his head. Tears pour from his eyes. My own head nearly explodes as I realize what I'm doing to him. Stop! Stop! I think. I catch his shoulders as he begins to crumple. I try to force myself to think healing, peaceful thoughts, but they slip through my racing mind, like smoke. He leans against me, breathing hard. His knees begin to buckle, and I fight a rising panic. I focus on my heart chakra and breathe with him. Gradually, he relaxes and pulls himself upright. He backs away from me. I won't look at him. I couldn't bear to see the terror in his eyes. "I'm sorry. I'm sorry. I'm so sorry." No words could make this right.

Sage, Logan, Ethan, Jo, and Cayde walk in. A silence descends, but only Ethan, Cayde, and Logan can guess what happened. I push past them, desperate for a space small enough to contain me.

Jo follows me up.

"What happened down there? Did Finn do something? Say something?" She means well, but I can't begin to explain.

"He didn't do anything," I say, but I keep my back to her.

She puts a hand on my shoulder. "Please, Elena, let me help you."

I spin around, more to pull away from her touch than to face off, but she backs up anyway, like she might need to do battle. "Jo, there's nothing you can do."

"Look, Lane, something's gotta change here. You keep pushing me away, and I'm beginning to feel like I don't know anything about you. One minute you want me here and the next you want me gone. I'm never sure which Elena I'm going to get. I know you've been through a lot, but so have I. Please. I'm here."

"Trust me, Jo, you don't want to know what's happening with me. In fact, you may not want to know me."

She steps forward, her arms open. "That's absurd. I love you, Lane."

I wish I could fall into her arms and tell her everything, but all she'd feel would be fear. I turn away. "Go away, Jo. Just go, okay?"

I don't hear her feet on the stairs, but when I turn back around, she's gone. No one else bothers me, though I half-expect Logan to show her face. Then again, she's not really the comforting type.

I lie on the bed and focus my attention on the stars. I suppose I fall asleep, because Logan makes an appearance in a strange dreamscape. We're standing in the middle of nowhere. There isn't a building, a tree, a rock, a road, or a blade of grass to be seen. The ground is powder-fine, blinding white sand. I have no idea how either of us arrived here, but she doesn't show the slightest shock at finding herself in this place with me. She turns and looks to the left. When I glance back, Logan's gone, and my mother's standing beside me. She puts one hand on my shoulder and points upward with the other. Above us, the sky's midnight blue, with a million points of light that form pictures across the canvas of my mind.

"You just need to gain a little focus. Stop trying so hard to control everything. Your emotions are raw from disuse," my mom says, staring up at the stars.

"What're you talking about?" I ask.

"Relax. Look up. Tell me what you see," she says placidly.

I look up, and the stars shift. An image of the first time I healed someone comes into focus, a girl named Amie who failed her math test. She was so disappointed in herself and upset about how her parents were going to react. I put a hand on her arm, and her mood turned from panic to calm, instantly. It took me almost a year and several other incidents to understand that I was the one causing the emotional shifts.

I watch myself heal Finn's angst a thousand times, then Sage's pain the first night we met by the swimming pool in the yard of this house. I see all the times I tried so hard to heal Ethan and failed.

I turn my head and there to my right I see Logan finding me and Ethan through her connection with my mother on the astral plane. Jamie's there, too, watching me, manipulating my emotions so I'll want to examine and explore my ability. I see the advertisement he put on that bulletin board, and I feel the need to make the call. I see our relationship begin, and the trust grow. I see his desire for me turn into my desire for him. I want to look away, but my mother leans in and whispers, "Stay with it; you won't have this chance again."

I nod and keep my eyes focused on the unfolding of my skills. I watch as Robineau and Meriwether push me harder and harder, until I risk my own health to make Ash and the kids at the hospital whole. I watch Ethan and me being pulled apart, isolated from each other, and I feel all my anguish and his. I wipe the tears away, so they won't obstruct my view.

I watch our friends working together and risking so much to get us out of PSI, though they don't understand why we'd want to leave. Their concern for our safety is overwhelming. I don't believe I deserve their devotion. From this vantage point, I wonder if it was worth all that it cost every one of us.

I watch the soldiers suffer because of me, the ones in the field and the one in the stairwell. I wish I could take it back.

Then I see myself hesitating and finally healing Finn just this side of death, and our journey back to life. I see myself retreating to the little room in the attic that's able to contain me and all the rage, guilt, pain, frustration, and love I feel all the time. I see Jo and Sage and Marco and Ethan all moving away from me, giving me the space I demand, but don't really want.

The story, my story, shapes itself into a constellation that tells it all and leaves it open, too. It seems as though it has always been there, a pathway through the firmament that chronicles my journey, but I can't fathom where the stars are leading now.

I turn to my mother, but Logan looks back at me. "Stellar navigation, shrimpo." She smirks, and I wonder if she's being sarcastic or providing some kind of ninja advice.

"How did you do that?" I ask.

"For real? I didn't do anything." She seems sincerely puzzled by my question.

"Then how?"

"All of time and space exists at once, as if on a ribbon. You get to see the ribbon sometimes, that's all I know. Or all I think I know." She lifts her hand from my shoulder. By the time I turn to thank her, she's gone, and I find myself looking down at my body, sleeping under the attic eaves. "How do I know what to do next?" I yell, but my voice only pulls me back into my body, and I'm awake. Ethan's curled into a chair at the far end of the attic by the window, where a beam of light streams in. He turns when the bed creaks as I sit up.

"Hey, E. What're you doing up here?" I ask, settling into the chair next to his.

"I thought you might want to talk to someone." He closes the sketchbook and pushes the pencil into the spiral wire at the top.

"Okay."

"Did something happen with Finn today?" Ethan has no gift for subtlety.

"Oh. I don't really want to talk about that," I say, and I get up to turn on some music.

"Whatever," he says. "We can talk about whatever you want. Come on. I never see you anymore."

I smile at him. "You don't need me anymore."

His eyes widen. "Why would you say that?"

"E, look at you now. You're like a real boy!"

He laughs. "So, I used to be made of wood? Is that what you're implying?"

"You know what I mean. You're, like, all grown up, kind of. You saved me, like a hero. Came up with the whole plan, big picture stuff with tons of logistical complications. I couldn't believe it. You don't need me anymore."

He shrinks down in the chair. "Lanie, I'll always need you. Why do you think I did all that? I had to."

I crouch down in front of him and put my hand on his knee. "Well, you don't need me, not like you did, but I sure as hell need you."

He brings his hand up to my face. "No worries, little sister. We'll navigate these stars together."

ℵ 17 ℵ

EPILOGUE: SEARCHING FOR A SONG

Lay down the map
Don't choose a destination
If you'll ride with me
I'll let you choose the station
Find a beat that'll keep our hearts hopin'
Find a love song that'll make our minds open
To the possibilities
Of you and me, of you and me
Keep searching for a song
I'll keep driving all night long.
　　"Driving All Night" – Luna Rayne, 2000

Time has a way of moving fast and slow, simultaneously. People have a way of staying the same and changing completely right before your eyes, without you noticing.

Ethan has just come into the kitchen, where Sage and Rachel are putting the finishing touches on our birthday cake. He's a little taller than Sage now, with a meager mustache and goatee, very hipster. His hair's cut shorter, so the curls are just a memory. The biggest changes in him aren't purely physical, however. He stands up straighter now, smiles more often and talks more easily. He puts an arm around Rachel and scoops up a fingerful of frosting that he eats before Sage can voice her protest.

"Hey! Keep your filthy hands out of the frosting!" Sage yells.

He holds up his hands. "I just got out of the shower. Totally clean, I swear." He smiles, then comes over to where I'm standing and puts his hands on my shoulders. "How long do we have to wait before we get to eat our cake?" he asks.

"Patience, grasshopper," I say. "Jesse still has to barbeque the steaks and corn."

He groans. "So, it's going to be hours and hours."

"Afraid so," Rachel chimes in.

"Where did everyone else go?" he asks.

"Jesse and Finn took Fiona and Cayde on some mysterious errand so we could get this cake finished without little fingers digging into it every five seconds," Sage says, giving Ethan a stern look.

"Oops," Ethan says, pretending to be chastened.

A car pulls up the driveway and raucous male voices punctuated by the bossy tones of a soprano toddler enter the house long before the door opens.

"Why can't I have any? If Ethan gets to drink it, I should get to, too! Come on. I'm sixteen!"

"No way!" Jesse says flatly. "Ethan's twenty-one now. That, my son, is the drinking age in this state. What kind of a father would I be if I let you drink beer illegally?"

"The awesome kind," Cayde says. "I'll bet Finn drank beer when he was sixteen."

Finn's laughing when they burst through the door. "Yeah, but you don't want to be like me, bud."

"Yes, I do," Cayde protests.

"Me too!" little Fiona chirps from Jesse's arms. Her entire entourage laughs.

"E-man! Jesse and Finn bought beer, and you get to drink it," Cayde says when he catches sight of my brother.

Ethan doesn't look all that thrilled. "How thoughtful," he says coolly.

Rachel stops decorating to observe the interaction. She looks even less thrilled about the prospect of Ethan drinking a beer than he does. Finn busts open the case of Fat Tire, pulls a Swiss army knife out of his back pocket, pops off the top, and hands one to Ethan and one to Jesse. He offers one to Rachel, but she points to her boob and waves it off, so he holds it out to me. I shake my head. Sage reaches for the bottle, but Finn pulls it away at the last second, so she has to move in closer to get it. He keeps pulling it backward, until she's more or less on top of him, trying to reach for it. Then he leans in and kisses her. Ethan grabs the beer out of his hand and passes it to Sage on the other side.

"Thanks," she says to Ethan. Finn shakes his head puts the rest of the bottles in the refrigerator.

Ethan looks uncomfortable holding the beer, like it might be poisoned. After a long pause, he brings it to his lips and takes a draw. We all watch as he swallows. "What?" he says, looking around the room. "None of you ever saw a guy drink a beer?"

Rachel washes her hands and takes the baby from Jesse. "Fifi, fairy!" she croons, kissing Fiona's neck over and over.

My little half-sister giggles with delight. Then she reaches around Rachel for Sage. "Sagey, Sagey, hold you!" she demands.

Rachel gives up and lets her climb over her arm like a little squirrel, onto Sage's back. Sage easily flips her around to the front, and they rub noses affectionately. They look like sisters.

"Ethan, grab the steaks," Jesse commands. Then he heads outside to ready the grill. Finn and Cayde follow, with Finn fighting off Cayde's attempts to grab his beer.

"Come on, man, don't be so uncool!" Cayde protests.

Ethan hands me his bottle and digs the steaks out of the fridge. I take a small sip and follow him outside. After I give the beer back to Ethan, I go to the garage and pull out as many lawn chairs as I can find. The weather's warm for February, so the gathering settles out around the pool and by the grill.

Before long, Hugo and Maureen show up with presents for both of us. They're giddy with excitement about some secret they have in store for us. Hugo joins the boys around the grill, and Rachel comes out with some chicken and sauce to add to the feast. I'm starting to feel a little overwhelmed by the noise and confusion, but Ethan looks oddly relaxed under the influence of the alcohol.

I don't dare drink. I have no idea what could happen to people if I lose control of my emotions. I live in nearly constant terror of hurting people, though that hasn't happened since the day I almost killed Finn in the kitchen over a year ago. I've made sure of that. I keep to myself, mostly. I go to work at the café and to voice lessons. I sing in the choir at the community college and occasionally do gigs with my teacher's band: weddings, parties, and funerals. Aside from that, I stay in the attic. Ethan, Jo, Sage, and my parents hang out up there with me, but the visits are never too long or stressful. This is the most social event I've attended since Gran's funeral.

Marco and Myra pull up as the steaks come off the grill. Jo must've invited them. Marco fits in instantly, like this is his family, while Myra keeps her hands and eyes on him at all times. She tells him how many beers he can have and what to eat, and he takes it all on the chin. Myra's even jealous of Maureen, who's trying to engage Marco in a discussion about avant-garde films and filmmakers.

After a while, Hugo, Cayde, and Finn run off to jump on the trampoline that Jesse set up behind the garage when we first returned from PSI. It's a wonder the thing hasn't collapsed from the stuff they do on it. Sage and Ethan have their feet in the water by the pool stairs. Ethan's smiling like the sun is shining just for him. I'm not sure anything good can come of their proximity. Sage has kept Ethan at arm's distance for a long time, and rightly so, but today they look like old times before PSI. I hope she's not getting his hopes up.

Jesse and Rachel have set up an iPod and speaker. Their happy hippy music spills out over the afternoon. They're completely enthralled with my little sister, who's dancing like only a thirteen month old can, to the delight of anyone who will watch.

Jo arrives as people begin heaping their plates. A part of me is happy to have an ally at the party, but her worried looks and incessant questions about how I'm doing wear thin quickly. I'm probably no better than she is, though. I wince when Finn hands Ethan his third beer. I'm about to check in with my brother when another car parks across the street. Two people get out and head toward us. My heart flutters and my breathing stops momentarily.

"Okay, now the party can begin!" Logan yells loud enough for everyone to look. She has about five piercings I've never seen and her hair's blue at the tips. She's dressed kind of steampunk chic. Hugo, Maureen, and I hurry toward her, but Cayde beats us all. He doesn't tackle her this time. Instead, he hugs her almost properly. She pulls away. "And who the hell are you?"

Cayde looks devastated. "C-C-Cayde. Shit, don't you remember — "

Logan can't keep a straight face. "Like I could forget a moron like you!"

"You bitch!" Cayde punches her playfully in the arm, and she pounds him back, then hugs him hard.

"Hey, shrimpo," she says to me. "You look shorter." I keep my eyes on her, trying hard to ignore Jamie, who's lingering behind her. "You're gonna need to talk to him at some point," Logan whispers after greeting the others. I nod. She looks across the yard, and her eyes light on Ethan, standing by Sage with a beer in hand. "Is that —? Oh my god! He's so different." She sweeps up the driveway, leaving me alone with Jamie.

"Hey," he says. "How are you?"

"I'm good," I say, but he knows I'm not, of course. My only consolation is that he looks far worse off than I feel. "You?"

"Not great," he admits. "PSI got closed down. No more neuro-inhibiters, kind of a limited supply of those on the street. Makes it tough for me to function day-to-day."

"I'm sorry." I am sorry he's suffering, despite what he did to me, to us.

"Man, Ethan looks great." Jamie smiles sincerely.

"He is, mostly. He just got a job at the university as a TA in the physics lab. His art's selling well at a couple of galleries and online." I leave out the fact that he still struggles with the nightmares and bedwetting.

"That's great," Jamie says, but he looks a little wistful.

"What're you doing here, Jamie? How did you get Logan to bring —" I don't bother finishing the question and, I doubt he'll bother to answer it.

"I. . . I missed you." He reaches for my hand, but I don't give it to him. I already feel the familiar confusion setting in, clouding my emotions and twisting them into alignment with his.

"Don't do that," I say.

"Do what?" he asks.

"You know. That thing where you make me feel what you do. Don't do it. Okay?"

"Sorry. It's a reflex, you know. If I don't do that, I just absorb whatever people around me are feeling. Your anger, for example. I would just rather feel my pain than your anger."

"I'll try to feel less angry," I say, but the truth is that I'm even madder now. I look away and try to rein it in.

"I have something for you." He hands me an envelope.

"What's this?" I'm a little frightened of what might be inside.

"Letters from the kids and soldiers you helped."

"Nothing from the soldiers I hurt."

"Don't be like that, Elena."

I turn away.

Jo comes out of the house and looks around until she sees me. I've told her very little about Jamie, but I have no idea what Ethan has said. In any case, she makes a beeline for us, and I cringe.

Jo and I have yet to make love, but I've been hoping against hope that today we'll find our way to each other. It's my birthday wish. I don't want Jamie to derail it.

"You must be Jamie," Jo says, smiling and holding out her hand, but there's something completely guarded and cold just under the surface. She puts her arm around me.

"Jo. It's nice to finally meet the girl Elena pined for." Jamie turns on the charm.

"It's nice to know she pined for me when she was with you." Jo's voice is fine sandpaper. She knows something.

Logan, Hugo, and Maureen come over with drinks. They hand a beer to Jamie. There's a flurry of hugging and back slapping. "So, what do you think of our surprise?" They look at Logan and Jamie, then back at me, hopefully.

"It's great," I say, summoning as much enthusiasm as I can.

"We ran into Logan a while back. Jamie's been keeping tabs on her. Seemed like a reunion was in order," Hugo says. Jamie's good, I think. Even long distances he's got people feeling what he wants.

"It's soup!" Jesse calls out, loudly enough to be heard blocks away.

"The food's ready. Come eat, baby," Jo says to me. I follow her into the kitchen, leaving Jamie to Logan, Hugo, and Maureen.

"I don't like that guy," Jo says once we're alone. "I don't trust him."

I drop the envelope on the counter and take her hand from where it rests on the spoon in the potato salad. I wait until she's facing me. "I don't trust him either, and I didn't invite him. In fact, if I had my way, the only person I'd be celebrating my birthday with would be you." She pulls me in and kisses me, soft and gentle, deep down into my seventh chakra. I'm about to kiss her back. Hell, I'm about to steer her up to the attic where we can be alone, but the sound of glass shattering outside has us suddenly racing for the door.

"What the fuck do you think you're doing?" Finn growls. Ethan jumps to his feet, and Sage follows. Shards of a beer bottle lay shattered over the deck, as though Finn threw his empty down on his way across the patio. "Keep your freaky little paws off Sage. When're you going to get it through your thick head —"

"She doesn't belong to you, Finn." Ethan's words slur slightly.

Finn moves in closer, and before another word's exchanged, Ethan throws a punch. It happens in slow motion. Finn catches Ethan's hand before it gets anywhere near his jaw and spins him around in a bear hug. Then he shoves Ethan hard, away from his chest, and Ethan sprawls onto the pavement on his knees. His palms catch the shards of glass, and he cries out. He stays down on his knees, breathing hard and trying not to cry as a dark stain spreads over his crotch. Sage and I both move at the same time, but Finn grabs Sage's arm to hold her back. I pull Ethan to his feet and usher him toward the house as fast as I can.

He turns his head and yells back over his shoulder, "I wish you were dead! You should be dead!" When we get inside, he pulls away from me. "Just leave me the fuck alone, Lane." He runs up the stairs.

"What did you do, E?" I yell up from the bottom landing.

"He kissed Sage," Cayde says from behind me. "He just planted one right on her lips. Never saw it coming," he says, in awe or horror, I can't tell which.

Rachel and Jesse come in, arguing.

"Let me, Jesse. Please, he's embarrassed and drunk and probably feeling pretty miserable. He's not going to want you to see him like that," Rachel says.

"He's my son," Jesse says, nearly defeated.

"He's my patient," Rachel trumps him. Jesse nods, and she heads up. I hear the knock on the door, but I have no need to spy on this scene; I've played it out with him a hundred times before. Well, all except the drunk part.

I go back outside. Maureen has scooped up the baby and Hugo's cleaning up the glass. The drama has dissipated. Sage and Finn are notably absent, presumably gone to his apartment over the garage to fight about what happened. Jo's talking to Logan. Not a matchup that makes me comfortable. I hurry back to Jo.

"Now, that's the Ethan I remember," Logan quips, but I don't smile.

"It's been over a year since he's had an accident," I say. "Jesse should've known better than to give him beer."

"It's fine, baby. He'll be fine," Jo reassures.

"I know, but couldn't Finn just let it go?" I ask.

"Obviously not," Logan says with a little too much enthusiasm.

"What are you? Finn's fan club?"

"Your brother kissed his girl, Lane," Logan says.

"Whatever." I walk back inside and sit with my plate in the living room. After a couple of minutes, Jo joins me. We eat our dinners in silence, but gradually I'm able to relax.

After a while, Rachel comes back down. "He's gonna sleep it off, I think."

"That's probably best," I say. "Should I go up?"

"You're fine here. He doesn't really want to see anyone."

"I can understand that," I say.

Rachel looks at me with a worry furrow crimping her brow. "You coming back out to your party?"

"In a bit," I say, giving her my best approximation of a smile.

After she's gone, Jo slides in closer and takes my hand. "You don't have to go back out there, you know."

"It's my party." The words come out far more heavily than I intend, and the prospect of passing through the kitchen archway seems daunting.

"It's your birthday. You get to do what you want on your birthday." Her voice is low and full of promise. We've both wanted this for so long that now as we finally fall together, it doesn't matter that the timing isn't ideal. Neither of us cares what the others think, so we join hands and head up to our attic sanctuary.

Words are completely superfluous. We don't rush, though there's no lack of passion. I savor every kiss like it's our first, or maybe our last. Her warm, gentle, musician hands play my body, like she's practiced this concerto a million times, and the performance is nothing short of brilliant. I'm not as adept, but my fumbling leaves us laughing and smiling, until I bring her to a climax that leaves us both breathless.

I fight the urge to sleep in her arms. I want to be present, fully present in this aftermath of what's truly my first time making love. There can be no one but Jo forever for me. I have no doubts now.

"We should go back down," Jo says, pulling away and sitting up.

"Yeah, people will talk," I giggle.

Jo doesn't laugh. She sits with her back to me.

"What?" I ask, putting my hand on her coffee and cream skin.

She stands and tugs on her clothes.

"Are you okay?" I ask.

"We shouldn't have. . . I shouldn't have —"

I can't speak. Tears threaten.

Jo comes back and sits beside me. "Oh, baby. It's not you. You. . . you're an angel fallen from heaven into my broken arms."

"No —" I say, but nothing else comes out.

"I have to do something. I've known for a long time that until I do it, I'm not going to be worth a damn to anyone who loves me."

I shake off my self-pity. This is about Jo's pain. "How can I help?" I manage to squeak.

Jo thinks about it for a few seconds. "You could come with me. Be there to have my back."

"You're going to see Sage's dad?" It makes sense.

She nods. "I need to take back my innocence. I want you to have it all. He shouldn't get to keep that piece of me." Her voice teeters on the edge. "Will you come?"

I take her in my arms and hold her, but I don't answer. I might not have killed those soldiers at PSI, and I managed to get control in time to save Finn, but I know with a certainty that cannot be debated that I'll kill the man who broke my Jo. If I killed Sage's father, I'd become the monster I fear I am already. What would Jo think of me if she knew? Fallen angel, indeed. I can't go with her, but I can't tell her why.

"You should go back down," I say. "I need to check on E."

Jo blinks blankly. "Ethan's down at the party. He's having a great time. Why would you need to 'check on' him?"

"Uh. . . there was the little matter of the drunken kiss. Punches were thrown."

Jo looks at me like I've lost my mind. "Having a little trouble with reality today, Lane?"

I open my mouth to protest, but I close it quickly when the reality that I'm having no trouble with at all dawns on me. "Never mind. I'll meet you down there," I say.

"Ethan!" I scream in my mind.

"Everyone's waiting for you for cake." He comes back, calm as a pond on a still summer day.

"What did you do?" I ask.

"What's the point of having superpowers if you don't use them?" he asks blithely.

"Ethan, you can't just mess with people's memories."

"Obviously, I can." He's indignant. "Don't make me sorry I didn't include you."

I swallow my thoughts, cut the connection on my side and hurry down the stairs.

When I push though the kitchen door, a cheer goes up from the party. They all start singing "Happy Birthday." Ethan steps forward and takes my hand. He leads me to the cake, where we blow out the candles together, like we have for the last twenty-one years. I hug him afterward, like we always do, but I can't look at him. Everyone rushes forward for a piece of cake, and I fade back, fighting a strange sense of foreboding that threatens me. I make my way to the end of the driveway and scan the sunny sky for a star to guide me. When I feel a hand on my shoulder, I turn, expecting to find Jo. Instead, Jamie stands behind me, far too close. "I know what Ethan did," he whispers. "I know what you're afraid of, too." He waits for it to sink in. "I can help you, you know."

I shake my head as the terror takes hold.

"I'm the only one who can help you, Elena."

ACKNOWLEDGEMENTS

I would like to thank all of the people who have been part of the Geodesy Series journey.

First, I would like to thank Helen Mayhew, who unwittingly turned *Safe Distances* into the *Geodesy Series* when after reading my first book, she said, "I can't wait to see what happens to these kids next!"

Next I would like to thank my daughter Skye for her endless patience, editing skill, and belief in me. Thanks Skye for the idea of having each story told by a different character!

I need to give a huge shout out to my beta readers, Kim Kent, Amie King, Helen Hayhew, and Matt Lacey. Your thoughtful reading and comments improved the story immensely.

In addition, this project would not be what it is without the photography of Paul Woodruff who did the *Stellar Navigation* cover and the photos in the book trailers. I also would like to thank Alicia Hartzell for her photography in the trailers and the cover of *Safe Distances.*

And speaking of the covers and trailers, thanks to the actors who became my characters and inspired me in so many ways: Hayli Kaminski as the face of Elena, Alesha Williams as the voice of Elena in the trailer, Kayleigh Rago as Sage (face and voice), Michael Johnson as Finn, and Jeremy Leavell as Ethan.

A very special thank you is due to my wonderful friend and talented artist Jeanne Hospod who brought Ethan's paintings to life on the website www.susan-michalski.com and in the book trailers.

(Check out her art at http://www.jeannehospod.com/).

I also need to tip my hat to Michael A. Lepore Jr. who composed and recorded the amazing original scores for the book trailers. The music rocks me sideways!

Also, a big thank you to Amie King at <u>Making a Scene Social Media Marketing</u> for tweeting and all that whatnot to sell my books.

Thank you, Jen Hritz for editing my books on a short deadline and for making me a better writer by being so hugely talented a writer yourself.

Finally, I want to thank all my friends, family, students, and companions for reading my books and reviewing them so favorably. All I ever wanted was to write books that people loved to read. You make my dreams come true!

ABOUT THE AUTHOR

Susan Michalski has been making up stories for as long as she could understand words. Because she rarely sleeps, reading and writing have filled the dark hours since childhood. With degrees in literature, drama, creative writing and secondary education, Susan has been able to find work as an actress, high school teacher, college instructor, web/UI designer, private tutor, online course writer, curriculum designer, technical writer, waitress and swim coach. She dreams of quitting her day jobs to live in an alternate reality full-time. Susan Michalski lives, works and occasionally sleeps in Austin, Texas, with her devoted dogs. *Stellar Navigation* is Book Two in the Geodesy Series. *Safe Distances* is Book One. Go to www.susan-michalski.com to learn more about her and her writing.

Keep reading for a sneak peek.

Gravitational Forces

Ethan's Story

Susan Michalski

GEODESY SERIES

BOOK 3

Gravitational Forces

Ethan's Story

Susan Michalski

ஐ CHAPTER 1 ௸

I USED TO . . .

"If you would be a real seeker after truth, it is necessary that at least once in your life you doubt, as far as possible, all things."

— René Descartes

Dr. Wiseman: Hi Ethan, I'm Dr. Wiseman.

I nod, trying to maintain eye contact He's the third one this year, and who knows how long he'll last, but I promised Rachel, so here we are. I look around the office. Cool institutional blue walls, modern art, nothing representational, overstuffed chairs that look like they came from someone's attic, and a big round glass table in the center with fidget spinners, Rubik's cubes, and nerf balls. I sit in a chair that is as deep in the corner of the room as possible with a view of the door. He sits directly across from me, so the table is between us.

"No couch." I state.

Dr. Wiseman: (smiling) Nope. Do you think I should get one?

I shrug and stare at him. Dr. Wiseman looks like tool. He's maybe late 40s or 50s, but fighting aging tooth and nail. He's sinewy like someone who never eats carbs and goes to the gym before and after work. Not married, no kids, I conclude. He looks up from the form I filled out in the waiting room.

Dr. Wiseman: I see your birthday was last week? How was that?

The memory washes over me like the slow-motion nausea of car sickness. I draw my arms in tighter. I'm not going to discuss that. I swallow, gnaw at my thumb nail, and he continues.

Dr. Wiseman: You turned 21. Right? That's a big milestone. How did you celebrate?

I suppress the pained grimace tugging at the corners of my mouth. "I got drunk," I say flatly. He laughs to let me know that this is totally normal. Nothing wrong there. I have no desire to enlighten him.

Dr. Wiseman: Your first time?

I nod and fix my gaze on the swirls of blue and green just over his right shoulder.

Dr. Wiseman: Not what you expected?

I didn't expect anything. I didn't even plan to drink. But since you asked, no I didn't expect getting drunk to be so completely humiliating. He doesn't press with another question, and I don't hurry to fill the silence.

"I didn't say that," I finally mumble, but I don't look at him.

Dr. Wiseman: You don't want to be here? Do you?

Understatement! The only therapist that ever gave a damn was Rachel. The worst of them drugged me, caged me, and manipulated me for her own twisted agenda. "I didn't say that either."

Dr. Wiseman: I know you're pretty attached to Rachel. How long has she been working with you?

He knows perfectly well how long she's been my therapist. I'm here because of all the crap about her being my stepmother now, but that's a specious argument. She's been with my father for well over two years. Before PSI. Since the fire. I ride another wave of nausea. I was a different person then, I remind myself. He set the fire, that other Ethan, the one I loathe, the one I wish I could eradicate from everyone's memory for all time. A smile tugs at my mind. I could do that, eradicate him from every memory one by one. I shake off the thought.

"Three years or so, I guess."

The guy looks at his notepad. He hasn't written a single thing yet, but he studies it nonetheless. After another long silence, he sighs.

Dr. Wiseman: Why don't we talk about your family. That's usually a good place to start. Would that be alright?

My family is definitely NOT a good place to start, but I'd rather talk about them than myself, so I nod. "What do you want to know?"

Dr. Wiseman: Let's start with your parents. What's their story?

Well, shit! Can of worms doesn't begin to describe my parents and their story. Besides I'm pretty sure the good doctor already knows this part of my sad history. "I don't know much about my parents," I say. I'd like to stop there, but I elaborate. "When Elena and I were four, my mom died, and my dad took off." I spare him the details about how she set the house on fire and burned alive while I watched, while I held her hand. I pull my sleeve down over the burn scar on my left arm and hand. "My grandmother kept us." I can't keep the bitterness out of my voice.

The guy is writing furiously now. I wait till he stops.

Dr. Wiseman: What was she like, your grandmother?

I scoff a little, and he starts writing again. "Iron-lady. Sage called her Iron-lady."

Dr. Wiseman: *She passed away?*

"A couple of years ago."

Dr. Wiseman: *I'm sorry for your loss.*

"Don't be." I sound angrier than I really am. "She didn't like *him* — I mean *me* — very much."

Dr. Wiseman: *Did she like your sister?*

I nod. "Everyone loves Lane … Elena."

Dr. Wiseman: *Really? Why's that?*

I shrug.

Dr. Wiseman: *Do you like her?*

"She's my twin!" A million thoughts, memories, and emotions close in around my throat. I would have died without Elena. She was my only friend, my care-taker, and confidant. She is the other half of me. There is no way to talk about her with words, so I don't. I don't tell him about how much I love her or about how angry I am with her about PSI and signing our lives away without even asking me. I don't tell him about how worried I am about her since we got back or about how hard it is to talk to her now.

Dr. Wiseman: *Do you still live together?*

I nod. "Grandmother left us her house in the will."

Dr. Wiseman: *Is it just the two of you?*

"Not exactly." I take a deep breath and let it out slowly. "Sage lives there too. And Finn in the garage apartment. And then there's Jo, who's there pretty much all the time too."

Dr. Wiseman: Finn? Who's that?

"My asshat cousin."

Dr. Wiseman: (laughing) And Jo?

"That's Lane's girlfriend. She's cool."

Dr. Wiseman: How so?

I don't have any idea how to convey the overall cool that is Jo. "She just is," I say. Jo has not had it easy. Shit happened with Sage's pervy dad. And Jo has every right to be pissed off and hate Sage, but that's the thing, she never judges or holds grudges. Jo is strong and clear-headed. She keeps Lane from going completely off the rails. Actually, she keeps us all from completely blowing apart.

Dr. Wiseman: OK. And Sage, how does she fit in to your family?

Sage. How does she fit in? I could start with the fact that we're all in love with her. Me, Lane, Jo, and Finn. We don't just love her; we're stupid in love with her. Sage is the reason I am. She brought me back into the world and made me want to be something more. My whole life is divided into two parts. Before Sage and after. The before part is where *he* lived. Then Sage came, and I was woke. There are no words.
"She's my step-sister, I guess. Rachel's daughter."

Dr. Wiseman: You guess?

"Technically, legally," I correct myself. He's kind of staring at me with one eye brow raised. "I don't think of her as a sister."

Dr. Wiseman: You have feelings for her?

Yeah. We aren't going there. "I have a half-sister too."

Dr. Wiseman: Okay.

"Fiona. She's Sage's half-sister too. She's almost two."

Dr. Wiseman: Right. She must be Rachel and your dad, Jesse's child?

I nod and look away.

Dr. Wiseman: Didn't they recently adopt a child too? A boy?

"Cayde."

Dr. Wiseman: He's just a little younger than you, isn't he? Do you get along?

Cayde is actually a lot younger than I am. He's sixteen, a sophomore in high school. But he's taller than I am and braver, and better in probably every way one human can be better than another. Cayde was my first friend aside from Sage. "Yeah, he's okay." I smile without meaning to.

Dr. Wiseman: And your dad, Jesse, he came back? What was that like?

I really haven't thought about it that way. When Jesse first came back, he was more like Finn's dad than mine. I think he was disappointed in what I was back then. He couldn't relate to me on any level, and I hated him for the bits and pieces I remembered about him. Now it's more like he's just some guy who's married to Rachel. I hardly think anything about him at all.

"I don't really care. It's not like he was ever a dad to me."

Dr. Wiseman: I can understand that. Families can be fraught with conflict. What are the best and worst things about your family?

Yup total tool. Who uses words like "fraught." And more importantly who asks questions like that. Unfortunately, now that he's put it out there, it's going to gnaw at my mind. Best thing — Twin powers. Lane and I are . . . connected and gifted or cursed depending on which of us you ask and on which day you ask it. Worst thing — Finn. It seems impossible to me that his mom and my dad were related. And even more fucked up, that our moms were in love. Dr. Phil would have a field day with my family tree.

"I don't know."

I cross my arms over my chest to stop chewing my fingernails. I think we're about done here. I'm just about to stand up.

Dr. Wiseman: Perhaps we should set some goals, Ethan. Talk about what you'd like to see come out of our sessions in the next few months.

My eyebrows go up, and I search the walls for some clue as what I'm supposed to say. Goals? Few months? I blink several times trying to wrap my mind around an answer. I have no clue. After only a short argument with Elena's voice in my head, I decide to go straight to the source to figure out what he wants me to say.

I can hear his thoughts a moment after he has them. The past is relative when it comes to my gifts, and I am good at seeing what's already happened, though I probably shouldn't according to Elena.

Wiseman has just finished running down the list of symptoms and my diagnosis. PTSD with regressive behavior disorder, social anxiety, isolation, enuresis. His mind lights on the last one. Yeah. I'm not talking about that. Rachel and I have spent the last year beating that drum. Alarms that woke up everyone but me, drugs that made me dehydrated and gave me hallucinations, bladder training that helped during the day at least, and even hypnosis, which was amusing, albeit embarrassing. Lost cause.

"Sex." I hear myself say out loud. "I want to have sex."

Dr. Wiseman: Okay. Sex. So what kind of work do you think you might need to do to achieve this goal?

I need to get rid of Finn, I think. Still, I wouldn't want homicidal ideation added to my diagnosis, so I keep that gem to myself. "You tell me." I say. Isn't that what I pay you for? He smiles again, but I don't.

Dr. Wiseman: I probably need to know a little more about you, Ethan. Is there a particular person you have in mind? Do you have any experience? What obstacles do you expect to encounter?

Okay! Okay! Enough questions already! So much for safe subjects. I think my head might explode.

"I kissed her. . . Sage. On my birthday." I blurt out.

Dr. Wiseman: "Oh. Rachel's daughter? Your sort of step-sister"

"I kissed her before too. A few times, but it was different then. I was different . . . then."

The good doctor can barely conceal his excitement. In his head he's been counting the number of words in each sentence I've uttered. He thinks he's getting through, wearing me down, finding an opening. Soon the floodgates will open, and I'll bare my soul. I shake my head.

Dr. Wiseman: How was it different this time?

"It just was. That's all. She was kissing <u>me</u>."

Dr. Wiseman: Do you mean she was kissing you back?

"No!" This is ridiculous. He doesn't get it. "She was kissing <u>me</u>, not him!" I watch the therapist's head spin in the way only therapists' can. He looks through me like he has telepathy. I know he doesn't, of course. He figures it out, and his eyes blink fast a couple of times.

Dr. Wiseman: You've changed a lot in the time you've known Sage and Rachel. Haven't you?

I shrug and look away. I really really don't want to talk about <u>him</u>.

Dr. Wiseman: Do you think Sage sees how far you've come?

"She's the only one who see me!"

Dr. Wiseman: You might be wrong about that. What about Rachel? What about your sister?

He leans forward and picks up a folder from the big round table. Damn, that thing is thick. I pull my focus back. Rachel and Lane loved him, the other Ethan; I'm not so sure how they feel about me. "I'm not going to talk about him," I say flatly.

A silence plays out between us while he adjusts his expectations. "I want to talk about how to get with Sage. That's what I want help with. That's what Rachel couldn't help me with." I say it quietly, like something I shouldn't even think, let alone say aloud.

Dr. Wiseman: Okay. (pause) Tell me more about your birthday party then. What happened after you kissed Sage?

"Finn happened. Finn always happens." Dr. Wiseman doesn't push me with another question. Even in his head he doesn't press. He waits patiently. "Before she could kiss me back, he came flying out of nowhere." The anger comes back like a bitter aftertaste. I ball my hands into fists. "He clocked me." I feel myself going down on my knees, the concrete tearing the skin on my knees, and the glass shards sinking into my palms.

Dr. Wiseman: Are Finn and Sage together?

Good question! I guess they are. I mean, she sleeps at his place way too often. But then again, no. I don't think she's really made up her mind who she wants to be with. Sage isn't really someone you can hold down with a thumb.

"Maybe. I don't know."

Dr. Wiseman: After you fought, did something else happen?

"Nothing." Except for the warm rush in my crotch, and the burn of humiliation. Then later in my room the ice-cold flex of power when I made them all forget. Despite Elena's nagging and warnings, I don't regret that. And I don't regret kissing Sage either. The only one who knows the whole story beside me is Lane, and she won't tell anyone what I did, what I can do. She has her own problems and demons to wrestle. She's as lost now as he was before.

I saw it over two years ago when I remembered this future. I painted us reversed in the mirror just before we went to PSI. She wouldn't listen. She didn't believe in him. She believes me now, though. Now that it's too late.

The shrink is staring at me, waiting for me to go on, but I'm done. This guy is not the kind of guy who wants to hear about remembering the future. It's hard enough to talk about the stuff he can handle. Rachel wants me to work with a male therapist. She thinks I need men

I can trust and look up to. She means well, but she's wrong.

"Sorry," I say. "I'm tired. Can we stop now?"

Dr. Wiseman: We can do anything you want. It's your dime. (long intake of breath) Do you mind if I say something, offer an opinion . . . about sex?

I glance up. I do mind, actually, but I feel myself nod. Social niceties, as my grandmother called them, are becoming oddly ingrained into my interactions. She would see that as a good thing. I'm not so sure.

Dr. Wiseman: Liking Sage, even wanting her is perfectly natural, Ethan. But you need to open yourself up to the possibility that this relationship may not work out, and that maybe there are other girls — women who could be right for you.

This asshole obviously isn't listening. Did he even bother to read my ridiculous file? No other girl would want me. Ever. He wanted to hear about obstacles. I could fill the rest of his billable hours for a week listing them. This is not making me feel better. In fact, it's pissing me off. I get up.

"I'm gonna go now. Okay?" I say. My hand is on the door knob before he answers.

Dr. Wiseman: See you next Tuesday then.

I can't get out of there fast enough. By the time I get into my Jeep, my hands are shaking. My throat and chest feel tight, like I'm having a heart attack, but I know I'm not. I take deep breaths and close my eyes. I count slowly backward from 100, and the panic passes. I won't try to analyze why this is happening. That would just pull me back into the attack. I turn over the ignition and back out of the parking space. Driving helps.

When I get home, Elena's in the kitchen. It's nice to see her downstairs.

"Coming in or going out?" I ask silently.

"Don't do that," she says out loud.

"Whatever you say," I think, smirking at her.

She rolls her eyes. "How's the new shrink?" she asks.

"He's an ass," I say. "Yours?" She shrugs.

"You didn't go!" I can't believe it. Maybe I can. I don't know.

"Not going at all is better than going and lying to someone you're paying to help you," she says.

"Were you spying?" I don't know why I'm asking. She wasn't there. I would have felt it.

"I just know you, little brother," she almost smiles.

I shake my head.

"Tomorrow's the big day, huh?" she says, keeping her back to me, so I won't notice the furrow in her brow, but her voice lacks its usual melody.

"Guess so." Talking about it is going to freak me out.

"Is Sage going with you?" She takes a diet soda out of the fridge and offers it to me. I shake my head. "Oh yeah, I forgot. Only water these days, right?" I nod. "Is that helping?"

"Yeah, sure," I say. I wouldn't tell her if it wasn't. "And no. I'm going to meet Dr. Roschan by myself. It's not like it's my first time setting foot on the campus. I don't need her to hold my hand."

"Okay," Elena says. "Good for you."

She doesn't believe me. Why should she? I don't believe myself. I want Sage to hold my hand, but I don't want to ask her. I don't want her to think of me like that anymore.

The screen door slams, and we both turn.

"Hey, wonder twins!" Sage's easy smile sparkles up to her eyes, and I try to hold her gaze, but she turns to Elena and wraps her in an embrace that makes my arms feel empty. Elena kisses her cheek and smiles back. Sage is one of the few people who can elicit a smile from my twin these days. I certainly have no such power over her. "Having a family meeting without me?" she asks.

"Not anymore," Elena teases. "I was just asking Ethan if you were going with him tomorrow."

"You don't have to." I jump in fast because I can see what Elena is doing. She has absolutely no faith in me.

Sage turns and winks at me. "I have to go in and meet with my advisor anyway, so you can drive me. Right, E?"

I open my mouth to argue, but Sage's mind is made up. My protests would probably sound pathetic, so I just nod. "Sure."

I swallow down an 8 ounce glass of water ten minutes ahead of my careful schedule and head up to my room, hoping Sage will follow. I stop just short of telepathically "inviting" her. Too desperate, and

Elena isn't necessarily wrong about the dangers of using our abilities. She's terrified that somehow someone will know and come after us from PSI or the government. We didn't exactly fulfill the contract she signed without reading it, and there were threats of prosecution for treason or something. Then again, we're kind of dead as far as anyone attached to that contract knows. Still, I worry about it too, but not enough to give it up. I think if they were coming, I would know anyway.

I shuffle through some papers I left on my desk without really thinking while I keep one eye on the door. Sage isn't coming. We used to spend hours and hours together every day just hanging out, but everything changed after PSI, after I messed with her memory in that hotel room. I didn't even know I was doing it, but it was the biggest mistake of my life. I would take it back if I could. I need to stop going over this again and again, so I head across the hall, to the room that used to be Elena's when we were growing up in this house. Now it's my art studio.

I have two oil paintings in different stages of completion leaning against the easel. They're commissions from the gallery that are way past due, but I'm just not inspired to work on them today.

I pick up the large sketch pad from the table beside my easel and a charcoal shard from the jar. I settle into the window seat that looks out over the yard and let my mind slip into the magical state above conscious thought. Sage is by the pool, sitting with her feet in the water. She's kicking at the surface with her toes. Her arms are stretched out behind her like wings. I'm too far away to see her face, but I have it memorized anyway. All I need to do is close my eyes, and her smile, all teeth and crinkles, is right in front of me.

I shade the underside of her arms, making them even more wing-like and place her poised on a rock over a waterfall, rather than the dull concrete of the swimming pool. I feel my senses slipping away as my hand, so practiced by previous drawings and paintings, etches the curves of her face. I could close my eyes, and each line and shadow would fall into place. A thousand years could pass without a pad and pencil, and I could scratch it into a rock, trace it with a stick in the sand. I know it that well. Drawing Sage makes me feel closer to her, connected in a way that maybe only sex could top. It's sensual and honest, like really knowing someone deep down.

My phone buzzes, shocking me out of the zone. I glance around and locate it across the room next to the charcoal. It's just a text. I'll check it later. I look down at what I've drawn and shudder. The face is all wrong. It doesn't look like Sage at all. I don't understand how I could have messed up that badly. I flip the page and close my eyes to get her back. When she's there, head back and hair cascading around her shoulders, I let the charcoal make contact with the page.

The skritch-scratch lulls me back to the day we fought, the day she came in to apologize, the day we first kissed, the day she meant it. I sink into the memory of her scent, all tangy and earthy from being outside. I remember the sketch pad in my lap and how I wanted so much not to look up. I was angry, and I felt betrayed. I thought she didn't want me, but then I did look up, and she was so close I could taste her scent. And her lips were so soft that I felt their touch all the way down my back and into my legs. I could taste her in my soul.

The phone buzzes again. Fucking thing. I lick my lips, which feel oddly dry. I shake it off and look down at the page again. What? The image looks identical to the one I drew before. The face is all wrong, too round with thicker more sensuous lips, large almond eyes, wider spread than Sage's, and brows that arch seductively. The body proportions and curves are off too. This girl's breasts are full and high, her shoulders and hips rounder. I flip back to look at the image from earlier. Same girl. No doubt. It's not Sage. My breathing becomes labored. There is something about this woman that scares and thrills me. I wrack my brain for a conscious memory of her either from my past or my future. I can't find her there. Yet.

A light tap on the door is followed by the creek of it opening a crack. "'Sup, bro?" Cayde keeps his voice down like he's entering a church or something. He shuffles around in the doorway nervously, like he's tamping down kinetic energy about to explode.

"Hey, brother!" I say. It's all the invitation he needs. He is my brother, not by blood, but by law and in ways that are far more important than any court document. I first met Cayde at PSI where he was the resident telekinetic guinea pig, and I was being pushed toward prescience. We were roommates and friends. Since my father and Rachel adopted him, he's mostly lost his abilities, most telekinetics do apparently. My gifts are growing stronger, but they have less to do with knowing the future and more to do with rewriting the past. We don't talk about PSI, about the drugs, the lies, the millions of manipulations, and unanswered questions.

"Whacha drawing?" He crosses the room in less than three lanky strides.

I pull the image from the pad with my fist and crumple it quickly. "Nothing good. It came out horrible!"

He reaches for it, but I shove it behind me into the corner of the window seat and close the drawing pad before I stand up. "Let's do something," I say.

"Wanna light up some zombies?"

I give him the yeah-right stare.

"Come on, man. It'll be awesome. Finn has the sickest system, and it's like right there." He points across the lot at the garage apartment. "You don't have to talk to him. Come on! Sage might be there."

I sigh, sit back down, and pick up my sketch book. "Never mind."

"Lame!" he yells throwing down his arms and stamping his feet. I look down. He stops moving and stares at me for a second or two, makes a noise of disgust with his tongue, and then he's out.

He's right; I'm lame, and for half a second, I consider chasing after him. Cayde is a good friend, and I owe him. He accepted me when I was unacceptable and taught me how to let go, how to have fun. I turn to the window and watch him cross the yard, past the pool where Sage was sitting a minute ago and up the stairs to the garage apartment where Finn lives. By blood and some cruel twist of fate Finn is my cousin, so he belongs in this house as much as I do. Our grandmother left him the garage apartment in her will. But in practice Finn is my enemy, my tormentor from all the way back in elementary school. Even if he hadn't stolen Sage from me, I still would have hated him with every fiber of my being.

My jaw tightens just thinking about him. I pick up my sketch pad and examine the image again. A change of subject is needed, so I close my eyes. I freeze frame Cayde in the moment when he threw down his arms in disgust. After I memorize the curves, angles, and shade, I open my eyes, pick up my charcoal, and let the image of my brother emerge on the page.

The next morning, I wake up early and let my current reality sink in. Today I will go to a job like millions of other guys my age. I will drive downtown to a college campus and park my car in a lot across the quad from the building I work at. On my way to the laboratory and lecture hall I will pass dozens of strangers who know nothing about me or the panic I will most likely be wrestling down with mantras and sheer willpower. I'll shake hands with a professor who believes in me and stand in front of a classroom and show other students how to think about physics. Pride and terror battle for control.

Despite my anxiety, it was a good night. No nightmares, and I am not in need of an immediate shower. I throw on my running clothes and rake a hand through my hair. At the bottom of the stairs, I look across the living room at Sage's door. This used to be so easy. I knock softly. The door flies open immediately. I take a step back, startled.

"Hey, you!" Sage smiles, and I forget to smile back. "Don't look so surprised to see me; I do live here," she says as she pulls her hair into a messy ponytail and heads into the kitchen.

While it's technically true that she lives here, occupying the suite that was my grandmother's when she was alive, it is also true that she spends many – too many – nights with Finn.

"So you wanna run together?" I ask quietly. She swallows a couple of gulps of water right from the faucet and turns to face me. She wipes her mouth with the back of her hand and knits her brow. I look away, ready to retreat in defeat.

"Do you really think you can keep up with me?" she asks.

I stifle a laugh. "I think, you can . . ." I unlock the door and open it slowly. ". . . eat my dust." I fly out the door with Sage just a step behind. At the end of the driveway, I turn to see her beside me, matching my pace stride for stride. I take a mental picture, so I can draw her later. Face flushed, wisps of brown hair framing her face, eyes forward like she is running into her future. The moment is perfection.

"You ready . . . for today?" she pants. The question is not heavy the way Lane would ask it.

"Sure," I say with as much nonchalance as I can muster. "What could go wrong?"

"Well . . . shall we count the ways," her eyes crinkle, and she shoulder butts me teasingly. I shoulder her harder, and she stumbles a little sideways, but recovers.

"Sure, let's count 'em out. Number one: I could pass out."

"Number two," Sage picks up the count, "You could get lost on campus and —"

"Please," I object. "I'm not going to get lost. And besides, that would be less embarrassing than say —"

"Forgetting your own name?" She gives me another shove.

And just like that Sage and I are laughing about the hundred real and unimaginable ways this day could go down.

"You're gonna be just fine," she says after the giggles subside.

"Yeah," I almost feel like I mean it too.

Too soon we're walking back up the driveway. Sage stops at the bottom of the stairs by the garage. "Meet you by the Jeep in an hour?" she asks. I glance up at Finn's door, and a cloud of anger moves in quickly. I shrug. She puts a hand on my arm for a microsecond, but then pulls away abruptly like my skin burns. I take a step back, but our eyes are locked. "Sorry," she says, but it's unclear to me whether she's sorry about leaving me to go to Finn, or she's sorry she touched me, or she's sorry she pulled away.

"It's fine," I reply at absolute zero, already moving away from her. After I'm inside, I glance back. Sage is still standing on Finn's porch, looking down at the main house. I imagine she's trying to fill the hole in her memory that *he* took from her and replaced with lies and half-truths. Nothing I say or do is likely to span the void between us that *he* - *I* created. I lean my forehead against the cold glass, close my eyes, and reach out for her thoughts.

"Hey, E?" Lane's voice makes me jump. "How was your run?" She looks past me through the glass and shakes her head slowly. "How many times do I need to tell you to stop?" Her voice has that shrill edge, more terrified than angry.

"I wasn't doing anything," I say without any conviction.

"Bullshit." She turns away from me, but I can see her hands are shaking.

"It's okay, Lane. PSI is over. No one is hunting us. They think we're dead. This isn't an episode of *Heroes* or *X-men*, ya know."

"Maybe," she mumbles, sitting at the table, and I join her. "But seriously, E, didn't we learn anything from those crazies at PSI?"

"Sure. We learned not to sign away our lives without reading all the fine print," I keep my tone light, but I'm poking the bear, and I know it.

"Fuck you!" she says flatly, getting up abruptly. "You know that wasn't my fault! You know Jamie was fucking with my head. Forget it, E. Have your fun, but there will be a reckoning." I can't control the scoff that comes out. "A reckoning!? You're kidding, right? I think you need to keep that appointment with your shrink, Sister, because you're sounding more than a little paranoid." I have to scream the last sentence because Elena has already retreated to her little hole up in the rafters. I shake my head, down my eight ounces of water, and hurry up the stairs to get ready.

After showering, I get dressed and set my watch alarm to vibrate every two hours to remind me to use the bathroom. I haven't used the watch in months, but today is not the day I want to suddenly fall off my strict regimen and end up having an accident. I set my jaw. That was *him*, the other Ethan. Not me. Fuck him! I've got this.

I gather my notes on the lab I will be leading a scant sixty minutes from now. I run through the procedures, the desired outcomes, the likely points of failure, and the complex calculations that come more easily to me than even drawing.

I'll have an hour and a half to kill between sections. I run into my studio to grab a sketch pad. The pages I discarded yesterday lie on the floor by the window seat. I pick them up, smooth them out, and allow the image of the woman I don't know to pull me in. Everything about her is pure seduction, full lips, fuller hips, eyes deeper than my dread. I fold the sketches in half and tuck them into the cover of the sketch book. I stuff the last item, a set of drawing pencils into my backpack and sling it over my shoulder.

I catch my image in the mirror that Elena never moved up to her rafter nest. I look small and scared like *him*. It stops me in my tracks. I turn to face myself, pick up my chin and square my shoulders. Better, but five-eight is never going to look tall. I pull down my shirt and smooth the collar. Shorter hair is a definite improvement. With that and the modicum of stubble I've been able to grow, I look maybe 17 instead of 12. I try on a stern expression, and sigh. I'm going to have overwhelm them with intellect because if I'm honest with myself, I have all the ferocity of pygmy hedgehog. Despite my underwhelming appearance that loser therapist is right about one thing. I've come a long way. Two years ago leaving the house was a major struggle. Now I'm not only going out, but I'm standing up in front of a room full of people. My stomach does a flip-flop. I attempt a smile that looks more like a grimace and settle on a steely-eyed nod.

"Ethan!" Sage yells from the foot of the stairs. "Let's get this show on the road, boi!" I smile for real and head down the stairs.

In the kitchen I'm surprised to see Rachel, Jesse, and little Fiona sitting at the table eating muffins. Everyone looks up when I walk in.

"EEEEE," Fifi squeals skipping over to me.

"Fifi-ona," I say, dropping my pack and scooping her into my arms. "Whatcha doing here?"

"Special day for E." She hugs me tight around the neck. "Happy special day."

"Thanks," I say flatly, putting her down. "I wish you wouldn't make this a big deal," I say to Rachel. "It's babysitting two classes one day a week, not President of the college."

Rachel smiles wryly and throws a weighted look at Jesse, my stranger-father, and he gets up from his chair to come over to me. I glare at her, but she points at my father. I turn to face him. He holds out his hand awkwardly, and I'm tempted to leave him hanging, but after an awkward second, I allow him to take my hand and pump my arm.

"We . . . I just wanted you to know . . . how . . .uh . . . proud . . . I am of you. You know . . . " His voice trails off, and I extract myself from his grasp.

"Okay," I say, avoiding their stares by picking up my pack. I wave goodbye on my way out, but I'm not sure it doesn't look more like a traffic cop telling them to stop. Jesse is trying, but the truth is I'm not. He hated me when I was four, and I hate him for that now. Whatever. I don't have the energy to waste on this family shit. Not today.

On the way to campus Sage keeps up a steady banter over the loud music she's chosen. I don't really hear either. I'm keeping my eyes on the road, and my mind is circling around the question of how I got here, to this moment. It's just like attending a class I tell myself, but the truth is that I haven't attended many classes in my life. I stopped going to school in about the sixth grade when my grandmother gave up any hope of me being "normal." After that, I more or less taught myself and got the credits I needed to graduate online. Learning was never a problem for me. I don't have an eidetic memory like my friend Hugo from PSI, but math especially has always been second nature.

A year and a half ago, just before PSI, I started taking online courses at the local college. Dr. Rochan was my first physics instructor. Back then he tried to get me to come in and take the class in person. It didn't happen until over a year later. Now I've gone as far as I can in physics as an undergrad, but I still have a few more core credits to get before I can apply for grad school - another complicated topic of discussion for all involved. I push it away. I focus on Dr. Rochan and the day he asked if I would TA for his classes. "You won't have to lecture or anything," he assured me. "Basically, I just need someone to show the neophytes around a laboratory and keep them from blowing up the building." I guess I didn't answer right away because he straightened up his bent spine and looked me directly in the eye before he added, "I think you're the man for the job," in the most clear and authoritative voice I've ever heard him use. That memory makes me smile.

Suddenly, I realize that I am in the faculty parking lot behind the humanities building. I inhale sharply. Sage turns off the music and stares at me. "I'm okay," I say. I pull into a parking space and keep my hands on the wheel as I take some deep breaths. Sage just sits next to me watching. After I count ten, I get out and lean against the door, looking out across the quad bustling with activity. Sage gets out on the other side and comes around the back with our packs.

A stray thought vibration shoots through my mind like a poison arrow. "This is a huge mistake. You're not ready."

I snatch the pack from Sage's outstretched hand angrily. In my mind I holler back defiantly, "Fuck you! How many fucking people on the quad can do this."

"Something I said?" Sage half jokes.

"Something you thou –," I stop. How many people can hear thoughts or put them in someone else's head. Aside from me and Lane, only one person I know of! Jamie Fleming, Dr. Meriwether's fucked up empath lapdog. I scan the quad for his dark hair and scarecrow form.

"You okay?" Sage's voice comes from far away, though I know she's standing right next to me. "Ethan? Earth to Ethan, come in!" I shake my head, and my hearing comes back into focus.

"Come on," I say louder than I mean to. "We're gonna be late."

We cross the quad quickly, but I don't stop looking for him. If Jamie is here and messing with me, Elena's paranoia may not be so off-base. At the door to the science building I realize that Sage is still beside me. Her advisor is in the humanities building right next to the parking lot. She holds the door open for me, but I don't go through.

"I thought you had an appointment with your advisor," I say with as much ice as I can muster through the panic clawing around the edges. A couple of frat types shove us out of the way.

"Neanderthals!" Sage yells after them, but they don't even notice. I hope they aren't in my class. She turns back to me and smiles. "Ah ha, you caught me. My appointment isn't for another half hour." She opens the door again, and I go through shaking my head.

"You don't need to — " my voice is shaking, so I stop talking.

"I know that, E." It feels like there's more she wants to say. I could just wait a second and dive into her memory, but it's too risky so I don't. We're in front of Dr. Rochan's office anyway, and he's just stepped into the hallway in front of us. The second I see him, the reality of the situation hits me. My throat contracts, and I can't inhale.

"Ah, Mr. Paige. So good of you to take this on. Just in time too." He reaches his hand forward to shake mine, and without conscious thought I reciprocate. There is a sharp jolt and a searing pain in my head as my perspective shifts, and I land inside one of Dr. Rochan's memories. A young woman is standing in front of him in the same hall with her arms wrapped around her body. She's weeping as she explains in stilted phrases that she can't be his TA anymore. I feel his frustration and compassion at odds as he pats her arm and tells her not to worry, even as he thinks, "Where will I get a new TA mid-semester?"

The shock of what I am seeing pulls me back to the present where my new boss is still holding my hand and shaking himself free of whatever memory of mine I cast him into. I pull my hand away and shove it into my pocket.

Shit! It's been a long time since I lost it like that. Fuck! I lean my back against the wall for support and look at Sage. Her eyes are huge as she puts a hand under Dr. Rochan's arm to support him. She's begun a steady stream of chatter to keep him and maybe me from processing what just happened, but he looks confused and slightly ill, pale, and sort of stricken. That can't be good, but I kind of don't care. I was hired out of desperation apparently. So much for being "the man for the job." The exit is just a few feet away. I could be back at my car and home in less than 20 minutes.

"Look at the time," Sage says too loudly and too suddenly. "Y'all are going to be late for class." She shoves me toward the stairway and steers us both into the lab. Roughly thirty pairs of eyes snap to attention, and the chatter subsides into a void of silence as we enter the room. After a maybe a couple of seconds that take an hour to go by, Rochan clears his throat.

"Settle down," he says out of habit I guess because the settling has already occurred. The thirty pairs of eyes exchange glances with each other, and a couple of students giggle.

"As you know, June, is no longer with us," he continues. Several students gasp audibly.

"She's pregnant, not dead," a woman in the front assures the gaspers.

"This young man . . ." he gestures toward me, . . . "Mr. Paige, will be taking her place as your teaching assistant. He will guide you through the labs and grade your writeups. Please treat him with the same respect you would afford me. I can assure you his skill and knowledge as a physicist are unimpeachable. Any questions?"

Immediately the room erupts. "How old are you? 12?" "Do you have a girlfriend? Boyfriend?" I swallow and put my hands on the desk in front of me to stop them from shaking. Rochan is already heading out the door, so it's all me.

I clear my throat and give them the icy stare I practiced in the mirror. "Any questions about physics?" I say without raising my voice. The questions stop as quickly as they started. "Okay, come get the lab."

The students file up to the front to grab the lab packets off the desk where Rochan left them. The flurry of movement drains the tension from the room and gives me the time I need to get my head in the game. By the end of the hour, my shaking has subsided, and I can make it through whole sentences without stuttering. Most of the groups complete the procedure and get acceptable results. I busy myself erasing the whiteboard as the students file out, so I don't have to risk any personal encounters. Sage is sitting on a bench outside the room when I come out.

"You survived," she says in mock surprise.

"It was touch and go for a minute there," I say, and she laughs. "Really?" I ask. "You find my trauma funny?" But I can't not smile.

"So how many girls wrote their digits on their assignments?" She gets up, and we start making our way toward the stairs.

"For real? What have you been smoking out here?"

"That many? Damn! And how many boys?"

"Stop." I say. "None of any gender."

"We'll see how long that lasts."

I cut her off at the end of the stairs. "Can you wait here a minute?" I ask. "There's something I need to do."

She looks down the hall at Dr. Rochan's office door. "What are you going to do?" she asks quietly.

I can't look at her. This is not something we talk about. She knows about what happened earlier. It happened with her the first time we met when I was still *him*. She knows about Elena and me and our gifts, but not about the details. She would be horrified maybe even terrified if we told her the truth. I think she suspects that our abilities are not all puppies and unicorns. I'm sure Finn reminds her daily about how dangerous I am, but I don't think she fully believes him. I don't want her to believe him.

"I'm just going to apologize for earlier. Maybe explain a little."

"Sure," she says. "I'll wait in the quad."

I watch her go through the doors before turning around. The truth is I could do this from anywhere, but it's easier if I'm physically closer to the person. For a second I reconsider, but I'm more afraid of what my mentor might now know about me than I am about being tracked down by Jamie or PSI goons. Through the small window in his office door, I can see Rochan hunched over the laptop on his desk. I close my eyes and reach into his memory. The one I want is easy to find. It's fresh and fuzzy like the memory of a dream for him. He won't miss it at all. I try to leave the others around it intact, but removing memories from other people's minds is not an exact science. The first time I did it, I shredded Sage's mind, but I have practiced this skill quite often since then.

When I'm done, Dr. Rochan looks up and our eyes meet. My heart skips a beat in a surge of irrational panic that I failed. Then he smiles in his usual vague way and waves me in. I stand awkwardly as he asks how my first class went. I tell him fine and try not to sound bitter. I wish I could erase my own memories too, sometimes. He reminds me about the second section, and I leave feeling relieved.

Sage is sitting on a bench in the quad. She's fully focused on her phone, texting someone. I am just about to take an ill-advised trip to spy on who she's talking to and what she's saying, when I hear the uninvited thoughts from the parking lot again.

"That went so well! You think you can control yourself? You can't! You can't control anything. Everyone on this campus can see how weak you are. You don't belong here."

I feel like I've been slammed against a wall or thrown on the ground, like the breath has been knocked out of me and my lungs are compressed and paralyzed, so I can't fill them. I stop walking. For the first time it occurs to me that maybe, just maybe these thoughts are my own, coming from a place inside where that other Ethan still lives. That thought is almost worse than the one that preceded it. A flush of panic washes over me, and my knees almost buckle.

A stranger passing by pauses to ask if I'm okay, but her voice is miles away and mine is nowhere to be found, so I just shake my head. Sage is beside me an instant later, telling the girl she's got it and that I'll be okay.

Time shifts forward several seconds, and I'm sitting on a bench with a water bottle in my hand. Sounds pull into sharp focus as does my vision. I take a deep disconcertingly shaky breath.

"Do you want to go home?" Sage's voice sounds sharp and tight. She didn't sign on for babysitting my panic attacks today.

I don't answer. I allow my conviction that someone else is wreaking havoc with my thoughts take root again. Where the fuck is that weasel, Jamie? I stand up and turn around, scanning the entire quad as quickly and thoroughly as I can.

"What the fuck is going on with you, Ethan?" Sage's voice gets higher pitched as her calm erodes.

This is not really something I can explain to her. If I tell her someone is fucking with my mind, the next stop will be the psych hospital.

"I'm fine now." I say, but her body language tells me she's not convinced. "I just need to eat something," I add, even though I'm not hungry. Still, it sounds like something that might make sense, and it makes Sage feel like there is something she can do to help.

I follow her across campus, concentrating on the search and on keeping my mind shut tight. No more fucking around. The café is buzzing. Packed with people, noise, and smells. Sage knows me well enough to know this is not my scene. She leaves me at an outside table and goes in to order.

I perch on the edge of a cold metal chair and close my eyes. I concentrate on breathing, counting four to inhale, holding for four, exhaling four, and holding for four again. The rhythm and counting is soothing. When Sage comes back with fruit, muffins, and coffee, I'm able to make conversation.

"Soooo . . . whachya looking for?" Sage asks tentatively.

"I thought I saw Jamie." Not a total lie.

"The tall guy from PSI? The one from your birthday party? The very guy who tried to convert Elena?"

I nod.

"That's weird. Why would he be here?"

I shrug. "Just thought I saw him."

"Well, shit. I got the impression you weren't best friends, but I didn't know he upset you this much."

"Now you know," I snap just a little and regret it immediately.

Sage pulls a book out of her backpack and pretends to read, so I fish out my pencils and sketchpad. When I open it, the two failed drawings from yesterday flutter out onto the table. Sage snatches them up before I can react. In a moment she has the paper spread out and is studying them.

"Argh! Don't look at that! It's not . . ."

"Wow! She's gorgeous." Sage exclaims holding on tight to the page so I can't pull it away. "Should I be jealous?"

I stop pulling. "What?" I shake my head. "I don't even know her." Sage looks me up and down like she thinks I'm lying. "Really. She's just a figment of my twisted imagination. I swear."

"Well, that's a huge relief," She says relinquishing the drawing. I stuff it back under the sketchpad cover.

The relief is all hers because between the concentration it's taking to block out the voice in my head and the uneasy feeling that the woman in that drawing gives me, I am barely keeping it together. I run my pencil over the page feigning concentration so Sage will stop staring at me. Finally, she at least pretends to read.

When I get to the classroom for my second section, Dr. Rochan is already there spreading out the lab papers. He greets me warmly when I enter. This time I opt for a nod and forgo the handshake. The students trickle in as I write the equations on the board. I work slowly, avoiding the moment when I'll have to face them, but when Dr. Rochan finishes his spiel and says my name. I turn around and raise a hand awkwardly. Fortunately, there's no Q&A this time, and the students just hurry forward to pick up the lab assignment and get started.

This group is all business, they raise their hands and ask a few pertinent questions, and then go heads down. Truthfully, I don't even take notice of their faces. While they work, I pull out my sketch pad to keep my mind occupied and closed off. When I flip it open, the loose pages flutter onto the desk and I leave them where they lay. I continue the sketch of Cayde, shading and blurring his image into life.

When there are just a few minutes left in the class, the students start coming up in a swarm to have me check their work and accept it. In less than a minute the calm of the last hour turns to chaos, and in the confusion the loose sketches of the mystery woman flutter off the table and onto the floor by the front row of desks. A tall boy with long thin fingers and a large nose thoughtfully scoops them up, and then rudely unfolds them to gawk. I reach forward and manage a small noise, but the desk is between us, and the crowd suddenly shifts away from me toward this young man, who is now passing around the drawings to the other students and looking toward the back of the room at a student who is still seated at a lab table with her back to me.

"Hey, Sam," one of the girls calls. "Turn around."

I'm frozen in terror. I already know what's going to happen next. This young woman, who I have never seen before in my life is going to turn around, and she's going to look exactly like my drawings. At best the pack will laugh it off as a bizarre coincidence, at worst they will be horrified and certain that I am some fucked up stalker or serial killer. I wish my superpower included the ability to stop time, rewind to the moment that I pulled the sketch book out of my backpack. No, further, to the moment I chose to put the drawings inside the sketchpad. I want to be able to turn the damn things to ash in that kid's hand. I want to be able to stay cool, but instead, one of three things is going to happen, I'm going to barf all over this table and the papers, or I'm going to piss myself in front of this room full of people, or I'm going to cry. Fainting would be better, but my luck isn't that good.

In slow motion as the girl, Sam, swivels toward the front, I turn toward the door to my right. If I can just get out of the room before their attention shifts back to me, I can clean up the mess later, like I did with Rochan earlier. Unfortunately, my feet are cemented in place.

Just as Sam's face comes fully around, and the attention shifts to me, a blond girl states the obvious, "Shit, Sam, these look just like you."

I feel the drill of her eyes on my forehead. I cannot lift my gaze to meet hers. I hear her footsteps echo as she moves to the front of the room. The papers crinkle as one of the other students pass them to her. The smell of cardamom and roses wafts past as the air swirls around us.

"They should look like me. I modelled for them." Her voice is gentle, calm, and lightly authoritative. The tension in the room dissolves, and my panic dissipates instantly, washed away in a wave of relief. I'm able to swallow and look her in the eye. She smiles knowingly as I nod my appreciation, and she passes the sketches back to me.

Time regains its normal cadence as the students continue checking in their labs and packing their bags to leave. I can't take my eyes off the girl from my drawing as she glides back to her desk and collects her belongings. She moves languidly like she has all the time in the world, and she does, because she has not yet handed in her paper, and I can't leave without it. A minute or two more passes and finally she is the only student left in the room. In that time I have thought of and discarded at least a dozen apology-explanations.

When she finally approaches the desk, I'm not the one who speaks first. "Those sketches —," she begins. "Not bad."

"Um . . . thanks." I mumble. That's not exactly what I expected. "I . . . I . . . um . . . thanks for uh . . . ya know . . . the save."

We make eye contact and holy fuck, it's electric. Not romantic electric. More like an electrical storm in my frontal cortex. I have to take a step back because I can't look away.

She purses her lips in thought, unperturbed by the intensity. "Sure. No sweat." Then she reaches out her open hand and without a trace of emotion asks, "Can have them?"

"Um . . . yeah. Okay," I say, finally tearing my eyes from hers. My hands shake as I extract the crumpled drawings from my backpack. Instead of handing them to her, I shove them across the desk without looking up. She drops her lab on the stack, but doesn't walk away. We are standing in awkward silence like that when Sage walks in.

"Hey, I was waiting in the hall and —" She comes to an abrupt halt when her eyes take in Sam. "Oh," she adds, exacerbating the awkwardness.

"Hi, I'm Samara." Sam stretches her hand out toward Sage.

"Sage," Sage replies.

"Well, nice to meet you both," Sam says heading out the door.

Sage waits till she's gone and then peaks out and down the hall before exploding. "That's her! The girl you drew! How? Like how did you?"

I sink down onto the stool and shake my head.

"Did you ever —?"

"No, Sage! I don't fucking know her!" My tone and volume are way too hostile. "Sorry."

"Shit, Ethan!"

Shit is right, I think. That girl, Samara, she didn't fucking ask a single question about how those drawings came to be.